no greater love

code blue hearts
book two

Cari Blake

This novel is entirely a work of fiction. The names, characters and incidents portrayed in it are the work of the author's imagination. Any resemblance to actual persons, living or dead, events or localities is entirely coincidental.

First edition

ISBN (IngramSpark-Print): 9798998947520

For Doc Speedy
A Navy Cross–decorated Corpsman who gave everything in service of others.
For the battles you fought on the battlefield—and the ones you still fight today.
You were the model for Nate.
You are a hero in every sense of the word.
This book is for you.

content warning

This book contains realistic depictions of emergency medical situations as experienced by healthcare providers, including:

- -A brief but emotionally challenging scene involving suspected child abuse. While handled with sensitivity and professional care, this content may be difficult for some readers.
- Combat-related PTSD and trauma, including descriptions of wartime injuries and casualties
- Pregnancy loss concerns and medical emergencies
- Depictions of racist harassment in a healthcare setting
- Family court proceedings involving child custody

These scenes are integral to the authentic portrayal of emergency medicine and the emotional toll on healthcare workers. They are written with respect for real survivors and are never gratuitous. The focus remains on the caregivers' professional response and emotional resilience.

If you or someone you know needs support regarding child

abuse, please contact the Childhelp National Child Abuse Hotline at 1-800-422-4453 or visit childhelp.org.

This book celebrates the strength of healthcare workers who face these difficult realities daily while maintaining their compassion and dedication to healing.

one

nate

THE BULLET STRUCK Lance Corporal Alvarez high in the chest, spinning him backward into the exposed street.

"CORPSMAN UP! CORPSMAN UPPP!"

The cry ripped through our radio nets as Alvarez collapsed into the open, dust billowing around him. From my position behind the Amtrak, I could see the dark bloom spreading across his desert camo. Pneumothorax, probably. Exsanguination risk. He had minutes, if that.

I was moving before the call ended, trauma bag already in hand, muscle memory from endless drills taking over. Three bounds to the corner, then a straight shot to Alvarez. Fifteen seconds, max.

"Doc, NO!"

Hands seized my plate carrier, yanking me backward with such force that my helmet slammed against the Amtrak's armored side. Staff Sergeant Miller's face was inches from mine, his features contorted with fury and fear.

"You stay put, Doc!" Miller's eyes were wild, spittle flying as he shoved me against the vehicle. "D'you understand me?"

"He's bleeding out, Staff Sergeant!" I struggled against his grip, my eyes locked on Alvarez's increasingly still form. The precious seconds ticking away. "I can reach him!"

"No, you fuckin' can't!" Miller roared. "That's exactly what those bastards want! They take out our corpsman, we're *all* fucked!"

"*I can*!" I screamed back, "HE NEEDS ME, STAFF SERGEANT! I CAN GET TO HI-"

"CORPORAL JONES! PRIVATE MACKEY! You grab Mr. Crawford here and make sure he doesn't move!" Two Marines materialized, physically blocking my path.

Over Miller's shoulder, I saw Hernandez—just another kid, barely nineteen—making a decision. Our eyes met for a split second.

"I got him, Doc," Hernandez called, already moving.

"Hernandez, don't—" Miller turned, but too late.

Hernandez sprinted from cover, a blur of desert camo against the dust-colored road. Three steps. Four. He was going to make it.

The insurgent machine gun opened up from somewhere in the abandoned apartment block; the familiar *duntduntduntduntdunt* death rattle of an RPK, 7.62mm rounds tearing through the air.

Hernandez jerked as the first rounds hit him, his body absorbing the impacts like hammer blows. But he kept moving, three more stumbling steps toward Alvarez before a final burst caught him squarely in the torso. He dropped to his knees, then fell forward beside the man he'd tried to save.

"Suppressing fire! Get some fire on that building! *Where's our goddamn air support?*" Miller screamed into his radio. Marines opened up, pouring rounds toward the suspected shooter position, but the damage was done.

I strained against the hands holding me back, my medical training screaming that I could still save them, while tactical awareness coldly calculated the survival odds at near zero in that kill zone.

"We need to move! *Now!*" Miller ordered, his voice cracking with strain. "Two men down. We need immediate QRF support and suppressive fire to recover!"

Minutes stretched into eternity. Through my scope, I could see

Hernandez's fingers twitching. Still alive. Still suffering. Just yards away, yet completely unreachable. Alvarez hadn't moved since falling.

Bullets pinged off the Amtrak, the metallic sounds a grotesque counterpoint to Hernandez's diminishing movements. I memorized each detail with clinical precision: the angle of Hernandez's sprawled legs, the exact pattern of blood spreading beneath him, the way his hand still clutched his weapon. The sun beating down, baking the blood into the dust.

"Doc." Miller's voice had softened, his hand now resting heavily on my shoulder. "There's nothing you can do right now."

He knew. He understood exactly what this was doing to me.

The QRF finally arrived with a Bradley, providing enough cover fire for a recovery team to dash out. I waited, medical kit ready, praying against probability.

"They're gone, Doc." The recovery team leader shook his head as they dragged the bodies behind cover. "Both of 'em."

I went through the motions anyway, checking for pulses I knew weren't there, performing assessments that couldn't change the outcome. Alvarez had bled out from his initial wound. Hernandez had taken seven rounds to the chest and abdomen.

I closed Hernandez's eyes with gloved fingers already stiff with his dried blood. Nineteen years old. He'd told me just yesterday about his plans to become a firefighter after his tour. He'd died because I was too valuable to risk.

"You did what you could," Miller said, his voice distant, mechanical. "You couldn't have saved them."

But I could have. I could have at least tried. I should have been the one to go. I knew trauma medicine. I might have stemmed the bleeding, bought precious minutes...

Instead, I had survived.

I jerked awake with a gasp, my hands clutching at sheets soaked with sweat. The bedroom was dark except for the soft glow of the digital clock: 0417. The nightmare had come earlier than usual tonight.

My hand trembled as I reached for the water glass by the bed, muscle memory from twenty years ago still sending signals to reach for a weapon that wasn't there. I drained the glass in three gulps, then swung my legs over the side of the bed, letting the cool floor ground me in the present.

Breathe in. Four count. Hold. Four count. Release. Four count.

The trembling subsided gradually. Twenty years since Fallujah, and still my body remembered. Still my hands wouldn't stay steady after these dreams.

Sleep was done for the night. I moved through the darkness of the house with practiced efficiency, pausing only to crack open Paige's door. The soft glow of her astronomy nightlight illuminated her sleeping form, one arm flung dramatically across the pillow, the rhythmic rise and fall of her chest a silent reassurance.

Safe. My daughter was safe.

In the kitchen, I started the coffee maker—prepped the night before, always—and checked my watch. Too early for a run, but plenty of time to review Paige's science homework and prep lunches.

By 0545, the house was filled with the smell of coffee and toasting bread. Paige's lunch was packed, her backpack double-checked, the day's weather forecast consulted and appropriate outerwear laid out.

"Dad?" Paige appeared in the doorway, hair mussed from sleep, squinting against the kitchen light. "Why are you always up so early?"

I smiled, folding down the top of her lunch bag with precision. "Early bird gets the worm, kiddo."

She yawned dramatically. "I guess that's okay if you like eating worms." At eleven, Paige had developed a wit that constantly surprised me. "Can I have cinnamon toast?"

"Already in the toaster." I slid a glass of orange juice toward her. "Calcium supplement?"

"Dad." The eye roll was impressive. "I'm not a baby. I'm *eleven*."

"Calcium for growing bones isn't just for babies." I held out the small tablet, our morning ritual unfolding exactly as it had for the past three years.

With another eye roll—she'd perfected the technique—Paige took the tablet. "Mrs. Swanson said she's bringing banana bread this morning."

"Did she now?" I poured a second cup of coffee, this one into the thermal mug Mrs. Swanson preferred. "That's the third time this month. We should get her something to say thank you."

"I did!" Paige said with a sly smile, crunching into her toast. "I made her a card in art class. And..." She hesitated, looking up at me through her lashes. "I maybe told her you'd fix her garbage disposal this weekend."

I raised an eyebrow. "Voluntelling me for home repairs now?"

She grinned, braces glinting. "You said we should always help people who help us."

"I did say that," I admitted, unable to hide my smile. "I'll bring my tools over on Saturday."

The soft knock at exactly 0615 announced Mrs. Swanson's arrival. I opened the door to find her holding a foil-wrapped package that was indeed emitting the heavenly scent of banana bread.

"Marion, you're spoiling us," I said, accepting the package while handing her the travel mug.

Mrs. Swanson waved away my thanks, her silver bob perfectly coiffed despite the early hour. "Nonsense. I had bananas going brown. Besides," she lowered her voice conspiratorially, "I've got a freezer full. My Austin and Mason loooove Nana's banana bread, but Harold will eat himself into diabetes if I leave it all at home before they come visit again."

At fifty eight, Marion Swanson was the closest thing to family Paige and I had. A retired middle school English teacher, she'd moved in next door five years ago and had almost immediately become our emergency contact, occasional babysitter, and de facto grandmother figure.

"Paige tells me you've got a garbage disposal with my name on it,"
I said, checking my watch. 0617. Right on schedule.

"That girl," Mrs. Swanson chuckled. "I mentioned it was making
a funny noise, and the next thing I know, she's promising your
mechanical expertise. But only if you have time, Nathan."

"For you? Always." I gathered my keys and badge. "Mrs. Swanson
will make sure you don't miss the bus." I dropped a kiss on the top of
Paige's head. "Homework's in the green folder."

"I know, Dad." Another eye roll, but she hugged me quickly.
"Don't get puked on today."

"I'll do my best." I nodded to Mrs. Swanson. "Thank you, as
always."

"Go save lives," she replied with a warm smile. "We'll be just
fine."

As I backed out of the driveway, I could see them through the
kitchen window—Paige animatedly talking, Mrs. Swanson listening
intently. The familiar comfort of knowing Paige was in safe hands
settled over me.

My hand had stopped trembling completely by the time I pulled
into the hospital parking lot at 0638. The nightmares might still
come, but the daylight hours were firmly under control.

This was the life I'd built for us—predictable, safe, carefully
structured. No room for variables, no space for surprises.

No room for failure.

I parked in my usual spot, Section C, Row 4, third space from
the end. Exactly eleven minutes from doorway to time clock if I
maintained my standard pace.

My phone buzzed as I gathered my bag. A text from Meghan, my
backup sitter for Thursday.

*Hey Mr. C, so sorry but I can't make Thursday morning anymore.
Got asked to cover a study group. Can still do pickup tho!*

I stared at the screen, the carefully constructed scaffolding of my
week already beginning to wobble. On Thursday, Mrs. Swanson had
her garden club meeting. I'd need to find someone to make sure Paige

got to school, and quickly, or else find someone to cover the first part of my shift in the ER.

The tremor in my hand returned, faint but unmistakable.

One problem at a time. I'd handle this. I always did.

I tucked the phone away and headed inside, my pace exactly as practiced, counting steps until the familiar rhythm steadied my hands once more.

The ER was already humming with morning activity. I clocked in at 0646—a minute later than my usual, but still within acceptable parameters. The night shift looked tired but relieved to see the day crew arriving.

"Morning, Nate," called Kirsten from behind the charge nurses' station, already deep in her handoff notes. "We've got a full house. Five admits waiting for beds upstairs, one discharge teaching in progress, and a lovely gentleman in Room 4 who's been asking for 'someone competent' every ten minutes since 0500."

"Charming," I said, pulling up the patient list on my tablet. "What's his story?"

"Post-op hip replacement complications, probably discharged too early, now waiting for a bed. Thinks nurses are his personal concierge service." Kirsten's expression was carefully neutral, but I caught the edge in her voice. "He's... particular about his care preferences."

I nodded, scanning over the digital greaseboard detailing patients and their chief complaints. Mrs. Brooks in Room 2 with chest pain, ruled out STEMI, now waiting for serial troponins. Mr. Rodriguez in Room 6 with diabetic ketoacidosis, stable but grumpy about the insulin drip. The usual morning mix of emergencies and frustrations.

"Where do you want me?" I asked.

"Triage," Kirsten said immediately. "University Hospital went on divert twice yesterday, and I can't imagine they'll skip it today. We need someone who can keep the waiting room from becoming a riot. Tasha is handling Fast Track, but she's..." Kirsten paused, glancing toward where I could see Tasha moving efficiently between patients. "She's in one of her moods today."

I followed her gaze and immediately understood what Maria meant. Tasha's professional mask was firmly in place, but there was something sharper in her movements, a defensive edge I'd learned to recognize. Someone had gotten under her skin.

"What happened?" I asked.

"Mr. McAllister in Room 4 happened. The one I mentioned." Kirsten's voice dropped to a whisper. "And Tasha... well, you know how she gets when people are assholes."

As if to emphasize this, the call bell chimed from Room 4. Kirsten responded immediately.

"How can I help you?"

"I need a nurse to come hold me," came Mr. McAllister's voice through the intercom. "I can't use the urinal by myself."

I saw Tasha's head snap up from her charting, her expression darkening. Kirsten looked uncertain, glancing between the room and the nurses' station.

"Perfect," I said, already moving toward Room 4. "I got it."

I knocked once and entered to find Mr. McAllister looking considerably less helpless than his request had suggested.

"Oh," he said, his tone shifting immediately. "I thought... well, I was expecting..."

"You said you needed help with the urinal," I said pleasantly, moving to the bedside table where the urinal sat. "I'm happy to assist."

"Actually, I think I might be able to manage after all," he said quickly.

I tilted my head, maintaining my helpful expression. "Are you sure? You said you couldn't do it yourself. I really don't mind helping. It's no trouble at all."

"No, no," he insisted, reaching for the urinal himself. "I'm feeling much stronger now."

"Wonderful," I said. "Recovery can be unpredictable that way. I'll be right outside if you change your mind."

I stepped back into the hallway, where Tasha was watching from the nurses' station. Her expression was carefully neutral, but I caught the slight nod of approval.

No woman should have to deal with that kind of manipulation disguised as patient care. It was predatory behavior, plain and simple, and I'd seen enough of it over the years to recognize it immediately.

"Hey," I said, approaching her at the desk. "If anyone asks you to do something like that again, come get me. I don't tolerate that."

Tasha's lips curved in a small smile. "My prince charming," she said.

"Oh, no," I replied quickly, feeling heat creep up my neck. "I'd do that for anyone. Any of the nurses. It's just... it's not appropriate."

"No," Tasha said, "I got that. I was just being a smartass."

"Oh," I said, then paused, realizing I had no idea how to respond to that. "Right. Well. Good."

She grinned at my obvious discomfort before heading back to her patients, leaving me standing there feeling oddly off-balance.

I made my way to the triage desk, settling into the familiar rhythm of assessments and decisions. Everything was going as well as it could for triage.

Then came Mr. Shifflett.

"What's going on today, sir?" I asked, clicking up a fresh assessment form on the digital greaseboard.

"I'm having kidney pain on my left side, and I'm pissin' blood," he replied without looking up from his phone. He plopped himself down into my assessment chair and held his arm out automatically when I approached with the blood pressure cuff, but his eyes never left his screen. "I'm pretty sure it's another kidney stone."

"You have a history of kidney stones?" I asked, wrapping the cuff around his bicep.

He nodded, thumbs flying over his screen. I waited for him to elaborate, but he seemed completely absorbed in whatever he was typing.

"How many days have you been having symptoms?" I asked, fingers poised over my tablet.

Silence. I glanced up to see him completely engrossed in his phone, either not hearing me or choosing to ignore me.

"Mr. Shifflett?" I tried again, keeping my voice polite but firm.

"Yeah, what?" he said, still not looking up.

"How many days have you been having pain?"

"Oh." He seemed to consider this briefly, his typing slowing momentarily. "I don't know... probably a couple."

"On a scale of zero to ten, with zero being no pain and ten being the worst pain you've ever—"

"Eleven."

I made a note without comment. "Any allergies I should know about?"

This finally got his attention. He looked up, biting his lip thoughtfully. "Let me think... Tylenol, ibuprofen, Aleve, Toradol, tramadol, Zofran, droperidol, Benadryl, and medical tape." He paused. "I think that's everything."

I documented the extensive list, then glanced at his medication history. "I see you're prescribed Vicodin and Dilaudid?"

"Yeah, but I'm out of those."

"And you take the Vicodin okay, even with your Tylenol allergy?"

"Yeah, my doctor said Tylenol was fine when it's mixed with other stuff, just not by itself."

"We'll probably need a urine sample and discuss getting a CT scan to check for stones."

"No way," he said, shaking his head. "I don't do radiation. It's bad for you."

I kept my expression neutral, though internally I noted the refusal. Considering kidney stones were consistently rated as being more painful than childbirth, someone genuinely suffering from them would typically want any test that might help diagnose and treat their condition. The reluctance to confirm the diagnosis he was claiming was... telling.

"I understand," I said diplomatically, meaning it in more ways than one.

After completing his assessment, I directed him to the waiting room. As he stood to leave, he finally looked directly at me.

"Hey, how long do you think the wait will be? I've got plans later, and my ride's coming in about forty-five minutes."

I felt my jaw tighten slightly. "We see patients based on medical priority, sir. I'll do my best to keep things moving efficiently."

"Can you just try to hurry it along?" he asked, already shuffling toward the waiting room, phone back in hand.

I watched him go, then turned back to my computer to complete his chart. As I typed, I found myself thinking about the morning's earlier incident with Tasha, about Mr. McAllister's manipulative behavior, about Mr. Shifflett's casual dismissiveness.

Just another beautiful day in emergency medicine.

But even as I thought it, I realized something had shifted since this morning. The tremor in my hands from the nightmare had completely disappeared. The familiar weight of the day's routine had settled around me like armor, steady and reliable.

The dreams might still come at night, might still drag me back. But here, in the controlled chaos of the ER, surrounded by colleagues I respected and problems I could actually solve?

Here, I was exactly where I belonged.

two
tasha

THE PROBLEM with Nathan Crawford wasn't that he was incompetent. The problem was that he was so aggressively competent, so relentlessly professional, that it made everyone else look stupid by comparison.

Take Tuesday morning's disaster: Mrs. Kellerman, sixty eight years old, diabetic, on dialysis three times a week, veins like spider webs under tissue paper. She'd been stuck four times already—twice by night shift, once by respiratory therapy trying to draw blood gases, and once by some overeager resident who'd insisted he could "definitely get this one."

Her arms looked like a war zone.

"I can't take much more of this, honey," Mrs. Kellerman said to me, tears leaking from the corners of her eyes. "I know y'all are trying, but..."

I looked at her arms, mapping the viable targets in my head. There, on the back of her left hand, I saw it— a tiny, threadlike vein that everyone else had probably dismissed as too small.

But I'd gotten smaller.

"Mrs. Kellerman," I said, pulling up a chair beside her bed, "I'm going to get this on the first try. I promise."

"Oh, sweetheart, that's what they all say."

"Well," I said, prepping my supplies with practiced efficiency. "I'm not 'they all.' I'm very good at this."

Nathan appeared at my elbow with the ultrasound machine. "Need help? I can get this set up for—"

"Won't need it," I said without looking at him. "But thanks anyway."

I felt his eyes on me as I slid the 22-gauge needle into that impossibly small vein, felt the tiny pop of entry, watched the flash of blood in the chamber. Perfect placement on the first stick.

"There we go, Mrs. Kellerman," I said, taping down the IV with satisfaction. "All done."

"Oh my God," she breathed, staring at her hand like I'd performed magic. "I barely felt that. You're amazing!"

I waited for the acknowledgment. The impressed look. The grudging respect that always came when I pulled off something the others couldn't.

"Nice work," Nathan said, already moving to hang Mrs. Kellerman's antibiotics. "That was textbook technique. Saved us from having to call for a midline."

That was it. No amazement. No 'how did you do that?' Just 'nice work' like I'd done something any competent nurse could manage.

"Textbook," I repeated flatly.

"Perfect angle, good vein choice, excellent patient communication," he said, checking the IV flow rate. "Mrs. Kellerman, thanks to Tasha, you're all set. This should run for about an hour."

I stared at him as he moved on to his next patient, completely oblivious to the fact that he'd just dismissed what was genuinely impressive work.

Textbook.

Like anyone could have done it.

Thursday brought Mr. Taylor, seventy four years old, readmitted for complications related to his gallbladder surgery, who'd been holding in our ER for a day and a half waiting for an inpatient bed to come free. The kind of patient who thought nurses were just there to fetch things and fluff pillows—which was apparently all the MedSurg nurses upstairs did, considering how reluctant they were to actually take report and get this man out of our trauma bay.

Because nothing said "efficient patient flow" like having a stable patient taking up space while we tried to manage actual emergencies around him. But here we were, providing what was essentially hotel service while waiting for the floor to *deign* to accept their admission.

"You're very gentle," he told Nathan as he helped him to the bathroom. "Not like some of these girls who just want to rush through everything. You really care about doing a good job."

"That's very kind of you to say, Mr. Taylor," Nathan replied, steadying the man's elbow. "All the nurses here are excellent. We all want you to get better."

Mr. Taylor harrumphed. "Well, you're different. More professional. You take your time, explain things properly."

"Yes," I said, my voice perfectly pleasant as I approached with his medications. "Nathan's very... nurturing."

I put just enough emphasis on the word to make it sound like something between a compliment and an observation about his maternal instincts.

Nathan glanced at me, that same mild, unreadable expression. "Thank you, Tasha."

Thank you. Not *'what's that supposed to mean?'* or *'are you questioning my competence?'. 'Thank you'.* Like I'd given him a genuine compliment.

Mr. Taylor, oblivious to the subtext, nodded enthusiastically. "Exactly! That's what I was saying. Very nurturing. You'd make a great father someday."

"I have a daughter, actually," Nathan said, helping Mr. Taylor back into bed. "She keeps me on my toes."

"Well, she's lucky to have you," Mr. Taylor said with the authority of someone who'd decided Nathan was his new favorite person.

I watched Nathan tuck the blankets around Mr. Taylor with the same methodical care he brought to everything, and felt something twist in my chest. Not anger, exactly. Something more complicated.

"Your pain medication is here, Mr. Taylor," I said, holding up the small cup of pills.

"Oh," Mr. Taylor said, taking the cup without really looking at me. "Thank you, dear."

Of course. Not *thank you for going through my medications with a fine-tooth comb to make sure the resident's NSAID order wouldn't cause me to bleed internally.* Just *'thank you, dear'*.

Nathan caught my expression this time, something shifting in his face. "Tasha spent time reviewing all your medications to make sure nothing would interact poorly," he told Mr. Taylor. "She probably prevented some serious complications."

"Oh," Mr. Taylor said again, this time actually looking at me. "Well. That's... thank you."

I waited for Nathan to move on, to go back to his other patients and leave me to stew in my irritation. Instead, he lingered.

"That was a good catch," he said quietly. "The warfarin-NSAID interaction. Most people would have missed it."

I blinked. He'd noticed. He'd actually been paying attention to my work, not just his own.

"It's my job," I said, but the words came out less sharp than I'd intended.

"Still. Good work."

He walked away then, leaving me standing there feeling oddly off-balance. It wasn't the praise that threw me; I was used to being good at my job. It was the *way* he'd said it. Like he actually meant it. Like he'd been watching my work with genuine respect, not just waiting for his turn to look competent.

I watched him stop at the next bed, where Mrs. Garcia was arguing with her daughter about discharge planning. His voice was patient, kind, as he explained the home care instructions for the third time. No condescension. No frustration. Just... professional competence mixed with genuine compassion.

The man was irritatingly impossible to dislike.

Which was exactly the problem.

I'd spent three years perfecting the art of keeping people at a distance. A sharp comment here, a perfectly timed eye roll there, just enough attitude to make sure no one got too comfortable, too familiar, too close. It worked. It kept me safe.

But Nathan Crawford didn't seem to notice my carefully crafted defenses. Or maybe he noticed and just... didn't care.

Either way, it was unsettling.

three
nate

5:45 AM came too early, as it always did on Saturday mornings. I'd been up since 5:15, moving through my pre-shift routine with the same methodical precision I brought to everything else. Shower, shave, uniform pressed and ready. Coffee brewing while I double-checked Paige's schedule for the day.

Mrs. Swanson was still in Chicago visiting her daughter, had been for three days now, and wasn't due back until later today. Which left me scrambling for childcare on one of the busiest days of the week.

"College Meghan", as she was listed in my phone's contact list, wasn't my first choice. Hell, she wasn't my fifth choice. But when you're a single parent with a 6:45 AM punch-in time... sometimes you have to make do with what you can get.

Meghan Morgan was a nursing student at the community college, recommended by Maria's cousin who worked in the cafeteria. Twenty years old, responsible enough to maintain a 3.5 GPA, and desperate enough for babysitting money to agree to spend her Saturday shuttling an eleven-year-old around the city. The plan was simple: meet in the Metro General parking lot at 6:30, hand off Paige for a day at the science museum and whatever else they could find to fill the time, then meet back at 7:15 PM when my shift ended.

It wasn't ideal—I hated not knowing exactly where Paige would be every minute of the day—but Meghan had promised to text me updates, and the science museum was safe, educational, and would keep Paige entertained for hours.

"Dad, you're doing the thing again," Paige said from the passenger seat, not looking up from her book.

"What thing?"

"The checking-your-watch-every-thirty-seconds thing." She looked at me with amused exasperation. "It's 6:25. We're here exactly on time, like always."

I forced myself to stop looking at my watch. The Metro General parking lot was starting to fill with the day shift arriving, but no sign of a beat-up Honda Civic with the dented front bumper.

"Just making sure we're coordinated," I said, scanning the lot again.

The digital clock on my dashboard flipped to 6:30 AM. No sign of Meghan.

"Dad?" Paige looked up from her book, concern creeping into her voice. "Shouldn't she be here by now?"

"She's probably just running a little late, sweetie." I kept my voice even, masking the anxiety that was already building in me.

Six thirty-two.

I pulled out my phone and dialed Meghan again. Straight to voicemail. Again.

"Hey, Meghan, it's Nate Crawford, Paige's dad. I'm in the ER parking lot waiting. Please call me as soon as you get this."

Paige shifted in her seat, closing her book; "*The Giver*" by Lois Lowry. She'd been engrossed in it all week, breaking my heart by pointing out that the main character had never seen color until after a special experience. "Dad, aren't you going to be late?"

"I've got a few minutes." The lie rolled off my tongue easily, alongside the forced smile. I'd been imbued with a rigid sense of duty

—show up fifteen minutes early or don't show up at all. The military had only reinforced that. But Metro General's HR department had reinforced it even further with their new "three strikes and you're out" attendance policy.

Six thirty-five.

I scrolled frantically through my contacts. Mrs. Smith from two doors down? No, she was at her daughter's for her baby's birth. The Thompsons? On vacation in Europe. Every name blurred together as my anxiety mounted.

Six forty.

"Dad?" Paige's voice was small now.

"It's okay, Paige. We'll figure it out." My fingers flew over the phone, sending a rapid text to Mrs. Swanson on the off chance she'd returned early.

> Mrs. S - Desperate situation. Are you back in town by any chance? Meghan no-showed, and I'm about to start my shift.

Six forty-three.

My stomach dropped as the reality set in. I was utterly screwed. Call in late and face a potential write-up that could jeopardize everything I'd worked for? Or bring my daughter into an ER filled with HIPAA violations waiting to happen, infectious diseases, and God knows what else?

Some choice.

Six forty-five. My official start time.

I stared at the steering wheel. Sophia would be looking for me. The night nurse would need to hand off report. Every minute I sat here was another mark against me.

Six forty-seven.

"Dad, I can stay in the car," Paige offered, looking so grown-up and serious that it broke my heart. "I've got my books. It's not even hot out."

"Absolutely not, Paige." The thought of leaving her alone in a parking lot made my skin crawl. "That's not safe, not even a little bit."

Six forty-nine.

A desperate plan formed. I'd punch in, find Sophia immediately, explain the situation, and... then what? Take the write-up? Beg for mercy?

"Okay, Paige, here's what's going to happen. We're going inside. I need to talk to my boss, Miss Sophia—you met her at the holiday party a while back—and we'll figure something out. Just... stay close to me, okay?"

She nodded solemnly, tucking her book into her cat-shaped backpack.

Six fifty-one.

We half-jogged across the parking lot, through the ambulance bay, and straight to the time clock. My badge swiped through with a merciful beep.

06:52.

Made it. Barely. But now came the hard part.

I guided Paige through the maze of corridors, hyperaware of every privacy curtain, every exposed patient chart, every potential hazard. The break room door loomed ahead, and I could hear the murmur of the day shift getting their assignments. Sophia would be there, clipboard in hand, wondering where the hell her usually punctual nurse was.

My hand on the doorknob, I looked down at Paige. "Remember, sweetheart, just—"

"Stay close and be quiet," she finished. "I know, Dad."

Then we were in, and every eye in the room turned to us. The sudden silence was deafening. I felt Paige shift closer to my side, and my face burned with shame. Eight years as an ER nurse, and I'd never felt more unprofessional than in this moment, standing in the staff break room with my eleven-year-old daughter at my side.

Sophia's eyes found mine, surprise quickly replaced by concern. "Nathan. The charge office, please?"

Thank God. At least I wouldn't have to explain myself in front of everyone.

I followed her, Paige trailing silently behind me, clutching her book like a talisman. Once inside the relative privacy of the charge office, the words spilled out in a desperate rush.

"Soph—Miss Mitchell. Ma'am, I apologize for the breach of protocol." I felt myself slipping into military formality, a defense mechanism against the crushing embarrassment. "My babysitter didn't show, no warning, no communication. I had no alternative childcare options available on short notice. I have no excuse."

Sophia's eyes softened. "Nathan, you could be on fire and you'd apologize for the smoke. Relax. It's okay."

I exhaled sharply, some of the tension leaving my shoulders. Still, the immediate problem remained.

She smiled cheerfully at Paige. "Hi there. I'm Sophia. Your dad's told me a *lot* about you."

Paige gave a small, polite nod. "Nice to meet you."

"Okay, Nate," Sophia continued, her voice even. "Deep breath. It happens." She paused. "She can't go out there. And you'll be worried sick if she's just tucked away somewhere." She glanced at the schedule. "Can you get someone to pick her up soon?"

I ran a hand over my face. "Working on it. My neighbor usually helps in a pinch, but she's out of town until this afternoon. I'm calling everyone I know."

"You could call out," she offered, though we both knew what that meant. "I can try to cover triage myself for a bit, or ask Maria to pull someone from the float pool, but... it'd count as an occurrence. And a late call-out."

The unspoken *"and you can't afford that"* hung in the air between us. Even one occurrence and I'd be on thin ice. With Paige, I couldn't risk it. Who knew when she might actually get sick and need me to stay home with her?

I shook my head, feeling the walls closing in. Then a knock at the door interrupted us, and Tasha Williams stuck her head in, coffee in hand.

"Oh my God, hiiiii, is this your daughter?" she asked, her eyes lighting on Paige. "The one who drew that heart valves picture you showed everyone!?"

I blinked, momentarily thrown by her enthusiasm. Tasha Williams, of all people, remembering Paige's science project?

Paige looked up at me, surprise evident. "You showed my drawing to people?"

My ears burned. "It was exceptional work."

Tasha leaned down to Paige's level. "I thought it was soooooo cool how you included the interatrial septum. Most people forget that's technically a fifth distinct area."

Paige brightened visibly, sitting up straighter. "Dad helped me build a model!"

"If you need someone to watch her," Tasha continued, turning to Sophia, "I could stay with her in the break room. Just until Crawford can sort something out." She shrugged. "I'm good with kids. Got a bunch of younger cousins."

I stared at her, utterly dumbfounded. Tasha Williams, the same nurse who'd rolled her eyes at me three days ago when I'd asked for her help with a difficult catheter, was offering to babysit my daughter?

"Are you sure, Tasha?" Sophia asked, her tone neutral but evaluating. "You'd be responsible for her. I'd need to pull you from the floor."

"I can handle it," Tasha replied, a flicker of her usual defensiveness in her voice. "For an hour or so. Give him time to make some calls."

Sophia made her decision quickly. "Okay, Tasha. Thank you. For one hour. Break room. I'll let Nathan and I handle Fast Track between us."

Relief washed over me, so profound that for a moment I thought my knees might buckle. "Tasha, I... thank you. Seriously. I owe you big time."

"No worries, Crawford," Tasha said, already turning to Paige. She gestured to the book in Paige's hands. "Is that '*The Giver*'?"

Paige nodded, holding it up. "For school."

"That's one of my favorites," Tasha said, her face lighting up with genuine enthusiasm. "The ending still makes me mad, though."

Paige's eyes widened. "You've read it?"

"Dystopian literature is kind of my thing," Tasha admitted, then looked at Sophia defensively. "What? I read!"

Sophia raised her hands in surrender. "Never doubted it."

I hesitated, then unzipped my backpack and handed Paige her lunch bag. "Your lunch. Protein bar for midmorning. Water bottle's full. Remember your inhaler's in the side pocket if you need it."

"*Dad*," Paige muttered, embarrassed. "I know."

"Want a juice box, Paige?" Tasha asked, already steering her toward the door. "We've got apple, orange, and prune... mmmmm, we should probably skip that last one."

Once Tasha and Paige were out of earshot, the door closing behind them, Sophia turned back to me with an expression I'd seen too many times—gentle concern mixed with unspoken questions.

"Are you okay, Nate?" she asked, lowering her voice. "Have you heard anything from... her?"

The careful way she avoided saying Sarah's name was deliberate, respectful. But it still landed like a blow. My jaw tightened involuntarily.

"No," I said, keeping my voice even. "Last I heard, a few years ago, she was somewhere in Florida. 'Finding herself.'" I couldn't help the short, humorless breath that escaped. "I still email photos of Paige to her folks, her grandparents. Never hear anything back. It is what it is."

I tried for casual dismissal, but the words tasted bitter. Eleven years of silence. Eleven years of Paige's first steps, first words, first day of school, science fair victories—all documented in carefully curated emails that disappeared into the void of Sarah's family's indifference. I'd even included my phone number. Not once had they reached out.

Sarah's abandonment had been clinical, almost elegant in its totality. No messy custody battles, no child support negotiations. She'd simply... gone. Left before the postpartum haze had fully cleared, while Paige still smelled of newborn and I was still fumbling through diaper changes with hands better trained for handling battlefield trauma than baby wipes.

"I need to find myself," she'd said, standing in our apartment doorway, a single suitcase beside her. *"I told you I wasn't ready for this. I'm not mother material, Nate."*

I'd nodded then, numb, Paige asleep in my arms. "The door's always open," I'd told her, the words automatic, dutiful. "She'll always know her mother loved her enough to make the right choice for herself."

A lie I'd perfected over the years, tailored to Paige's age and understanding. The closest I'd ever come to dishonesty with my daughter. But I'd die before I let Paige carry the weight of thinking she'd been left behind as an inconvenience.

Now, looking at Sophia's sympathetic face, I felt the familiar ache of wondering if I was enough. If Paige needed more than I could give her. A mother figure. A woman's guidance. The older she got, the more aware I became of my limitations.

But dwelling on it wouldn't change anything. Sarah was gone. Paige had me. We managed.

"Thank you, Sophia," I said, shifting the subject, my voice thicker than I'd intended. "For trusting Tasha with her. I don't know what I would have done."

"Tasha stepped up. And you needed a solution," Sophia replied with a small smile. "Go make your calls, Nate. Find a real babysitter. And Tasha just earned herself some serious good karma."

My sense of fairness flared up immediately. "I can have HR take an hour or two of my sick time or PTO to pay for her time," I offered. Tasha was doing me a personal favor. She shouldn't lose income because of my crisis.

Sophia waved me off. "Nate, this is real life, and real life is messy. If we asked corporate or HR, they wouldn't have let this happen at all, but that's why they pay me to figure these things out. Tasha can stay punched in." Her smile deepened. "You're an asset to our department. And you're our friend. You'd do the same for any of us."

Friend. The word caught me off guard. I'd spent so long keeping my colleagues at a professional distance—partly from military habit, partly from the fierce need to protect Paige from any more abandonment. But here was Sophia, casually claiming me as one of their own.

An unexpected warmth spread through me... immediately followed by guilt. Did I deserve this kindness? This flexibility? Every minute I spent in this office was a minute another nurse had to cover for me, a disruption to the careful system we all relied on.

I nodded, allowing a flicker of gratitude to show before pulling out my phone. Back to the task at hand. Efficient. Practical. That was my role. That was what I could control.

As I scrolled through my contacts, Sophia slipped out, leaving me alone with my thoughts. I found Mrs. Swanson's number, my thumb hovering over the call button.

For just a moment, I allowed myself to wonder—as I did on the hard nights, the lonely nights—whether Sarah ever thought about Paige. Whether she ever looked at the calendar and realized it was her daughter's birthday. Whether she ever regretted walking away.

Then I shook it off. What Sarah did or didn't feel was irrelevant. She'd made her choice. I'd made mine. Every day since Paige was born, I'd chosen her, would keep choosing her, would build my life around ensuring she never felt the void Sarah had left.

I pressed "call" and pushed thoughts of Sarah firmly away. The present needed my attention. Always had. Always would.

four
tasha

METRO GENERAL WAS quiet when I arrived, the calm before the inevitable storm of a Saturday morning. I was running just late enough to be annoying, but not late enough to get called out for it. The perfect sweet spot.

I pushed through the staff entrance, my travel mug of coffee clutched tightly in one hand, mentally preparing myself for another day of bodily fluids, entitled patients, and doctors who thought "nurse" was synonymous with "personal servant." At least my scrubs were fresh, and my coffee was strong enough to strip paint. Small victories.

The break room would be packed with the day shift getting their assignments, but I needed to refill my water bottle before facing humanity. As I approached, the door burst open, and I nearly collided with Nathan Crawford—Metro General's most annoyingly punctual nurse—looking frazzled in a way I'd never seen before.

And he wasn't alone.

A girl of about eleven or twelve trailed behind him, clutching a backpack shaped like some cartoon character and a paperback book. Her dark hair was pulled back in a messy ponytail, and she had blue braces that flashed briefly when she nervously bit her lip.

Crawford's kid? Had to be. Same serious eyes, same way of standing, like she was trying to take up as little space as possible.

I stepped back, watching as Sophia immediately took control of the situation, ushering Crawford and his daughter into the charge office. Through the glass, I could see Crawford's rigid posture, the tension in his shoulders. The little girl looked small and out of place, clearly trying to be invisible.

"Babysitter drama," Maria muttered from beside me, appearing, like she always did, out of nowhere. "Poor Nate!"

I took a sip of my coffee, affecting nonchalance. "Not my circus, not my monkeys."

But I kept watching. The kid... Paige. That was her name. Was fidgeting with the book in her hands. *The Giver*. I remembered that book from school. Pretty heavy stuff for a tween, but Crawford's kid was probably as serious as he was.

Wait. I remembered now. A few weeks back, Crawford had been showing around a picture Paige had drawn for a science project. Something about heart valves, way beyond what an eleven-year-old should be capable of. He'd been so damn proud, practically bursting at the seams, even though he tried to play it cool. "Just sharing some interesting anatomical information," he'd claimed, fooling absolutely no one.

I'd taken a look, more out of boredom than interest. The kid had included the interatrial septum in her analysis of heart valves. Most *adults* wouldn't catch that.

Through the glass, I could see Sophia's expression shift from stern to sympathetic. Crawford looked like he was drowning. The kid looked like she might cry any second. After a moment, they all disappeared from the break room, heading for the charge nurse's office.

"What do you think will happen?" I asked Maria, keeping my tone disinterested.

Maria shrugged. "He'll probably have to call out. With the new attendance policy, that'll be rough." She lowered her voice. "HR's been on the warpath lately."

I frowned. Crawford was a pain in the ass with his military precision and his constant "by the book" attitude, but he was also one of the few nurses who always had your back in a crisis, who never complained when shifts ran long, who took the difficult patients without whining.

And that kid. Something about her quiet determination to be brave, the way she clutched that book like it was a lifeline... it reminded me of my cousin Alexis at that age. Scared but trying so hard not to show it.

Before I could overthink it, I found myself walking toward the charge office. I knocked once, decisively.

Three faces turned toward me as I opened the door. Crawford looked shell-shocked, Sophia looked calculating, and Paige... Paige just looked lost.

Something twisted in my chest, unfamiliar and uncomfortable.
Damn it.

"Oh my God, hiiiii, is this your daughter?" I blurted, channeling my inner enthusiastic babysitter voice. "The one who drew that heart valves picture you showed everyone!?"

Paige looked up, clearly startled. "You showed my picture to people?"

Crawford's ears reddened. "It was exceptional work."

I leaned down slightly to Paige's level, surprising myself with how genuine my interest was. "I thought it was soooooo cool how you included the interatrial septum. Most people forget that's technically a fifth distinct area."

Paige brightened visibly, sitting up straighter. "Dad helped me build a model!"

The words tumbled out before I could stop them: "If you need someone to watch her, I could stay with her in the break room. Just until you can sort something out." I shrugged, trying to look casual, like this wasn't completely out of character for me. "I'm good with kids. Got a bunch of younger cousins."

Crawford stared at me like I'd grown a second head. Sophia's eyebrows nearly hit her hairline.

"Are you sure, Tasha?" Sophia asked, her voice neutral but her eyes sharp. "You'd be responsible for her. I'd need to pull you from the floor."

"I can handle it," I replied, a defensive edge creeping into my voice. What, they thought I'd *corrupt* the kid? "For an hour or so. Give him time to make some calls."

Sophia made her decision quickly. "Okay, Tasha. Thank you. For one hour. Break room. I'll let Nathan and I handle Fast Track between us."

Crawford looked at me like I'd just thrown him a life preserver in a hurricane. "Tasha, I... thank you. Seriously. I owe you big time."

His sincerity was so unexpected it made me uncomfortable. "No worries, Crawford," I said, already turning to Paige, desperate to change the subject. I gestured to the book in her hands. "Is that '*The Giver*'?"

Paige nodded, holding it up. "For school."

"That's one of my favorites," I said, genuinely excited now. "The ending still makes me mad, though."

Paige's eyes widened. "You've read it?"

"Dystopian literature is kind of my thing," I admitted, then caught Sophia's surprised look and felt instantly defensive. "What? I read!"

Sophia raised her hands in surrender. "Never doubted it."

Crawford hesitated, then unzipped his backpack and handed Paige a smaller bag. "Your lunch. Protein bar for midmorning. Water bottle's full. Remember your inhaler's in the side pocket if you need it."

"*Dad*," Paige muttered, embarrassed. "I know."

I bit back a smile. He was so painfully earnest. It was actually kind of... sweet? No, not sweet. Thorough. Professional. Something like that.

"Want a juice box, Paige?" I asked, already steering her toward the door. "We've got apple, orange, and prune... mmmmm, we should probably skip that last one."

Paige giggled, a quiet sound, but real. My heart did a weird little flip.

Once in the break room, I settled Paige at the corner table, away from the main traffic. "So, '*The Giver*,' huh? How far are you?"

"Jonas just left the community," she said, touching the book cover. "With Gabriel."

"OooOOOoooh, the great escape," I nodded. "What do you think happens to them?"

Paige shrugged, but her eyes were alive with curiosity. "The book makes it seem like they find Elsewhere, where there's music and colors. But my friend Tyler thinks they just freeze to death."

I laughed. "Tyler sounds cheerful."

"He likes zombie movies," Paige explained solemnly.

"Of course he does," I said, grinning. "Want to know what I think?"

"What?"

"I think they make it. I think the memory of music becomes real music. I think they find people who remember how to feel things, how to see color." I leaned in conspiratorially. "And I think the sequel proves me right."

Paige's eyes widened. "There's a sequel?"

"There's four books total," I informed her. "I've got the whole set at home. Maybe I could lend them to you sometime."

Paige nodded eagerly, then hesitated. "My dad says I should only borrow books if I can return them within two weeks. He says it's respectful of other people's property."

Of course he did. "Well, maybe we can work something out," I said. "Your dad comes here pretty often, after all."

Paige smiled, a small, shy thing. "Okay."

We chatted about books for a while, and I was impressed by how articulate she was. Not just smart, but thoughtful. No wonder Crawford was so proud of her.

"Want to see a cool trick?" I asked suddenly, grabbing a tongue depressor from a supply drawer.

"Sure," Paige said, looking intrigued.

I rummaged through another drawer and found some medical tape. "When I was about your age, my mom worked night shifts at a hospital. Sometimes I'd have to hang out while she finished paperwork. One of the nurses taught me how to make these."

I folded the tongue depressor in half, securing it with tape, then cut small triangular notches on both sides. With a few more folds and twists, it resembled a butterfly. I added a few more details with a Sharpie, and voilà.

"A butterfly!" Paige exclaimed, delighted.

"Here," I said, handing it to her. "You can color it later if you want."

Just then, the break room door opened, and Crawford stuck his head in. He looked surprised to find us both smiling, Paige holding her new creation.

"Everything okay?" he asked, his eyes darting between us.

"We're good," I said, straightening up, suddenly self-conscious. "Just talking books and making butterflies. Regular stuff."

He nodded, a strange expression crossing his face. "I'm still trying to reach Mrs. Swanson. Thank you again, Tasha."

"No big deal," I said, waving him off. "Paige is cool. We're vibing."

Paige giggled at that, and Crawford's eyes softened as they landed on his daughter. For a brief moment, I glimpsed something in his expression—a fierce, protective love that was almost painful to witness.

Then he was gone, back to his calls and his patients.

"Your dad really loves you," I said without thinking.

Paige nodded, serious again. "He's the best dad ever. He tries really hard."

"I can tell," I said softly.

We spent the next half hour making more butterflies, talking about school, and comparing notes on our favorite books. When Crawford returned, announcing that Mrs. Swanson was on her way, I felt an odd pang of disappointment.

When the older woman arrived, Paige gathered her things. Then, to my complete surprise, she gave me a quick, shy hug.

I froze for a split second before awkwardly patting her shoulder. "See you around, kiddo," I managed. "Let me know what you think about the ending of that book, okay?"

As Paige left with her father and Mrs. Swanson, I found myself watching them go. Crawford's hand rested lightly on Paige's shoulder, guiding her, and she looked up at him with complete trust.

Something twisted in my chest again, that same unfamiliar feeling. It wasn't envy, exactly. Maybe... wistfulness? A strange sense of having glimpsed something precious and rare.

Then Maria appeared at my elbow, eyebrows raised suggestively. "Look at you, playing Mary Poppins."

"Shut up, Maria," I muttered, the spell broken. "The kid's not terrible. And Crawford owes me coffee for a month."

"Mmm-hmm," Maria hummed knowingly.

I grabbed my stethoscope, slinging it around my neck. "I'm going to get report. Some of us have actual work to do."

But as I headed for the nurses' station, I couldn't quite shake the image of Paige's smile when she'd held that paper butterfly, or the raw gratitude in Crawford's eyes when I'd offered to help.

It was just one weird morning, I told myself.

It didn't mean anything.

five
nate

"LISTEN TO ME," I said quietly but firmly to the nervous-looking volunteer EMT clutching his clipboard. "You *cannot* spring these things on us."

My tone was controlled, but inside I was *pissed*. We'd received a squad report describing a "87-year-old lady, feeling a little weak today" from one of the local nursing homes, only to discover—on arrival—that the patient was barely coherent, with a body temperature of 89.9 degrees, completely incontinent of *blood* and pressure (literally) in the toilet.

The volunteer rescue squads often had these problems. This particular one was largely staffed by pre-med and medical students from the local college, kids with grand visions of doctorhood who thought volunteering as an EMT would be the perfect stepping stone for their careers. I understood how important it was to train these folks—they might well be taking care of me someday, a thought that made me shudder—but it didn't make it any easier to deal with the constant cycle of "*How hard could this really be?*" becoming "*Oh God, I don't know what the fuck I'm doing*" as students rotated through the squad.

"If you're bringing me a severely hypothermic patient with active GI bleeding and systolic pressure in the 60s, I need that information *before* they roll through our doors," I continued, keeping my voice measured despite the frustration coiling inside me. "What did you chart her temperature at when you first assessed her?"

The young man glanced down at his clipboard. "Um, we didn't actually... I mean, the nursing home staff told us her vitals were stable this morning, so we just—"

"*Stop right there.*" I cut him off, unable to hide my incredulity. "You took the nursing home's word for it? *Without checking yourself?*"

He shifted uncomfortably. "They're—I mean—"

"Let me explain something that will serve you well if you ever make it to med school," I said, leaning in slightly and putting an edge of drill instructor sharpness into my tone. "Rule number one in emergency medicine: Never, *ever* trust what a nursing home tells you about a patient's condition. Not because they're bad people, but because they're understaffed, undertrained, and overwhelmed. Half the time, the person who called you hasn't even seen the patient themselves."

His face fell as I continued, "That 'feeling a little weak today' could mean anything from fatigue to full septic shock. That 'hasn't eaten much' could mean they haven't taken food or fluids in three days. And 'seemed fine this morning' often translates to 'nobody's checked on them since yesterday afternoon.'"

I gestured toward the trauma bay where the patient was now surrounded by staff working frantically. "That woman has probably been deteriorating for days. Her core temperature is 89.9. That doesn't happen in an hour. She's been bleeding internally long enough to drop her pressure to critical levels. And now instead of coming in as the critical patient she is with resources ready, she rolled in as a 'weak elderly woman' and we're playing catch-up."

The young man swallowed hard. "I didn't realize—"

"This is what separates the people who should be in medicine from those who shouldn't," I said, my voice quieter but no less intense. "It's not about the fancy degrees or memorizing the Krebs cycle. It's about developing the healthy skepticism and critical thinking that keeps patients alive. *Always. Check. Vitals. Yourself.* Always question what you're told. Assume the worst until proven otherwise."

I took a deep breath. "Look, I'm not trying to crush your spirit. But that woman deserved better, and so will every patient you encounter. This job isn't a line on your med school application. It's people's lives."

The terrified young man—who I'd probably be calling "doctor" in less than a decade, *sigh*—nodded frantically before scurrying off. I closed my eyes, took a deep breath, and exhaled slowly.

"Looks pretty rough," Maria remarked as I walked back to the charge desk.

"Yeah," I admitted, shaking my head. "She doesn't look good. Good chance she gets admitted to the 7th floor."

Maria winced and nodded. There was no 7th floor; our hospital stopped at six. The 7th floor was *above* the hospital.

Well. I thought it was a better euphemism than "the basement room" or "being discharged to JC."

"What techs do we have free right now?" I asked aloud, mostly to myself. "Maria, would you ask Arushi and Kevin to help Deonna get that patient stabilized?" That would leave my triage nurse without assistance, but I didn't see much other choice.

"You got it," Maria confirmed.

Acting as charge nurse during Sophia's absence was like juggling chainsaws while reciting the periodic table. This is why I preferred triage and loathed being in charge. Triage was mechanical: assess, decide, move. This was like conducting an orchestra playing in a burning semi traveling 75mph down the road.

Sophia was infinitely better at this than I was. But she was off gallivanting around New Zealand with that Kiwi paramedic boyfriend of hers, and I'd agreed to pick up a couple of her shifts. Sigh. To be fair, I did owe her—not just for helping out with Paige, but for so many things I'd lost count of over the past few years.

My phone vibrated in my pocket. Normally, I'd ignore it until a break, but the school's number flashed on the screen. My heartbeat accelerated immediately.

"This is Nate Crawford."

"Mr. Crawford, this is Ms. Wilson from Riverdale Elementary." The assistant principal's voice held that careful neutrality school administrators perfect, the one that says 'don't panic yet, but something's wrong.'

"Is Paige hurt!?" I asked, a pang of adrenaline shooting through my heart.

"Not hurt, no. But there's a... situation. Paige has locked herself in the bathroom and refuses to come out. She's been in there for almost forty minutes. We've tried talking to her, but she just says she wants to go home."

A dozen scenarios flashed through my mind, none good. Bullying. Illness she was hiding. Anxiety attack.

"Has something happened? Was there an incident with another student?"

"Not that we're aware of. She seemed fine during morning classes. Her teacher said she asked to use the restroom during math, and that's when this started. We wouldn't normally call for a bathroom issue, but she sounds quite upset, and she specifically asked for you."

I glanced around the ER, dubiously, trying to do mental arithmetic that kept coming back with an impossible answer.

"Mr. Crawford? Are you able to come to the school?"

The hard reality settled over me. I couldn't leave. There wasn't a single other "charge trained" nurse on the schedule, and we were barely holding things together as it was.

"I'm in the middle of an emergency situation at the hospital." The words felt like ash in my mouth. "I can't leave right now."

Ms. Wilson's sigh carried through the phone. "I understand, but Paige is quite distressed. Our school nurse would normally handle this, but she's only here Mondays and Wednesdays due to budget cuts."

"Is there anyone there who can stay with her until I can get free? Maybe Coach Lynn?" Paige liked her gym teacher, one of the few adults at school she talked about.

"Coach Lynn is on a field trip with the fourth grade. Mr. Crawford, we're doing our best, but we can't leave her in there indefinitely, and if she won't come out—"

"I understand." My mind raced, searching for a solution. Mrs. Swanson was visiting her daughter in Chicago. My list of emergency contacts was woefully short. "Let me see if I can find someone to come. Can you give me ten minutes?"

"Of course. We'll keep trying to talk to her."

I hung up, frustration and helplessness warring within me. Who could I call? The question pounded in my head as I quickly documented vitals. Paige's world was small—my parents had both passed away, and I didn't have any close family, both by emotion and geography, and that meant our support system was equally limited.

Then an unexpected face flashed in my mind: Tasha.

Tasha, who'd watched Paige during my babysitter crisis. Tasha, who'd bonded with her over books and tongue depressor butterflies. Tasha, who was off duty today.

Tasha, who had no real reason to help me again.

But I was out of options.

I grabbed our contact list of staff phone numbers, stepped into the medication room, pulled out my phone, and dialed.

The phone rang four times. I was about to hang up when her voice came through, immediately defensive.

"Look, Crawford, I'm already in overtime this week, so unless you're offering double call pay, there's no way I'm getting off this couch—"

"No, no, it's not that. I—" I faltered. This was unprofessional, inappropriate, probably crossing a dozen boundaries. "I'm sorry to call on your day off."

"Yet here we are." Her tone was dry, but the defensiveness had vanished. "What can I do for you? Everything okay?"

"No." The single syllable felt like defeat. "I need a favor. A big one."

There was a pause, then a rustle of movement. "I'm listening."

"It's about Paige. She's having some kind of... issue at school. She's locked herself in the bathroom and won't come out. We're slammed, Sophia's on the other side of the world, there isn't another charge-trained nurse available. I can't leave."

"Is she hurt?"

"They don't think so. They don't know what's wrong. I just—" I inhaled sharply, hating the weakness in my voice. "I don't have anyone else to call."

Another pause. I could almost hear her weighing her options, calculating the imposition.

"What's the school?" Tasha asked finally.

Relief washed over me so intensely my knees almost buckled. "Riverdale Elementary. You'd need to talk to Ms. Wilson in the front office, I'll call and tell them you're coming, and that you're authorized to pick her up and take her to our house if necessary." I rattled off the address.

"I'll be there in twenty. And Crawford?"

"Yeah?"

"Breathe. Kids have emergencies. It happens."

"Thank you, Tasha. I—" What could I possibly say? "I owe you. Again."

"Start a tab," she replied, but there was a lightness in her voice that hadn't been there before. "I'll text you when I have her."

I hung up, immediately calling the school back. "Ms. Wilson? I'm sending Tasha Williams, she's a colleague and an emergency department nurse. Paige knows her. She has my permission to help however necessary and to take Paige home if needed."

The weight on my chest lightened incrementally. Tasha was capable, smart, and she'd been surprisingly good with Paige before. Whatever was happening, she could handle it.

I just hoped Paige would let her.

six
tasha

I **WAS HAVING** the most delicious dream about lying on a beach with a mojito and Chris Evans when my phone shattered the fantasy. Chris, you see, had just offered to apply my sunscreen with those impossibly perfect hands of his onto places the FDA doesn't even regulate. So when I saw Crawford's name on the screen of my phone, I almost sent him straight to voicemail—emergency room trauma could wait until my actual shift—but some impulse made me answer.

His voice was tight with the strain of someone barely holding it together. Paige was in trouble. He had one else to call. Woe is him. Please help.

Now I was pulling into Riverdale Elementary's parking lot, wondering what the hell I was doing. This wasn't my problem. Wasn't my kid. Wasn't my responsibility.

But something in Crawford's voice had gotten to me. The iron control he wore like armor had cracked, just for a moment. And somewhere in that crack, I'd seen something real.

Besides, I liked Paige. The kid had substance.

The school's front office was the same beige-and-inspirational-poster combo as every elementary school in America. The harried-looking woman at the desk looked up as I entered.

"May I help you?"

"I'm Tasha Williams. Nate Crawford sent me for Paige."

The woman's expression immediately shifted to relief. "Ms. Williams, thank you for coming. I'm Andrea Wilson, the assistant principal." She lowered her voice. "Paige is still in the girls' bathroom near the cafeteria. She still won't come out, though we've assured her she's not in trouble."

"Has she said anything specific about what's wrong?"

"Just that she wanted her dad." Ms. Wilson sighed. "Fifth grade can be tough socially. We've had incidents of bullying, though Paige hasn't reported any."

"I'd like to try talking to her alone," I said. "Kids can be funny about audiences."

Ms. Wilson led me through the cheerful corridors decorated with student artwork and science projects. Outside the bathroom door, a female teacher was speaking softly through the door.

"Paige, honey? There's someone here from your dad."

I nodded to the teacher. "I've got this."

Once she'd retreated to a discrete distance, I leaned against the wall beside the bathroom door. "Hey, Paige. It's Tasha. From the hospital. '*The Giver*'? Butterfly maker extraordinaire? Remember?"

Silence. Then a small, muffled voice: "My dad sent you?"

"Yep. He's stuck at work with some major emergencies, so I'm the B-team. Lucky you."

A wet-sounding sniffle. "I want to go home."

"I bet you do. But first, think you can unlock the door? Just for me? These hallway tiles are hideous, and I'd rather not be seen hanging out here too long."

A pause. Then the soft click of a lock. I slipped inside quickly, locking the door behind me.

Paige sat on the floor in the corner, knees pulled to her chest, arms wrapped around them. Her face was blotchy from crying, hair escaping from her ponytail. She looked so small and miserable that something in my chest squeezed unexpectedly tight.

"Hey, kiddo," I said, keeping my voice casual as I sat on the floor beside her, leaving space between us. "Rough day?"

She nodded, not meeting my eyes.

"Want to tell me what's going on? I'm pretty good with emergencies. It's kind of my whole job."

Paige buried her face against her knees. "It's embarrassing."

"More embarrassing than the time I accidentally set off the fire alarm at my high school because I was trying to microwave a Snickers bar?"

That earned me a quick glance. "Why would you microwave a Snickers?"

"I thought it would taste like a warm brownie. It does *not*. It becomes lava." I smiled. "So, what's up? Stomach bug? Threw up in class? Wardrobe malfunction? I've seen it all, kiddo."

Paige hesitated, then stage whispered, "*I'm bleeding.*"

Ahhhhhh. Everything clicked into place. "First time?"

She nodded miserably. "And I don't have any... stuff. Dad made me this emergency kit thing, but I took it out of my backpack because I needed room for my science project materials."

"That tracks," I said, nodding sagely. "Science has a way of being inconsiderate to female biology. You've got blood on your pants?"

Another nod, more tears welling up. "Everyone's going to know. Amber Miller already asked if I was okay because I looked weird during math."

"Amber Miller sounds kinda nosy," I said. "But I get it. It's scary the first time, even when you're prepared. And at school? *Ugh*, the worst."

"Dad told me it would happen eventually." Paige sniffled. "He bought all these different kinds of pads and we sat at the kitchen table while he opened the packages and tried to figure out how they worked. He kept reading the instructions and saying 'Wait, that can't be right' and then trying again."

"What happened?" I asked, fascinated by this mental image.

"He stuck one upside down at first," Paige said, a small smile breaking through her tears.

That startled a genuine laugh out of me. "I can just picture it. Your dad with his serious face, battling adhesive strips."

"He finally called one of the ladies he works with—Maria, I think —and put her on speakerphone. She was laughing so hard. But then she helped us figure it out."

"Your dad is something else."

"He does his best," Paige said with a fiercely defensive note that made me like her even more.

"He absolutely does," I agreed. "And now, so will we. Here's the plan: I've got a pad in my purse. You're going to use it, then take off your jacket and tie it around your waist. We're going to walk out of here with our heads high, and I'm taking you home. Sound good?"

Relief washed over her face. "You have one? Right now?"

"Never leave home without it." I pulled the wrapped pad from my purse. "Want me to step out?"

She shook her head. "Can you... explain again how to use it? It's been a while since..."

For the next few minutes, I walked her through the basics, answering her questions with the same straightforward tone I'd use for any medical procedure. By the time we finished, her tears had dried, and she'd tied her purple jacket around her waist.

"Perfect," I said. "Can't see a thing. Ready to make our escape?"

She took a deep breath and nodded. "Thank you for coming."

"No problem, kiddo. That's what... friends are for."

We emerged from the bathroom with dignity intact. Ms. Wilson tried to ask questions, but I smoothly intercepted.

"Paige isn't feeling well. Her dad asked me to take her home. I'm an emergency department nurse, and I've got it from here."

As we walked to my car, I glanced at Paige. "We're making a pit stop before home."

"Where?" she asked, sliding into the passenger seat.

"Walgreens. Mission critical: supply run. One pad isn't going to cut it, and we need to properly equip you for the battle ahead."

A ghost of a smile appeared on her face. "Dad calls emergencies 'missions' too."

"Your dad's a pretty smart guy."

The local Walgreens was mercifully quiet. I guided Paige to the feminine hygiene aisle, which she approached with the caution of someone walking into a minefield.

"Okay," I said, gesturing to the wall of products. "Welcome to Puberty Paradise. Let's talk options."

Paige stared wide-eyed at the overwhelming selection. "There are so many."

"Intimidating, right? Let's break it down." I picked up different packages. "These are for lighter days, these for heavier. These have wings—little sticky tabs that fold under your underwear to keep everything in place. Personally, I'm Team Wings, but it's dealer's choice."

She studied the packages seriously. "Which ones are easier?"

"For beginners? Definitely pads. We'll save the tampon talk for another day."

She selected a package of junior-sized pads with wings. "These?"

"Perfect choice. Now, let's get you some backup underwear too, because accidents happen to the best of us."

We added a pack of plain cotton underwear to our basket, then wandered down another aisle where I tossed in some gentle wipes.

"Last but not least," I said, steering us toward the candy aisle, "medicinal chocolate. Doctor's orders."

Paige hesitated. "Dad says chocolate is an occasional treat."

"Today is 100% an occasion." I gestured grandly at the selection. "Choose your weapon."

She selected a large Hershey's bar with almonds, her smile growing a little more genuine.

At the checkout, I noticed her eyeing the items with apprehension as the cashier scanned them.

"Don't worry," I said quietly. "No one cares what we're buying, promise. To her, we're just another transaction."

As if to prove my point, the cashier barely glanced up as she bagged our items. "That'll be $33.47."

Back in the car, Paige clutched the bag to her chest. "Thank you."

"No biggie. Consider it your welcome package to the Secret Society of Menstruating People. It's an exclusive club."

She giggled, a small, brief sound—but music to my ears after her tears earlier. "Does it get easier?"

I started the car, considering how honest I wanted to be. "Yes and no. The logistics get easier. You figure out your rhythm, what products work for you. The cramping... well, ibuprofen helps. But the overall experience? It becomes normal. Just another part of life."

She nodded, digesting this. "Dad explained all the biology. The uterine lining and hormones and stuff."

"I bet he did," I said, unable to keep the amusement from my voice.

Twenty minutes later, we were pulling into the Crawford driveway. Paige had been quiet during the drive, occasionally shifting uncomfortably in her seat.

"Cramps?" I asked.

She nodded. "A little."

"We'll get you set up with a heating pad. Your dad probably has ibuprofen somewhere too."

The house was exactly what I'd expected: modest, meticulously maintained, with a small front yard so perfectly mowed it looked like it had been trimmed with scissors. Inside was just as tidy—everything in its place, nothing unnecessary or frivolous. It reminded me of military housing, which I supposed made sense.

"I'll text your dad that we're home," I said, pulling out my phone.

Got her. We're at your place. She's fine.
No need to rush home.

CRAWFORD

> What happened? Is she hurt?

Nothing serious. She's OK. I've got this.
We'll talk when you get here.

CRAWFORD

> Thank you. ETA 7pm at earliest.
> Emergency contact list on fridge if you
> need to leave.

Roger that, Captain. Go save lives.

I found Paige in the kitchen, rummaging through a drawer. "Dad keeps the ibuprofen in here somewhere..."

"Let me help you get settled first. Go change into something comfortable. And take these," I added, handing her the Walgreens bag. "Bathroom first, then comfy clothes."

While she was changing, I explored the kitchen, looking for supplies... The pantry was organized with military precision—canned goods in perfect rows, cereal boxes aligned by height. I found chamomile tea, which my mom always made for cramps, and put the kettle on.

In a drawer near the stove, I discovered a folder labeled "PAIGE - MEDICAL." Curiosity got the better of me. Inside, behind the standard medical forms and immunization records, was a section labeled "Puberty."

What I found inside nearly made me choke.

Nathan Crawford had created what could only be described as the world's most comprehensive period preparation guide. Color-coded diagrams of different menstrual products. Flow charts about hormonal changes. A literal timeline prediction based on the average age of menarche for girls of Paige's demographics. Notes on potential emotional changes. A shopping list with specific brands recommended by "online parenting forums for single fathers." And two articles he'd taken a highlighter to, one from WIRED titled "Aunt

Flo Doesn't Have to Suck (That Much)" and another from *The New York Times* titled "The Best Period Kit is the One You Make Yourself."

"Oh my God, Nate," I whispered, torn between laughter and an unexpected wave of tenderness. "Jesus."

The most touching part was a handwritten note on hospital stationery:

Questions Paige might be too embarrassed to ask (per r/AskReddit)
- Will everyone know? (No, but it might feel that way)
- Does it mean something's wrong if it starts earlier/later than friends? (No)
- Is it normal to feel emotional? (Yes)
- Will it hurt? (Sometimes - heating pad, ibuprofen)

The man had thought of everything, consulted everyone from Reddit to *The New York Times*, but forgot the most basic reality: that a preteen girl might take the emergency kit out of her backpack.

Crawford, I thought, shaking my head, *you brilliant, overthinking dork. You are trying so hard to be both mom and dad, and doing an amazing job, but some things just need a woman's touch.*

"That's Dad's period bible."

I jumped, quickly closing the folder. Paige stood in the doorway in sweatpants and an oversized t-shirt with a NASA logo.

"Sorry, I was looking for ibuprofen."

"It's okay." She sat at the kitchen table. "Dad made that when I was ten. He stayed up three nights in a row working on it."

The kettle whistled, giving me a moment to compose myself. "Your dad is very... thorough."

"He says proper preparation prevents poor performance. It's his favorite saying."

I poured her tea and found the ibuprofen in a different drawer, neatly labeled "Pain Relief - NSAID." Of course.

"How are you feeling now?"

She shrugged. "Okay, I guess. Dad told me all about periods. The hormones and stuff. He even told me about cervical mucus changes."

I nearly spat out my tea. "'Cervical mucus'!? Oh, *honey*."

"Is that... not normal?"

I couldn't help laughing. "Your dad is amazing, Paige. But some things are just better coming from another woman. Not because he doesn't know his stuff—clearly he does—but because he hasn't lived it."

She nodded slowly. "Like how he knows all about broken bones but still freaked out when I broke my wrist last year."

"Exactly."

As the afternoon progressed, we settled into a surprisingly comfortable routine. I found a heating pad in a cabinet, and we camped out on the couch. Paige mentioned a book she was reading, which led to a debate about the best fantasy series, which led to her showing me her bookshelf.

She gradually relaxed, her initial embarrassment fading. I showed her how to track her period on a calendar app. We talked about school, about her science project on water filtration, about her best friend Zoe.

At some point, I realized I was enjoying myself. Not just tolerating the situation, but actually having fun with this serious, bright kiddo who was so clearly Crawford's daughter in every way that mattered.

Around four, I heated up some soup I found in the freezer (labeled "Chicken Noodle - Homemade"). We were eating at the kitchen table when Paige looked up suddenly.

"Did you know my mom left when I was a baby?"

The question caught me off guard. "I think your dad mentioned it once."

She nodded, stirring her soup. "I used to think she left because of me. But Dad says she just wasn't ready to be a mom, and that was about her, not about me."

"Your dad's right."

"Sometimes I wonder what it would be like to have a mom. For stuff like today. It's really nice having another girl around." She glanced up. "But Dad does pretty good."

"He does better than pretty good, Paige. He's kind of incredible."

"Yeah." She smiled, a flash of braces. "He is."

The front door opened at exactly 7:27 PM. Nathan appeared in the kitchen doorway, still in scrubs, his face lined with fatigue but eyes immediately seeking out Paige. He came over and wrapped her up in a bear hug, twirling her around once before setting her back down.

"Hey, sweetheart. You okay?"

Paige nodded. "I'm fine, Dad. Tasha helped me."

Relief washed over his features. "Good. That's good." He turned to me. "Tasha, can I talk to you for a minute?"

I followed him into the living room, where he turned to me with an intensity that was almost uncomfortable.

"What happened? Is she okay? Why was she locked in the bathroom?"

"She got her first period. At school. No supplies."

Understanding dawned on his face, followed by a complex mix of emotions: relief, empathy, and something that looked almost like wistfulness.

"Ah." He ran a hand through his short hair. "The emergency kit. I should have checked."

"You can't anticipate everything, Crawford."

"I should have," he insisted. "I knew this was coming. The statistical window for—"

"Oh my God, you dork, shut *up*! You did *not* talk about 'statistical windows' with Paige!" I couldn't help the laugh that escaped.

A faint flush colored his cheeks. "I may have used more age-appropriate language."

"Like 'cervical mucus'?"

His flush deepened. "She told you about that?"

"Relax, Crawford. You did good. Better than most dads would have. But some things... well, they're just easier coming from someone who's been there."

He nodded slowly. "I'm aware of my limitations."

"They're not limitations. They're just... differences." I paused. "She's a really great kid, Nate. You're doing an amazing job with her."

Something shifted in his expression at the use of his first name. Something warm and surprised.

"Thank you," he said simply. "For today. For being there for her. For..."

"Handling the cervical mucus discussion?" I suggested, raising an eyebrow.

A real smile broke through then, transforming his face. "Among other things."

We stood there for a moment, something unspoken passing between us. Then Paige appeared in the doorway, her hair damp from a shower, dressed in fuzzy pajamas with planets on them.

"Dad?" she asked hesitantly. "Before Tasha goes..." She shifted from one foot to the other. "Could I maybe have her number? For my phone? In case I have more... questions?"

Nate blinked, clearly caught off guard. Paige had told me he had a strict policy about her Gabb phone—a basic device that only allowed calls and texts to a carefully vetted list of contacts.

"It's just," Paige continued into the silence, "sometimes there's stuff that's easier to ask another girl about."

I watched Nate's face as he processed this request, the internal struggle visible in the slight furrow of his brow. This wasn't just about exchanging phone numbers, this was about expanding Paige's circle of trust beyond the tightly controlled boundaries he'd established to keep her safe.

"I think that's a great idea," I said lightly, trying to ease the moment. "I promise not to share any state secrets or teach her how to hotwire a car."

A smile tugged at the corner of his mouth. "That's exactly what I was worried about." He turned to Paige. "Go get your phone, sweetheart."

Paige's face lit up, and she darted back toward her room.

"Thank you," I said quietly once she was gone. "That means a lot."

"I trust you with her," Nate replied simply.

The words hung between us, weighted with significance. For Nathan Crawford, there was no higher compliment.

Paige returned with a simple phone in a purple case. As I added my contact information, I felt the responsibility that came with this permission. This wasn't just about being available for period questions—this was an invitation into their carefully constructed world.

"All set," I said, handing it back to Paige. "Text me anytime, okay? Even if it's just to talk about books or complain about homework."

Paige clutched the phone to her chest, beaming. "Thanks, Tasha!"

"I should get going. Got plans tonight."

It was a lie, but the intensity of whatever was happening in that quiet living room was becoming too much.

Nate's face fell, disappointment flashing briefly before he composed himself. "Are you— ahh. I... of course." He walked me to the door. "Tasha. Really. I don't know how to thank you for this."

"Buy me coffee sometime," I said, the words escaping before I could think better of them. "Good coffee, not the ER sludge."

He blinked, surprised, then nodded, a hint of renewed warmth in his eyes. "Deal."

As I drove home, I found myself smiling at nothing in particular. The day had been unexpected in every way—especially in how much I'd enjoyed being part of the Crawford family's world, even briefly.

My phone buzzed as I pulled into my apartment complex:

UNKNOWN

Hi Tasha it's Paige Crawford!

I saved the contact before responding:

> Hey kiddo! How are you?

PAIGE

Good! Dad made me tea and we're watching Great British Bake Off. ☕🍰

> Perfect recovery plan. That's a quality show.

PAIGE

I like when the cakes fall apart. 😂💥🍰

I laughed out loud at that.

> Same! The disasters are the best part.

PAIGE

Thank you again for today. It was really scary but you made it better. 😊➡️😊

> Anytime, Paige. For real. That's what the number is for.

PAIGE

I've never asked Dad for anyone's number before. Just Miss Swanson and my friends parents.

The significance of this wasn't lost on me. Another text came through:

PAIGE

I'm glad he said yes.

Something warm unfurled in my chest.

Me too, kiddo. Get some rest. Tell your
dad the tea was a good call.

PAIGE

Goodnight Tasha!

I set my phone down, that unexpected warmth still spreading through me. Something was changing between Nate and me. Something I wasn't sure I was ready for, but couldn't seem to stop.

And strangely enough... I wasn't sure I wanted to.

seven
nate

I FINISHED my third straight trauma assessment of the night, signing off on the chart before sliding it into the completed rack. The board was finally clearing after the chaos of a two-car MVA that had sent five patients our way. Now, in the temporary lull, I allowed myself a moment to breathe.

Maria was leaning against the nurses' station, absorbed in her phone, her expression shifting between smiles and frowns as she scrolled Instagram.

"Checking up on our world travelers? I hope Sophia's having a better time than *this*," I said, gesturing to the general chaos of the emergency department around us.

"Madison's been posting like crazy," Maria replied, turning her phone toward me. "Look at these mountains! And the lake! God, I need a vacation."

I studied the images, full of breathtaking landscapes, shimmering lakes, a vineyard stretching toward distant mountains. Professional quality scenery, but something felt off.

"Lots of landscape shots," I observed. "Not many people."

"I noticed that too." Maria's brow furrowed. "And Sophia hasn't responded to my text from yesterday. Just a thumbs-up emoji."

"Could be busy," I offered, though my own instincts were prickling. "Or bad cell service."

"Maybe." Maria scrolled further, unconvinced. "But Madison's been posting hourly updates, so the service can't be that bad. And look—this was from this morning. Sophia's in it, but she looks... off. And no Jack."

The photo showed Madison beaming in front of a vineyard, Sophia beside her with a smile that looked fine, superficially, but after years of knowing her, I recognized right away as her "just going through the motions" smile.

"Something's not right," Maria declared, maternal concern evident in her voice. "Sophia was so excited about this trip. About Jack's family."

"Could be jet lag," I suggested, but even I didn't believe it. In the years I'd known Sophia Mitchell, I'd never seen her rattled. Not during mass casualties, not during codes, not even when dealing with administration. Whatever had put that look on her face wasn't trivial.

"Mmm-hmm." Maria's skepticism matched my own. "You know Jack a bit, right?"

I nodded, remembering our brief conversations. The Kiwi paramedic had reminded me of the New Zealand Defense Force guys I'd worked with in Basrah rebuilding the hospital there—straightforward, competent, no bullshit. We weren't close, but there was a mutual respect there.

"We've talked a few times," I acknowledged. "Seems like a solid guy."

"Maybe you could check in with him? Casually?" Maria suggested, her expression all innocent concern, though I wasn't fooled by the matchmaker gleam in her eye. "Just to make sure everything's okay?"

I frowned. "Talked a few times" meant we'd exchanged probably fifty, maybe a hundred words. I wasn't one for inserting myself into other people's business in any circumstances, but here, the suggestion was particularly absurd. If my daily word count with people I genuinely cared about hovered around single digits, my desire to "check in" with an acquaintance was somewhere in the negative numbers. Paige would probably say I had the emotional involvement skills of a cactus.

But on the other hand, Sophia was a colleague I respected, someone who'd had my back more than once.

"I'm not one for getting involved in other people's business," I said, mirroring my internal dialogue, more in an effort to convince myself than Maria.

"It's not getting involved," she insisted. "It's showing concern for a colleague. Very professional."

She tilted her head, giving me that look I'd seen her use on reluctant specialists. "Besides, Sophia would do it for you in a heartbeat."

Ooooooof. *That* hurt. Damn it. Maria knew exactly which buttons to push. Sophia *had* been there for me more times than I could count, never asking questions, just stepping up when needed.

"Fine," I grumbled. "*One* text. But I'm not playing relationship counselor."

Maria's victory smile was insufferable. "Of course not. Just checking in. Very casual. Very professional. Very demure."

I rolled my eyes as I walked away, but I was already composing the message in my head. Nothing intrusive, nothing that suggested I was prying. Just a casual check-in, one professional to another. As I rounded the corner toward the break room, I pulled out my phone.

> Jack, mate. Nate Crawford here. Hope the trip's going well. Heard from Maria things might be a bit quiet on Sophia's end. Just checking in, make sure you're all showing her a good Kiwi welcome.

I hit send before I could overthink it, then tucked the phone away as the trauma alert sounded again. Whatever was happening in New Zealand would have to wait—Metro General's never-ending parade of emergencies demanded my full attention now.

A half hour later, I finally had a moment to check my phone. Jack had responded:

> JACK
>
> Bit of a hiccup, mate. Working through it. She's seeing the sights. Thanks for checking.

That confirmed my suspicions. Something had definitely happened. I hesitated, then sent what I thought was a safe closing message:

> Hiccups happen. She's a tough one, our Sophia. You need anything, say the word. I've known her for years if you need advice.

There. Professional courtesy extended, obligation fulfilled. I slipped the phone back in my pocket, confident that would be the end of it. I was halfway through my charting when my phone buzzed again. Jack's name lit up the screen. My stomach dropped as I read his message:

> JACK
>
> Actually, mate, if you've got a minute, I could really use some insight. I lied to her about something really big. If you've seen her get really angry, what worked to get back in her good graces?

"Oh, you done fucked *up*," I said aloud—and loudly—drawing startled looks from two of my nurses and a passing resident.

"Patient care," I muttered, gesturing vaguely at my phone. "Bad lab values."

What the hell was I supposed to do with this? I'd offered advice as a polite formality, not expecting to actually dispense relationship wisdom. And this guy was asking about making things right with Sophia Mitchell after lying to her? I knew Chief Petty Officers at

Great Lakes who would have withered under the kind of fire Sophia could bring to bear. I'd seen seasoned doctors back away from her when she was in righteous-fury mode defending her patients or nurses. The resident who snapped his fingers at her two years ago had *literally never been seen in the ER again.*

My fingers hovered over the keyboard.

I could ignore it. Claim I was busy with patients. God, that was so tempting.

Awww, hell.

> What exactly did you lie about?

I typed instead, immediately regretting the decision to engage. The three dots appeared, disappeared, then appeared again.

JACK

> Can't go into details. Just know it wasn't anything harmful, but it was fundamental. An omission that changed how she sees me.

Fundamental but not harmful? Fundamental but not harmful?!? What does THAT mean? My mind raced, trying to square that circle, but came up empty. What the hell could he have done that fit *that* description and had Sophia Mitchell ready to bring the thunder? Before I could respond, he texted again:

JACK

> On a scale of 1-10, how fucked am I?

I considered everything I knew about Sophia Mitchell. Her incredible competence. Her absolute and utter intolerance for bull-shit. The way she valued honesty above almost everything else, especially after what she'd been through with her ex.

I typed back honestly.

> 11. But not necessarily permanently
> fucked.

I hesitated, then added:

> Look, I'm the last guy who should give
> relationship advice. But I know Sophia.
> She doesn't do games. If you fucked up
> so bad it doesn't fit in a text, you better
> just own it and then pray as hard as you
> can to whatever deity will listen.

I hit send and immediately felt like an idiot. What the hell did I know about fixing relationships? My longest relationship in the past five years had been with my coffee maker.

The phone buzzed again.

> JACK
>
> Thanks, mate. That actually helps. I can
> do that. I owe you.

"Who are you texting?" Maria asked, appearing beside me with suspicious timing.

I quickly pocketed my phone. "No one."

"Mmm-*hmm*." Her knowing look was insufferable. "'No one' named Jack, perhaps? From New Zealand?"

"Don't you have specialists to page, Maria? We're still waiting on the wet read for that vascular ultrasound. Let's get to it," I deflected.

"I'm multitasking," she replied smoothly, leaning against the counter with no intention of leaving. "So Jack texted back, huh? Must be serious if he's actually responding to your attempt at emotional support."

I glared at her. "You really have nothing better to do than monitor my text messages?"

"Not really," she said cheerfully. "This is the most interesting thing to happen since Dr. Brown got stuck in the elevator with that guy from Pharmacy she's been avoiding for months." She patted my arm. "You're a good friend, Nate. Whether you admit it or not."

She sauntered off, looking pleased with herself, while I tried to remember when exactly I'd agreed to be anyone's "good friend."

But as I worked through my notes, I kept thinking about Jack's situation. The poor dumb bastard had no idea what he was up against if he'd truly hurt Sophia. But the fact that he was desperate enough to ask me—practically a stranger—for advice... sigh.

Even I could admit that said something about how much he cared.

Hell, he might just stand a chance after all.

eight
tasha

SOME DAYS you were just *on*. Today was one of those days.

First, there was the HVAC tech in Room 2, writhing in agony with what looked like the worst case of conjunctivitis I'd ever seen. Three residents had already been in there, throwing around words like "chemical burn" and "industrial accident," when I asked the simple question: "What exactly were you working on when this started?"

"Just routine maintenance," he'd said through gritted teeth. "Checking the sterilization units in the hospital's ventilation system."

Bingo. "Did you look directly at any of the UV lights?"

The sheepish pause told me everything I needed to know. UV keratitis—essentially a sunburn on his corneas from ultraviolet exposure. Not rocket science, but apparently none of the doctors had thought to ask about UV exposure when dealing with an HVAC tech complaining of severe eye pain.

Twenty minutes later, Dr. Lee was writing him a prescription for eye drops and strict instructions about eye protection, looking slightly annoyed that a Fast Track nurse had solved what the residents had been puzzling over.

Then came Mrs. Henderson, sweet sixty-eight-year-old grandmother who needed an MRI for her knee pain. The night shift nurse had already cleared her through the screening—no pacemaker, no surgical implants, all good to go.

Except I actually read the screening form.

"Mrs. Henderson," I said carefully, "the form asks about *any* metal piercings. Are you sure you don't have any?"

She blushed adorably. "Well, I do have one, but it's in a... very unusual place. Would that matter?"

I kept my expression perfectly professional. "If it's anywhere that would be painful as hell when the MRI kicks on, then yes, it absolutely matters." Absolutely *no* judgment from me! If Grandma wants to have fun, Grandma can have fun! "That's exactly why we do the complete screening on everyone."

Crisis averted. The MRI tech thanked me profusely when I called to update the orders. Apparently, discovering a clitoral hood piercing *after* the machine was running would have been, ahh... *problematic*.

I was feeling pretty good about my clinical decision-making when EMS rolled in with what should have been a straightforward finger injury.

The kid—and he really was just a kid, early twenties at most—was practically hyperventilating on the stretcher, cradling his left hand like it might fall off. His index finger was swollen and obviously painful, but from what I could see, it wasn't mangled or deformed.

"Got it slammed in a heavy door about an hour ago," the EMT reported to Sophia, freshly returned from her globetrotting adventures and thrown right back into the crucible of the ER. "Significant pain, some swelling. We splinted it."

Sophia glanced at the board, which was already packed. "Send him to triage. We'll get him worked up when—"

"Wait," I interrupted, watching the kid's face. He'd gone pale at the word "triage," probably imagining another hour of waiting with a throbbing finger. "What exactly did you tell him about the injury?"

The EMT, a young volunteer who looked like he was maybe nineteen himself, shifted uncomfortably. "Well, you know, with that kind of trauma to the finger, there's always a chance it might need amputation if there's significant damage to the—"

"*Amputation*?" I stared at him. "You told a kid with a slammed finger that he might need amputation?"

"I mean, it's always a possibility with crush injuries—"

I looked at the kid's finger again. Swollen, yes. Bruised, definitely. But the nail bed looked intact, there was no obvious laceration, and he had full range of motion despite the pain.

"Sophia," I said, making a decision, "just send him to Fast Track. I think I can take one more."

She raised an eyebrow but nodded. "Your call."

Twenty minutes later, I had the kid comfortable with an ice pack and pain medication, his x-ray ordered, and his anxiety significantly reduced after I'd explained that his finger was almost certainly just bruised, not dangling by a thread.

"So I'm not going to lose it?" he asked for the third time.

"Not unless you're planning to stick it in a blender," I said dryly. "You'll be sore for a week or two, but all your digits should remain attached."

He actually smiled at that, the first time since he'd arrived. As a transporter wheeled him off to radiology, I felt pretty good about the whole interaction. It would have been completely appropriate to send him to triage—we were slammed—but sometimes a little extra effort made all the difference.

That's when *she* arrived.

"*Excuse* me, I need to speak to someone about my son's treatment," announced a woman who had clearly perfected the art of demanding to speak to managers. She was maybe fifty, wearing what I'd learned to recognize as "*I have money and you will respect me*" casual wear, and radiating the kind of entitled energy that made my teeth itch.

"What can I help you with?" I asked, keeping my voice pleasant.

"My son was brought here with a serious hand injury, and I need to know exactly what's been done and what the treatment plan is. I also need access to his medical records."

I blinked. "I'm sorry, what's your son's name? We don't have any children here with hand injuries."

She rattled off a name that made me pause. "Wait, you mean the *adult* patient? The twenty-something guy with the finger injury?"

"Yes, and I demand to know—"

"Ma'am," I interrupted, "that's an adult patient we're talking about. I can't discuss anything with you without his explicit permission. You're welcome to talk to him directly when he gets back from radiology—assuming you have a visitor badge?"

Her face flushed red. "That's ridiculous! I'm his mother! I have every right to know what's happening with his medical care!"

"Actually, you don't," I said, maintaining my professional tone despite the spike of irritation. "HIPAA laws are very clear about patient privacy, even for family members. Unless he's given us written permission to share his information with you, I legally cannot discuss his case."

"This is outrageous! I want to file a complaint! I'm being treated rudely and denied basic information about my own child!"

"Your *adult* child," I corrected. "And I'm sorry you feel that way, but—"

"Is there a problem?" Sophia's voice cut through the rising tension as she approached, her expression professionally concerned.

"This person wants access to their son's medical chart," I explained, keeping my voice level but shooting Sophia a look that said *help me out here.*

Sophia nodded seriously, her face taking on an expression of helpful understanding. "Oh, of course! For a minor, we absolutely have to allow parental access to medical records." She turned to the woman with professional interest. "How old is your son, ma'am? Ten? Twelve?"

The woman stammered slightly. "Twenty-four."

"Twenty-four?" Sophia's eyebrows shot up in apparent surprise. "Twenty-four years old?"

"Yes."

"Well," Sophia said, her voice taking on that deadly polite tone I'd learned to recognize, "I'm sorry, ma'am, but Tasha here is absolutely correct. Unless you want us to break a multitude of federal and state laws regarding patient privacy, I cannot give you information from an adult patient's chart without his explicit written permission."

"But I'm his mother—"

"You're not suggesting we break the law, are you?" Sophia asked, her expression perfectly innocent.

The woman opened and closed her mouth a few times, clearly wanting to argue but recognizing she was on the losing side. With a final huff of indignation, she stalked off toward the waiting area.

"Good job sticking to your guns on the privacy issue," Sophia said once the woman was out of earshot. "The kid might not have cared if we shared that information with his mom, but we do things the right way here."

I nodded, but I could feel my irritation still simmering. "It's just frustrating, you know? There are people who've been waiting in triage for hours, and I went out of my way to get that kid seen quickly because he was obviously struggling. The EMT had him convinced he was going to lose his finger. And then all I get is grief from his helicopter mother."

"Welcome to the ER," Sophia said with a slight smile. "Where no good deed goes unpunished."

Something about her smile caught my attention. There was a lightness to it I hadn't seen before, a relaxed quality that was distinctly un-Sophia-like. She looked... content. Happy, even.

"Speaking of good deeds," I said, studying her face, "you seem remarkably chipper today. Did you have... *fun*... in New Zealand?" I let the question hang with just enough implication to make my meaning clear.

Sophia's smile widened, and instead of her usual deflection or professional redirect, she actually looked almost... smug?

"Let's just say it was... educational," she replied, and there was definitely something in her voice that hadn't been there before.

"'*Educational*'?" I pressed, grinning despite myself. "I gotta know: what kind of '*education*' are we talking about here?"

"The kind that's none of your business," she said, but she was still smiling, and there was color in her cheeks that suggested I was right on target.

"Damn, Sophia!" I laughed, bouncing slightly on my toes, unable to contain my excitement. "Okay! Okay! I see you! Here I was thinking you were all work and no play, but apparently you've been holding out on us! Did you—" I gasped audibly. "Oh my GOD, did you join the mile-high club? *Please tell me you joined the mile-high club!*"

"Tasha!" Sophia hissed, glancing around the ER, but she was fighting back laughter.

"What? It's a perfectly reasonable question! You were on a very long flight!" I was practically vibrating with curiosity now, completely forgetting where we were. "Or wait—was it the accent? Because honestly, that accent would do things to me too. Like, I get it. Completely."

From across the nurses' station, I caught Nate watching us with an expression somewhere between amusement and mild horror. He shook his head slightly, the kind of look an older sibling might give a particularly exuberant younger one.

"I have no idea what you're talking about," Sophia said primly, but the effect was ruined by the fact that she was practically glowing.

"Oh, but you *do*. You *absolutely* do," I said, lowering my voice but not my enthusiasm. "And honestly? Good for you. Really. It's nice to see you... I don't know, properly sexed-up, I guess."

"Jesus, Tasha," Sophia muttered, but she was still smiling.

"What? Life's too short not to get some! Especially with hot foreign guys who probably know what they're doing." I paused, struck by a thought. "Oh *God*, please tell me he knows what he's doing. Because if Sophia Mitchell finally lets someone past the ice queen fortress and he turns out to be disappointing in bed, I will personally—"

"Tasha." Sophia's voice carried a warning, but there was warmth underneath it. "You need to stop talking. Now."

I grinned, completely unrepentant. "Fine, fine. But just so you know, I'm living vicariously through you right now. My dating life is nonexistent, so I need details. Not right now, obviously, but later. Over drinks. Many drinks."

For a moment, something softer crossed her expression. "Thanks, Tasha. That... means more than you know."

As she walked away, I found myself reassessing everything I thought I knew about Sophia Mitchell. Maybe the ice queen thing had been more about protection than personality. Maybe she just needed the right person to help her thaw out.

Either way, seeing her this happy was oddly satisfying. If someone as controlled and guarded as Sophia could find whatever it was she'd found in New Zealand, maybe there was hope for the rest of us.

Though watching the kid's mother pace around the waiting area like a caged tiger, I was reminded once again why I preferred keeping my professional and personal lives completely separate.

Some people's family dynamics were just too complicated to navigate.

Give me a straightforward medical emergency over relationship drama any day of the week.

nine
nate

THE ER WAS A CONTROLLED HUM, the usual Tuesday afternoon rhythm. I was halfway through documenting a sepsis workup when I heard it. The tone first—condescending, hostile—then the words, slithering across the bay like poison.

"Don't you people *ever* listen? I said I need a real nurse."

My shoulders tensed automatically. Nothing good ever followed "you people." My gaze lifted from the computer, shifting to Bay 4 where Tasha was checking vitals on a middle-aged white guy with an expensive watch and a face twisted in contempt.

"Sir," Tasha responded, her voice controlled with a practiced neutrality I recognized from my time in the service, "I'm administering your medication as ordered by the doctor. If you have concerns about your treatment plan, I'd be happy to page Dr. Lee."

I should have gone back to my charting. Not my patient, not my problem. But something about the set of Tasha's shoulders held my attention. The careful way she kept her face composed despite the hard glitter in her eyes.

"I don't want your kind touching me," the man—Jensen, according to the board—sneered. "Get me someone competent.

Someone who actually earned their position instead of filling a quota."

My fingers stilled on my keyboard, a red haze at the edges of my vision.

Tasha's expression never faltered, her professional mask firmly in place. "Sir, I'll be monitoring your pain levels, but please use the call button if you need anything else. Dr. Lee will be in shortly."

She turned to leave, and I should have looked away then. Would have, if Jensen hadn't muttered the slur under his breath—just loud enough to be heard, just soft enough to maintain plausible deniability.

A single word, ugly and deliberate.

Tasha's step faltered, almost imperceptible. Her spine straightened, shoulders squaring. But she kept walking, kept her composure, kept her dignity.

Something hot and dangerous uncoiled in my chest.

The anger wasn't new. It's always there, banked low like embers, waiting for oxygen. What was new was its sudden, overwhelming intensity. The roaring in my ears. The taste of metal in my mouth.

Before I registered moving, I was across the room, my pen clattering forgotten on the counter. All I could see was Jensen's smug, hateful face and Tasha, standing there, taking it, because that's what she had to do.

But I wasn't going to.

My voice, when it came, wasn't my own. It was deeper, harder, a sound dredged up from a place I kept locked down tight. The voice that had called cadence for miles on the tarmac of Naval Training Center Great Lakes. The one that could make recruits piss their pants at fifty yards.

"YOU WILL *NOT* SPEAK TO HER LIKE THAT!"

The ER went dead silent. I felt, more than saw, heads turn. Jensen, startled, actually recoiled. Then his pasty face mottled with anger. "Who the hell do you think you are? You can't talk to me like that! I'm a patient! I'll have your job! I'll sue this whole damn hospital!"

I was moving before I realized it, a straight line from the nurse's station to Bay 4. The rage was a living thing now, coiling in my gut, demanding release. My voice dropped, but it was the low growl of a cornered animal. I almost threw my arm, finger pointed angrily, towards the doors marked EXIT at the far end of the hallway.

"*YOU GET THE FUCK OUT OF MY EMERGENCY DEPARTMENT!*"

"I'll have you arrested! Assault! You're threatening me!" Jensen shrieked, scrambling back on the gurney.

A cold calm settled over me then, the kind that always came before the storm in the sandbox. My vision narrowed. "Try me," I said, and the words were flat, devoid of heat, which somehow made them more dangerous. "I would *love* to explain to the District Attorney *exactly* why I felt the need to remove a threat from this ER. I'd relish detailing every single word, you—"

"ENOUGH!"

Sophia's voice. Sharp. Absolute. It sliced through my rage like a scalpel. I froze, my retort dying on my lips. She was standing at the entrance to the bay, and her eyes weren't on Jensen. They were on *me*. And they were radiating an authority that even in my current state, I couldn't ignore.

"OUT! Nate, hallway. *Now!*"

The command was a physical blow. *Me?* Out? Confusion warred with the receding tide of adrenaline. I wanted to argue, to explain, but one look at her face—the unwavering steel in her eyes—and I knew. I was seconds from crossing a line. A very bright, very final line.

She didn't wait. She turned to Jensen, who was looking smug. "And *you*. *You* will leave." Her voice was ice. "Dr. Lee," she called, her tone sharp, "is Mr. Jensen medically stable for discharge?"

Dr. Lee, bless his usually oblivious soul, was already at the bedside. His face was granite, all traces of his usual charm gone.

"Patient presented with a minor abrasion, received irrigation and a dressing. Vitals stable. No indication for further acute medical intervention. He's clear for discharge."

"You heard the doctor," Sophia said to Jensen. "Your treatment here is complete. Security will escort you to the exit. I am personally filing a trespass order. If you ever set foot on hospital property again for anything less than a life-threatening emergency, you will be arrested. Am I clear?"

Jensen sputtered, but the fight was gone. Security, who'd materialized like ghosts, flanked him. I watched him go, then Sophia turned back to me. Tasha was a pale shadow behind her, her eyes wide, fixed on me.

"My office, Nate. *Now.*"

I followed her, the walk down the hall feeling like a mile. The adrenaline had leached away, leaving a bone-deep weariness and the cold dread of what was coming.

In her office, the door closed, and the small space felt suffocating. I didn't know what to do with my hands, my body. Instinct took over. Heels together. Back straight. Arms locked, thumbs on the seams of my scrubs. Eyes front. The familiar brace of military attention.

Sophia's voice was quiet, but it cut deeper than any shout. "Nate. You're not in the Navy anymore. You can't hide behind that bearing. Not here."

I didn't move. Couldn't.

"Look at me."

Slowly, I forced my gaze to meet hers. The disappointment in her eyes was worse than anger.

"They pay me an extra dollar an hour to kick out racists," she said, her voice low. "That's my job. Yours is to take care of patients. Even the assholes." She took a step closer, almost in my face. "You were *seconds* away from putting your hands on him, Nate. *Seconds.* And then what? You go to jail? Maybe. You lose your license? Possibly. You lose your job here? *Guaranteed.*" Her voice softened, but the words were like hammer blows. "What about Paige? What happens to her when her father is in jail or can't work?"

Paige. The name was a punch to the gut. My carefully constructed world, the one I'd built to protect her, was teetering. Because of me. Because I'd lost control.

"When you blow up like that," Sophia continued, her voice regaining its edge, "*you* become the story. The headline won't be, 'Racist Patient Verbally Abuses Nurse.' It'll be, 'ER Nurse Assaults Patient.' And we won't get to say he was spewing vile hate. Because we're not allowed to. HIPAA doesn't give a damn about justice; it cares about patient privacy, even for the ones who deserve none."

My gaze dropped to the scuffed linoleum. She was right. Of course, she was right.

"You're off the floor for the day. Go home, Nate." She paused, and I braced myself. "And I'm sorry, but I have to write you up for this. This is too big. Administration will be involved. I don't have a choice."

Her voice caught on the "I'm sorry," a tiny tremor that somehow made it worse.

There was nothing to say. No defense. I'd crossed a line. A big one. I nodded slowly, the movement feeling stiff, unfamiliar. My shoulders, which had been locked back, sagged.

"I understand, Sophia," I said, my voice raspy, barely recognizable. "I... I put you in an impossible position. I am sorry for that." I met her eyes then, a flicker of the man I used to be, the one who'd faced down worse than Jensen. "But I'm not sorry he knows he can't talk to her that way." The words were out before I could stop them. A beat of silence. "I shouldn't have lost control," I added, the admission costing me. "It won't happen again."

I turned and walked out of her office, out of the ER, the weight of what I'd done settling over me like a shroud. I didn't look at Tasha, didn't look at anyone. Just walked.

But as I pushed through the doors into the corridor, the image of Tasha's face flickered in my mind—those wide eyes fixed on me, that expression I couldn't quite read. Not the gratitude I'd half-expected, but something more complex. Concern? For me? After the way I'd just detonated? Or was it just shock? Disappointment that the guy who fumbled through explaining periods to his daughter, who relied on *her* to rescue Paige from a school bathroom, could also lose his damn mind like this?

The Tasha who'd handled Paige's period emergency with such unexpected kindness and humor... what would she think of this? I shoved the thought away, a fresh wave of shame washing over me. I had bigger problems. A write-up. Possibly a suspension. A conversation with Paige about why Daddy was home early.

And somewhere beneath it all, the unsettling realization that the control I'd fought so hard to maintain since coming home, through therapy, through sobriety, through the rigid routines that structured our lives... it was more fragile than I'd allowed myself to believe.

All it had taken was one word, not even directed at me. One ugly word aimed at a colleague. A colleague who'd shown Paige, and me, a surprising amount of grace just a short while ago.

So why had it shattered my control so completely?

Each step felt heavy, the future uncertain. Paige. My job. Everything felt fragile, breakable. And it was all my own damn fault.

ten

tasha

THE WORST PART wasn't the words themselves.

I'd heard worse. Growing up as one of the few Black girls in honors classes, working my way through nursing school, even here at Metro General—racist assholes were nothing new. You developed thick skin, learned to document everything, kept your face neutral while you fantasized about creative ways to make their IV insertions especially memorable.

No, the worst part was the look on Nate's face afterward.

I'd seen him handle every kind of chaos the ER could throw at us. Code Blues where he moved with surgical precision. Trauma cases that would make seasoned doctors flinch. Difficult families, belligerent drunks, the woman last month who'd thrown her bedpan at Dr. Ward's head. Through it all, Nathan Crawford remained the same: calm, controlled, professionally competent.

I'd never seen him lose it. Not once.

Until today.

"You okay?" Sophia appeared at my elbow as I finished charting the racist asshole's discharge. Her voice was carefully neutral, but I caught the concern underneath.

"I'm fine," I said automatically, not looking up from the computer screen.

"Tasha."

Something in her tone made me glance over. Sophia's expression was gentle but direct—the look she got when she was about to have one of those conversations that made everyone uncomfortable but needed to happen anyway.

"Really, I'm okay," I said, meaning it mostly. "It's not like it's the first time some ignorant piece of shit has—"

"I'm not asking about him," Sophia interrupted softly. "I'm asking about you. About what just happened with Nate."

Right. Because Nate Crawford, model of professional restraint, had just screamed at a patient to get the fuck out of his emergency department. And then I'd had to watch Sophia march him out of the bay like a misbehaving toddler, while he stood there looking ashamed and furious and something else I couldn't quite name.

"I didn't ask him to do that," I said quickly.

"I know you didn't." Sophia's voice was matter-of-fact. "But he did it anyway. That had to be... complicated."

Complicated. That was one word for it.

On one hand, yeah, it was gratifying to see someone stand up for me. To see that patient's smug expression crumble when six feet of pissed-off Navy veteran told him exactly where he could shove his bigotry. For about thirty seconds, I'd felt protected in a way I'd never experienced before.

But then reality kicked in. I couldn't get away with what Nate had just done. If I'd lost control like that, if I'd screamed at a patient —even a racist piece of shit—I'd be facing suspension, possibly termination. The investigation would focus on my "unprofessional behavior," not the patient's hate speech. That was just how it worked.

"It was," I admitted finally.

Sophia nodded, not pushing for more details. Which I appreciated. The last thing I needed was a well-meaning white woman trying to explain racism to me or telling me how I should feel about what had happened.

"If you need anything," she said instead, "resources, someone to talk to, time off to process—just let me know. Okay?"

"Okay."

She squeezed my shoulder briefly and moved on to deal with the next crisis, leaving me alone with my thoughts and a half-finished discharge summary.

I tried to focus on my charting, but my mind kept drifting back to Nate's face. The way his jaw had tightened when he'd heard that word. The cold fury in his voice when he'd ordered the patient out. The strange, almost vulnerable look he'd given me before Sophia had dragged him away.

Nathan Crawford had just risked his job for me. His spotless professional record, his ability to provide for Paige—he'd put all of it on the line because some asshole had disrespected me.

I wasn't sure what to do with that.

The rest of my shift passed in a blur of routine cases and careful normalcy. A few of my coworkers asked if I was okay, offering the kind of surface-level sympathy that let them feel good about themselves without actually engaging with the ugliness of what had happened. I smiled and nodded and told them I was fine, because that was easier than trying to explain the complicated knot of emotions sitting heavy in my chest.

By the time I clocked out, I still hadn't seen Nate. Word was he'd been sent home for the day, which meant he was probably sitting in his perfectly organized house, beating himself up for losing control and worrying about the write-up Sophia would have to file.

The thought bothered me more than it should have.

———————————

I spent the next two days watching Nate from across the ER, trying to figure out how I felt about what had happened.

He was back to his usual self—calm, competent, professional. If anything, he seemed more controlled than before, like he was overcompensating for his moment of explosive anger. He was polite when our paths crossed, nodded when I made suggestions about patient care, treated me exactly the same as he treated every other nurse.

But there were moments when I caught him looking at me with an expression I couldn't quite read. Something careful and searching, like he was trying to gauge my reaction to him, to what he'd done.

It should have been awkward. It should have made things weird between us.

Instead, I found myself thinking about the night Paige had her period emergency. The way he'd trusted me with his daughter, the most precious thing in his world. The gratitude in his eyes when I'd helped them through that crisis. The careful way he'd asked if I'd be willing to stay in Paige's life, to be someone she could turn to when she needed a woman's perspective.

Nathan Crawford didn't trust easily. I'd figured that out months ago. But when he did trust someone, when he let them into his carefully constructed world, he defended them with everything he had.

Even when it cost him.

Thursday afternoon, I made my decision.

"Sophia," I said, catching her between patient rooms. "Remember what you said the other day? About if I needed anything?"

She looked up from her tablet, immediately alert. "Of course. What can I do?"

"I could use something, if you think it'll work." I took a breath, feeling suddenly nervous. "Does your daughter babysit?"

Sophia's eyebrows rose slightly. "Madison? Sometimes. For family friends. Why?"

"I want to ask Nate out. Properly. But he'll never leave Paige with just anyone, and I don't want him worrying about her the whole time." I paused, then added, "I figured if it was your daughter, someone he knows and trusts..."

A slow smile spread across Sophia's face. "I think that could be arranged. Madison would love to hang out with Paige."

"You think she'd be up for it?"

"Are you kidding? She's been bored out of her mind this week. A night playing big sister to an eleven-year-old sounds like exactly the kind of responsibility she'd eat up." Sophia's smile turned slightly mischievous. "Should I ask what you have planned?"

"Nothing too scandalous," I said, though I could feel heat creeping up my neck. "Just... dinner. Maybe dancing."

"Mmmhmm." Sophia's expression was knowing, but she didn't push. "I'll talk to Madison tonight. When were you thinking?"

"Tomorrow? If that works for everyone."

"I'll text Madison right now to ask," Sophia promised. "But Tasha? Good for you. He's a good man. He deserves someone who sees that."

As I walked away, I felt something settle in my chest. A sense of rightness, like I was finally doing something I should have done weeks ago.

Nathan Crawford had stood up for me when it mattered. Now it was my turn to show him that some risks were worth taking.

eleven
nate

I'D BEEN REPLAYING Tuesday's incident in my head for three days straight, and it wasn't getting any better.

The write-up from Sophia sat in my personnel file like a ticking bomb. The shame of losing control in front of my colleagues ate at me every time I walked into the ER. But worst of all was the uncertainty—the way Tasha had looked at me afterward, an expression I couldn't read, couldn't decode, couldn't get out of my head.

I'd risked everything for her. My job, my reputation, Paige's security. And I still didn't know if she was grateful or horrified.

"Crawford."

I looked up from the supply cart I'd been organizing with unnecessary precision to find Tasha approaching. She moved with her usual confidence, but there was something different in her expression—something purposeful that made my stomach clench with anxiety.

"Tasha," I replied, keeping my voice carefully neutral.

"You got a minute?" She glanced around the busy ER, then back at me. "I wanted to ask you something."

This was it. She was going to tell me the incident had made her uncomfortable, that my loss of control had crossed a line, that we needed to maintain strictly professional boundaries going forward. I'd been dreading this conversation for three days.

"Of course," I said, setting down the IV tubing I'd been arranging for the third time.

"Would you like to have dinner sometime?" she asked. "Or coffee? Whatever you're comfortable with."

I blinked, certain I'd misheard. "I'm sorry?"

"Dinner. You and me. Like a date." Her tone was matter-of-fact, but I caught the slight uncertainty underneath. "Unless you're not interested, which is totally fine—"

"No," I said quickly, then realized how that sounded. "I mean, yes. I'm interested. I'm very interested. I just... I didn't expect..."

A small smile tugged at the corner of her mouth. "Good. I was thinking tomorrow night, if that works for you."

"Tomorrow?" My mind immediately went to logistics. "I'd need to arrange childcare for Paige. Mrs. Swanson might be available, but it's short notice—"

"Actually," Tasha interrupted, and her smile widened, "I already talked to Sophia. Madison's going to hang out with Paige tomorrow night. Sleepover, if that's okay with you? Sophia said she'd love to do it."

I stared at her, trying to process this information. "You... talked to Sophia? About babysitting? For us?"

"Well, technically I talked to her about Madison babysitting so I could ask you out properly." Tasha's expression was almost smug now. "I figured you'd never leave Paige with just anyone, and Madison's great with kids."

She'd planned this. She'd thought through the one obstacle that would have made me hesitate and solved it before I even knew there was a problem. The consideration behind that gesture made something light and buoyant expand in my chest.

"That's... very thoughtful," I managed.

"I have my moments." She paused, and when she spoke again, her voice carried a hint of mischief. "So, about dinner. I was thinking we could try this place I've been wanting to check out. It's called Whiskey River. It's a honky-tonk."

The word sent my thoughts scattering in twelve different directions. A honky-tonk. Tasha Williams, a Black woman, was asking me, a white man, to a honky-tonk. On our first official date.

My brain immediately started spiraling. Was this a test? Was she checking to see if I'd make assumptions about her musical preferences based on her race? Was she expecting me to object, to suggest somewhere more "appropriate"? Or was she deliberately choosing a venue that would make me uncomfortable, some kind of social experiment about my biases?

But then I looked at her face and saw the barely contained amusement there, like she was watching me work through exactly this mental gymnastics routine. And I realized... she was messing with me. Not cruelly, but... playfully. Testing my assumptions, yes, but in a way that felt more like gentle teasing than serious judgment.

"A honky-tonk," I repeated carefully.

"Yep. Country music, line dancing, the whole nine yards." Her eyes sparkled with barely suppressed laughter. "Problem with that?"

"No," I said slowly. "No problem at all. I just... wouldn't have expected..."

"What? That I'd like country music?" She tilted her head, her expression innocent except for the devil in her eyes. "What kind of music did you think I liked, Nate?"

"I have no idea what kind of music you like," I said honestly. "We've never talked about it."

"You're a smart guy." Her smile softened, becoming more genuine. "And now you'll find out. Tomorrow night. Seven o'clock work for you?"

I nodded, still trying to catch up with this conversation. "Seven's perfect."

"Great. I'll text you the address." She turned to go, then paused. "Oh, and Nate? Don't overthink it. It's just dinner and music."

But as I watched her walk away, I knew there was nothing

"just" about any of this. Tasha Williams had just turned what should have been a simple dinner invitation into a masterclass in assumptions, privilege, and getting to know someone beyond the surface.

And despite my spinning head and racing heart, I was looking forward to it more than I'd looked forward to anything in years.

———

Friday evening found me standing in front of my bedroom mirror, trying to decide between the blue button-down and the gray one for the third time. Paige sat on my bed, offering commentary with the brutal honesty only an eleven-year-old could muster.

"The blue one makes your eyes look nice," she said, not looking up from the friendship bracelet she was making for Madison. "But you've changed shirts four times now, Dad. It's getting weird."

"I'm not nervous," I lied, switching back to the blue shirt.

"You reorganized the spice rack twice today. You only do that when you're really nervous."

I paused in my buttoning. "The spice rack needed organizing."

"Uh-huh." Paige looked up at me with those too-perceptive eyes. "Are you nervous about your date with Tasha?"

"It's not..." I started to say it wasn't a date, then realized that was exactly what it was. "Maybe a little."

"Why? You like Tasha. She likes you. Madison says her mom thinks you guys would be good together."

"Madison said that?"

"Yep. She also said Tasha was really excited about tonight." Paige grinned. "She asked Sophia to borrow some fancy earrings."

The image of Tasha getting dressed for our date, caring enough about it to borrow jewelry, stirred something indefinable inside me.

"Dad?" Paige's voice was softer now. "Are you going to marry Tasha?"

The question caught me completely off guard. "Paige—"

"Because if you did, I wouldn't mind. She's nice. And she knows about periods and stuff, which is good."

"Noted," I said weakly. "But we're just... getting to know each other."

"Okay." Paige went back to her bracelet. "But just so you know, if you do marry her, I call dibs on being flower girl."

Before I could figure out how to respond to that, my phone buzzed with a text.

TASHA

Ready to pick me up, cowboy?

Despite my nerves, I smiled as I typed back:

NATE

As ready as I'll ever be.

At exactly six, I was loading Paige and her overnight bag into the car for the drive to Sophia's house. She chattered excitedly about her plans with Madison while I tried to calm my nerves.

"Madison says she's going to teach me how to French braid," Paige said, bouncing in her seat. "And we're going to make friendship bracelets and watch movies. She even said we could stay up until ten!"

"That's very generous of her," I said, pulling into Sophia's driveway.

The Mitchell house was a modest two-story that somehow managed to look both lived-in and welcoming. Sophia opened the door before we even knocked, Madison appearing behind her with a grin.

"Right on time," Sophia said, stepping aside to let us in. "Madison's been planning activities all afternoon."

"We're going to have the *best* time," Madison announced, immediately claiming Paige's bag. "Come on, I'll show you my room."

As the girls disappeared upstairs in a flurry of excited chatter, I found myself standing in Sophia's living room feeling oddly nervous.

Not about the date—well, not entirely about the date—but about this moment of domestic normalcy, this glimpse into what family life looked like when it wasn't just you against the world.

"She'll be fine," Sophia said gently, reading my expression. "Madison's great with kids."

"I know. I just—"

"Dad worry. I get it." She smiled. "Trust me, they'll have more fun without us hovering."

"*Kia ora*, Nate."

I turned to see Jack emerging from what looked like a home office, laptop in hand. He looked more relaxed than I'd ever seen him at the hospital—jeans and a rugby shirt instead of his paramedic uniform, hair slightly mussed like he'd been running his hands through it.

"Jack," I nodded. "How's it going?"

"Can't complain, mate. Just catching up on some paperwork." He set the laptop aside and studied me for a moment. "You look nervous. Big night?"

"Something like that."

Jack's expression shifted, becoming more serious. "Listen, I wanted to thank you again. For the advice you gave me during that whole... situation. Really helped me sort my head out."

I knew he was referring to whatever had happened between him and Sophia in New Zealand—the "hiccup" he'd mentioned in his texts. "No need to thank me. From what I can see, you two worked it out."

"Yeah, we did." Jack glanced toward Sophia, who was tidying up the kitchen, and his expression softened. "Though I have to say, you were right about one thing. I'm a *damn* lucky man. Kicking way past my coverage on this one."

I followed his gaze to Sophia, thinking about everything I knew about her— her competence, her strength, the way she'd handled my crisis with Paige's babysitter like it was nothing. "She's not usually one for second chances, so she must like you an awful damn lot."

"Yeah, mate, you're not joking." Jack shook his head, a slightly amazed smile crossing his face. "Still can't quite believe she took me back after I mucked things up so thoroughly."

"Well, you must have done something right."

"Eventually." He paused, then looked at me directly. "But seriously, I appreciate the hell out of the advice you gave me. I owe you one big."

"Nah," I said, meaning it. "You don't owe me anything. It's what friends do."

Jack's expression warmed. "Well, I appreciate it all the same."

Before I could respond, the sound of giggling from upstairs reminded me why I was here. Sophia appeared with a knowing smile.

"You should get going," she said. "Tasha's probably already wondering where you are."

"Right." I called up the stairs. "Paige! I'm leaving!"

"Bye, Dad!" came the muffled response. "Have fun on your date!"

"No worries, Mr. C," Madison added, her voice carrying down the hallway. "We've got this handled!"

Jack caught my expression and grinned. "Madison's got a good head on her shoulders. Paige is in excellent hands."

"I know." I grabbed my keys. "Thanks again, both of you."

"Go," Sophia said, practically pushing me toward the door. "And Nate? Have fun. You deserve this."

Twenty minutes later, I was pulling into the parking lot of Tasha's apartment complex, and my nervousness had been completely overtaken by curiosity. She lived in one of those converted warehouse buildings down by the river—industrial brick and huge windows, the kind of place that screamed urban professional rather than struggling nurse.

I found her building and texted:

Here

Coming down

came the immediate reply.

I got out of the car to wait, and when the lobby door opened, every coherent thought in my head evaporated.

Tasha stepped out wearing dark jeans that hugged every curve and a burgundy top that made her skin seem to glow from within. Her hair was down, falling in soft waves around her shoulders instead of the practical ponytail she wore at work, and she was wearing silver earrings that caught the light when she moved.

I'd always known she was attractive. I could appreciate her looks the way you might admire a painting in an art gallery, with professional detachment and aesthetic appreciation.

But this... this was different. Tonight she wasn't just attractive. Tonight she was absolutely *devastating*.

"You clean up nice, Crawford," she said as she approached, and her smile was warm and knowing, like she could see exactly what her appearance was doing to me.

"You look..." I started, then lost track of my words as she stepped closer, close enough that I could smell her perfume—something warm and spicy that made me want to lean in and breathe deeper. "Amazing. You look amazing."

"Thank you." She seemed pleased by my reaction, which only made her more beautiful. "You ready for this?"

"Define ready," I managed, opening the passenger door for her.

She laughed as she slid into the seat, a sound that made my breath catch a little. "Come on, Crawford. Let's see if you can handle a little country music."

As I walked around to the driver's side, I caught her watching me through the windshield, and the heat in her gaze made something low in my stomach clench with anticipation.

Whatever happened tonight, I was pretty sure my carefully controlled world was about to get turned upside down.

twelve
tasha

THE DRIVE to Whiskey River was surprisingly comfortable. I'd expected awkwardness, maybe some nervous small talk, but instead we fell into an easy rhythm. Nate was a careful driver—of course he was—but not obsessively so. He asked about my week, listened when I complained about Dr. Ward's latest bizarre comment, even laughed at my impression of Mrs. Boitnott from Room 3 who'd insisted her chest pain was caused by "too much thinking."

"Too much thinking?" he repeated, glancing over at me with amusement.

"Apparently her brain was working so hard, it was pulling blood away from her heart." I shook my head. "She was very serious about this theory."

"And the actual diagnosis?"

"Acid reflux. From the gas station burrito she'd eaten an hour before."

His laugh was genuine, warm, and I found myself studying his profile in the dashboard light. He had good hands on the steering wheel, long fingers, no wedding ring tan line. I'd noticed that at work, of course, but tonight felt different. Tonight I was allowed to look.

"What?" he asked, catching me staring.

"Nothing. Just... you seem more relaxed than usual."

"It's the shirt," he said with mock seriousness. "The blue brings out my eyes. Paige told me so."

"Paige has excellent taste."

The honky-tonk was exactly what I'd expected—neon beer signs, sawdust on the floor, the kind of place where everyone knew the words to every song and nobody cared if you couldn't line dance. Perfect for my purposes.

Nate held the door for me, ever the gentleman, and I watched his face as we walked in. He looked... curious. Not uncomfortable, not judgmental, just interested. Like he was genuinely wondering what I was up to.

Good. Let him wonder.

We found a table near the dance floor but not so close we'd get trampled by enthusiastic two-steppers. The waitress—all big hair and bigger smile—took our drink orders. I got a beer, he asked for the same.

"Just one?" I asked.

"Yes, please. Two is my limit." He said it matter-of-factly, without explanation, and I filed that information away for later consideration.

The conversation flowed easier than I'd expected. He asked about my family, and I found myself telling him about being the middle child, about trying medical-surgical nursing first and hating every minute of it.

"ICU was even worse," I said, taking a sip of my beer. "All that monitoring, all those drips, sitting there for twelve hours, watching numbers on a screen. I lasted exactly three shifts before I begged to be transferred."

"But you love the ER."

"I love Fast Track," I corrected. "I know they stuck me there because I was new, figuring maybe I wasn't ready for the acute care side. But honestly? I like the pace. You never stop moving, never get bored. And the patients might seem 'easier,' but that's not always true."

"Like the epiglottitis case," he said, and I was surprised he remembered.

"Exactly. Guy comes in for a sore throat, gets triaged to Fast Track, and I'm the one who caught that his voice was getting muffled. If he'd sat in the waiting room for another hour..." I shrugged. "Dr. Lee nailed the cric, though. Have to give him credit for that."

"Lee's a smartass, but he handled that with swagger," Nate agreed. "Jumped right up on the bed, did the whole thing without flinching."

"Yeah, well, he used to hit on me until I..." I paused, smiling at the memory. "Let's just say he doesn't anymore."

Nate's eyebrows rose. "Should I ask?"

"Probably better if you don't. But he's been very professional ever since."

The band took the stage then—three guys in cowboy hats and a woman with a voice that could make angels weep. They opened with something slow and sad, but by the third song they'd shifted into something more upbeat. The dance floor filled with couples doing the two-step and the Cotton-Eyed Joe.

That's when the magic happened.

The opening notes of "Friends in Low Places" filled the air, and I watched something shift in Nate's expression. His foot started tapping under the table. His fingers drummed against his beer bottle.

"Oh no," I said, grinning. "You know this song."

"Everyone knows this song."

"Not like *you* know this song."

He was trying to look innocent, but I could see the war playing out on his face. Professional Nate versus... whoever this was who wanted to sing along to Garth Brooks.

Whoever this was won.

When the chorus hit, Nathan Crawford—serious, controlled,

military-precise Nathan Crawford—opened his mouth and belted
out every single word with a perfect baritone country twang. Not just
mumbling along, but really singing, with feeling and enthusiasm and
zero self-consciousness.

I was absolutely *gone*.

I'd seen him handle medical emergencies with calm competence.
I'd watched him father his daughter with tender devotion. But this—
this goofy, uninhibited, secretly-country-music-loving side of him—
was a revelation.

"Holy shit," I breathed when the song ended. "You're full of
surprises."

He had the grace to look embarrassed. "I went through a phase in
the Navy."

"A phase?"

"Okay, fine. I still listen to country music when I'm cleaning
house. Happy?"

I was more than happy. I was enchanted. "What else don't I know
about you, Nathan Crawford?"

"Probably a lot."

The band shifted to something slower, and couples moved onto
the dance floor in various states of coordination. Nate glanced
toward them, then back at me.

"I should probably mention I'm not much of a dancer," he said.

"That's okay. I'm not much of a follower."

But we went out there anyway, finding a spot where we wouldn't
get in anyone's way. He held me carefully, respectfully, one hand on
my waist and the other holding mine. We swayed more than danced,
but it was perfect.

"This is nice," I said, close enough to his ear that he could hear
me over the music.

"Yeah, it is."

I could feel the warmth of his body through his shirt, could smell
his cologne—something clean and masculine that made me want to
bury my face in his neck. When the song ended, we stayed like that

for a moment, close enough that I could feel his breath on my forehead.

"Tasha," he said softly.

"Yeah?"

"Thank you. For this. For..." He seemed to be searching for words. "For seeing something in me worth taking a chance on. It means a lot to me."

My heart did something complicated. "Nathan."

"Yeah?"

"Take me back to your place."

The drive back to his place was charged with anticipation. We didn't talk much, but the air between us hummed with possibility. When he pulled into his driveway, we sat there for a moment, both of us knowing what came next but neither wanting to rush it.

"Are you sure?" he asked finally.

"I'm sure."

Inside, he turned on a single lamp in the living room, casting everything in warm, golden light. We stood there looking at each other, suddenly awkward again, like teenagers who didn't know what to do with their hands.

"Do you want some coffee? Or water? I could—"

I silenced him by stepping close and putting my hands on his chest. "Nate."

"Yeah?"

"Stop thinking so hard."

He laughed nervously, some of the tension leaving his shoulders. "I can't help it. It's been... it's been a while since..."

"How long is a while?"

He looked away, color creeping up his neck. "Since before Paige was born."

I blinked. "Since... what now?"

"Eleven years," he said quietly. "Give or take."

I stared at him, trying to process this information. "Eleven years!? Nathan, that's not 'a while,' that's a geological epoch."

"I know how it sounds—"

"Wait." I held up a hand, my mind reeling. "You're telling me you haven't been with anyone since Paige's mother left?"

He nodded, looking uncomfortable.

"You were a veteran. A single dad raising an amazing daughter. You were even in nursing school." I was talking faster now, trying to wrap my head around this. "How were those girls not throwing their panties at you?"

"Tasha—"

"No, seriously. A hot single dad in scrubs who was devoted to his daughter? I'm honestly shocked half those nursing students didn't get pregnant just from their ovaries practically staging a revolt in your presence."

He laughed despite himself. "It wasn't like that."

"A hundred horny co-eds were *begging* you to fuck them and you told them *no*? For your *daughter!?*"

The crude words hung in the air between us, but I wasn't embarrassed. I was amazed. Awed, even.

"Paige needed stability," he said simply. "She needed to know that she could count on me, that I wouldn't bring people into her life who might leave again. So I made a choice."

And there it was. The thing that made Nathan Crawford different from every other man I'd ever known. Not just his competence or his kindness, but this—this absolute, unwavering devotion to his child that had led him to sacrifice his own needs for over a decade.

"Jesus, Nathan," I whispered. "You're..."

"What?"

"You're extraordinary."

I stared at him, the full weight of what he'd just told me settling in my chest. Eleven years. He'd been alone for eleven years, not because no one wanted him, but because he'd chosen his daughter over every-thing else. Over every opportunity, every moment of loneliness, every basic human need for companionship.

And now he was here, with me, letting me in. Trusting me with the most precious thing in his world.

I kissed him then, pouring all my admiration and desire and growing feelings into it. He responded immediately, his arms coming around me, pulling me closer. When we broke apart, we were both breathing hard.

"Tasha," he said against my lips.

"Take me to bed, Nathan. Please."

He did.

———

The bedroom was dim, the bedside lamp casting soft golden light across the rumpled sheets. Nate's hand was warm and steady in mine, but everything else felt electric—like the air had changed the moment the door shut behind us.

He pulled me gently against him, and I kissed him like I meant it. Because I did. Because I'd never meant anything more.

His fingers threaded into my hair, one hand slipping to the small of my back. I could feel how tightly he held himself in check, the tension just beneath the surface. When I deepened the kiss, pressing my body into his, he let out the smallest, roughest sound—half surrender, half warning.

"Tasha," he murmured, his breath brushing my jaw. "You're sure?"

I answered by sliding my hands beneath his shirt, dragging my palms up over his chest, feeling the heat of his skin and the thud of his heart.

"I've never been more sure."

He pulled back slightly, and the look in his eyes—raw, vulnerable, fiercely determined—nearly undid me completely.

"I've wanted this for so long," he confessed quietly, his voice rough with honesty. "Wanted you. But I couldn't let myself... not with Paige to think about."

I reached up, cupping his face in my hands. "I'm here. We're here. And she's safe."

Something shifted in his expression then—relief, gratitude, pure want—and that was all it took.

He kissed me harder then—hungry, unguarded, no longer holding back. The kind of kiss that made my knees buckle and my pulse race. The kind that made me forget everything but his name.

We undressed each other in fits and starts, half-drunk on adrenaline and anticipation. I tugged his shirt over his head and ran my hands across his bare chest, memorizing the curve of muscle, the scars I wanted to learn by heart. He stripped off my blouse with reverence and heat in equal measure, his eyes drinking me in like I was something he wasn't sure he deserved but had decided to worship anyway.

When he leaned down to kiss the curve of my shoulder, I shivered. When his mouth trailed lower, I gasped.

He caught my eye. "Tell me if you want me to stop."

"Don't you dare," I whispered.

We tumbled onto the bed in a tangle of limbs, skin against skin, every inch of him driving me wild with want. He kissed down my body slowly, savoring, teasing, making me arch and moan and beg for more. And then he moved lower, tasting me with a thoroughness that left me breathless.

By the time he came back up, I was shaking. He kissed me again, and I could taste myself on his lips.

"Nathan," I said, voice wrecked. "Please. I need you."

The look he gave me was pure fire. "You have me."

He moved over me, strong and careful and completely overwhelming, and when he finally entered me, I swore the earth shifted. I clutched at him, anchoring myself to the solid, burning reality of us.

He set a rhythm that was slow but deep, every thrust deliberate, like he needed to memorize how we fit together. I matched him beat for beat, every movement a promise, every gasp a surrender.

"God," he whispered into my neck. "You feel like—like coming home."

I tangled my fingers in his hair, pulling him closer, desperate to get closer still. The pressure built fast, relentless, curling in my belly like a fuse about to blow.

"Nathan," I gasped. "I'm—"

"I've got you," he whispered. "I've got you, Tasha."

And then I shattered.

Pleasure slammed through me, wild and blinding. I cried out, nails digging into his shoulders, body arched into his. He followed a heartbeat later, groaning my name as he buried himself deep, his control finally breaking.

We clung to each other, shaking, kissing like we were still trying to catch up with what we'd just done. I couldn't stop touching him —his back, his jaw, the sweat-slick strands of hair at his temple. He kissed the curve of my breast, my collarbone, the corner of my mouth, like he was afraid I might vanish if he let me go.

"I should've done that a long time ago," he said hoarsely.

"No," I said, smiling up at him. "It was right now. It had to be now."

He held me tighter, pressing a gentle kiss to the top of my head. "Thank you. For tonight, for everything."

"Don't thank me yet," I teased lightly, hoping to ease the tension that had returned to his shoulders. "I'm not done with you."

He chuckled softly, pressing another kiss to my forehead. "Good."

We lay in quiet comfort, the night wrapping around us like a promise. Yet even in that perfect stillness, I felt a subtle tension in Nate's body, something lingering just beneath the surface. It was a reminder that for all the gentleness and tenderness we'd shared, Nathan Crawford was a man carrying scars...

Both seen and unseen.

thirteen
nate

THE DUST CAME FIRST. Always the dust.

Fine particles hung suspended in shafts of morning light, cutting through blown-out windows. The air tasted like chalk and cordite. My boots crunched over pulverized concrete and shell casings as our squad advanced through the partially collapsed building.

"*Clear*," came the whispered confirmation from the point man, hand signal reinforcing the message.

We moved in ranger file, deeper, room by room, the distant rattle of gunfire elsewhere in the city a constant soundtrack. Three days into Operation Phantom Fury, and Fallujah had become a warren of firefights, ambushes, and booby traps.

I adjusted my trauma bag, the weight of it reassuring against my hip. Three emergency casualty evacuations in the last 24 hours. All successful. All Marines who would see home again because our training had held, because the golden hour hadn't been squandered.

The squad leader held up a fist. We froze.

Muffled voices ahead. Arabic, rapid and tense. The squad leader used hand signals. Two, maybe three fighters in the room beyond the partially open door. Ready positions.

Then everything accelerated.

The door kicked in. Shouts of "MARINES!" and "GET DOWN!" in English and broken Arabic.

Gunfire erupted, deafening in the confined space. The insurgents had been waiting. Return fire immediately. Plaster dust and concrete chips sprayed as rounds impacted walls.

A flash of movement from behind a fallen bookcase. Fast. Small.

Thompson, on edge after losing his fire team leader yesterday, swung his rifle toward the movement—

"NOOOOO!" The shout died in my throat, but it was too late.

A child. A little girl. Seven, maybe eight years old. She had darted from her hiding place, perhaps toward her parents, perhaps in blind panic.

The sound of Thompson's rifle seemed to echo longer than the others.

The girl crumpled, pink shirt darkening to crimson. Her mother's scream was high, keening, primal, and cut through the ringing in my ears.

"CEASE FIRE! CEASE FIRE! CIVILIANS!" the squad leader bellowed.

I was moving before the last insurgent hit the floor, shedding my rifle, trauma bag already open. I skidded to my knees beside her tiny form.

GSW to the abdomen. Too much blood. Too much damage for a child her size. But my hands moved anyway, training taking over where hope faltered.

Not her. Not a child. Not on my watch.

Her father cradled her head, weeping in Arabic, words I didn't understand but meaning I couldn't miss. Her mother rocked back and forth against the wall, palms bloodied where she'd clawed at the concrete.

"Get me an evac! NOW!" I shouted, my voice cracking as I frantically packed combat gauze into the wound. "I need pressure here! Someone hold pressure!"

Her father tried to help, his hands shaking as he pressed where I showed him. Blood seeped between his fingers, too much, too fast.

"No, no, no," I muttered, ripping open another packet of hemostatic gauze with my teeth. "Stay with me, kiddo. Please. Stay with me."

Her pulse weakened beneath my fingers. Her breathing became shallow, irregular. Her eyes, wide with fear and incomprehension, began to lose focus.

"Goddammit, more pressure!" I barked to no one in particular, shoving another Marine's hands onto a secondary wound. "We need blood! Where's the fucking evac?!"

"Doc, there's no evac coming in time," Miller said, his voice steady but gentle. "You know that."

I ignored him, working frantically, methodically, my training a litany in my head. Stop the bleeding. Maintain the airway. Treat for shock.

"Come on, sweetheart," I pleaded, switching to chest compressions as her breathing stuttered. "Come on. Don't do this."

Her mother wailed, a sound so primal it seemed to vibrate in my bones. Her father spoke rapidly in Arabic, pressing his forehead to his daughter's, tears falling onto her increasingly pale face.

"She's losing too much blood," I said to Miller, to anyone listening. "I need a line in. I need fluids. I need—" My voice broke. What I needed was a fully-equipped trauma center, not a dusty room in a half-demolished building with a limited field kit. What I needed was to be back home, in Virginia. What I needed was to have never come here.

But I kept working. One compression. Two. Three. Pause to check. Nothing. Again.

"COME ON!" I screamed, abandoning all pretense of professional detachment. Sweat and tears mingled on my face, dropping onto her still chest. "BREATHE, GODDAMNIT!"

I was aware of the room falling silent around me except for the mother's keening and my own desperate counting. I was aware of

Thompson sinking to his knees, of Miller standing helplessly nearby. But they receded to the periphery as my world narrowed to the tiny figure beneath my bloodied hands.

One compression. Two. Three.

Her gaze had emptied. The frantic rise and fall of her chest, now only moving because of my hands, stilled when I paused.

"Doc." Miller's hand on my shoulder. "Doc, she's gone."

"No." I shook him off, resumed compressions. "No, she's not. She can't be."

I ripped open another field dressing. Packed another wound that had stopped bleeding only because there was no more pressure behind it.

"She just needs more time. She just needs—" My voice caught as I felt the first signs of rigor already setting in around her jaw. Even then, I couldn't stop. "She's just a kid. She can't—"

"Doc." Miller's voice firmer now, his grip on my shoulder tightening. "She's gone. We need to move."

Thompson had curled in on himself, rocking slightly, tears cutting clean tracks through the dust on his face. "We shouldn't even be here, man, we shouldn't even fuckin' be here..."

I stared at my bloodied gloves, at the combat gauze soaked black, at the tiny, still figure beneath them. Time seemed to bend inward on itself.

I couldn't save her.

I hadn't saved her.

fourteen
tasha

THE SHEETS still held the warmth of our bodies, tangled together in the soft darkness of Nate's bedroom. I drifted in that peaceful space between sleep and wakefulness, muscles pleasantly sore, mind unusually quiet. It had been good. It had been *better* than good. The careful control Nate maintained in every aspect of his life translated to a focused intensity that left me breathless. But there had been tenderness too, vulnerability in his eyes that I hadn't expected.

A slight movement beside me drew me partway back to consciousness. Nate shifted in his sleep. I reached for him without opening my eyes, palm finding the solid warmth of his chest, feeling the steady rhythm of his heart.

The rhythm that suddenly wasn't steady at all.

His breathing changed first—quickening, becoming shallow. Then his body tensed beside me, muscles coiling like springs. A small sound escaped him, something between a whimper and a groan.

"Nate?" I murmured, still half-asleep.

He jerked suddenly, violently. His arm flung out, narrowly missing my face.

I sat up, fully awake now, switching immediately to assessment mode. His heart was racing; he was breathing fast and shallow, sweating profusely.

"No," he mumbled, head thrashing on the pillow. "No... get me an evac... bleeding out..."

My stomach dropped as understanding dawned. PTSD. Not just the garden variety stress reaction, this was a full-blown episode.

"Nate," I said, more firmly this time, but careful not to touch him. Startling someone in this state could be dangerous— for both of us. "Nate, you're having a nightmare. You're safe. You're home."

"Can't stop the bleeding." His voice was different—younger, desperate. Tears leaked from the corners of his closed eyes. *"Muta'asif... muta'asif..."*

I didn't recognize the words, but the anguish was universal.

"She's just a kid," he choked out. "Thompson, NO!"

His body convulsed, back arching off the bed. I hit the bedside lamp switch, flooding the room with sudden light. Nate's eyes were open now, but unseeing, fixed on horrors I couldn't perceive.

"Nate," I said, keeping my voice calm but firm. "Nate, honey. It's Tasha. You're at home. You're safe. It's 2025. We're in your bedroom."

His eyes darted around the room, wild and confused. Sweat plastered his hair to his forehead.

"I need you to breathe with me," I continued, making my own breathing deliberate and audible. "In through your nose. Out through your mouth."

Slowly, agonizingly, he began to come back. His eyes focused, found mine, recognition dawning with visible relief and then—worse —shame.

"Tasha." His voice was raw. "I—I'm so sorry."

"No, sweetie, no. Don't apologize," I said, keeping my tone light and warm despite the ache in my chest. "I've woken up screaming about forgetting to study for exams. Your nightmares are at least justified."

He sat up, drawing his knees to his chest in an unconsciously

protective gesture that reminded me so much of Paige that my throat
tightened. He rubbed his hands over his face, trying to erase the
evidence of tears.

"That hasn't happened in... a while," he said finally.

I waited, giving him space, though every instinct urged me to pull
him into my arms.

"What were you saying?" I asked after a moment. "It sounded
like... 'muta' something?"

"*Muta'asif*," he said softly. "It's Arabic. It means 'I'm sorry.'"

The words hung in the quiet room. I reached out slowly,
telegraphing my movement, and placed my hand on his arm. The
muscles beneath my fingers were still rigid with tension.

"Iraq?" I asked simply.

He nodded, eyes fixed on some middle distance. "I was nineteen.
Almost twenty. Just a stupid kid who thought I was invincible." His
laugh was hollow. "I volunteered to go. Didn't want to be stuck on
some ship in the middle of the ocean. Pretty dumb idea to join the
Navy, I guess, but I wasn't exactly thinking things through back
then."

I let the silence stretch, knowing he needed to find his own way
through this.

"Most of my time there was... I don't want to say routine, because
there's nothing routine about war. But it was sporadic. You'd go
weeks with nothing, then suddenly you're taking fire. You kind of get
used to people taking shots at you." His voice took on a detached
quality. "You can't leave the compound without expecting an impro-
vised explosive device attack. But it wasn't... it wasn't sustained
combat."

His hand found mine, fingers intertwining almost desperately.

"Then they came asking for volunteers. They didn't have enough
corpsmen for an operation."

A tear slipped down his cheek, and this time he didn't try to
hide it.

"I wasn't prepared. None of us were. Not for Fallujah."

The horror in his voice made me shiver despite the warmth of the room. I'd heard about Fallujah, of course. But it had only just barely made it into my American History class in high school. It wasn't *really* real, it was just another entry in a textbook. Not something that had marked the man beside me so deeply that two decades years later, he still couldn't escape it in his dreams.

"They told us it was clear of civilians, but there were..." His voice caught. "There was a little girl."

Understanding clicked into place—the nightmare, the desperate pleas, the Arabic apology. The little girl from Iraq and his fierce protection of Paige. The pieces of Nate Crawford suddenly aligned in a way that made my chest ache.

"You don't have to tell me," I said softly.

"I do," he insisted. "I need to. I've never... I've never told anyone. Not really. Not everything."

I nodded, shifting closer to him, our sides touching. An anchor to the present as he revisited the past.

And then he told me. Everything. The clearing operation in Fallujah. The insurgents using a family as human shields. Thompson firing at movement. The little girl in the pink shirt. His desperate attempts to save her. The parents' anguish. The Arabic words he'd hastily memorized from a military phrasebook. "I'm sorry. I'm sorry. I'm sorry."

By the time he finished, tears were flowing freely down his face, and his body shook with the force of emotions long suppressed. I didn't hesitate now—I pulled him against me, his head on my shoulder, his tears warm against my skin.

"I couldn't save her," he whispered. "I was supposed to save people. That was my job. But I couldn't save her."

"You tried," I said, threading my fingers through his hair. "Nate, you tried everything possible."

"It wasn't enough."

The words hung between us, and suddenly I understood so much more about him. His obsessive preparation for every aspect of Paige's life. His rigid control. His reluctance to let anyone else in.

"Is that why you push yourself so hard with Paige?" I asked gently. "Because you couldn't save that little girl?"

He stiffened slightly, then relaxed with a shuddering exhale. "Maybe. Probably. I don't know." His voice was muffled against my shoulder. "I just know I can't fail her. I can't... I can't let anything happen to her."

"You haven't," I assured him. "You haven't failed her. She's amazing, Nate. She's smart and kind and resilient. That's because of you."

He pulled back slightly, eyes searching mine with a vulnerability that made my heart twist. "You think so?"

"I know so. And I'm a pretty good judge of character."

A ghost of a smile touched his lips. "Since when?"

"Hey," I nudged him gently, relieved at the tiny spark of humor. "I chose you, didn't I?"

His smile faded, replaced by something more serious, more intense. "Why did you? Choose me, I mean."

The question caught me off guard. Why had I? I'd spent so long keeping everyone at arm's length, protecting myself with sarcasm and attitude. But somehow, this serious, damaged, beautiful man had gotten under my defenses.

"Because you see me," I said finally. "The real me. Not the façade. And because..." I hesitated, then decided he'd been brave enough tonight to deserve my honesty. "Because I see you too. All of you. The nightmares and the spreadsheets and the fierce way you love your daughter. And I think all of it is... worth choosing."

His eyes widened slightly, something like wonder crossing his face. For a moment, I thought he might cry again. Instead, he leaned forward and kissed me—softly, reverently, like I was something precious.

When we broke apart, I could see exhaustion etched in the lines of his face. "You should try to sleep," I said.

Fear flickered in his eyes. "The dreams might come back."

"I'll be right here," I promised. "I'm not going anywhere."

I guided him back down to the pillows, pulling the sheet over us both. He curled toward me, his head resting against my chest, arm draped across my waist. I stroked his hair, humming softly, some half-remembered lullaby my grandmother used to sing.

As his breathing finally evened out into sleep, I stared up at the ceiling, my mind racing. This wasn't what I'd signed up for. This was complicated, messy, far beyond the casual relationship I'd convinced myself I wanted.

But as I felt Nate's steady heartbeat against my side, I realized with startling clarity that I didn't want casual. Not with him. I wanted this—all of it. The nightmares and the healing. The pain and the joy.

I wanted to be the person he could fall apart with.

And somehow, that was the most terrifying and beautiful realization I'd ever had.

fifteen
tasha

"YOU'RE BRINGING a man to the reunion? And his child?" My mother's voice over the phone held the same tone she used when I announced I was going to nursing school instead of pre-med. Equal parts surprise, suspicion, and grudging curiosity.

"It's not a big deal, Mom." I stirred the pasta sauce on Nate's stove, phone wedged between my shoulder and ear. "We've been seeing each other for awhile. Figured it was time."

"How long have you been 'seeing each other'?" I could hear the air quotes.

I glanced toward the living room where Nate and Paige were locked in an intense game of Scrabble. Three months since that night. Three months since he'd broken down in my arms. Three months of carefully navigating whatever this was between us.

"Long enough," I replied.

"Mmm-hmm." The sound was loaded with implication. "And this man is...?"

"A nurse at Metro. He works in the ER with me."

"His name, Tasha Marie."

I sighed. "Nathan Crawford."

"'Nathan'?"

"Yes. 'Nathan'."

A pause. "And how old is Nathan Crawford?"

I closed my eyes briefly. Here we go. "Thirty-nine."

"Thirty-nine." She repeated the number flatly. "And you're twenty-seven."

"Yes, Mom. I can do basic subtraction."

"Don't get smart with me. And his child? Where's the mother?"

"She left when Paige was a baby. Nate's raised her alone. She's eleven. She's great." I surprised myself with the defensiveness in my voice.

Another long pause. "And is he...?"

"White? Yes, Mom. Does that matter?"

"You know very well it doesn't matter to me. But I'm not everyone who's going to be at this reunion. There's Uncle Earl to consider, and your cousin Janelle just went through that awful breakup with—"

"Mom, if it's going to be a problem—"

"Don't you put words in my mouth, young lady. I didn't say it was a problem. I'm just preparing you." Her voice softened marginally. "Are they important to you? This man and his daughter?"

The question caught me off guard. Were they? The answer came easier than I expected.

"Yes. They are."

"Then they're welcome. I'll tell your Aunt Patricia to make extra of her mac and cheese. That child's too skinny in the pictures you sent."

I blinked. "What pictures?"

"The ones from the science fair. You texted them to me last week. Don't act like you didn't."

I had. I'd been so proud of Paige's volcano project, not because it was spectacular (it wasn't), but because I'd helped her fix the wiring the night before when Nate was on shift. It had felt... significant.

"Right," I said. "Well, we'll be there. Sunday at noon."

"One small thing," Mom said, her casual tone setting off immediate warning bells. "Your father's bringing Deanna."

My grip tightened on the wooden spoon. My father's third wife. Twenty-nine years old. Two years older than me.

"Great," I said flatly.

"And Marcus is coming with his wife and the twins."

My older brother. The golden child. The doctor.

"Fantastic."

"And Jasmine got into Howard pre-med. She'll want to talk to you about it."

My perfect little sister, following the path I was supposed to take.

"Anything else? Is Michelle Obama stopping by? Maybe Beyoncé?"

"Don't be dramatic, Tasha Marie. I'm just giving you the lay of the land." A pause. "I'm looking forward to meeting your young man. And his daughter."

After we hung up, I stood staring at the sauce, wondering what cosmic glitch had prompted me to invite Nate and Paige to the Williams family reunion. It had seemed like a good idea three days ago, after Nate had casually mentioned that Paige seemed to thrive around other kids, but their social circle was limited.

"Something wrong with the sauce?" Nate's voice startled me. He stood in the kitchen doorway, concern etching his features.

"No, just... stirring."

"You've been 'just stirring' for five minutes." He moved beside me, close enough that I could feel his warmth. "Was that your mom?"

I nodded.

"Having second thoughts about Sunday?" he asked quietly.

"No. Maybe. I don't know." I set the spoon down. "My family is... a lot."

"Most families are."

"Not like mine." I turned to face him. "There's going to be at least thirty people there. Kids running everywhere. My grandmother's going to interrogate you. My brother's going to give you the third degree. My aunt's going to ask if you know how to cook anything besides 'white people food.' And that's just the first hour."

Nate smiled, that small, genuine smile that still made my stomach flip. "I served in Iraq, Tasha. I think I can handle your family."

"Ehhhhh... don't say I didn't warn you." I forced lightness into my tone, but something of my real anxiety must have shown through.

His expression softened. He reached out, tucking a stray curl behind my ear. "Hey. What's really bothering you?"

I looked away. "I just... I don't do this. Bring people home. Especially not..." I gestured vaguely between us.

"Especially not older white guys with pre-teen daughters?"

I winced. "That sounds terrible when you say it out loud."

"But accurate."

I met his eyes finally. "It's not you. Or Paige. It's... complicated."

"Most important things are." He didn't push, didn't demand explanations. Just stood there, steady and patient.

Something in his quiet acceptance loosened the knot in my chest. "My dad's bringing his new wife. She's twenty-nine."

Understanding dawned in his eyes. "Ah."

"And my brother's going to be there with his perfect wife and his perfect twin boys and his perfect medical practice. And my sister just got into pre-med, which is what I was supposed to do before I 'settled' for nursing."

"Settled?" His eyebrow rose. "You're one of the best nurses in the ER."

"Try telling my family that. Marcus puts people to sleep for a living and he's practically royalty."

"He's an anesthesiologist?"

"The youngest one at Johns Hopkins," I confirmed with an eye roll. "We've all heard. Repeatedly."

Nate was quiet for a moment. "We don't have to go."

The simple statement, free of judgment or pressure, made something in my heart twist painfully. "No, I want to. I want them to meet you. And Paige." I took a breath. "I just want you to be prepared. For the chaos. For the questions. For... all of it."

He stepped closer, his hands finding my waist. "I think we can handle it."

"Even Paige?"

His smile widened. "Especially Paige. She's been talking about nothing else since you mentioned your cousin has a trampoline."

I laughed despite myself. "It's more of a death trap with springs, but yes."

"Then it's settled." He leaned in, pressing a soft kiss to my forehead. "Now, can we eat? Paige is forming revolutionary movements in the living room over hunger."

As we set the table together, I tried to shake the lingering unease. It wasn't just introducing Nate to my family that had me tied in knots. It was the realization that I cared—deeply—what they thought of him. Of us. Of whatever this was becoming.

And that terrified me more than any family reunion ever could.

Sunday arrived with merciless sunshine and humidity that turned the air to soup. I'd changed outfits three times before settling on a yellow sundress that my mother had bought me last Christmas (a strategic choice). Nate wore khakis and a blue button-down that made his eyes look even more intensely green. Paige had agonized almost as much as I had, finally choosing a purple skirt and white top, her hair in neat braids that I'd helped with the night before.

My parents' house was a forty-minute drive from Nate's place in the suburbs. As we turned onto the familiar street, my stomach clenched at the sight of cars lining both sides.

"That's... a lot of vehicles," Nate observed, his calm facade cracking slightly.

"Told you. Thirty people, minimum."

Paige leaned forward from the backseat. "Are there really going to be that many kids?"

"At least ten," I confirmed. "Most of them are monsters. You'll fit right in."

She grinned, braces flashing. "Awesome."

We found a spot three houses down. As we walked back, I could already hear music and laughter from the backyard. Nate reached for my hand, giving it a reassuring squeeze. I was grateful for the anchor.

"Ready?" he asked.

"No," I admitted. "But let's do it anyway."

We entered through the side gate, and the full chaos of a Williams family reunion hit us like a wall. The spacious backyard was transformed—tables laden with food, coolers overflowing with drinks, children shrieking as they ran through sprinklers. And everywhere, family. Aunts, uncles, cousins, second cousins, family friends who'd been around so long they might as well be blood.

"Tasha!" My mother's voice cut through the noise. Loretta Williams approached, resplendent in a teal dress and matching headband, arms outstretched. "Finally, you made it."

She embraced me briefly, then immediately turned her attention to Nate and Paige. I watched her eyes make a lightning-fast assessment—taking in Nate's posture (military straight), his age (evident in the silver at his temples), and his eyes (warm but guarded).

"You must be Nathan," she said, extending her hand. "I'm Loretta Williams. Tasha's mother."

"It's a pleasure to meet you, Mrs. Williams," Nate replied, his handshake firm. "Thank you for having us."

"And this must be Paige," my mother continued, her expression softening as she looked at the girl. "My, aren't you pretty as a picture."

Paige smiled shyly. "Thank you for inviting us, ma'am."

"Ohh, listen to those manners!" Mom looked impressed. "Well, come on back. Everyone's dying to meet you. Paige, honey, the other children are over on the trampoline. Though you might want to get some food first."

"Mom, give them a minute to breathe," I protested.

"There's no time for breathing at a Williams reunion, you know that." She linked her arm through Nate's, effectively separating him from me. "Nathan, let me introduce you to my husband, Carl. He was military too, you know. Marines."

As she swept Nate away, I met his eyes over her head. He gave me a small smile that said, *I've got this*. Paige looked up at me questioningly.

"Go ahead," I told her. "The trampoline's through there. Try not to break anything vital."

She hesitated. "Are you sure?"

The concern in her young face touched me. "I'm sure. Go have fun. I'll come find you soon."

As Paige scampered off, I took a deep breath and plunged into the crowd. Within minutes, I was surrounded.

"Girl, you didn't tell us you were bringing a whole man to the reunion!" My cousin Aisha materialized beside me, cocktail in hand. "And he's *fine*! Little salt and pepper action going on."

My first instinct was to launch into explicit detail about exactly *how* fine Nate was—the way his shoulders looked in that blue shirt, what those hands could do, how his voice sounded when he—but then I caught sight of Paige bounding across the yard, and something in me shifted.

I was more than just *Tasha-who-brought-a-hot-guy-home* now. I was part of something bigger, more important.

Sigh.

"It's not a big deal," I finally muttered, snagging a drink from a passing tray.

"Oh, it's a *big* deal. Aunt Patty is already planning your wedding. And Grandma Rose just asked if his 'people' are from here or 'up North.'"

I groaned. "It's been five minutes."

"It's been five years since you brought anyone home," Aisha countered. "What did you expect?"

Before I could reply, my brother Marcus appeared, his twin boys hanging off his legs like little koalas.

"Little sis," he greeted me with a one-armed hug. "Mom says you brought a boyfriend. And he's old enough to be your father."

I bristled. "He's thirty-nine, not sixty."

"Hmm." Marcus studied me with the same assessing gaze he probably used on patients. "Is it serious?"

"It's... evolving."

"That's not an answer."

"That's all you're getting."

He sighed dramatically. "Always so difficult. You know Mom's worried."

"Mom's always worried about something."

"She wants you to be happy."

"I *am* happy."

Marcus raised an eyebrow. "Are you? Because you don't seem happy right now. You seem stressed."

I barely resisted the urge to dump my drink on his perfectly pressed shirt. "I'm fine."

"If you say so." He extricated himself from his sons. "Boys, go find your mother. Tell her Aunt Tasha's here." As they ran off, he fixed me with one last look. "Just be careful, Tash. Relationships with that kind of age gap can be complicated."

"Says the man who married his college sweetheart and never looked at another woman," I shot back.

"Some of us just get it right the first time," he replied with infuriating smugness before disappearing into the crowd.

I downed half my drink in one go, feeling the tension build in my shoulders. This was exactly why I'd hesitated to bring Nate and Paige here. Every interaction felt loaded, every comment a potential minefield.

I made my way around the yard, fielding questions about Nate, about my job, about when I was going to "settle down properly" or "come to my senses and go to medical school." By the time I spotted my grandmother holding court under the elm tree, I was ready to fabricate an emergency at the hospital.

"There's my Tasha," Grandma Rose called, patting the seat beside her. "Come sit with your grandmother."

I obeyed, leaning in to kiss her papery cheek. At eighty-one, Rose Williams was still sharp as a tack and twice as dangerous.

"Where's this man of yours?" she asked without preamble.

"Mom kidnapped him," I replied. "Probably interrogating him in the garage."

She chuckled. "Your mother means well."

"Does she?" The question slipped out before I could stop it.

Grandma Rose fixed me with a penetrating look. "She wants for you what she thinks will make you happy. Problem is, she doesn't always know what that is." She patted my hand. "Neither do you, sometimes."

I looked away. "I'm doing fine, Grandma."

"I didn't say you weren't. But you've always carried that chip on your shoulder. The one that says you have to do everything differently from what's expected, just to prove you can."

"That's not fair."

"Isn't it? You were brilliant enough for medical school. Everybody knew it. But you chose nursing because your father pushed too hard for medicine." She held up a hand when I started to protest. "I'm not saying nursing isn't a fine profession. Lord knows we need good nurses more than we need mediocre doctors. But I wonder sometimes if you make choices based on what you want, or based on what will surprise everyone else."

The words hit uncomfortably close to home. "Nate's not like that. He's not a choice I made to shock anyone."

Her eyes softened. "Then he must be special indeed."

Across the yard, I spotted Nate emerging from the house with my mother, both of them laughing about something. The sight was so unexpected it made my breath catch. He looked... comfortable. At ease in a way I hadn't expected.

"He seems like a good man," Grandma Rose observed, following my gaze. "Steady. The quiet kind who sees more than he says."

"He is."

"And the girl? His daughter?"

"Paige. She's amazing. Smart, kind. She reminds me a little of Jasmine at that age, but more serious."

"And how do you feel about being in her life? That's a big responsibility, loving someone else's child."

The question startled me. I'd been so focused on navigating my relationship with Nate that I hadn't fully considered what it meant for Paige.

"I care about her," I said finally. "A lot. More than I expected to."

"That's the thing about love," Grandma Rose said. "It never comes the way you think it will. Never looks like what you planned."

Before I could respond, a commotion near the trampoline drew our attention. My heart sank as I recognized one voice rising above the others—my father's new wife, Deanna.

"I said *no roughhousing*! You're going to hurt someone smaller!"

I was on my feet and moving before I fully processed what was happening. As I approached, I saw Paige standing near the trampoline, face flushed, while Deanna towered over her.

"What's going on?" I asked, stepping between them.

Deanna turned, her perfect features arranged in a mask of concern. "Oh, Tasha. The older kids were getting too rough on the trampoline. I was just making sure everyone stays safe."

I looked at Paige, whose expression was a mixture of confusion and embarrassment. "Were you roughhousing?"

She shook her head. "We were playing a game. Taking turns."

"She pushed my Jason," Deanna insisted, gesturing to her four-year-old son—my stepbrother—who was indeed crying nearby. "He could have been hurt."

"I didn't push him," Paige said quietly. "He fell when he was trying to do a flip. I tried to catch him."

I believed her instantly. Paige wasn't the type to push smaller kids —if anything, she was too careful, too conscious of others.

"I'm sure it was an accident," I said, keeping my voice level. "Right, Jason? Did Paige push you, or were you trying to do a flip?"

The little boy, momentarily distracted from his tears, looked up. "Flip," he admitted. "But I fell."

Deanna's perfect features hardened. "Well, regardless, I think the big kids should let the little ones have a turn now."

"That's fine," I said smoothly. "Paige, why don't you come meet my grandmother? She's been asking about you."

As we walked away, Paige leaned close. "I really didn't push him, Tasha."

"I know you didn't, kiddo," I assured her, squeezing her shoulder. "Deanna just likes to make everything a bigger deal than it is."

"Who is she?"

"My father's new wife."

Paige processed this. "She's really young."

I laughed, unable to help myself. "Yes, she is."

"Why doesn't she like me? She doesn't even know me."

The innocent question pierced me. "It's not about you, Paige. Some people just... need to feel important by controlling situations. It doesn't reflect on you at all."

She nodded, seeming to accept this. "Your family is really big. And loud."

"Too much?"

"No," she said thoughtfully. "It's kind of nice. Different, but nice. Dad's so quiet all the time. Sometimes our house feels too... empty."

The observation, so simple yet profound, hit me hard. I'd never thought about what it might be like for Paige, growing up in that orderly, often silent house with just Nate. How different from this— the noise, the chaos, the overwhelming presence of family everywhere you turned.

"Well, if you ever need some noise, you know where to find us," I said lightly.

"Could we come back sometime? For a regular visit, not just a special occasion?"

A feeling like a slow sunrise spread through my chest. "I'd like that. I think Grandma Rose would too."

By the time we reached Grandma's shaded spot, Nate had found his way there too. He was sitting beside her, listening intently as she showed him what appeared to be old family photos. The sight of them together—his head bent respectfully toward hers, her gnarled hand gesturing animatedly—made my throat tighten unexpectedly.

"There you are," Nate said, looking up with evident relief. "Your grandmother has been showing me pictures of you as a teenager. The braces phase was particularly enlightening."

"*Grandma*!" I protested.

She cackled. "Every young man should know what he's getting into. Besides, I only showed him the nice ones. Not the ones where you shaved half your head."

"You shaved your head?" Paige asked, eyes wide.

"Just half. It was a phase."

"A statement," Grandma corrected. "Everything with you was a statement."

Nate's eyes met mine, warm with amusement and something deeper. "Still is," he said softly.

The moment was broken by my father's arrival. Thomas Williams, distinguished in his golf shirt and khakis, approached with the confidence of a man who'd never doubted his place in the world.

"There's my girl," he boomed, enfolding me in a cologne-scented hug. "Finally decided to grace us with your presence."

"Hi, Dad," I said, extricating myself. "This is Nate Crawford and his daughter Paige."

My father's handshake was a challenge, his smile not quite reaching his eyes as he assessed Nate. "Thomas Williams. Tasha's father. I understand you're a nurse at Metro."

"Yes, sir," Nate replied, unfazed by the subtle emphasis on 'nurse.' "Emergency department."

"Noble profession. Though with your military background, I'd have thought you'd aim higher. Officer track, perhaps, or medical school."

I tensed, but Nate's expression remained pleasant, almost thoughtful. "Well, sir, I considered it," he said with that same respectful tone, "but I enjoy working for a living."

The comment landed with such casual, good-natured delivery that it took my father a beat to process it. Nate's smile never wavered, his posture still respectful, as if he'd just made pleasant small talk about the weather.

"Emergency nursing suits me," Nate continued seamlessly. "The challenge, the pace. And it allowed me to be present for Paige while she was growing up. Single parenting requires certain sacrifices."

I bit the inside of my cheek to keep from grinning. Nate had delivered that repartee with such perfect, polite timing that my father couldn't tell if he'd just been zinged or complimented. He'd managed to defend his career choice, acknowledge his military service, and subtly remind my father about the value of being present for one's children, all while maintaining perfect respectful demeanor.

The pointed reference to parenting wasn't lost on my father, whose own career had kept him absent for much of my childhood. But neither was the "work for a living" comment, judging by the slight tightening around his eyes.

"Indeed," he said stiffly. "Well, you must try the barbecue. Carl's been smoking it since dawn."

As he retreated, I let out a breath I hadn't realized I was holding.

"That went well," Nate murmured.

I turned to face him fully, unable to suppress my grin any longer. "Did you just tell my father you work for a living?"

His eyes crinkled with suppressed laughter. "I have no idea what you mean."

"You absolute menace," I said, and before I could second-guess myself, I rose on my toes and kissed him as a reward for handling my father with such perfect, respectful sass.

When I pulled back, his expression had shifted to something warmer, more surprised.

"What was that for?"

"For being you," I said simply. "Better than expected doesn't even cover it. Although I'm surprised he didn't mention your age."

"Oh, he did," Nate said with a slight smile. "When you were getting drinks. Right before he asked about my 401k and whether I had life insurance."

"Dad!" I was mortified.

"It's fine. I'd ask the same things if a man my age was dating Paige in fifteen years."

The casual reference to a future so distant startled me. Nate rarely spoke in those terms, his life with Paige carefully contained in present tense.

The afternoon progressed in a blur of food, music, and constant conversation. I watched as Nate navigated my family with unexpected grace—discussing military history with my uncle, gardening with my stepmother, sports with my cousins. He was a chameleon, adapting to each new interaction with the same quiet competence he showed in the ER.

Paige, meanwhile, had been fully absorbed into the pack of children, her initial shyness dissolving as she joined in their games. I caught glimpses of her laughing, running, completely at ease in a way I rarely saw at school functions or the hospital.

It was nearing sunset when I finally escaped to the kitchen, seeking a moment of quiet. I stood at the sink, running my wrists under cool water, a nurse's trick for regulating body temperature.

"Hiding?"

I turned to find my mother in the doorway, an empty platter in her hands.

"Regrouping," I corrected.

She set the platter down and moved beside me. "Your young man is quite something."

"He's not 'my young man.' He's just... Nate."

"Mmm-hmm." She busied herself loading the dishwasher. "He's good with people. Respectful. Even got your brother talking about something besides his practice." She closed the dishwasher with a decisive click. "And that girl of his. She's lovely, Tasha. Bright. Well-mannered."

"She is," I agreed cautiously, waiting for the criticism that usually followed her compliments.

It didn't come. Instead, my mother said, "He looks at you like you hang the moon."

I blinked, caught off guard. "What?"

"When you're not watching. He looks at you like..." She hesitated, uncharacteristically searching for words. "Like you're the answer to a question he's been asking for a very long time."

Heat crept up my neck. "Mom—"

"I'm just saying. I see it." She turned to face me fully. "Does he make you happy, Tasha?"

The question echoed Grandma Rose's earlier comments and Marcus's skepticism. Did Nate make me happy? It seemed too simple for what we were to each other.

"He makes me... more," I said finally. "More honest. More myself. More willing to try things that scare me."

My mother's eyes softened. "Then that's enough for me."

She reached out, adjusting the strap of my dress with a familiar gesture that transported me back to childhood. "You've always been my stubborn one. My fighter. Even as a little girl, you had to do everything your own way." Her hand lingered on my shoulder. "It used to worry me. Now I think maybe it was preparing you for this."

"For what?"

"For loving people who need your kind of strength. That man out there—he carries something heavy. I can see it in his eyes. And that child, growing up without a mother..." She squeezed my shoulder. "They need someone who doesn't back down. Who isn't afraid of the hard parts."

My throat tightened unexpectedly. "I don't know if I'm that person, Mom."

"I do." Her certainty was absolute. "You get that from me."

The kitchen door swung open, and Nate appeared, looking slightly overwhelmed.

"Sorry to interrupt," he said. "But your grandmother is insisting Paige try her secret recipe banana pudding, and I'm concerned about the amount of bourbon I watched her add to it."

My mother laughed. "Don't worry, the alcohol cooks off. Mostly." She patted his arm as she passed. "I'll go rescue your daughter."

When we were alone, Nate leaned against the counter, exhaling heavily. "Your family is..."

"A lot?" I supplied.

"Extraordinary," he corrected. "Overwhelming, yes. But extraordinary."

I studied him. "You look tired."

"I am," he admitted. "But it's a good tired. Like after a challenging shift when everything went exactly right."

I moved closer, drawn to the quiet space he created even in my mother's chaotic kitchen. "And did everything go right today?"

"I think so." His hand found mine, fingers intertwining. "Your grandmother threatened me with bodily harm if I hurt you, but she also gave me her secret cornbread recipe, so I think I'm on solid ground."

I laughed. "Grandma Rose doesn't give that recipe to anyone."

"She said I needed feeding up. Apparently, I'm too skinny."

"Everyone's too skinny for Grandma Rose."

His thumb traced circles on the back of my hand. "Paige is having the time of her life. I haven't seen her this... free in a long time."

"She's a great kid."

"She likes you, you know. A lot."

The simple statement hung between us, heavy with implication. This wasn't just about Nate and me anymore. There was Paige to consider, her heart, her needs.

"I like her too," I said softly. "More than I expected to."

He nodded, understanding what I wasn't saying. "This is complicated, isn't it?"

"Very."

"Worth it?"

I looked at him—this serious, damaged, beautiful man who'd somehow become essential to me. Who'd shown me parts of myself I hadn't known existed.

"Yes," I said. "Worth it."

The kitchen door swung open again, this time revealing Paige, face flushed with excitement.

"Dad! Tasha! Come quick! Uncle Carl is bringing out the fireworks!"

Nate's eyebrows shot up. "Fireworks?"

"It's not a Williams family reunion without something catching fire," I explained, tugging him toward the door. "Consider yourself officially initiated."

As we followed Paige into the gathering dusk, I felt a strange peace settle over me. This day hadn't gone as I'd feared. There had been no disasters, no unforgivable faux pas. Just family, in all its messy, complicated glory, making room for two more people I cared deeply about.

And if my father's sidelong glances or Deanna's pinched smiles suggested not everyone was entirely on board—well, that was family too. The hard parts came with the good. Always had, always would.

Later, watching Nate laugh as my uncle's modest fireworks display went slightly awry, Paige safe beside him, I realized something.

I hadn't brought them here to get my family's approval. I'd brought them because, somewhere along the line, they had become *my* family too. A different kind, perhaps. Newer, more fragile. But family nonetheless.

And for the first time in a very long time, I wasn't afraid of what that might mean.

sixteen
nate

THE HOUSE FELT UNNATURALLY quiet after the chaos of the Williams family reunion. I stood in the kitchen, mechanically washing the few dishes we'd accumulated, while the events of the day replayed in my mind like a highlight reel.

Paige had lasted exactly thirty seconds in the car before succumbing to what could only be described as fun exhaustion. One moment she was chattering about the trampoline and her new friend Ayla, the next she was out cold, head lolled back against her car seat, mouth slightly open. I'd carried her into the house like a sack of potatoes, her arms dangling limply as I navigated the front door. She hadn't even stirred when I tucked her into bed, still wearing her purple reunion dress.

When was the last time I'd seen her that happy? That... free?

I dried my hands and moved to the living room, settling into my usual spot on the couch. The silence should have been peaceful, but instead it felt loaded with the weight of everything that had happened today. Everything that was changing.

Carl Williams clapping me on the shoulder, his weathered face split by an enormous grin. "A 'Devil Doc', huh? Well, I'll be damned. You boys saved more Marine asses than we could count." The unexpected acceptance from Tasha's stepfather, a man who'd seen his own share of combat, had caught me completely off guard. When he'd started defending my nursing career to anyone within earshot—"This man saved Marines in Fallujah, show some damn respect"—I'd felt something loosen in my chest that I hadn't even realized was tight.

Then there was Thomas Williams, Tasha's father, with his pointed questions about my career choices and his obvious disappointment that I hadn't "aimed higher." The condescension in his voice when he'd said the word "nurse" had been unmistakable. But Tasha had been watching, and when I'd delivered that old military line about working for a living, her eyes had lit up like Christmas morning.

The kiss she'd given me afterward—spontaneous, warm, proud—had been worth every awkward moment with her father. "You absolute menace," she'd called me, and I'd found myself grinning like an idiot.

I leaned back against the couch cushions, a strange restlessness settling over me. Today had been... good. Better than good. Paige had been welcomed into a huge, chaotic, loving family. I'd been accepted, even defended.

So why did I feel like I was standing on the edge of a cliff?

The answer came with unwelcome clarity: because I'd let them in. Both of them. Tasha and her entire extended family. I'd let Paige experience what it felt like to be part of something bigger than our carefully constructed world of two. And more terrifying than that... I'd let myself experience it too.

Letting people in meant they could leave. And if Tasha left— when she inevitably realized that a forty-year-old single father with PTSD and a mortgage wasn't worth the complications—she wouldn't just be leaving me. She'd be leaving Paige. And Paige had already been abandoned once by someone who was supposed to love her unconditionally.

My mind drifted, unbidden, to another time. A gas station. Paige barely four months old, Sarah gone for three weeks, and me driving home from Paige's babysitter on fumes because I'd miscalculated the sudden new distance between paydays. My card had been declined at the pump, my checking account showing a balance of $0.47, and I'd found myself searching the car for loose change like some kind of desperate scavenger.

I'd come up with $1.82 in sticky quarters, grimy dimes, and lint-covered pennies scraped from under the seats and dashboard. Enough to get us home. Barely.

The gas station attendant—a kid barely out of high school—had looked at my handful of change like I'd offered him something diseased. "Eww," he'd said, actually recoiling as I counted it out on the counter. I'd been carrying Paige in her car seat, her tiny face peaceful in sleep, completely unaware that her father was counting pocket change to get them home.

I'd wanted to explain. To tell this kid that I was a veteran, that I was in school, that this was temporary. But pride had kept my mouth shut, and I'd simply waited while he reluctantly accepted my money, his expression making it clear what he thought of me.

That night, I'd sat in this same position, Paige finally asleep in her crib, and made myself a promise. Never again. Never would I let us get that close to the edge. Never would I risk the stability I was building for her, not for anyone or anything.

I'd kept that promise for eleven years. Built walls. Maintained distance. Kept our world small and safe and predictable.

And now here I was, having spent the day watching my daughter bloom in the chaos of someone else's family, seeing her experience joy I couldn't provide on my own. Watching Tasha navigate between her world and ours with an ease that should have terrified me.

The strangest part was that it didn't.

I waited for the familiar anxiety to kick in. The voice that usually started cataloging all the ways this could go wrong, all the reasons I should pull back, protect what we had. But it didn't come. Instead, I felt... calm. Settled in a way I hadn't experienced in years.

Tasha had been texting with Paige regularly since the period emergency. Not just crisis management, but genuine conversation about books and school and silly things that made Paige laugh. She'd helped my daughter through one of the most potentially traumatic experiences of growing up, and she'd done it with such grace and humor that Paige had actually enjoyed it.

Today, watching her with my family—because that's what the Williams clan had felt like, family—I'd seen something else. The way she'd automatically cut Paige's food into smaller pieces. How she'd reminded her to drink water when she was running around. The steel in Tasha's eyes when Deanna had tried to make Paige feel bad about the trampoline incident. The way she'd stepped between them without hesitation, her voice calm but absolutely unyielding. "I'm sure it was an accident." Not just defending Paige, but doing it with such natural authority that even Deanna had backed down.

That wasn't the behavior of someone who was planning to disappear.

Tasha Williams was already part of our life. Not hovering at the edges, waiting for permission to enter, but fully integrated into the fabric of our daily existence. And somehow, without my noticing, I'd stopped being afraid of that.

I pulled out my phone, scrolling through the photos from today. Paige on the trampoline, arms spread wide, pure joy on her face. Tasha laughing at something Grandma Rose had said. The three of us together in front of the house, Paige between us, all of us smiling like we belonged there.

We looked like a family.

Before I could second-guess myself, I opened my email and started typing.

Dear Mr. and Mrs. Davis,

I hope this email finds you well. I wanted to share some photos from a family gathering we attended this weekend. As you can see, Paige had a wonderful time and made some new friends.

I also wanted you to know that I've been seeing someone—Tasha Williams. She's a nurse at the hospital where I work, and she's been a wonderful, positive presence for Paige as she's navigating these big growing-up years. She's been very good to both of us.

As always, I'll continue to keep you updated on Paige's life and activities. Please know that you're welcome to reach out anytime if you'd like to talk or if you have any questions. I know how much you love Paige, and I want you to know she's happy and thriving.

Best regards,

Nathan Crawford

I attached the best photos from the day—Paige's radiant smile, the three of us together—and hit send before I could overthink it.

It was the right thing to do. Sarah's parents deserved to know that their granddaughter was happy, that there was someone new in her life who cared about her. And if I was being honest with myself, I wanted them to see what I'd found. What we'd found.

For the first time in eleven years, I wasn't afraid of tomorrow. I wasn't calculating risks or preparing for disaster. I was simply... hopeful.

Leaning back against the couch, I closed my eyes and let myself imagine what that might feel like long-term. What it might mean to stop living in survival mode and start living in possibility.

The thought should have terrified me.

But it didn't.

I set the phone aside and walked quietly down the hallway. Paige was still out cold, her hair fanned across the pillow, one arm curled around her stuffed axolotl. I leaned in, kissed her forehead, and whispered the same thing I had a thousand times.

"We're okay, baby girl."

But this time... I was really starting to believe it.

seventeen
tasha

ROOM 8 WAS SUPPOSED to be routine. A fifteen-month-old girl with UTI symptoms—fussiness, low-grade fever, foul-smelling urine. The kind of case I could handle in my sleep.

The little girl—Mia, according to her chart—sat on the exam table in a pink onesie covered with tiny elephants, her wispy blonde hair pulled into two small pigtails with purple elastic bands. She was clingy but not screaming, which was already a win. Her mother, Jessica, looked exhausted in the way only parents of sick toddlers could manage.

"She's been cranky for two days," Jessica explained, bouncing Mia gently on her hip. "Won't eat much, keeps grabbing at her diaper. I thought it might be a UTI because my sister's daughter had one around this age."

I nodded, making notes. "Good instinct. Let's get a sample and see what we're dealing with."

Getting a clean urine sample from a fifteen-month-old required patience and creativity. I applied the adhesive-backed collection bag carefully while Jessica distracted Mia with her phone, playing some mindless kids' song on repeat. The whole process took twenty minutes, but we finally had what we needed.

"Lab should have results in about an hour," I told Jessica as I labeled the specimen. "In the meantime, let's get her some Tylenol for the fever and see if she'll take some juice."

Jessica nodded gratefully. "Thank you so much. I was worried I was overreacting."

"You did exactly right bringing her in," I assured her. "Better safe than sorry with little ones."

I sent the specimen to the lab and moved on to my other patients. Room 12 had a construction worker with a gnarly laceration that needed suturing. Room 4 was a college student with what appeared to be strep throat. Standard Friday afternoon in the ER.

I was charting the strep throat case when my phone rang. Lab extension.

"Fast Track, this is Tasha."

"Hi Tasha, this is Mike in the lab. I have critical results that need to be reported directly to a nurse or physician, not just uploaded to the system."

I frowned, pulling up my patient list. "Which patient are you calling about?"

"It's, ahh, Room 8. Mia Johnson."

Room 8. Mia. The UTI case. I felt a flutter of confusion. "Room 8? That's a routine urinalysis for a possible UTI. What's critical about that?"

"The culture came back positive for Neisseria gonorrhoeae."

The bottom dropped out of my stomach. I stared at my computer screen, at Mia's sweet face in the photo Jessica had shown me earlier—the one where she was laughing in a sandbox, dirt smudged on her cheek.

"Are you... are you sure?" I managed.

"Confirmed positive. The patient is fifteen months old, correct?"

"Yes." My voice sounded strange to my own ears. "Yes, that's correct."

"Okay, I'll upload the results now, but I needed to make sure you were aware, given the... circumstances."

I hung up and sat staring at the phone for a long moment. Gonorrhea. In a fifteen-month-old baby.

There was only one way that could happen.

I stood up slowly, my legs feeling unsteady. I needed to find Sophia. I needed to call Dr. Lee. I needed to... I needed to go back to Room 8 and somehow explain to Jessica that her daughter's infection wasn't what she thought it was.

My hand flew to my mouth, bile rising. I swallowed hard, fighting it down.

Sophia. I needed Sophia.

I found Sophia at the charge desk, reviewing staffing assignments for the next shift.

"Sophia," I said quietly. "I need to talk to you. *Now*. It's about Room 8."

She looked up, immediately reading something in my expression. "What's wrong?"

"Lab just called with critical results. The fifteen-month-old with UTI symptoms." I lowered my voice. "She's positive for gonorrhea."

Sophia's face went perfectly still.

"Have you told the mother yet?"

"No, I... I just got the call."

"Okay." Sophia stood up, her expression shifting into the controlled competence I'd seen her use during mass casualty events. "Let's get Dr. Lee involved. I'll page him now. And we'll need to call Child Protective Services."

My stomach clenched tighter. "The mother... she's going to ask me how this happened."

"I know." Sophia's voice was gentle but firm. "We'll handle it together. But first, let's make sure we have all the facts straight."

Dr. Lee arrived within minutes, his usual easy demeanor replaced by professional gravity when Sophia quietly explained the situation. Together, the three of us approached Room 8.

Jessica looked up hopefully when we entered. Mia was sleeping in her arms, finally peaceful after the Tylenol had brought her fever down.

"How are the results?" Jessica asked. "Is it what we thought?"

I glanced at Sophia, who gave me an almost imperceptible nod.

"Jessica," I said, pulling up a chair so I could sit at eye level with her. "The lab results showed that Mia does have an infection, but it's not the typical UTI we were expecting."

"What do you mean?" Jessica shifted Mia slightly, protective instincts already kicking in.

"The culture came back positive for an infection called gonorrhea," Dr. Lee said gently. "I know that's probably not a word you were expecting to hear in relation to your daughter."

Jessica blinked, confusion clear on her face. "Gonorrhea? But that's... how could Mia have that?"

I watched her mind work through the implications, saw the exact moment when the pieces started to fall into place... and then the desperate scramble to find another explanation.

"Oh!" Jessica's face brightened with sudden understanding. "Oh, I bet I know what happened. I had that same infection recently. My boyfriend, he..." Her cheeks flushed. "He cheated on me. We worked things out, but before I knew I was infected, I took a bath with Mia. She loves playing in the tub with me. That has to be how she got it, right?"

The hope in her voice was heartbreaking.

"Jessica," Sophia said softly, "I understand why you'd think that, but unfortunately, that's not how this type of infection spreads. Gonorrhea can only be transmitted through direct sexual contact. It can't be passed through bath water or casual contact."

"But then how...?" Jessica's voice trailed off, her eyes growing wide with dawning horror.

"We need to ask you some questions," Dr. Lee said gently. "Has your boyfriend ever been alone with Mia? Even for short periods?"

"I... yes, but..." Jessica's voice became smaller. "He babysits her sometimes when I work late shifts. He's good with her. She likes him. She never seemed scared or..."

The words died in her throat as the full implications hit her. The color drained from her face.

"No," she whispered, almost inaudibly. "No, that's not... he wouldn't... he loves her. He tells me how much he loves her all the time."

Then she began to cry. Not the quiet tears of a worried mother, but the soul-deep, keening wail of someone whose world had just shattered. Mia stirred in her arms, whimpering at the sound.

I had heard people cry before. In the ER, you hear every kind of grief—the sharp grief of sudden loss, the exhausted grief of prolonged illness, the angry grief of unfairness. But I had never heard anything like the sound Jessica made. It was primal, devastating, the sound of every assumption about safety and love being ripped away.

Sophia immediately moved to gently take Mia from Jessica's arms, holding the sleepy toddler while her mother fell apart. Dr. Lee was already on his phone, making the necessary calls.

"I'm so sorry, Jessica," I said, my own voice thick with tears I was desperately trying to hold back. "I know this is devastating. But we're going to take care of Mia, and we're going to make sure she's safe."

"How could I not know?" Jessica sobbed. "How could I not protect her? She's my baby. She's my everything. How could I let this happen?"

"This is not your fault," Sophia said firmly, still holding Mia. "Do you understand me? This is not your fault. You brought her here because you knew something was wrong. You did exactly what a good mother does."

But Jessica was beyond hearing reassurances. She was lost in the horror of what had been done to her child, what she had unknowingly allowed to happen.

I excused myself and walked quickly to the bathroom, where I locked the door and leaned against the sink, trying to regain control.

My hands were shaking. My stomach felt like it was full of broken glass.

When I came back out, Sophia was waiting for me in the hallway.

"You okay?" she asked.

"Yeah," I lied automatically.

"Tasha." Her voice was gentle but firm. "I've been doing this for fifteen years. I've seen too many of our colleagues—good nurses, smart nurses, dedicated nurses—who we've lost forever because they didn't want to ask for help. We see the worst things in the world, and we're good at helping people through them, but we're awful at helping ourselves."

I nodded, not trusting my voice.

"You know what the most dangerous thing is?" Sophia continued. "When we start thinking, 'What right do I have to complain or be sad when so many other people have it so much worse?' It's a fallacy. Just because someone else's pain is visible doesn't mean yours doesn't matter."

"I'm fine, Sophia. Really."

"This is a hard thing to see and go through," she said, ignoring my deflection. "If you need help processing it, we have grief counselors available. I'm going to get you that information this afternoon. And if you need anything else, anything at all, I'm here. Anytime. Really."

I managed a thin smile. "Thank you."

"Also," Sophia said, glancing back at the charge desk, "we're overstaffed today. I need to send someone home early."

I stared at her. In three years at Metro General, I had never once seen us overstaffed. Not even close.

"Sophia, you don't have to—"

"Four o'clock is fine," she said, as if I hadn't spoken. "Get out of here. Go home. Rest."

I looked at her for a long moment, seeing the kindness behind the professional facade, understanding that she was giving me exactly what I needed, even if I couldn't ask for it.

"Sophia," I said as I gathered my things. "Does it ever get easier? Does it ever... go away?"

Her expression softened, and for just a moment, I saw the weight she carried—fifteen years of cases like Mia, fifteen years of being the rock everyone else leaned on.

"No," she said quietly. "It doesn't. But you learn to carry it. And you don't carry it alone."

I nodded and headed for the parking garage, pulling out my phone as I walked. I scrolled to Nate's contact, my thumb hovering over the call button.

He was probably having a nice day off with Paige. I didn't want to ruin that. But I also couldn't go home to my empty apartment and sit alone with what I'd just witnessed.

Before I could talk myself out of it, I hit call.

"Hey," Nate's voice was warm, relaxed. "This is a nice surprise. What's up?"

"Are you busy?" I asked, trying to keep my voice normal.

"Just hanging out with Paige. She's building some kind of architectural marvel with Legos. Why?"

"Could I... would it be okay if I came over? I know it's last minute, and if you have plans—"

"Of course," he said immediately, and I could hear the shift in his voice, the way it became more alert. "Everything okay?"

"Yeah," I lied. "Just... had a rough shift. Thought maybe I could see you both."

"Absolutely. We'll order pizza. Paige will be thrilled."

"Thank you," I said, and had to end the call before my voice broke.

As I drove toward Nate's house, I tried to push the image of Mia's innocent face out of my mind. Tried to stop hearing Jessica's devastating sobs. Tried to forget the moment when I'd had to explain to a mother that the person she trusted with her child had destroyed that child's innocence.

But I couldn't. It sat in the pit of my stomach like a stone, heavy and sharp-edged.

I needed to see Paige safe and happy. I needed to see Nate's fierce protectiveness in action. I needed to remember that there were good people in the world, people who would die before they let harm come to a child.

I needed to remember that love could be trusted.

Even if I wasn't sure I believed it anymore.

eighteen
nate

"DAD?" Paige looked up from her elaborate Lego city. "Who was that?"

"Tasha. She's coming over for dinner."

Paige's face lit up like Christmas morning. "Really? Can we show her my new book? And can we make s'mores? Oh, and I want to show her how I finally got the bridge to stay up!"

"Sure, kiddo. We'll do whatever makes her happy." I ruffled her hair. "She had a hard day at work, so let's make sure she has a good time here, okay?"

Paige nodded solemnly. At eleven, she was already developing the same protective instincts I had. "Like when you have the dreams and need quiet time?"

Sometimes my daughter's emotional intelligence caught me off guard. "Sort of like that, yeah."

By the time Tasha's car pulled into the driveway forty-five minutes later, Paige had reorganized her entire Lego display and I'd ordered pizza from the place that made Tasha's favorite margherita. Through the front window, I watched her sit in her car for a long moment before getting out, like she was gathering herself.

When I opened the door, she looked perfectly normal. Professional smile in place, shoulders squared, every inch the competent ER nurse I worked with every day. But you could see the cracks if you knew where to look—the slight tightness around her eyes, the way her hands clenched and unclenched at her sides.

"Hey there," I said softly, stepping aside to let her in.

"TASHA!" Paige bounded into the hallway, launching herself at Tasha with the enthusiasm of a golden retriever.

Tasha caught her in a hug, and I watched her hold on just a beat too long, her arms tightening around Paige's small frame like she needed the contact.

"Hey, kiddo," Tasha said, her voice steadier now. "I hear you've been doing some engineering today."

"Want to see? I built an entire city! With a working drawbridge!" Paige grabbed Tasha's hand, tugging her toward the living room.

For the next three hours, Tasha threw herself into being with us with an intensity that would have seemed normal to anyone who didn't know her well. She admired every detail of Paige's Lego city. She helped us build an even more elaborate bridge. She laughed at Paige's jokes and listened with rapt attention to a detailed explanation of why certain structural elements were more stable than others.

But I noticed the way she kept reaching out to touch Paige— smoothing her hair, adjusting her sleeve, letting her hand linger on Paige's shoulder. I noticed how she watched me interact with my daughter, something almost hungry in her expression.

During dinner, Paige regaled us with stories from school, and Tasha hung on every word like it was the most fascinating thing she'd ever heard. When Paige got pizza sauce on her chin, Tasha was there with a napkin before I could even reach for one.

"Can we watch a movie?" Paige asked as we finished eating. "The new one I got from the library?"

"What movie?" I asked.

"'The Princess Bride.' Mrs. Davidson said it was a classic and I needed to see it immediately or I was deprived."

Tasha laughed, the first genuinely relaxed sound I'd heard from her all evening. "Mrs. Davidson is absolutely right. That's practically required viewing."

We settled on the couch, Paige between us, her head gradually migrating to rest against Tasha's shoulder as the movie progressed. Tasha's arm came around her automatically, and I watched something in her expression soften.

By the time Westley was storming the castle, Paige was fast asleep, her breathing deep and even. Tasha looked down at her with such tenderness it made my chest tight.

"I should put her to bed," I whispered.

Tasha nodded, carefully extricating herself so I could scoop Paige up. My daughter was getting too big for me to carry easily, but I managed to get her to her room and tucked into bed without waking her.

When I came back to the living room, I found Tasha curled into the corner of the couch, knees drawn up, staring at nothing. The facade had finally cracked.

"Hey," I said softly, settling beside her. "You want to talk about it?"

She shook her head, then seemed to change her mind. "Tell me a story about you and Paige," she said quietly. "Something good. Something... normal."

"Okay, hmmm." I said, shifting so she could lean against me if she wanted to. "Let me tell you about nursing school."

She nestled into my side, her head finding the hollow of my shoulder.

"Paige was barely six months old when I started," I began. "Single dad, living on GI Bill money and whatever I could make working weekends at a clinic. I was terrified I wouldn't be able to handle both."

"But you did."

"Barely. The first semester, I had to bring her to class twice because my babysitter fell through. I was sure they'd kick me out of the program." I smoothed Tasha's hair absently. "The first time, she was maybe eight months old, and I had this English class with a strict attendance policy. One absence dropped your grade a full letter."

"With a baby!?"

"Right? It was aimed at frat boys who wanted to sleep off hangovers, not single parents dealing with sick babysitters. But they wouldn't make exceptions." I felt the old frustration rise up. "So I brought her in her carrier, all swaddled up, praying she'd sleep through the lecture. And she did—didn't make a peep for ninety minutes."

"Good girl," Tasha murmured against my chest.

"The professor barely noticed. But afterward, this smug graduate assistant held me back and told me I wasn't 'taking the class seriously' and that I 'shouldn't be here' if I couldn't arrange proper childcare. Then he marked me absent anyway."

"What a dick."

I laughed softly. "I almost failed that class. Had to do extra credit just to scrape by with a C." I paused, remembering. "But you know what? My nursing professors were completely different. When they found out about Paige, they went out of their way to help. Professor Martinez used to bounce her on her knee while I took exams. Dr. Kim kept a Pack 'n Play in her office."

"They understood."

"They understood that sometimes life doesn't wait for convenient timing. That being a parent doesn't make you less capable—it makes you more determined." I pressed a kiss to the top of her head. "I wouldn't have made it through without them."

"Tell me another one."

I studied Tasha's face in the dim light from the TV. Whatever she'd seen today, she obviously needed to remember that good things existed.

"Another one?" I asked. "Another one. Ahhh... hmmm... oh, I know! Let me tell you about Paige's singing phase. When she was about four, maybe five, she went through this phase where she had to sing constantly. Not normal kids' songs, mind you. Educational songs. Scientific songs." I chuckled at the memory. "Tell me if this surprises you, because this one is burned into my memory forever."

I cleared my throat and began to sing in a soft, but deliberately overdramatic, sing-song voice:

"When there's water vapor in the air,
it condenses, forming clouds!
Saturation, condensation,
bring about the cloud formation,
when there's water vapor in the air!"

Tasha burst out laughing, the sound bright and genuine. "Oh my God, that is one thousand percent Paige. Where did she even learn that?"

"I don't even know. Some educational TV show. She must have heard it once and decided it was her new favorite song. She'd sing it in the grocery store, in the car, during bath time. The other parents at the playground thought I was raising some kind of tiny meteorologist."

"That's so adorable," Tasha said, still chuckling. "I can picture her little serious face, belting out cloud formation facts."

"She was so proud of herself too. Like she was sharing the most important information in the world." I smiled at the memory. "One time, she—"

I stopped. Tasha's laughter had shifted, becoming something else entirely. Her shoulders were shaking, but the sound coming from her throat wasn't amusement anymore. She was crying. Not the controlled tears of someone trying to hold it together, but deep, wrenching sobs that shook her entire body.

"Hey," I said softly, pulling her closer. "Hey, hey, hey. Sweetheart! What happened? What's wrong?"

"I can't," she gasped. "I can't stop seeing her face. This little girl, fifteen months old, and someone... someone hurt her, Nate. Someone she trusted. Someone her mother trusted."

My blood went cold. I didn't need details. I'd seen enough cases in the ER to know exactly what she was talking about.

"Oh, Tasha. I'm sorry. I'm so sorry you had to see that."

"She was so little. So innocent. And her mother..." Tasha's sobs intensified. "The sound she made when we told her. I've never heard anything like it. Like her whole world just ended."

I held her tighter, my own throat closing up. "Yeah. Yeah. I've been there, too." A pause. "Did they get the bastard that did it?"

"I don't know. The police were called. CPS took the baby." She looked up at me with red, swollen eyes. "How could someone do that? How could anyone look at a child and think..."

"I don't know, hon," I said honestly. "Some people are just broken in ways that can't be fixed."

"I keep thinking about you with Paige," she continued, her voice raw. "The way you protect her. The way you love her. And I can't understand how someone could take that trust, that innocence, and destroy it."

I thought about all the ways I tried to keep Paige safe. The careful vetting of babysitters. The self-defense classes I was already planning for when she got older. The way I still checked on her every night before I went to bed, just to make sure she was breathing.

"I grew up without that," Tasha said quietly. "My parents... they weren't monsters. They weren't abusive. But they were never really there, you know? My dad was always working. My mom thought emotions were inconvenient. I learned early not to need too much from anyone."

"Tasha—"

"But watching you with Paige, seeing how you are with her... it's like seeing something I never knew existed. This fierce, unconditional protection. This safety." Fresh tears started. "And today I saw what happens when that safety gets stolen. When someone destroys it."

I didn't know what to say. How do you comfort someone who's just witnessed one of humanity's worst failures? How do you restore faith in goodness when evil has shown its face so clearly?

"You saved her," I said finally. "That little girl? You saved her. You got her away from the person who was hurting her."

"But we were too late. The damage is already done."

"The physical damage, maybe. But you gave her a chance at healing. At safety. That matters, Tasha. That matters a lot more than you know."

She was quiet for a long moment, her breathing gradually evening out. "I think I'm falling in love with you," she said suddenly. "With both of you. And it terrifies me because I don't know how to trust that it's real. That it won't disappear."

My heart stopped. Not because of the confession—I'd been falling in love with her too, had been for weeks—but because of the raw vulnerability in her voice. The fear.

"It's real," I said softly. "Whatever this is between us, it's real."

"How do you know?"

"Because you're here. Because when your world got turned upside down today, you came to us. Because you held my daughter like she was precious. Because you're crying over a baby you'll never see again." I tilted her chin up so she could see my face. "Because I've spent eleven years building walls to keep people out, and somehow you've gotten past every single one."

She hugged me then, desperate and needy, and I poured everything I had into hugging her back. All my own fears about letting someone in. All my gratitude that she'd chosen us. All my determination to be the safe harbor she'd never had.

We might have stayed like that all night, but a small voice from the hallway interrupted us.

"Tasha? I had a bad dream."

Paige stood in the doorway in her space-themed pajamas, hair mussed from sleep, looking young and vulnerable.

Without hesitation, Tasha was off the couch and crossing to her. "Oh, sweetheart, come here." She gathered Paige into her arms, and my daughter melted into the embrace like she'd been waiting for it her whole life.

"Want to tell me about it?" Tasha asked, leading Paige back to the couch.

"There were these scary men trying to get into our house, and Dad wasn't here, and I couldn't find him anywhere."

I started to get up, but Tasha was already settling onto the couch with Paige in her lap, stroking her hair with the kind of instinctive tenderness that couldn't be faked.

"That does sound scary," Tasha said softly. "But you know what? Your dad would never let anything happen to you. He'd fight off a hundred scary men before he'd let anyone hurt you."

"I know," Paige said, snuggling closer. "But in the dream, I couldn't find him."

"Well, he's right here now. And so am I. You're safe, baby girl."

I watched them together—Tasha holding my daughter, Paige trusting her completely—and felt something fundamental shift in my chest. This wasn't just about Tasha and me anymore. This was about family. The kind of family I'd never dared to hope we could have.

"Can I stay with you guys until I fall asleep?" Paige asked.

"Of course," Tasha and I said at the same time.

We rearranged ourselves on the couch, Paige curled between us, her head on Tasha's chest, my arm around both of them. I watched Tasha hum softly, some lullaby I didn't recognize, her hand making gentle circles on Paige's back.

Within minutes, Paige was asleep again, but none of us moved. We stayed there in the soft glow of the TV, holding each other, holding onto this moment of peace after a day that had shown us how fragile safety could be.

"Thank you," Tasha whispered.

"For what?"

"For letting me come here. For giving me this." She looked down at Paige, then back at me. "For showing me what love is supposed to look like."

I pressed a kiss to her temple, breathing in the scent of her hair, the warmth of her skin. "Thank you for trusting us with it."

Outside, the world continued to turn, filled with its mixture of beauty and horror. But inside our living room, wrapped around each other in the darkness, we had created something perfect and safe and real.

nineteen
tasha

"YOU THINK you're ready for triage? The real deal this time, not just covering for five minutes?"

Sophia's question caught me off guard. I looked up from my charting, remembering that brief stint covering for Nate when he'd had to step away. That had been manageable; a few routine patients, nothing too complex.

"Flying solo. Well, not completely solo. Nate'll be right there with you. But you'd be primary for a full shift." She studied my face. "Triage isn't for the faint of heart, Tasha. You don't have to deal as much with some of the more complex stuff, like the nursing home patient covered in God knows what, the gunshot wound that needs immediate stabilization. But triage is different."

I set down my pen, giving her my full attention.

"The triage nurse is arguably more responsible for patient flow than I am," Sophia continued. "You have to make snapshot judgments about patients. You have to theoretically wrangle every patient in the waiting room, and if you have ten, twenty, thirty people waiting, that adds up fast. People pile up at your desk, so you need focused assessments that get all the information you need without taking too long. But that's balanced against the fact that if you miss something, if you screw up something subtle..." She paused. "That's on your conscience."

I felt a flutter of nervousness mixed with something else—excitement? Pride? Those five minutes covering for Nate had gone smoothly, but a full shift was entirely different.

"Not just any nurse can do triage, especially not here at Metro General," Sophia said. "It's recognition of your clinical skills. Also, fair warning—triage nurses always get their asses beat because it's not easy. But you're ready for it, if you want it."

Two weeks ago, I would have jumped at the chance without hesitation. Now, after the Mia case, after falling apart in Nate's living room, I found myself hesitating. What if I missed something? What if I wasn't as ready as Sophia thought?

"You'll be shadowing Nate for the first few hours," Sophia added, reading my expression. "He's one of the best triage nurses we have. Learn from him, then take the lead when you're comfortable."

I took a deep breath. "Okay."

Sophia smiled. "Good. Go find Nate. He's expecting you."

I found Nate at the triage desk, reviewing charts with the same methodical precision he brought to everything. He looked up when I approached, and I saw something soften in his expression—the same gentle concern he'd shown me that night on his couch.

"Ready to see how the other half lives?" he asked, gesturing to the chaos of the waiting room beyond the glass partition.

"Define ready." I hesitated, then added quietly, "What if I'm not as prepared as Sophia thinks?"

Nate's expression grew serious. "You've got the best instincts in the department, Tasha. Trust them."

The simple confidence in his voice steadied me. "Let's do this."

The first patient was Mrs. Rodriguez, a regular who came in monthly for medication refills she could get at any urgent care clinic. Nate handled her with patient professionalism, explaining once again that the ER wasn't the right place for routine prescriptions, while I watched his technique—how he kept his voice calm, his questions focused, his documentation precise.

"The key," he murmured to me as Mrs. Rodriguez left, "is not to get frustrated with the frequent flyers. They're usually here because they don't have anywhere else to go."

The second patient was a middle-aged man who approached the desk with a slight grimace.

"I've been having back pain," he announced.

Nate's fingers moved to the keyboard. "Okay, sir. Did you injure yourself recently? Lift something wrong? How long has this been going on?"

"Five years."

Nate's hands stilled. He looked up with a perfectly neutral expression. "Well, sir, you got here just in the nick of time. Did something change in the character or nature of your pain that made you come in today?"

"No."

I bit my lip to keep from smiling as Nate calmly directed the man to the waiting room.

The third patient was a college kid with obvious food poisoning, retching into a basin. Straightforward triage—IV fluids, anti-nausea meds, probable discharge in a few hours. I watched Nate's hands as he started the IV, steady and sure.

Then came Mr. Swanson.

"What allergies do you have, sir?" Nate asked, fingers poised over the keyboard.

"Advil," Mr. Swanson replied confidently.

I watched Nate start typing "ibuprofen" into the allergy field.

"No, no," Mr. Swanson said, leaning forward to see the screen. "Advil."

Nate paused, looking up. "Yes, sir. Ibuprofen."

"No, I can take ibuprofen. I just can't take Advil."

I felt my left eye twitch involuntarily. Nate's expression remained perfectly neutral, but I caught the slight tightening around his own eyes.

"Ah," Nate said carefully. "Well, name-brand Advil has orange dye in it. Are you allergic to that?"

"No, no. Just the Advil part."

I bit the inside of my cheek to keep from laughing. Nate slowly deleted "ibuprofen" from the allergy field and typed in "Advil, not ibuprofen."

"Let someone else wrestle with that one," he murmured to me after Mr. Swanson left.

We moved through a few more cases when the man with back pain approached the desk, looking slightly annoyed.

"Hey, I didn't know I'd have to wait this long," he said. "I'm just gonna go and make an appointment with my family doc."

Nate looked up with the same deadpan expression. "That's probably a good idea, sir."

By the next patient, something had shifted. I found myself anticipating Nate's questions, reaching for supplies before he asked. When an elderly woman came in complaining of chest pain, I was already pulling up the EKG machine while he took her history. We moved around each other like dancers who'd been practicing the same routine for years.

From the corner of my eye, I caught Sophia watching us from the charge desk, a small smile on her face.

Then came the moment that surprised us both. A young mother arrived with her toddler, both of them in tears. The child had been crying inconsolably for hours, and the mother was convinced something was terribly wrong.

"He won't eat, he won't sleep, he just screams," she sobbed. "I know something's wrong. I know it."

Nate started his assessment, but the toddler only screamed louder at his approach. I stepped forward without thinking.

"Hey there, little guy," I said softly, crouching down to the child's eye level. Something about my voice seemed to catch his attention. "That's some impressive lung capacity you've got there."

The crying reduced to hiccups. I pulled out my stethoscope and made it into a pretend telephone.

"Hello? Yes, this is Dr. Tasha calling about a very important patient," I said into the stethoscope. "Really? He's the strongest crier you've ever heard? Wow."

The toddler giggled, reaching for the stethoscope. In the sudden quiet, I could hear it—the telltale wheeze of a reactive airway.

"Mild asthma exacerbation," I said quietly to Nate. "Probably triggered by crying, which made him cry more."

Nate nodded, already reaching for the nebulizer. Twenty minutes later, the little boy was breathing easily and playing with toys in his mother's lap.

"That was sharp, picking up on the wheeze with all that screaming. Good instincts," Nate said as they left.

Before I could respond, chaos erupted in the waiting room.

"Excuse me! EXCUSE ME!" A man's voice, loud and increasingly frantic. "I need to be seen RIGHT NOW!"

Through the glass, I saw a middle-aged man in a business suit pushing past other patients, his face flushed with panic. He practically ran to our desk, leaning over it with wild eyes.

"I'm bleeding to death," he gasped. "I'm going to die. You have to help me now!"

Nate remained calm, but I could see him shift into high-alert mode. "Sir, I need you to take a deep breath and tell me what's happening."

"I'm bleeding internally! There's blood everywhere! I've been bleeding for hours!" The man—Mr. Hendricks, apparently—was practically hyperventilating.

"Okay, sir. Can you tell me about any changes to your diet recently? What have you had to eat or drink today?"

Mr. Hendricks waved his hand dismissively. "You're not taking me seriously! I'm BLEEDING TO DEATH! I don't have time for twenty questions!"

Nate's jaw tightened almost imperceptibly. "Sir, I understand you're scared. We're going to take good care of you. But I need you to work with me here."

"I need a doctor! Now! Not a nurse asking me about my lunch!"

I felt my own temper flare at the dismissive tone, but Nate just nodded calmly. "Let's get you back to a room and figure out what's going on."

Because of his dramatic presentation, Mr. Hendricks got bumped ahead of several other patients who had been waiting longer. As one of our ER techs wheeled him to the main treatment area, Nate leaned over and whispered in my ear.

"He's loud, which is usually a good sign. It's the quiet ones who tell you they're dying, matter-of-fact, that you *really* worry about. That 'sense of impending doom' is no joke. We take this guy seriously because of what he's saying, but the way he's saying it... usually means we have a little more time to figure it out. Still, never get complacent."

In Room 6, Mr. Hendricks was still agitated, pacing back and forth despite our attempts to get him on the gurney. His vital signs were completely normal—blood pressure, heart rate, oxygen saturation all within normal limits.

"I need a stool sample," Nate said. "If you're having GI bleeding, we need to confirm it."

"I KNOW I'm bleeding! Look!" Mr. Hendricks gestured wildly toward the bathroom.

I glanced in, and sure enough: there was bright red color in the toilet bowl. My stomach dropped a little. Maybe this wasn't as routine as I'd thought.

We got an IV started—Mr. Hendricks barely flinched, too focused on his panic—and drew blood for a complete workup. His hemoglobin, hematocrit, and coagulation studies all came back normal. No signs of blood loss.

Twenty minutes later, the stool sample results came back. I read them twice to make sure.

"Heme negative," I said quietly to Nate. *No blood detected.*

"Interesting." Nate pulled up a chair next to Mr. Hendricks, who had finally calmed down enough to sit on the gurney. "Sir, I need to ask you again about what you've had to eat or drink today. And I need you to really think about it, because it's important."

Mr. Hendricks looked sheepish now, some of his panic having subsided with the normal test results. "I... well, I had my usual coffee this morning. And then around ten, I tried that new Berry Blast Juggernaut from the smoothie place downtown. The seasonal one."

I felt understanding dawn. "The bright red one? With the special holiday coloring?"

"Yeah, that's the one. But I don't see how—" He stopped mid-sentence, his eyes widening. "Oh. Oh, God."

"That Berry Blast Juggernaut has an awful lot of food dye in it," I said gently. "It can... well, it can make things look pretty dramatic on the way out."

Mr. Hendricks' face went through several shades of red that had nothing to do with food coloring. "You mean I... the blood wasn't..."

"Not blood, sir. Just dye."

The silence in the room was profound. Mr. Hendricks buried his face in his hands.

"I am so, so sorry," he said, his voice muffled. "I was so scared, and I... I was rude to you both. I thought I was dying."

"It's okay," Nate said, and I could hear the genuine compassion in his voice. "When you think you're in danger, it's natural to panic. We see it all the time."

We discharged Mr. Hendricks with instructions to avoid red-dyed beverages if he didn't want a repeat performance. He apologized three more times on his way out, shaking both our hands.

The moment the door closed behind him, I felt it start- a giggle that bubbled up from somewhere deep in my soul. I tried to hold it back, but when I looked at Nate and saw his lips twitching, I lost it completely.

"Berry Blast Juggernaut emergency," I gasped between laughs.

"The seasonal one," Nate added, and that set me off again.

We were both laughing so hard we had to lean against the wall for support. Every time we started to calm down, one of us would say "bright red" or "bleeding to death" and we'd start up again.

"I thought we were gonna have to hang a couple units of uncross-matched blood to gravity," Nate said, wiping tears from his eyes.

That image—universal donor blood running wide open through an IV, as fast as physics would allow—made me laugh even harder. "The look on his face when he realized..."

"I thought he was going to melt into the floor," Nate said.

It felt so good to laugh. Really laugh, the kind that makes your stomach hurt and your cheeks ache. After the heaviness of the past few weeks, the breakdown and all the emotional intensity, this moment of pure absurdity was exactly what I needed.

"You know what the best part is?" I said as we finally started to recover. "He's going to tell this story at parties for the rest of his life. 'Remember that time I went to the ER because I thought I was dying from a smoothie?'"

"His friends are never going to let him live it down," Nate agreed. "Especially if he tells them about pushing past other patients in the waiting room."

I grinned at him. "This job is insane."

"The best kind of insane," he replied, and something in his expression made my heart do a little flip.

We stood there for a moment, still smiling, and I realized something had shifted between us. Not just back to normal—forward to something new. Working together like this, sharing the ridiculous and the profound, felt natural in a way I hadn't expected.

From across the department, I caught Sophia's eye. She was still watching us, but now her expression held something that looked like approval. Like she was seeing exactly what she'd hoped to see.

"So," I said, "what's next? Someone allergic to the alphabet? A patient convinced they're turning into a werewolf?"

"Don't jinx us," Nate warned, but he was still smiling. "In this place, anything's possible."

As we headed back to triage, I felt something settle into place inside me. This was more than just doing the job—this was finding my place in it. Finding my rhythm, my confidence, my partnership with someone who brought out the best in my clinical skills.

It was about realizing that I was exactly where I was supposed to be.

twenty
nate

SATURDAY MORNING FOUND us in my kitchen, the kind of lazy domestic scene I'd never imagined having with anyone other than Paige. Tasha was at the stove making pancakes while I packed Paige's lunch for a sleepover at her friend Zoe's house later. Paige herself was sprawled at the kitchen table, supposedly doing math homework but mostly providing running commentary on everything we were doing.

"Dad, you're cutting the sandwich wrong," she informed me without looking up from her worksheet. "Zoe's mom cuts them diagonally. It tastes better that way."

"Ah yes, the scientific principle of diagonal sandwich superiority," I said, refolding the sandwich. "How could I forget?"

"You're so weird," Paige said, but she was grinning.

"Speaking of weird," Tasha added, flipping a pancake with unnecessary flair, "your daughter just asked me if I knew the difference between a numerator and a denominator. I told her I'm a nurse, not a mathematician."

"But you figured it out anyway," Paige said loyally. "You're smart."

I watched them interact, this easy back-and-forth that had developed over the past few months, and felt that familiar warmth in my

chest. Paige had taken to Tasha in a way that still surprised me sometimes—not just accepting her presence in our lives, but actively
seeking her out for everything from homework help to discussions
about which hair products worked best.

"So," I said, settling at the table with my coffee, "big week
coming up."

Paige's head snapped up from her math. "Five days until
graduation!"

The excitement in her voice was infectious. Fifth grade graduation (officially called "Fifth Grade Recognition Ceremony" by the
school district) was apparently the social event of the year in Paige's
world. She'd been planning her outfit for weeks and practicing
walking in a straight line without tripping, which she'd demonstrated for us approximately forty-seven times.

"I still can't believe you're going to middle school," Tasha said,
bringing a stack of pancakes to the table. "When did you get so
grown up?"

"I've always been this grown up," Paige said seriously. "You just
didn't know me when I was little."

"Fair point," Tasha laughed.

As we ate breakfast, listening to Paige's detailed analysis of which
of her classmates were most likely to trip during the ceremony
(apparently Marcus Dawson was the odds-on favorite), an idea
started forming in my mind. Paige's graduation was next Friday. I'd
been planning to take her somewhere special afterward, just the two
of us like always. But sitting here, watching Tasha help Paige with her
math while stealing pieces of bacon from my plate, I realized I wanted
something different this time.

I wanted to see how we'd work as a family.

"Hey," I said as Paige headed upstairs to get ready for her sleepover. "You have any plans for next weekend?"

Tasha looked up from loading the dishwasher, eyebrow raised.
"Depends. Why?"

"Paige graduates Friday. I was thinking we could do something to celebrate. Like a weekend trip."

"What kind of trip?" Her tone was cautious, but I caught the hint of interest.

"Camping."

Her face went through several expressions in rapid succession—surprise, horror, then what looked like mild panic. "Camping!? Are you trying to kill me? My idea of roughing it is a hotel without room service. Bugs? Sleeping on the ground in a tent? Noooooo, thank you. Hard pass."

I started to explain, but Paige chose that moment to thunder back down the stairs, overnight bag in hand, apparently having developed supernatural hearing where the word "camping" was concerned.

"Did someone say camping?" Her eyes were wide with excitement. "Oh, please, Tasha! Camping would be so cool! We could make s'mores and tell ghost stories! Please?"

I watched Tasha's resolve crumble in real time as she looked from Paige's pleading face to mine, clearly realizing she was outnumbered by the Crawford family united front.

"Alright, alright," Tasha sighed dramatically. "How can I say no to that face? Besides, it's not every day someone graduates from fifth grade. But if I see a spider bigger than my thumb, I'm sleeping in the car. I guess I'll have to go buy industrial-strength bug spray... and maybe a hazmat suit."

"Actually," I said quickly, "I was thinking we could rent a cabin. At the campground. So, you know, technically camping for Paige, but with actual beds and plumbing. And air conditioning."

Tasha's relief was visible. "Oh, *thank God*. You had me picturing myself with a sleeping bag and a prayer."

Booking the two-bedroom beachside cabin made my wallet wince, and I saw Tasha raise an eyebrow when I mentioned the price later. "Well," she'd said, "with that cabin price, looks like we're officially on a 'pack our own groceries and cook every meal' kind of vacation. Hope you like my famous peanut butter and jelly, Paige."

Paige was already bouncing on her toes. "Can we have a campfire? Can we roast marshmallows? Can we go swimming? Can we leave right after graduation?"

"All of the above," I promised,

"Perfect," Tasha said. "My ear infection should be completely gone by then, so I can actually enjoy the water."

I was already pulling up the campground website on my phone. "There's this place about three hours from here, right on the beach..."

The graduation ceremony itself was everything you'd expect from an elementary school production- adorable, endless, and featuring at least three kids who forgot which way to walk across the stage. Paige looked impossibly grown up in her cap and gown, and when they called her name, I felt that familiar mix of pride and terror that came with marking time.

"She looks so mature," Tasha whispered beside me, and I realized she was feeling it too. This strange bittersweet pride in a child who wasn't technically hers but somehow had become ours to worry about and celebrate.

After the ceremony, Paige was so excited about our trip that she demanded we pack the car that very evening.

"We have to get there as early as possible," she insisted, dragging her suitcase down the hallway. "What if all the good spots are taken? What if we miss the sunrise? What if—"

"Breathe, kiddo," I said, but I was already helping her load beach supplies into the back of my SUV.

"Can you wake me up really early?" she asked Tasha. "Like, super early so we can get there first thing?"

Tasha looked at her with mock horror. "You want me to wake up at ER shift times on my day off?" She paused dramatically. "Only for you, kid. Only for you."

Saturday morning arrived with Paige knocking on my bedroom door at 6:30 AM sharp, fully dressed and ready to go. By the time I'd stumbled to the coffee pot, Tasha was already at my front door with an overnight bag and a travel mug that suggested she'd made peace with the early departure time.

"Morning, sunshine," she said, then stood on her toes to steal a quick kiss that tasted like coffee and made me considerably more awake.

"Ready for the great outdoors?" I asked.

"Define ready," she said, but she was smiling.

The drive took us along scenic back roads that wound through farmland and small towns, windows down, music playing. We'd somehow managed to create a compromise playlist that included Paige's pop favorites, Tasha's R&B, and my classic rock without anyone complaining too much.

About an hour into the drive, we passed a massive cornfield that stretched to the horizon.

"Wow," I said, gesturing toward the endless rows. "Just look at all that corn. It's a-maize-ing!"

The silence in the car was profound.

"Dad," Paige said finally, "that was terrible."

"I thought it was pretty good," I protested.

"It was corn-y," Tasha added, then immediately looked horrified at herself. "Oh no. It's contagious."

"Ugggghhhhhhhh," Paige said with the long-suffering tone of someone who'd been dealing with dad jokes for eleven years. Thankfully, she recovered quickly.

"Are we there yet?" she asked as we passed a sign for a roadside attraction called "Pirate's Paradise Mini Golf."

"We were *already* there, we're on the way back home now," I said automatically.

"DAD!" But Paige was giggling despite herself. "Can we stop at the pirate place?" she added before I could answer her original question. "Please? It has a shipwreck!"

I glanced at Tasha, who was already grinning. "We're on vacation," she said. "Might as well embrace the full tourist trap experience."

Pirate's Paradise turned out to be a delightfully cheesy eighteen holes of mini golf winding around fake palm trees, treasure chests, and a fiberglass pirate ship that had definitely seen better decades. Paige attacked each hole with scientific precision, studying angles and taking practice swings, while Tasha and I provided color commentary that she pretended to find annoying.

"She's lining up the shot," I announced in my best golf announcer voice. "The crowd is silent. The pressure is enormous."

"That windmill looks pretty intimidating," Tasha added. "Are you sure you're ready for this level of competition?"

"Watch and learn," Paige said, and proceeded to nail a hole-in-one that had us both cheering loud enough to embarrass her thoroughly.

By the time we reached Ocean Waves Campground, it was late afternoon and all of us were singing along to whatever came on the radio. The campground was exactly what I'd hoped for—busy enough to feel alive but not overcrowded, with families setting up around picnic tables and fire pits, kids running around with fishing nets and beach buckets.

Our cabin was small but perfect, with knotty pine walls and windows that actually opened to let in the ocean breeze. The master bedroom had a double bed covered in a quilt that had seen better days but was clean and comfortable. When Paige saw the second bedroom with its bunk beds, she let out an actual shriek of delight.

"TOP BUNK!" she shrieked, scrambling up the ladder before we'd even set our bags down.

Over her head, Tasha and I exchanged a look full of shared amusement and something deeper—the quiet satisfaction of seeing someone you love this happy.

"Alright, kiddo," I said, "what's first on the agenda?"

"Beach!" Paige said immediately. "I want to see if there are any turtle nests! And build the world's greatest sandcastle! And jump waves! And—"

"Breathe," Tasha laughed. "We have the whole weekend."

But even as she said it, I could see she was caught up in Paige's enthusiasm. This woman who'd claimed to hate the idea of camping was already digging through our bags for sunscreen and beach towels, asking Paige if she wanted help braiding her hair back before we hit the sand.

We spent the rest of Saturday afternoon at the beach, and it was everything Paige had hoped for and more. After claiming our spot with an umbrella and chairs, Paige immediately began construction on what she declared would be the most architecturally sophisticated sandcastle in the campground's history.

"You missed a spot," Tasha said, pointing to a streak of white sunscreen along my jawline as I helped Paige haul water for her moat.

"Dad always misses a spot," Paige added without looking up from her engineering project. "Last time we went to the community pool, he looked like he had racing stripes."

"Oh, don't worry. *I'll* make sure he doesn't miss any spots next time," Tasha said with a tone and grin that made me look at her more sharply.

"Yes, *ma'am*," I said, and meant it.

The rest of the afternoon passed in a blur of wave jumping, sand-castle construction, and the kind of lazy family time I'd never quite experienced before. When Paige insisted on "jumping the waves"— which required both Tasha and I to hold her hands while she "flew" over the incoming surf—I found myself watching Tasha's face, seeing the pure, unguarded joy there as we swung Paige over another wave.

I didn't know I could have this, I thought as we set Paige down safely in the shallow water and she immediately demanded to do it again. *I thought this kind of happiness was for other people.*

But here it was, simple and real and ours.

twenty-one
tasha

SUNDAY MORNING DAWNED bright and clear, with Paige's excited chatter drifting through the thin cabin walls before my alarm had even gone off. I could hear her negotiating with Nate about whether 7 AM counted as "sleeping in" on vacation (apparently, it did not).

By the time I'd dragged myself out of bed and into the small kitchen, Nate was already making coffee while Paige bounced around the cabin in her swimsuit, beach bag packed and ready to go.

"Morning, beautiful," Nate said, handing me a mug. "Someone's been up since sunrise making plans for today."

"We need to get to the beach early," Paige explained with the serious tone of a military strategist. "Before all the good spots are taken. And I want to check on my sandcastle from yesterday."

"Your sandcastle," I said, taking a grateful sip of coffee, "was destroyed by the tide, kiddo. That's what happens to sandcastles."

Paige looked genuinely shocked by this information. "All of it?"

"All of it," Nate confirmed gently. "But that means you get to build an even better one today."

Her face brightened immediately. "Can we make it bigger? With more towers? Oh, and can we try boogie boarding today? I saw some kids doing it yesterday and it looked so cool."

I glanced at Nate, who was trying not to smile. "I've never actually boogie boarded," I admitted.

"Neither have I," Paige said. "We can learn together!"

And that's how I found myself an hour later, standing in knee-deep water with a foam board under my arm, getting instruction from an eleven-year-old who'd watched exactly three other kids attempt this activity.

"You have to wait for the right wave," Paige said with complete authority. "Not too big, not too small. And then you jump on and ride it in."

"Sounds simple enough," I said, though watching the other boogie boarders, it looked like there was significantly more skill involved than Paige's explanation suggested.

Nate waded out to join us, his own board tucked under his arm. "Famous last words," he said.

My first attempt was a complete disaster. I mistimed the wave, got tumbled head over heels, and came up sputtering with sand in places sand should never be. Paige and Nate were trying very hard not to laugh.

"Maybe start with smaller waves?" Nate suggested diplomatically.

"Maybe start with a different sport," I muttered, but I was already wading back out. I was not going to be defeated by a piece of foam and some water.

It took me six tries, but I finally caught a wave that carried me all the way to shore, Paige cheering like I'd just won an Olympic medal. The rush of riding that wave, the simple joy of Paige's excitement, the way Nate was grinning at me when I stood up—it was pure happiness in a way I hadn't experienced since I was a kid.

"Again!" Paige demanded. "Do it again!"

We spent the next hour taking turns with the boards, Paige getting braver with each wave while I slowly got less terrible at reading the water. Nate, predictably, was naturally good at it—something about his military training probably gave him better balance and wave-reading skills than us civilians.

I found myself watching him as he helped Paige position herself on her board, the patient way he explained how to paddle, how to time the wave. His shoulders were already getting tan, and there was something about seeing him in full dad-mode that made my heart do complicated things.

"You're staring," he said, catching me looking when Paige ran off to rinse sand out of her board.

"I'm appreciating," I corrected. "There's a difference."

"Appreciating what, exactly?"

"The view," I said, gesturing vaguely at his chest, then grinned when he actually blushed a little. "Also, you're really good with her. It's... attractive."

"Just good with her?" he asked, stepping closer.

"Good with me, too," I admitted, then splashed him before he could get too smug about it.

After lunch, we headed to the campground pool, where Paige immediately made friends with a group of kids who were organizing an elaborate game that seemed to involve a lot of screaming and splashing. Nate and I claimed chairs in the shade and watched her careen around the pool like a tiny, determined torpedo.

"She's going to sleep well tonight," I observed.

"That's the plan," Nate said, though I caught him looking at me in my bikini with an expression that suggested his thoughts weren't entirely focused on Paige's bedtime.

"What?" I asked, even though I knew *exactly* what.

"Nothing," he said, not very convincingly. "Just... this is nice."

"Yeah," I said softly. "It is."

We sat in comfortable silence, watching Paige attempt to teach her new friends some elaborate diving technique she'd apparently invented on the spot. The afternoon sun was warm on my skin, and I felt more relaxed than I had in months. Maybe years.

This was so different from anything I'd grown up with. My

family vacations had been tense, scheduled affairs; my father checking his phone constantly, my mother making lists and getting frustrated when things didn't go according to plan. There had been no spontaneous boogie boarding, no lazy afternoons by the pool, no sense that the point was just to enjoy each other's company.

Watching Nate with Paige, the easy affection between them, the way he could be completely present without needing to be anywhere else or do anything else... it was a revelation. This was what love looked like in practice. Not grand gestures or dramatic declarations, but patient attention, shared laughter, the simple pleasure of being together.

"Tasha!" Paige called from the pool. "Come see this dive!"

I dutifully admired her cannonball, which soaked three other kids and earned her a stern look from a lifeguard. When she climbed out to demonstrate her technique on dry land first, I found myself thinking about how naturally I'd slipped into this role-- not trying to be her mother, but just being someone who cared about her, who celebrated her small victories and helped her learn new things.

It felt right in a way that surprised me. I'd never been particularly maternal, but with Paige, it was easy. She was smart and funny and kind, and she made me want to be the kind of adult who deserved her trust.

"You're good with her too, you know," Nate said quietly, following my gaze.

"She makes it easy."

"No," he said seriously. "You make it *look* easy. But I see how much thought you put into it. How careful you are with her feelings. It means everything to me."

I felt my throat tighten unexpectedly. "She's a pretty great kid."

"Yeah, she is." He paused. "We both got lucky."

Later, as the sun began to dip, we found ourselves near the campground's activity center where a surprisingly intense cornhole tournament was underway. Paige, naturally, wanted to watch.

"Come on," Nate said after a particularly impressive throw by a woman who looked like she could bench press him. "Think you can handle a little friendly competition?" He gestured to an empty set of boards.

I smirked. "Ohhhh, you have no idea what you're getting into."

He raised an eyebrow, intrigued. "Yeah?"

What followed was, to put it mildly, a slaughter. My Uncle Earl, a man who considered cornhole an Olympic-level sport, had drilled its intricacies into us from childhood. Nate, it turned out, was a rank amateur. Bag after bag, mine sailed through the air with a satisfying thud, landing squarely in the hole or very near it. His... did not.

His jaw literally dropped after my third straight "cornhole" - the term for getting the bag directly in the hole. Paige was screaming with laughter, cheering me on like I was a professional athlete.

"Where," Nate finally managed, looking utterly bewildered as I sank another perfect shot, "did you learn to do *that*?"

I winked, dusting off my hands. "Family reunions. My Uncle Earl takes his cornhole *very* seriously. You pick up a few things."

He just shook his head, a reluctant grin spreading across his face.

Afterwards, we walked along the beach as the sun set, supposedly looking for turtle nests but really just enjoying the cooler air and the sound of the waves. Paige ran ahead of us, collecting shells and examining every piece of seaweed for signs of marine life.

"No turtles yet," she reported back, "but I found three really good shells and what might be part of a crab."

"Definitely part of a crab," Nate agreed solemnly, examining her treasure.

The stars were just starting to appear when we made it back to the cabin. Paige was finally showing signs of fatigue, though she was fighting it with everything she had.

"Can we have a campfire tomorrow night?" she asked, curled up on the small couch between us. "With s'mores? Real ones?"

"Absolutely," I said. "I'll teach you the proper s'more construction technique."

"There's a technique?" Nate asked.

"Oh, there's definitely a technique. Golden brown marshmallow, perfectly melted chocolate, graham crackers that don't crack when you bite them. It's an art form."

Paige giggled. "Tasha knows everything."

"I don't know everything," I protested. "I just know s'mores."

"And boogie boarding," Paige added. "Eventually."

"Very eventually," I said, making her laugh again.

She fell asleep on the couch twenty minutes later, despite her insistence that she wasn't tired. Nate carried her to her bunk bed, and I found myself watching from the doorway as he tucked her in, the gentle way he brushed her hair back from her face, the soft "good night, kiddo" he whispered before turning on her nightlight.

"She's out cold," he said, joining me on the small front porch.

"Beach days will do that," I said, settling into one of the plastic chairs. "I'm pretty tired myself."

"Good tired?"

"The best kind of tired." I looked out toward the ocean, listening to the waves. "I've never done anything like this before."

"Beach vacation?"

"Family vacation," I corrected. "Growing up, our trips were more like military operations. Schedules, itineraries, my father checking his Blackberry every five minutes. This is... different."

"Different how?"

I thought about it, trying to put into words what I was feeling. "Peaceful. Like the point is just to be together, not to accomplish something or check items off a list." I glanced at him. "Like maybe I've been missing out on something important."

Nate reached over and took my hand. "Well, you're here now."

"Yeah," I said, squeezing his fingers. "I am."

We sat there until the campground settled into evening quiet, just holding hands and listening to the ocean. Tomorrow would bring more beach time, more laughter, more of whatever this was we were building together. But for now, it was enough to sit here in the soft darkness with this man and his daughter who were somehow becoming my family too.

For the first time in my adult life, I wasn't thinking about what came next or what I should be doing differently. I was just grateful for what I had right here, right now.

twenty-two
nate

MONDAY MORNING BROUGHT perfect beach weather and Paige's declaration that it would be "the most epic sandcastle day in the history of sandcastles." We claimed our usual spot early, and she immediately began work on what she called "The Fortress of Ultimate Awesomeness."

The morning passed in our established rhythm—sandcastle construction, wave jumping, and Paige making increasingly elaborate plans with her "new best friend" Brooklyn and the other kids she'd befriended. Around ten-thirty, Brooklyn came running over with a flyer clutched in her hand.

"Paige! Look! They're doing tie-dye today from eleven-thirty to one! And they give you lunch! Can you do it? Please say you can do it!"

Paige's eyes went wide as she read the flyer. "Dad, can I? Please? It's tie-dye! And lunch! And Brooklyn's doing it!"

I made a show of considering it seriously, stroking my chin like I was weighing the pros and cons of a major life decision. "Hmmmm, I don't know..."

Paige's face fell slightly, and she turned those devastating puppy dog eyes toward Tasha. The look of betrayal was so complete that Tasha immediately stepped in.

"NATHAN..." she said in a voice of mock authority, then paused. "Wait, what's your middle name?"

"Uh... James?" I said, confused by the sudden interrogation.

"NATHAN *James CRAWFORD*!" Tasha declared with the kind of stern tone usually reserved for major infractions.

Paige dissolved into delighted giggles, and I couldn't help but grin at both of them.

"Alright, alright," I said with an exaggerated sigh. "I suppose we can manage without you for an hour and a half."

We packed up our beach gear a little early and walked Paige to the recreation center, where she practically bounced with excitement as she joined the group of kids gathering for the activity.

"See you at one!" she called, already deep in conversation with Brooklyn about color combinations.

Tasha and I waved goodbye and found ourselves standing outside the rec center, suddenly aware that we had ninety minutes of completely unscheduled time.

"Well," I said, looking at her. "Now what?"

"I'm sure we can think of something," she replied, and something in her tone made me look at her more carefully.

For a moment, we just stared at each other as the same idea occurred to us simultaneously. I could see it in the way her eyes widened slightly, in the slow smile that curved her lips.

"Race you back to the cabin?" she said.

And suddenly we were both grinning like teenagers.

twenty-three
tasha

WE WERE PRACTICALLY sprinting by the time we reached the cabin, both of us giggling stupidly, crashing through the door in a blur of tangled limbs and urgency. Nate barely got the lock clicked before I was pressed against him, my fingers already sliding beneath his shirt.

"How long do we have?" I breathed against his lips.

"Hour and a half," he murmured, gripping my waist, pressing his mouth to mine. "Maybe two if we're lucky."

"More than enough," I said, pulling him closer until our bodies fit together perfectly. Every stolen glance from the weekend, every lingering touch and whispered flirtation came flooding back, propelling us forward in a rush of laughter and desire.

"You know," I teased as Nate's lips grazed down my neck, lingering just long enough to make me shiver, "I'm starting to suspect you planned this."

He laughed softly against my skin, his breath warm, his fingers already teasing at the ties of my bikini top. "*Me*? Manipulate circumstances just to get you alone in a secluded beach cabin? *Never.*"

"Liar," I accused, then gasped as his mouth found that spot just below my ear. "Oh my God, we're totally those people now. The ones who ditch the kid for a quickie."

"We are not—" he started to protest, but I cut him off with a kiss.

"We absolutely are, and I'm not even sorry about it," I grinned against his mouth, feeling giddy and reckless and twenty-seven. "We're like horny teenagers at summer camp."

"Horny teenagers?" he raised an eyebrow, amusement dancing in his eyes.

"*Very* horny teenagers," I confirmed solemnly, then dissolved into laughter at his expression. "What? You're the one who orchestrated an elaborate childcare scheme just to get me naked."

I laughed, swatting his chest, but my amusement turned into a sigh as my bikini top slipped away, baring me completely. Nate's eyes darkened, his gaze heated and hungry, roaming over my exposed skin with unmistakable desire.

"You're gorgeous," he murmured, voice thick with admiration.

We left a trail of discarded clothing as we stumbled through the tiny cabin, Nate kicking aside his shorts and my cover-up falling forgotten. The afternoon sun streamed through the cabin's windows, painting golden streaks across his bare chest and highlighting every taut muscle, every faded scar. He caught me staring and smiled softly, reaching out to cup my cheek.

"I love you," he whispered, his thumb brushing gently over my lower lip.

"I love you too," I replied, my heart racing as I pulled him onto the narrow bed. We laughed breathlessly when we bumped into the wall, the bed creaking beneath us. "Very smooth."

"Always," he chuckled, shifting beside me, propping himself up on an elbow. His eyes locked on mine as his hand traced a slow, deliberate path from my collarbone down between my breasts, fingertips trailing heat in their wake. My breath hitched, anticipation sending goosebumps scattering across my skin.

"I've thought about this all weekend," he admitted, voice rough with desire.

"Only the weekend?" I teased breathlessly, my own fingers tracing down the hard planes of his chest, exploring the tight muscles of his abdomen, enjoying how his breathing quickened under my touch.

"Longer," he confessed, leaning in to kiss me deeply, hungrily, his mouth coaxing mine open as his tongue teased and explored.

Our playful touches quickly shifted into something deeper, more urgent. His hands moved down my sides, fingers tightening on my hips as he pulled me closer. I moaned softly as his mouth explored my neck, his kisses growing hotter, more possessive, each one igniting a fresh spark deep inside me.

When his mouth moved lower, his tongue tracing the sensitive curve of my breast, I arched into him, my fingers tangling in his hair. "Nate," I whispered urgently.

His eyes flicked up to mine, dark and playful. "What do you need, Tasha?"

"You," I breathed, pulling him back up into a fierce, heated kiss. "Now."

He shifted over me, every movement deliberate, every muscle tensed as he slid slowly inside me. I gasped sharply, overwhelmed by the intensity of the connection, the sensation of being filled completely, perfectly. Our rhythm began slowly, tenderly, savoring each other as if we had all the time in the world.

But patience soon gave way to passion. Our hips met with increasing urgency, bodies slick with sweat, hearts pounding in sync. Nate's hands roamed possessively, mapping every inch of my skin, gripping my thighs as he pulled me closer, deeper, sending waves of pleasure crashing through me.

"God, Tasha," he groaned, voice thick with raw need, his forehead pressed against mine. "You feel incredible."

My nails dug into his shoulders, breathless whispers and heated sighs filling the air between us. Pleasure built steadily, relentlessly, driving us both closer to the edge. His movements became more insistent, each thrust deeper, harder, his breath ragged against my ear.

"Come with me," he urged, his voice a husky plea.

His words tipped me over the edge, my climax hitting with a force that left me trembling and gasping his name. Nate followed immediately after, burying his face against my neck, his body shaking as he found his release, whispering my name like a prayer.

We lay entwined for several moments, hearts racing, breathing unsteady. Nate brushed a gentle kiss across my forehead, his thumb tracing lazy circles on my hip.

"That was worth the wait," I murmured softly, smiling up at him.

"Every second," he agreed, voice warm with satisfaction.

Eventually, laughing and touching, we stumbled into the tiny bathroom. The shower was warm, steam curling around us as we stepped beneath the spray. I ran my soapy hands over Nate's chest, marveling at the slick warmth of his skin under my palms. He pressed me gently against the tile wall, his body a comforting, solid weight against mine.

He paused, wrapping his arms around me tightly, holding me in a tender embrace beneath the cascading water.

"What are you doing?" I asked softly, smiling up at him.

"Feeling every inch of you," he whispered, his voice reverent. "Making sure this is real."

My heart fluttered wildly. Playfully, I tipped my head back. "Nate, have you ever seen '*Top Gun*'?"

He blinked, amused. "Of course."

I leaned in, lips brushing his ear. "Take me to bed or lose me forever."

He grinned, eyes bright with delight. "Yes, ma'am."

And he did—slowly, luxuriously, until the water ran cool, our bodies moving together effortlessly, indulgently. This time was about exploration and connection, about tasting and teasing, hands caressing slippery skin as our mouths found new ways to claim each other.

When pleasure took us again, it was slow and deep, Nate

capturing my cries against his lips, our bodies pressed so close it was impossible to tell where he ended and I began.

Clean and presentable once more, we headed back to collect Paige, who was proudly displaying her vividly tie-dyed shirt.

"Look what I made!" she exclaimed, practically bouncing with joy. "We learned color theory! Did you know red and blue make purple?"

"Revolutionary," Nate said solemnly, examining the shirt with exaggerated awe. "Definitely your new favorite."

"What did you guys do?" Paige asked, stuffing her creation into her beach bag.

Nate and I exchanged a secret glance, both fighting laughter.

"We checked out some local attractions," I said smoothly.

"Explored some interesting new areas," Nate added casually, his lips twitching.

"Sounds boring," Paige declared. "You should've tie-dyed. It was way more fun."

We laughed, Nate ruffling her hair affectionately. "We managed to entertain ourselves."

The rest of the day was filled with poolside lounging, packing up, and exchanging contact information with Paige's new friends. That evening, we gathered around our last campfire, making s'mores as Paige recounted every detail of her day and her ambitious plans for future crafts.

"Can we come back every year?" she asked hopefully, cuddling against my side. "Make it a tradition?"

"I think that's a great idea," I said warmly, glancing at Nate.

He nodded firmly. "Annual Crawford family beach trip. Sounds perfect."

Family. The word resonated deeply, filling my heart with a sense of belonging and love I'd never imagined for myself.

Later, as Nate carried a sleeping Paige to her bunk, I banked the fire and waited for him on the porch, the cool night air soothing against my skin.

He joined me shortly after, sliding onto the seat beside me and taking my hand. "She's out like a light."

"Good tired," I murmured. "The best kind."

We sat quietly, listening to the waves and the distant murmurs of other campers. Tomorrow we'd return home to everyday routines and responsibilities, but for tonight, it was just us—our own little world, perfect and complete.

"Thank you," I whispered.

"For what?"

"For this. For including me, for showing me how good this can feel." I gestured around us, encompassing the cabin, the beach, and everything we'd shared. "I didn't know I could have this."

"Thank you for being here," Nate replied softly, squeezing my hand. "For wanting us."

We lingered there until exhaustion gently drew us back inside, falling asleep wrapped around each other, the steady rhythm of Nate's heartbeat beneath my ear.

———

Tuesday morning brought the bittersweet business of packing up and checking out. Paige dragged her feet through every task, clearly hoping to delay our departure as long as possible.

"Do we have to leave today?" she asked for the fourth time as we loaded our sandy, sun-faded belongings into the car. "Can't we stay just one more day?"

"I wish, kiddo," Nate told her gently. "But we all have to get back to work."

"Work is stupid," Paige declared with the fervor of someone who'd never had to pay rent. "Beaches are better."

"I can't argue with that logic," I said, taking one last look at the ocean before getting into the passenger seat. "But beaches will still be here next summer."

"Promise?" Paige asked from the backseat.

"Promise," Nate and I said in unison, which made her giggle despite her melancholy.

The drive home was quieter than our trip out had been, all of us lost in our own thoughts and the gentle sadness that comes with the end of something wonderful. But it was a comfortable quiet, the kind that comes from being completely at ease with each other.

Paige dozed in the backseat for most of the journey, her tie-dye shirt clutched in her arms like a talisman. Every so often, she'd wake up and share a random memory from the trip—the sandcastle with working battlements, the way the campfire sparks had looked like shooting stars, the s'mores we'd made beside the campfire.

"Can we really come back next year?" she asked drowsily as we passed the exit for home.

"Absolutely!" Nate said, catching my eye in the rearview mirror. "The annual Crawford family beach trip is officially a tradition now."

There it was again. *Crawford family.* The words still sent a warm flutter through my chest. Not Nate and Paige plus their friend Tasha. Not a trial run or an experiment. *Family.*

As familiar landmarks started appearing outside the windows, I found myself thinking about how much had changed in just four days. Not just between Nate and me, though our relationship felt deeper and more settled than ever. Something about myself, about what I wanted from life, about what home meant.

For the first time in my adult life, I wasn't looking ahead to the next challenge or accomplishment. I wasn't thinking about what I should be doing differently or better. I was just happy with what I had right here, right now.

I was happy being part of this family we'd built together—this imperfect, wonderful, completely unexpected family that had somehow become the center of my world.

"Almost there," Nate said as we turned onto his street, and I felt that familiar mix of relief and reluctance that comes with coming home from a perfect trip.

But as we pulled into his driveway, all three of us sun-tired and sandy and completely content, I realized something important had been decided over the past four days. Not through any grand declaration or dramatic moment, but through the simple accumulation of small joys—wave jumping and s'mores and tie-dye shirts and the way Paige had fallen asleep against my shoulder by the campfire.

And for the first time in my life, that felt like enough.

Nate turned off the engine and we all sat there for a moment, nobody quite ready to break the spell of our perfect weekend. Then Paige stirred in the backseat, stretching and yawning.

"Do I have to unpack everything today?" she asked, though she was already gathering her beach treasures—shells, the tie-dye shirt, a piece of driftwood she'd insisted was "perfectly shaped."

"Just the essentials," Nate said, popping the trunk. "We can deal with the rest tomorrow."

I was pulling our cooler out of the back when I noticed it-- a white envelope taped to the front door.

"Nate, what's that?" I asked, nodding toward the house.

He looked up from where he was gathering beach chairs. "Huh. That's weird. I don't know. Probably a delivery notice or something from a neighbor."

I went back to organizing our sandy beach gear, making sure Paige had all her treasures accounted for. She was chattering about where she wanted to display her shells, completely oblivious to anything but the joy of being home with her vacation memories.

"Can we order pizza tonight?" she asked. "As, like, a celebration of our last vacation day?"

"I think that sounds perfect," I said, hefting her beach bag. "We can have a 'last vacation day' at home, just the three of—"

I looked up to see that Nate had stopped moving entirely. He stood frozen by the front door, the envelope open in his hands, his face drained of all color.

"Nate?" My voice came out sharper than I intended. "What's wrong?"

He didn't answer. Didn't even seem to hear me. He just stood there, staring at whatever was in that envelope like it contained the end of the world.

"What is it?" I asked again, moving toward him.

Wordlessly, he held out the papers. My eyes scanned the official letterhead, the legal terminology, and my heart sank as the words registered.

NOTICE OF PETITION FOR MODIFICATION OF CUSTODY

Sarah Elizabeth Davis...

"Oh, Nate," I breathed. "Oh, honey."

"Hey Dad, what's wrong?" Paige's voice came from behind us, bright and curious. "You look funny."

I turned immediately, moving to intercept her before she could see Nate's face, before she could sense the wrongness that had suddenly infected our perfect homecoming.

"Nothing, baby," I said, gently steering her toward the front door. "Just some boring grown-up mail. Let's get inside and figure out that pizza situation, okay? We can make this the best last vacation day ever."

Paige looked between Nate and me, clearly sensing something was off, but she allowed herself to be guided toward the house. "Can we get the one with the garlic knots?"

"Absolutely," I said, fishing Nate's keys from his numb fingers to unlock the door. "With extra garlic. Go wash your hands and we'll look at the menu."

As Paige disappeared inside, I looked back at Nate. He was still standing there like a statue, the papers trembling in his hands.

"Just give me a minute," he said, his voice hollow. "I need... I need to understand what this means."

I nodded, my heart breaking for him. "Take all the time you need. I've got Paige."

I went inside, closing the door gently behind me, leaving Nate alone with whatever bomb had just exploded in his hands. But I could see him through the window, standing in our driveway like a man who'd just watched his whole world crumble.

Sarah. After eleven years of silence, she was back.

And she wanted Paige.

twenty-four
nate

THE PAPERS SAT on my kitchen counter like a live grenade, and I couldn't stop staring at them. Sarah Elizabeth Davis. The name that had once meant everything to me, then nothing, and now...

I poured myself a glass of water with hands that wouldn't stop shaking, my mind spinning back to another version of myself—one I'd worked so hard to forget.

Biloxi, Mississippi. September 2005.

The smell hit you first... mold, sewage, and something else, something organic and wrong that you learned not to think about too hard. Hurricane Katrina had come and gone a week ago, but the devastation still looked fresh, like the storm had just finished carving through the Gulf Coast with deliberate cruelty.

I was supposed to be helping coordinate relief efforts, but mostly I was just trying not to throw up. My fatigues were already soaked through with sweat despite the early morning hour. My head felt like someone had been using it for target practice, and I wanted a drink- a beer, a shot, *anything*- so bad, I was shaking.

I hadn't yet fully recovered from the night two weeks ago, the night Chief Petty Officer Parker had found me passed out in my rack at 0400, reeking of vodka and vomit.

Based on the empty bottle he found on the floor, Chief Parker calculated, with the same clinical precision I'd later learn in nursing school, that my blood alcohol content had probably peaked somewhere north of .4. Potentially lethal. *Should* have been lethal.

"You know what you did, Crawford?" Parker had said, personally marching me to the shower and pouring black coffee down my throat until I could stand upright. "You not only almost destroyed your entire military career, you almost fucking *died*."

I'd nodded, but honestly, neither prospect had seemed particularly tragic at the time.

"Lucky for you, there's a hurricane bearing down on the Gulf Coast, and they need volunteers for disaster relief. So I told the CO you'd volunteered to deploy to Biloxi to ride it out at the Seabee base and help with recovery efforts." His voice carried the kind of disappointed authority that cut deeper than any formal reprimand. "We'll deal with your other problems when you get back. *If* you get back."

That's how I'd ended up in Mississippi, supposedly coordinating with relief organizations and the USNS *Comfort*, but mostly just trying to stay sober long enough to not get anyone killed.

Then the Red Cross nurses showed up, and everything changed.

There were about twenty of them, a motley crew of women ranging from fresh-faced twenty-somethings to silver-haired veterans who looked like they'd seen every disaster the world could throw at them. They'd been deployed from hospitals across the country— Minnesota, Oregon, Texas, everywhere—and they moved with the kind of practiced efficiency that reminded me of the best corpsmen I'd known.

"You Crawford?" The woman addressing me was maybe forty-five, with salt-and-pepper hair pulled back in a no-nonsense ponytail and eyes that missed nothing. "I'm Linda Kowalski, team supervisor. We're told you're our Navy liaison."

"Yes, ma'am," I managed, trying to project competence despite feeling like death warmed over.

"Good. We need someone who knows military logistics and won't faint at the sight of blood." She looked me up and down with the kind of assessment I recognized from battlefield triage. "You look like hell, sailor, but you're standing upright, so you'll do."

What followed were the longest and most educational weeks of my life.

These women—and they were all women, I realized, which challenged every stupid stereotype I'd carried about nursing being somehow "lesser" than what we did as corpsmen—were nothing like I'd expected. They worked eighteen-hour days in conditions that would have broken lesser people. No electricity, no running water, no real medical facilities. Just skill, determination, and an apparently bottomless well of compassion.

I watched them deliver a baby in a Walmart parking lot while the mother waited in line for FEMA assistance, the asphalt so hot it burned through the soles of our boots. I saw them counsel a man who'd lost his entire family while simultaneously treating his infected wounds and helping him fill out insurance paperwork. They were nurses, social workers, therapists, and case managers all rolled into one.

"How do you do it?" I asked Linda one evening as we cleaned up after treating what felt like our thousandth patient of the day. "How do you just... keep going?"

She looked at me with those sharp eyes, and I had the uncomfortable feeling she could see straight through to the mess I was inside.

"You do it because someone has to," she said simply. "And because tomorrow there'll be another person who needs help, and the day after that, and the day after that. You can either be the kind of person who shows up, or you can be the kind who finds excuses. But you can't be both."

The truth of her words hollowed me out, because I knew *exactly* which kind of person I'd been since coming back from Iraq. The excuse-finding kind. The kind who drowned his problems instead of facing them.

Two weeks later, when Hurricane Rita threatened to make landfall and the evacuation order came down, I got to see what "showing up" really meant.

"All non-essential personnel need to evacuate immediately," the Red Cross coordinator announced during our morning briefing. "Buses will be here in two hours."

I expected the nurses to start packing, to follow protocol like any sensible person would. Instead, Linda stood up and crossed her arms.

"We're not leaving," she said, her voice carrying the kind of quiet authority that brooked no argument.

"Ma'am, I understand your dedication, but—"

"No, you don't. You don't understand at all." Another nurse, a young woman from Portland whose name I'd never learned, was on her feet now too. "These people have been through hell. They've lost everything. We're not abandoning them now just because another storm might come through."

One by one, all twenty nurses stood up. To a person, they refused evacuation.

"These people are suffering," Linda said, speaking for all of them. "They've been through enough. Evacuate if you want to, but we're not leaving."

I stared at them—this ragtag group of women from every corner of America, every age and background you could imagine—and felt something shift inside my chest. Something that had been broken since Fallujah.

They weren't leaving. When faced with danger, with the easy option of walking away, they were choosing to stay. They were choosing the people who needed them over their own safety.

Rita never made landfall with any real force, but that wasn't the point. The point was that twenty nurses had looked at a community full of scared, desperate people and said, unequivocally, "*We're not leaving you.*"

I'd never seen anything like it.

I blinked, the memory fading, and found myself back in my kitchen, staring at legal papers that threatened to take away the most important thing in my world. My hands had stopped shaking, but I felt hollow.

I'd carried that memory with me through the rest of my enlistment, through my separation from the Navy, through years of aimless drifting that followed. I took random classes at the community college—intro to psychology, basic computer skills, whatever filled the schedule and qualified for my GI Bill benefits. Nothing with any real direction or purpose, just... existing.

That's where I met Sarah, in a completely pointless "Introduction to Philosophy" class that I'd only taken because it met the general education requirements and fit my work schedule at the warehouse.

She was twenty-seven, like me, working at a coffee shop and taking random classes without any clear goal. We were both killing time, both avoiding making real decisions about our lives. She had an easy laugh and didn't ask too many questions about why a former Navy corpsman was taking freshman-level classes with eighteen-year-olds.

When she got pregnant, neither of us knew what to do.

"I don't think I want to be a mother," she'd said, sitting on my couch with the pregnancy test in her hands. "I don't think I'm cut out for it."

"Whatever you decide, I'll support," I'd told her, and I'd meant it. "One hundred percent, whatever you choose."

We'd gone to Planned Parenthood together, where they'd separated us so Sarah could make her decision without pressure. The counselors were amazing. Non-judgmental, informative, completely supportive of whatever choice she made. When we left, I'd told her again: Whatever she decided, I'd respect it completely.

She chose to keep the baby.

"Okay," I'd said, and something had crystallized in my mind with startling clarity. "Then I need to get my shit together. I can't keep drifting around if I'm going to be somebody's father."

Sarah's pregnancy was brutal. Preterm premature rupture of membranes at twenty-six weeks, which meant months of hospital bed rest and medical bills that nearly bankrupted me. But I was there every day, bringing her books and drinking terrible hospital coffee, holding her hand through the fear and uncertainty.

When Paige was born—tiny and perfect and completely helpless —I'd felt something I'd never experienced before. Not just love, but purpose. This small person needed me, depended on me completely, and for the first time since Iraq, I felt like I had a reason to be alive.

Sarah had looked at our daughter like she was a beautiful stranger.

Three months later, she was gone.

"I told you from the beginning I wasn't cut out for this," she'd said, standing in our apartment doorway with a single suitcase. "I tried, Nate. I really tried. But I can't do it. I'm not mother material."

I'd held Paige—three months old and completely innocent—and watched Sarah walk away. And in that moment, sitting alone with my daughter in our tiny apartment, Linda Kowalski's words had come back to me with startling clarity.

You can either be the kind of person who shows up, or you can be the kind who finds excuses. But you can't be both.

I looked down at Paige, sleeping peacefully in my arms, completely trusting that I would take care of her.

I had to become the kind of person who showed up.

That was when I'd remembered the Red Cross nurses and their unwavering commitment. The way they'd refused to abandon their post when things got dangerous.

I'd applied to nursing school the next week.

That was when the military bearing had really kicked in. Not just for Paige, but for me. Because if I fell apart, she fell apart. If I failed, she suffered.

Eleven years of holding it together. Eleven years of being enough for both of us. Eleven years of proving to myself that I could be the kind of person who showed up, day after day, no matter what.

And now Sarah was back, with lawyers and legal papers and the biological claim that trumped everything I'd built.

I looked down at the custody petition again, and all those old voices started whispering in my head. The ones that said I wasn't enough. That I'd never been enough.

I couldn't save those Marines in Fallujah.

I couldn't save the little girl in the pink shirt.

I couldn't make Sarah want to stay.

And now, apparently, I couldn't even keep the daughter I'd raised from the moment she drew her first breath.

Maybe I'd been fooling myself all along. Maybe Tasha and this perfect weekend had been just another temporary thing, another good moment before the inevitable collapse.

Maybe I really wasn't enough, and it never had been.

And maybe Sarah was just here to prove it.

twenty-five
tasha

BY THE TIME Nate came inside twenty minutes later, I had Paige settled on the couch with a movie and a promise that pizza was on the way. She'd accepted my explanation about "boring grown-up paperwork" with the resilience of an eleven-year-old who'd had four perfect days and wasn't going to let anything ruin her mood.

"Is *The Emperor's New Groove* okay?" I'd asked, scrolling through streaming options.

"I've never seen it," Paige had replied, already curled up with her stuffed axolotl.

"Oh, you're in for a treat. I probably watched this a hundred times when I was your age."

Now, as Nate finally walked through the front door, his face looked like he'd aged a decade in the space of our conversation. The legal papers were clutched in his hand, and his eyes had that hollow look I recognized from the worst trauma cases in the ER.

"Pizza will be here in thirty minutes," I said quietly, nodding toward the living room where Paige was already giggling at Kuzco's antics. "She's good for now."

He nodded and sank onto one of the kitchen chairs like his legs had given out. I sat across from him, close enough to reach out if he needed it but giving him space to process.

"I haven't felt like this since Iraq," he said finally, his voice barely above a whisper.

My heart clenched. I'd seen glimpses of what his service had cost him, but he'd never put it in those terms before.

"Tell me what you're thinking," I said gently.

He set the papers on the table between us, smoothing them out with shaking hands. "I always thought... if Sarah ever wanted back in Paige's life, she'd call. Maybe send an email. We'd talk about it like adults." He laughed, the sound bitter. "I never imagined lawyers and court papers and... this."

I picked up the documents, scanning the legal language with growing unease. "Modification of custody. That's not just asking for visitation, Nate. She's asking for joint custody."

"I know." His voice cracked. "After eleven years. Eleven years of nothing, and now she wants to take Paige away from the only life she's ever known."

"Why now?" I asked, though I suspected I already knew. "What changed?"

"I sent an email to her parents. About us. About you being part of our lives." He buried his face in his hands. "This is all my fault. I opened the door."

"No," I said firmly. "This is not your fault. You shared good news with people who should have been happy for you. For Paige. If they passed that information to Sarah with malicious intent, that's on them."

He looked up at me, and I could see all his old fears written across his face. "What if she's right? What if Paige needs her biological mother? What if I've been selfish keeping them apart?"

"Nate." I reached across the table and took his hands. "Listen to me. Sarah walked away when Paige was three months old. She made her choice. You didn't keep them apart—she chose to leave."

"But she's her mother--"

"No," I interrupted, more forcefully than I'd intended. "Being a mother isn't about biology. It's about showing up. It's about being there when your child is scared or sick or just needs someone to listen. You've been doing that for eleven years. YOU are her parent."

He was quiet for a long moment, staring down at our joined hands. "What if I'm not good enough? What if I never was? What if she realizes she'd be better off with Sarah?"

The broken way he said it made my heart ache. This man who'd raised an incredible daughter, who'd built a life from nothing, who'd taught me what real love looked like... and he *still* couldn't see his own worth.

"You're good enough," I said, gripping his hands tighter. "You're more than good enough. And if you don't want to believe it for yourself, then believe me when I tell you. You're so good that I fell in love with you, Nate. With both of you. With the family you built and the man you are."

His eyes widened, and for a moment the fear was replaced by something else—wonder, maybe, or disbelief.

"You telling me that..." he said slowly, "this should be one of the happiest days of my life."

The words hung between us, beautiful and tragic. Here we were, finally saying what we'd been feeling for months, and it was happening in the shadow of the worst possible threat.

"It will be again," I promised. "We're going to fight this. Together."

"How? She has lawyers. Real lawyers. And I... I don't know anything about custody law. I've never had to think about it."

I could see him starting to spiral again, that military bearing kicking in as he tried to figure out how to handle this crisis alone. But he wasn't alone anymore.

"Hey," I said, squeezing his hands to get his attention. "Look at me. I'm here. This is us now, not just you. You don't have to be strong enough for the world all by yourself anymore."

Something shifted in his expression—relief, maybe, or the beginning of hope.

"We don't tell Paige anything yet," I continued. "Not until we understand what we're dealing with. But Nate, you need to know—I'm not going anywhere. Whatever this takes, however we need to fight it, I'm in. All the way."

He nodded, and I could see some of the tension leaving his shoulders. Not all of it—this was still a nightmare—but enough that he could breathe again.

"I love you too," he said quietly. "In case that wasn't clear."

I smiled despite everything. "It was getting pretty clear, yes."

From the living room came the sound of the poison for Kuzco, the poison chosen especially to kill Kuzco, Kuzco's poison, along with Paige's delighted laughter. Our normal life, continuing just a few feet away, while we sat in the kitchen planning how to protect it.

"So what do we do?" he asked.

"First, we read every word of these papers. Then we figure out what Sarah actually wants and what she's legally entitled to. Then we make a plan."

"Together?"

"Together," I confirmed. "That's what families do."

The word settled between us, solid and reassuring. Whatever was coming, we'd face it as a family. All three of us.

Even if one of us didn't know the battle had started yet.

twenty-six
nate

FOUR DAYS. Four days since that envelope destroyed our perfect homecoming, and I still couldn't shake the feeling that I was standing on quicksand. Every time Paige giggled, every time she talked about our next beach trip, every normal moment felt like something I was about to lose.

I'd read the custody petition so many times I could recite it from memory. *Petitioner seeks joint custody based on changed circumstances and the best interests of the minor child.* Legal language that somehow made eleven years of 2 AM feedings, homework battles, and bedtime stories disappear into irrelevance.

"Dad, you're doing the thing again," Paige said from across the breakfast table.

"What thing?"

"The staring-at-nothing thing. You've been doing it all week." She pushed her cereal around the bowl. "Is it about work?"

"Just thinking about grown-up stuff, kiddo. Nothing for you to worry about."

The lie tasted bitter. Everything about this was for her to worry about, but she didn't know it yet. Couldn't know it yet. Not until I understood what we were facing.

My phone buzzed on the counter. Unknown number, local area code. My hand hesitated over it.

"Aren't you going to answer?" Paige asked.

I forced a smile. "Probably spam."

But something in my gut knew better. I picked up on the fourth ring.

"Hello?"

"Nate?" The voice was different... older, more tentative.

But unmistakable.

"It's Sarah."

The kitchen suddenly felt too small. I stood abruptly, gesturing to Paige that I needed to take this outside. She rolled her eyes at adult weirdness and went back to her cereal.

I stepped onto the back deck, closing the door carefully behind me. "Sarah."

"I know the papers were a shock." Her voice carried a rehearsed quality, like she'd practiced this speech. "My lawyer insisted it was the best way to... formalize things. I just want to be involved in Paige's life. I've made mistakes, I know, but I've changed. Can we meet? Just to talk about what's best for her?"

My jaw clenched. *What's best for her?* As if she had any idea what that meant.

"You've been gone for eleven years," I said, keeping my voice level. "Not a call. Not a card. *Nothing.*"

"I know." A pause, then her voice dropped to something that almost sounded vulnerable. "I wasn't ready then, Nate. I was young and drowning. But I'm ready now. I'm in therapy, I have a stable job —marketing, actually. Remote work with good benefits. I even bought a place in Rosewood Hills. Three bedrooms, big yard. The kind of place a kid would love."

The specificity of it set off warning bells. Like she'd prepared a resume for motherhood.

"I want to know my daughter," she continued. "My therapist says it's crucial I re-establish this relationship before I... before I move forward with my life. Paige deserves to know her real family."

Real family. As if eleven years of bedtime stories and scraped knees and science projects didn't count.

"She barely knows you exist," I said.

"And whose choice was that?" The words came out sharp, almost accusatory, with an edge of entitlement that reminded me of the Sarah who'd walked out our door eleven years ago. Then, as if catching herself, she softened again. "I'm not blaming you, Nate. You did what you thought was best. But she has a right to know her mother, doesn't she?"

The worst part was, buried under all my anger and fear, some part of me wondered if she was right. What if Paige did need her mother? What if I'd been selfish somehow, keeping them apart?

"I need to think about it," I said.

"That's all I'm asking. Just think about it. I'm staying in town, at the Hampton Inn. I can meet whenever works for you." Another pause. "Nate? I really have changed. I want to prove that to you. To both of you."

After I hung up, I stood on the deck, staring at nothing. The morning sun felt too bright, too normal for what was happening.

The sliding door opened behind me. Tasha stepped out, coffee mug in hand. She'd been staying over more often since we got back, and Paige had stopped commenting on it.

"I heard you come out here," she said quietly. "Paige said you got a weird call."

"Sarah."

Her expression hardened immediately. "What did she want?"

"To meet. To talk. To be involved." I scrubbed a hand over my face. "She says she's changed."

"Bullshit." The word came out sharp and immediate. "Nate, you can't seriously be considering—"

"She's Paige's mother."

"No, she's not." Tasha set her mug down hard on the patio table.

"She's the woman who gave birth to Paige. There's a difference. A mother stays. A mother shows up when her kid is sick or scared or just needs a hug. A mother doesn't disappear for over a decade and then waltz back with lawyers."

"I know that."

"Do you?" She studied my face, and I could see the worry in her eyes. "Because you've got that look. That 'honor and duty' look that's going to make you do something stupid."

"It's not stupid to consider what's best for Paige."

"What's *best* for Paige is the life she has. With you. With *us*." She stepped closer, her hand finding mine. "Sarah doesn't get to disrupt that just because she finally decided she wants to play mommy."

"She mentioned a house in Rosewood Hills," Nate said. "Three bedrooms. Big yard."

"How convenient," Tasha muttered. "Just happens to have the perfect kid-friendly setup after eleven years of nothing."

"And something about her therapist saying she needs to re-establish the relationship before moving forward with her life."

She froze. "Moving forward how? New husband? Boyfriend who wants kids?"

"She didn't say."

"Of course she didn't. But she's painting a picture, isn't she? Stable job, nice house, therapy. Like she's checking boxes on some 'good mother' application."

I rubbed my face. "Maybe she really has gotten her life together."

"Or maybe someone in her life wants a ready-made family and she needs to secure her claim on Paige first." Tasha caught herself before she went further down that path. Thursday would tell us more. "Sorry. I'm just... the timing is too convenient, Nate. Right after you tell her parents about us? About me?"

"What if Paige needs—"

"Stop." Tasha's voice was firm but not unkind. "Stop doing that thing where you convince yourself you're not enough. Paige doesn't *need* Sarah. She needs the father who's been there every single day of her life. She needs stability and love and the family we're building."

"The door was always open," I said quietly. "I told Sarah that when she left. That I'd never stand between her and Paige if she wanted to be involved."

Tasha sighed, and I could see her shifting tactics. "Okay. Let's say you meet with her. What's your plan? What are you hoping to accomplish?"

"I don't know. Maybe understand what she really wants. Maybe see if she actually has changed."

"And if she has? If she's done the work and she's stable and she genuinely wants a relationship with Paige?"

The question I'd been avoiding. "Then we figure out what's best for Paige. Slowly. Carefully. With Paige's feelings at the center of every decision."

"And if she hasn't changed? If this is about money or image or some guy who wants her to have kids?"

"Then she doesn't get near Paige."

Tasha studied me for a long moment. "You're going to meet with her no matter what I say, aren't you?"

"I have to. If I don't, she'll use it against me. Say I'm alienating Paige, keeping them apart out of spite."

"This is exactly what she wants," Tasha said. "She's already got you second-guessing yourself, already got you worried about looking like the bad guy."

She was right. I knew she was right. But knowing something and feeling it were different things.

"Come with me," I said suddenly.

Tasha blinked. "What?"

"To meet with her. Come with me. You'll see things I miss. You'll keep me from falling into old patterns."

"She won't like that."

"Then she doesn't have to meet with me."

A small smile tugged at Tasha's lips. "Look at you, setting boundaries already."

"I'm trying." I pulled her closer. "I know you think this is a
mistake."

"I think Sarah is manipulative and selfish and doesn't deserve a
second of your time," Tasha said. "But I also know you. You need to
do this or you'll torture yourself with what-ifs. So yes, I'll come. And
I'll be watching her like a hawk."

"Thank you."

"Don't thank me yet. If she says one thing that feels off, I'm
calling her on it. Honor and duty be damned."

I kissed her forehead. "I'm counting on it."

From inside, Paige called out, "Dad! I'm gonna be late!"

Normal life, demanding attention. I squeezed Tasha's hand and
headed back inside to grab Paige's backpack and my keys.

"Everything okay?" Paige asked as we headed to the car.

"Everything's fine, kiddo."

"Is Tasha mad about something?"

"No, honey. Why would you think that?"

"She looked mad when you were on the phone. Like, scary mad.
Like when Miss Deanna yelled at me."

My heart clenched. Even when we tried to protect her, Paige saw
everything.

"She's not mad," I said carefully. "Just protective. She cares
about us."

"Good," Paige said simply. "We need someone scary on our side
sometimes."

If only she knew how much we were about to need exactly that.

twenty-seven
tasha

I **WATCHED** Nate's car disappear around the corner, Paige chattering away in the passenger seat about some science project, completely oblivious to the storm heading our way. My coffee had gone cold, but I stayed on the deck, trying to process what had just happened.

Sarah had called. Of course she had. The legal papers were just the opening salvo—now came the manipulation disguised as reasonable requests. And Nate, honorable to a fault, was already falling for it.

I understood why. God help me, I understood him well enough by now to see every button Sarah was pushing. The guilt about Paige not having a mother. The promise he'd made to keep the door open. The deep-seated fear that he wasn't enough.

But understanding didn't make it any less frustrating.

My phone buzzed. A text from Maria at the hospital.

MARIA

You coming in today? We're already short-staffed and it's barely 8.

> Day off, remember? Ask someone who
> doesn't have a family crisis brewing.

MARIA

> Everything okay?

I hesitated, then typed:

> Nate's ex showed up. The one who
> abandoned them.

My phone immediately rang.

"Shut UP," Maria said without preamble. "After eleven years? What does she want?"

"Custody. She filed legal papers and everything."

"That bitch." Maria's outrage was immediate and complete. "She can't just—wait, can she? Legally?"

"That's what we're trying to figure out."

"What does Nate say?"

I sighed. "He wants to meet with her. Talk things out. See if she's really changed."

"Oh honey, *noooo*. That man's too good for his own good sometimes."

"Tell me about it. He's so worried about doing the right thing that he can't see she's playing him."

"You going with him?"

"He asked me to."

"Good. Someone needs to watch his back." Maria paused. "How's Paige?"

"She doesn't know yet. We're trying to keep things normal until we understand what we're dealing with."

"Poor baby. She adores Nate." Maria's voice softened. "You okay, Tash? This can't be easy for you either."

The question caught me off guard. Was I okay? I was angry, protective, ready to fight. But underneath that...

"I'm scared," I admitted. "Not for me. For them. They're finally happy, Maria. We're finally... building something. And this woman who threw them away wants to wreck it all because what? She's suddenly ready to be a mom?"

"Biology doesn't make you a mother," Maria said firmly. "Showing up does. Being there does. Love does. You've been more of a mother to that girl in the last few months than Sarah's been her whole life."

"Maria, I-"

"No, listen. I've watched you with her. The period emergency? The way you handled that? That's mom stuff, Tasha. That's showing up when it matters."

"Her actual mom is back now."

"Her *biological* mother. There's a difference. And if she thinks she can waltz in and claim Paige like some forgotten toy, she's got another thing coming." Maria's protective fury was almost as strong as mine. "You need backup? Legal advice? Someone to accidentally run her down in a dark parking lot?"

"Maria!"

"I'm just saying. We protect our own here."

After we hung up, I went inside and started cleaning. It's what I did when I needed to think: aggressive organization of other people's spaces. Nate's kitchen was already pretty organized, but I found things to do. Reorganizing the spice rack. Wiping down baseboards. Anything to keep my hands busy while my mind raced.

What was Sarah's real game here? After eleven years of silence, why now? The timing couldn't be coincidental. Right after Nate emails about us, about our relationship, she suddenly wants back in?

I thought about the woman Nate had described. "Young and drowning", she'd said on the phone. Unable to handle motherhood. Walking away because it was too hard.

I got that, actually. The being overwhelmed part. The feeling like you weren't cut out for something everyone expected you to do naturally. But I couldn't imagine looking at Paige—tiny, perfect, trusting Paige—and choosing to leave.

My phone buzzed. Nate.

NATE

Set up a meeting for Thursday afternoon.
Neutral location - coffee shop on Broad
Street. You still willing to come?

Try and stop me.

NATE

Thank you. I love you.

I love you too. Even when you're being
too honorable for your own good.

NATE

It's a character flaw.

It's one of the reasons I fell for you, you
noble idiot.

Thursday. Two days to prepare for whatever manipulation Sarah was planning. Two days to figure out how to protect the family that had become mine without Nate realizing I was ready to go to war for them.

Because that's what this was—war. Sarah had fired the first shot with those legal papers. Now she was trying to draw Nate into negotiations, make him think this could be settled peacefully.

But I'd grown up with parents who used reasonableness as a weapon, who could make you feel guilty for having boundaries, who knew exactly how to phrase requests so saying no made you the bad guy.

I recognized the playbook, even if Nate didn't.

The front door opened, and I heard familiar footsteps. Nate was back already.

"Forget something?" I called out.

He appeared in the kitchen doorway, looking sheepish. "Yeah. You."

"I'm not a thing you can forget."

"No, but..." He crossed to me, pulling me into his arms. "I got halfway to dropping Paige off and realized I didn't kiss you goodbye properly. Felt wrong."

"You drove all the way back to kiss me goodbye?"

"Is that stupid?"

I stretched up on my toes to kiss him, slow and thorough. "No. It's perfect. You're perfect."

"Far from it."

"Perfect for me," I corrected. "Perfect for Paige. Perfect for us."

He held me tighter. "What if I mess this up? What if I make the wrong choice?"

"Then we'll figure it out together. That's what we do now, remember? Together."

"Together," he repeated, like he was still getting used to the word.

"Now go! You've got to drop Paige off at Zoe's *and* get to work before Sophia writes you up for being late."

"She won't. She likes you too much to punish me."

"Don't test that theory."

After he left—with another kiss that made me consider calling in sick myself—I finished my angry cleaning and tried to prepare myself for Thursday.

Sarah thought she was dealing with the same Nate she'd left eleven years ago. Overwhelmed, alone, grateful for any scrap of help or approval.

She was about to learn how much had changed.

Because Nate wasn't alone anymore. He had me, and I'd learned to fight dirty from the best of them.

Game on, Sarah. Game on.

twenty-eight
nate

THE COFFEE SHOP on Broad Street was deliberately neutral...
not somewhere I'd been with Tasha, not anywhere that held
memories. Just a generic space with exposed brick walls and the
aggressive smell of espresso. I'd arrived fifteen minutes early, partly
out of military habit and partly because I needed time to steady
myself.

Tasha sat beside me, her hand resting on my thigh under the
table. Not possessive, just... present. A reminder that I wasn't doing
this alone.

"You okay?" she asked quietly.

"Define okay."

"Fair point." She squeezed my leg gently. "Remember, we're just
listening today. No commitments."

I nodded, but we both knew it was much more complicated than
that.

The door chimed, and there she was.

Sarah looked... different. Not dramatically so, but in a thousand
small ways that added up to someone I barely recognized. Her hair
was shorter, styled in a way that probably cost more than our
monthly grocery budget. Designer jeans, soft cashmere sweater,

subtle jewelry that whispered money. She'd gained maybe twenty pounds, but it suited her. She looked healthy, settled. Successful.

She spotted us immediately, and something flickered across her face when she saw Tasha. Just for a second, then it was replaced by a careful smile.

"Nate." She approached our table with studied casualness. "Thank you for meeting me."

"Sarah." I stood—automatic courtesy drilled in by years of military service—but didn't offer my hand. "This is Tasha Williams."

"Of course." Sarah's smile never wavered as she extended her hand to Tasha. "I've heard wonderful things."

Tasha shook her hand briefly, professionally. "I'm sure you have."

If Sarah caught the edge in Tasha's voice, she didn't show it. She settled into the chair across from us, movements careful and deliberate. Everything about her seemed rehearsed.

"Can I get you something?" I asked, defaulting to politeness.

"Just water, thanks. I've already had too much caffeine today." She laughed, light and self-deprecating. "Nervous energy."

I went to the counter, grateful for the brief escape. When I returned with her water, Sarah was studying Tasha with an expression I couldn't quite read.

"So," Sarah said, wrapping her hands around the glass. "I imagine you have questions."

"Just one," Tasha said evenly. "Why now?"

Sarah's eyes flicked to me, then back to Tasha. "Because I'm finally in a place where I can be the mother Paige deserves. I know that might be hard to believe—"

"You're right," Tasha cut in. "It is hard to believe."

"Tasha." My voice carried a gentle warning, but Sarah held up a hand.

"No, it's okay. She's protective of you both. I respect that." Sarah took a breath, and when she spoke again, her voice had a vulnerable quality that seemed almost genuine. "I was working at a coffee shop, taking random community college classes with no direction. I was drowning, and I knew--I *knew*--I was going to damage that beautiful little girl if I stayed."

She looked directly at me then. "Leaving was the hardest thing I've ever done. But staying would have been selfish."

"And coming back now isn't?" Tasha asked.

"Maybe it is," Sarah admitted, and the honesty of it caught me off guard. "But I've done the work. Three years of therapy. Getting my degree. Building a career. I needed to become someone worthy of being in Paige's life."

"She needed you when she was three months old," I said quietly. "Not eleven years later."

"I know." Her voice cracked slightly. "God, Nate, I know. There's not a day that goes by that I don't think about what I missed. First words, first steps, first day of school. But I can't change the past. All I can do is try to be better going forward."

She reached into her purse and pulled out a small photo album. "My therapist suggested this. Said it might help you understand."

I didn't want to look, but my hands were already reaching for it. The first page showed Sarah in the cap and gown of a college graduation. The next, her at what looked like a marketing conference, giving a presentation. A house with a sold sign. Professional headshots. Certificates of completion from various therapy programs.

"It's like a resume," Tasha said, her tone neutral but her meaning clear.

Sarah flushed slightly. "I know how it looks. But I wanted you to see that I'm stable. That I can provide for Paige."

"Paige doesn't need providing for," I said, closing the album. "She has everything she needs."

"Materially, yes. But what about emotionally? Doesn't she deserve to know her mother?"

"She deserves stability," Tasha said. "She deserves to not have her life disrupted by someone who—"

"I'm not trying to disrupt anything," Sarah interrupted, and for the first time, she sounded genuinely distressed. "That's the last thing

I want. My therapist says forced relationships never work. I don't want to traumatize Paige. I just... I want a chance to know her. To let her know me. And if it's not working, if she's uncomfortable or unhappy, I'll step back."

The words were exactly what someone in my position would want to hear. Too exact.

"What does 'step back' mean to you?" Tasha asked.

Sarah blinked. "I'm sorry?"

"You say you'll step back if it's not working. What does that look like? Do you disappear for another eleven years? Do you maintain some kind of distant contact? What?"

"I..." Sarah faltered for the first time. "I haven't thought that far ahead."

"Maybe you should," Tasha suggested. "Because Paige isn't an experiment. You can't just try on motherhood and return it if it doesn't fit."

Sarah's composure cracked, just for a moment. Something sharp flashed in her eyes—anger, maybe, or calculation. Then it was gone, replaced by understanding.

"You're right," she said softly. "I need to think about all possibilities." She turned to me. "Nate, I know I have no right to ask for your trust. But I'm asking anyway. Let me prove that I've changed. Let me show you that I can be good for Paige."

"How?" The word came out rougher than I intended.

"Start small. Maybe... coffee? Somewhere public, with you there. Just an hour. Let her get to know me slowly, at her pace. No pressure, no expectations."

It sounded so reasonable. So carefully considered. Everything designed to make saying no seem cruel.

"I need to think about it," I said.

"Of course." Sarah stood, leaving the photo album on the table. "Take all the time you need. I'm not going anywhere."

She paused at our table, looking down at us. "I know you don't believe me, but I'm grateful to you, Nate. For raising her. For being the parent I couldn't be. And Tasha..." She smiled, something sad in it. "She's lucky to have someone who'll fight for her. Even against her own mother."

Then she was gone, leaving us in the coffee shop with her carefully curated evidence of transformation.

"That was..." Tasha started, then stopped.

"Yeah."

"She's good."

"Very good."

"You want to believe her."

I scrubbed my hands over my face. "I want to believe people can change. That making a mistake at twenty-eight doesn't define you forever."

"This wasn't forgetting to pay a parking ticket, Nate. She abandoned her infant daughter."

"I know."

"Do you?" Tasha turned in her chair to face me fully. "Because she's saying all the right things, and you're sitting here looking like you're actually considering it."

"What choice do I have?" The words came out sharp with frustration. "If I say no, she files for immediate custody. Claims I'm alienating Paige. And maybe she wins, maybe she doesn't, but Paige gets dragged through court either way."

"So you're going to give her what she wants?"

"I'm going to do what's best for Paige."

"Which is?"

"I don't know!" The admission ripped out of me. "I don't know what's best. Maybe Paige does need to know her biological mother. Maybe keeping them apart is selfish. Maybe—"

"Stop." Tasha's hand found mine. "Stop spiraling. Let's think about this logically. What do we actually know?"

I forced myself to breathe. "Sarah has resources now. Money, stability, a good lawyer."

"All of which appeared very conveniently just as she decides she wants to play mom."

"She seems genuine about the therapy."

"Or she's very good at seeming genuine."

"She said she'd step back if it wasn't working."

"She also couldn't define what that meant when I pushed her on it."

I looked at Tasha, really looked at her. She seemed tired, stressed. There were shadows under her eyes I hadn't noticed before.

"You okay?" I asked. "You look exhausted."

"These back to back shifts are killing me lately," she admitted. "I used to bounce back faster. Must be the stress of all this."

"I'm sorry. I'm putting you through—"

"Don't you dare apologize." Her voice was fierce. "We're in this together, remember? I just... I see what we have, Nate. What we're building. And yeah, right now it feels like the sun went out, but it's not. It's an eclipse. Temporary. We'll get through it."

"How can you be so sure?"

"Because I know you. And I know Paige. And I know that what you've built together is stronger than whatever Sarah's trying to do." She squeezed my hand. "Even if you can't see it right now."

We sat there for a moment, holding hands across the table where Sarah's photo album still lay. Evidence of a life rebuilt, or a carefully constructed weapon—I couldn't tell which.

"I have to let her meet Paige," I said finally. "Once. Supervised. If I don't, she'll use it against me."

Tasha nodded slowly. "I know. I hate it, but I know."

"Will you be there?"

"Try to stop me."

"She won't like that."

"Good." Tasha's smile was sharp. "Let her not like it. Let her show her true colors when she doesn't get exactly what she wants."

"And if she doesn't? If she really has changed?"

"Then we'll deal with that too. Together." She stood, pulling me up with her. "Come on. Let's get out of here. This place reeks of manipulation and overpriced coffee."

As we left, I grabbed Sarah's photo album. Evidence, maybe. Or just props in whatever game she was playing. Either way, I'd need to study it, look for cracks in the facade.

Because Tasha was right about one thing—this was an eclipse, not an ending. I just had to have faith that the sun would come back out.

Even if I couldn't see how just yet.

twenty-nine
tasha

THE DRIVE back to Nate's house was quiet, both of us processing what had just happened. I kept replaying Sarah's performance in my head—because that's what it was, a performance. Every gesture calculated, every word chosen for maximum effect.

"She's going to want primary custody," I said as Nate pulled into his driveway.

He cut the engine but didn't move to get out. "What makes you say that?"

"Because she's not really interested in 'starting small.' That whole song and dance about coffee dates and stepping back? That's to make you lower your guard." I turned to face him. "She's checking boxes, Nate. Showing she tried to be reasonable, that you were the one who made things adversarial."

"Maybe she really does want to take it slow."

"Did you see her face when she saw me? Just for a second before she put the mask back on?"

He was quiet for a moment. "Yeah."

"I'm a complication she didn't expect. Living proof that Paige has a mother figure already." I laughed, but there was no humor in it.

"God, the way she said 'she's lucky to have someone who'll fight for her.' Like I'm the nanny getting too attached."

"You're not—"

"I know what I am to Paige. And to you." I touched his face, feeling the tension in his jaw. "But Sarah doesn't see it that way. To her, I'm just an obstacle."

We went inside, where the evidence of our life together was everywhere. Paige's school photos on the fridge, mixed in with pictures from our beach trip. My nursing textbooks on the coffee table next to Nate's meal planning notebook. Three sets of shoes by the door.

"I need to call Sophia," I said suddenly.

Nate looked up from where he was staring at Sarah's photo album. "Why?"

"Because she's been through this. The ex coming back, the threats, the legal stuff. She'll know what to watch for."

He nodded slowly. "Good idea."

I found Sophia's number in my phone and hit call. She answered on the second ring.

"Tasha? Everything okay?"

"Not really. Are you free to talk?"

"Always. What's going on?"

I gave her the abbreviated version; Sarah's return, the legal papers, today's meeting. When I finished, Sophia was quiet for a long moment.

"Let me guess," she said finally. "She was perfectly reasonable. Understanding. Just wants what's best for Paige."

"Exactly."

"And she had evidence of how much she's changed. Therapy, career, stability."

"A whole photo album."

Sophia laughed, but it was bitter. "They all read from the same playbook. Troy did the same thing. Showed up claiming he'd been to therapy, found religion, whatever. All he really wanted was to hurt me for leaving."

"What did you do?"

"Gave him exactly what he asked for—supervised visitation with Madison. Documented everything. Every no-show, every manipulation, every time Madison came home upset." Her voice hardened. "It took six months, but eventually he showed his true colors. The judge saw right through him."

"Six months," I repeated, feeling sick. "Of putting Madison through that."

"It was hell," Sophia admitted. "But it was the only way to protect her long-term. If I'd refused from the start, he could have painted me as the vindictive ex keeping him from his child."

"That's what Sarah's counting on."

"Probably. But here's the thing. Nate has eleven years of being the only parent. That matters. Sarah can't just waltz in and claim equal rights after abandoning her baby."

"Tell that to her lawyer."

"Her lawyer's playing a game too. Hoping you'll be so scared of losing that you'll settle for shared custody without a fight."

I sank onto the couch, suddenly exhausted. "I hate this. Paige is happy. We're happy. Why does Sarah get to blow that up just because she finally decided she wants to play mom?"

"Because biology gives her the right to try," Sophia said gently. "But trying and succeeding are different things. You and Nate need a lawyer. A good one."

"He wants to give her a chance first. One supervised visit."

"That's probably smart, actually. Shows good faith." Sophia paused. "But Tasha? Document everything. Every word, every gesture, every response from Paige. Build your own evidence file."

After we hung up, I found Nate in the kitchen, making Paige's lunch for tomorrow with mechanical precision. Turkey sandwich, apple slices, granola bar, juice box. The same lunch he'd made a thousand times.

"Sophia says we need a lawyer," I said.

"After the visit. See how it goes first."

I wanted to argue, but I could see the weight he was carrying. The impossible position Sarah had put him in: refuse and look like the bad guy, or agree and risk everything.

"When are you going to tell Paige?" I asked.

"Tonight. She deserves to know." He sealed the sandwich in a container with shaking hands. "How do I explain that the mother who abandoned her wants to meet her? How do I make that okay?"

"You tell her the truth. Age-appropriately, but the truth."

"Which is what? That Sarah was young and overwhelmed? That she's better now?" He laughed bitterly. "Or do I tell her that this is probably about money or a new boyfriend or God knows what else?"

I wrapped my arms around him from behind, feeling the tension in his shoulders. "You tell her that Sarah gave birth to her but wasn't ready to be a mom. That she's asked to meet her. That it's Paige's choice whether she wants to."

"What if she says yes?"

"Then we support her. We're there every step of the way. And when Sarah inevitably disappoints her, we're there for that too."

He turned in my arms, pulling me close. "I don't know what I'd do without you."

"Lucky for you, you won't have to find out."

We stayed like that until we heard Paige's key in the lock. After-school program until 4:30, same routine every day. The normalcy of it made my chest ache.

"Hey Dad! Hey Tasha!" She bounced into the kitchen, backpack sliding off one shoulder. "Guess what? Maya's having a sleepover for her birthday and I'm invited! Can I go?"

"When is it?" Nate asked, and I could see him filing the information away, already thinking about how it might conflict with whatever Sarah had planned.

"Two weeks. We're going to watch movies and make friendship bracelets and Maya's mom said we could stay up until midnight!"

"Sounds fun," I said, ruffling her hair. "Hey kiddo, why don't you get started on homework? Your dad and I need to talk to you about something in a bit."

Paige's face immediately shifted to worry. "Am I in trouble?"

"No, baby. Nothing like that."

"Is someone sick? Did something happen to Mrs. Swanson?"

"Everyone's fine," Nate assured her. "Just... some grown-up stuff we need to discuss. Go do your homework first, okay?"

She nodded but I could see the wheels turning. Paige was too smart not to pick up on the tension.

After she headed to her room, Nate and I looked at each other.

"Together?" I asked.

"Together," he confirmed.

An hour later, homework allegedly complete, Paige sat between us on the couch, looking smaller than usual. Nate had that careful expression he got when he was about to deliver difficult news.

"Sweetie," he started, then stopped, running a hand through his hair. "Okay. So. You know how sometimes we've talked about your biological mom?"

Paige went very still. "The one who left when I was a baby?"

"Yes. Well, she... she contacted me. She wants to meet you."

"Why?"

Trust Paige to cut straight to the heart of it.

"She says she's in a better place now. More stable. She'd like to get to know you."

"But she didn't want to know me before."

"It's complicated, baby. Sometimes adults make choices that—"

"That's stupid," Paige interrupted, which was so unlike her that both Nate and I blinked. "She didn't want me when I was little and now she does? That doesn't make sense."

"You're right," I said. "It doesn't make a lot of sense."

Paige looked at me, then at Nate. "Do I have to?"

"No," Nate said immediately. "You don't have to do anything you don't want to."

"But?" Paige was too perceptive to miss the hesitation.

"But it might be good to meet her once. Just to see. If you hate it, we don't do it again."

"Will you be there?"

"Absolutely."

"Both of you?"

Nate glanced at me. "If that's what you want."

"I want Tasha there too." Paige's hand found mine. "Is that okay?"

"Of course it is," I said, squeezing gently.

Paige was quiet for a long moment. Then: "What's she like?"

"I don't really know anymore," Nate admitted. "She seemed... different. Older. More put together."

"Is she pretty?"

The question caught us both off guard. Such a kid thing to wonder about.

"She's... yes, she's pretty," Nate said carefully.

"Prettier than Tasha?"

"Hey!" I protested, trying to lighten the moment. "I'm right here!"

Paige smiled a little. "I'm just asking."

"No one's prettier than Tasha," Nate said, and the simple certainty in his voice made my throat tight.

"That's right," Paige said. Then, more quietly: "What if I don't like her?"

"Then we leave," Nate said. "Simple as that."

"What if she doesn't like me?"

Oh, this kid. I pulled her into my side. "Then she's an idiot. Because you're the best kid in the entire world."

"You have to say that."

"Doesn't make it less true."

Paige leaned into me, and I felt the weight of her trust like a physical thing. This little girl who'd already been left once, being asked to open herself up to that same person again.

"Okay," she said finally. "I'll meet her. Once."

"You're sure?" Nate asked.

"No. But you think I should, right?"

The raw honesty of it broke my heart. Nate looked like he'd been punched.

"I think..." he started, then stopped. "I think you're brave. And whatever you decide, we've got you."

"Promise?"

"Promise," we said together.

Later, after Paige was in bed, Nate and I sat on the back deck despite the evening chill. He'd been quiet since our talk with Paige, that thousand-yard stare I recognized from his PTSD episodes.

"She's going to hurt her," he said finally. "Sarah's going to disappoint that little girl, and there's nothing I can do to stop it."

"Maybe. Or maybe Paige will see right through her the way she saw through the whole situation tonight."

"She shouldn't have to. She's eleven. She should be worried about sleepovers and friendship bracelets, not whether her biological mother actually wants her."

"You're right. But this is the hand we've been dealt."

He was quiet for a moment. "Did you mean what you said? About documenting everything?"

"Yes. Sophia thinks—"

"No, I mean... you're planning for war. Getting ready to fight this all the way."

I turned to face him. "Aren't you?"

"I keep hoping it won't come to that. That Sarah will see how happy Paige is and back off."

"And if she doesn't?"

"Then yes. War." His voice went hard in a way I rarely heard. "She can visit. She can pretend to care. But she's not taking my daughter."

"Our daughter," I corrected softly.

He looked at me, something vulnerable in his eyes. "You mean that?"

"Every word. I know I'm not her mother, but—"

"You *are*, though." Nate cut me off. "In every way that matters, you're her mom. Have been for months now, Tasha."

The words hit me unexpectedly hard. I'd been so focused on protecting them that I hadn't let myself really feel the weight of what we'd become to each other.

"I love her," I said simply. "I'd do anything to protect her."

"I know. That's why I need you there. When Paige meets Sarah. Because I'll be too busy hoping for the best to see what's really happening."

"And I'll be watching Sarah like a hawk."

"Exactly." He pulled me closer. "We make a good team."

"The best," I agreed.

But as we sat there in the dark, I couldn't shake the feeling that we were about to be tested in ways we couldn't imagine. Sarah had played her opening move perfectly—reasonable, understanding, impossible to refuse without looking petty.

What would her next move be? And would we be ready for it?

I thought about Paige asking if she had to meet Sarah. The resignation in her voice when she'd agreed. Eleven years old and already learning that sometimes you had to do things that might hurt you, just to prove you'd tried.

It wasn't fair. None of this was fair.

But fair didn't matter anymore. All that mattered was protecting our family.

Our family. The word settled into my chest, warm and certain despite everything.

Sarah might have given birth to Paige, but we were her family. And I'd burn the whole world down before I let anyone hurt her.

Even—*especially*—her biological mother.

thirty
nate

I PACKED Paige's comfort items into her small backpack with mechanical precision, trying to keep my hands steady. Her tie-dye shirt from the beach trip, carefully folded. The stuffed axolotl she'd had since she was six. A granola bar, because eleven-year-olds got hungry at the worst possible moments.

Tasha paced my kitchen like a caged animal, her agitation filling the room.

"She was fucking twenty-eight years old, Nate," she said, stopping mid-pace to face me. "Twenty-eight. She was older than I am right now."

I kept folding, kept packing, because if I stopped moving, I might fall apart entirely. "Tasha—"

"No, you listen to me. She wasn't some scared sixteen-year-old who got pregnant in high school. She wasn't eighteen and overwhelmed. She was a fully grown adult woman who looked at her three-month-old baby and decided it was too hard."

My hands stilled on the backpack zipper. "She was struggling. People make mistakes when they're drowning—"

"Bullshit." The word came out sharp enough to cut glass. "You don't get to abandon your baby just because keeping your head above water got difficult. You know what you do when you're drowning? You learn to swim. You ask for help. You don't hand your infant to someone else and disappear for eleven years."

I looked up at her, seeing the fierce protectiveness in her eyes, the way she was ready to go to war for us. "What if she really has changed? What if—"

"Then she can prove it over months and years of consistent effort, not one supervised coffee date." Tasha moved closer. "Nate, I need you to hear this. I see what she's doing. The therapy resume, the perfect house in the suburbs, the 'I'll step back if it doesn't work' promise she couldn't define when I pushed her on it. This isn't about Paige. This is about Sarah needing something from Paige."

"You think I don't see it?" My voice was quiet, strained. "You think I want to put Paige through this?"

"Then why are we doing it?"

"Because if I say no, she goes to court claiming I'm alienating Paige. And maybe she wins, maybe she doesn't, but either way, my daughter gets dragged through a custody battle that could have been avoided." I zipped the backpack with more force than necessary. "At least this way, I control the terms."

"Fine," she said. "But I'll be watching everything. Every word, every gesture, every manipulation. And when she shows her true colors- and she *will*- I want you to remember this conversation."

I stood, slinging Paige's backpack over my shoulder. "I hope you're wrong."

"I hope I am too," she said softly. "But I'm not."

The coffee shop on Elm Street had been Sarah's suggestion, and I'd agreed without thinking it through. Now, watching Paige's face as we approached the entrance, I wondered if we should have asked *her* where *she* wanted to meet.

"Dad," Paige said quietly, "my stomach feels funny."

"Nervous?" I asked, crouching down to her level.

She nodded, clutching her axolotl tighter. "What if she doesn't like me?"

The question gutted me. After everything—the abandonment, the years of silence, the legal papers—my daughter was worried about being likable enough for the woman who'd walked away from her.

"Hey," I said, touching her chin gently. "That's not how this works, okay? She's the one who asked to meet you. And if she doesn't appreciate how amazing you are, that's her problem, not yours."

Tasha knelt beside me, her voice fierce but gentle. "You are perfect exactly as you are, kiddo. Anyone who doesn't see that isn't worth worrying about."

Paige nodded, but I could see the tension in her small shoulders. We were asking an eleven-year-old to navigate an emotional minefield that fully grown adults struggled with.

Inside the coffee shop, Sarah was already waiting at a corner table, and my first thought was that she looked like she was playing a role. The outfit was calculated—designer jeans that, once again, probably cost more than my weekly grocery budget, but casual enough to seem approachable. A soft sweater in what I recognized as Paige's favorite color. Even her hair looked professionally styled to appear effortlessly maternal.

She stood when she saw us, her smile bright but somehow artificial. "Hi, Paige. Wow... you look so much like your dad."

Paige blinked, but said nothing. I noticed Sarah didn't crouch to meet Paige at eye level, didn't wait for any cue from my daughter about what kind of interaction she was comfortable with. She just dove in.

"I'm so excited to finally meet you," Sarah continued, her voice light and enthusiastic. "I brought you something."

She reached into an expensive-looking bag and pulled out what had to be a hundred-dollar art set, replete with professional colored pencils, sketchbooks- the works. The kind of gift that screamed money but showed absolutely no knowledge of what Paige actually enjoyed.

"Thank you," Paige said politely, but she didn't reach for it. Sarah's smile flickered for just a moment, her fingers tightening imperceptibly around her water glass.

We settled at the table, Paige between Tasha and me, Sarah across from us. I watched Tasha cataloging every detail, her expression carefully neutral but her eyes sharp.

"So," Sarah said, folding her hands on the table, "tell me about yourself, Paige. What's your favorite color?"

"Blue," Paige answered, her voice flat.

"Oh, how lovely! Mine too. What about your favorite book?"

"I don't really have one."

"Favorite animal?"

"Maybe axolotls. Or sloths."

Sarah's eyes lit up with what looked like practiced enthusiasm. "Sloths! Oh, that's wonderful. I saw a sloth at a rescue center in Costa Rica last year. They're such fascinating creatures—did you know they only defecate once a week? And they can rotate their heads 270 degrees!"

Paige looked confused, clearly not following the adult reference or understanding why someone would go to Costa Rica to see sloths. I saw her eyes dart to me, then to Tasha, seeking something familiar in this strange interaction.

"That's... neat," Paige said, because I'd raised her to be polite even when she was uncomfortable.

I tried to help, to bridge the growing awkwardness. "Paige, why don't you show Sarah the shirt you made at the beach? The tie-dye one?"

Paige pulled the shirt from her backpack and held it up briefly, but she didn't offer it to Sarah to examine more closely. It was a small thing, but telling.

"You're so creative!" Sarah beamed. "I used to love crafts too when I was your age. I made bracelets, painted rocks, all sorts of things."

Everything was about Sarah. Every response circled back to her own experiences, her own interests. She wasn't learning about Paige; she was trying to find ways to make herself relatable.

thirty-one
tasha

I WATCHED Paige's body language with growing alarm. She was tucking into herself, shoulders hunching, eyes darting between Nate and me like she was looking for rescue. This wasn't a nervous child warming up to someone new. This was a kid who sensed something fundamentally wrong but couldn't articulate what.

Sarah kept pushing, seemingly oblivious to Paige's discomfort.

"I have a wonderful house now," Sarah was saying, "with a big yard and a pool. There's even a craft room where we could do projects together. When you come visit, we could—"

"Why would I visit you?" Paige interrupted, her voice small but clear.

Sarah's smile flickered for just a moment before returning full force. "Well, because I'm your mother, sweetie. We have so much time to make up for."

Paige was quiet for a long moment, her gaze distant and intent. When she finally spoke, her voice had that matter-of-fact quality only children possessed, able to cut straight through adult bullshit with devastating simplicity.

"No, you're not," she said, looking directly at Sarah. "Tasha's my mom."

The words hung in the air like a grenade with the pin pulled. I felt my heart simultaneously soar with fierce pride and sink with the knowledge of what Paige had just handed Sarah's lawyers.

Sarah's smile froze on her face, and for just a second—less than a heartbeat—I saw something cold and furious flash in her eyes. Not hurt. Not the pain of a mother being rejected by her child. This was anger at Paige herself, rage that an eleven-year-old wasn't playing the role Sarah needed her to play.

"Oh," Sarah said, her voice artificially bright, "that's... well, that's very sweet that you care about Tasha. But I'm your biological mother, Paige. That's a special bond that—"

"I don't want a special bond," Paige said, and there was steel in her voice that reminded me exactly whose daughter she was. "I already have everything I need."

The temperature at the table dropped about twenty degrees. Sarah's composure was cracking, and I could see her struggling to maintain the maternal facade.

"Maybe we should wrap this up," Nate said quietly, recognizing the signs.

"Of course," Sarah said, but her voice was tight now. "It was lovely meeting you, Paige. I hope we can do this again soon."

"I don't," Paige said with devastating honesty. "Can we go home now, Dad?"

As we gathered our things, I caught Sarah watching Paige with an expression that made my skin crawl. It wasn't sadness or longing or even hurt. It was calculation. Like she was already figuring out how to use this interaction to her advantage.

Outside the coffee shop, Paige immediately reached for both Nate's and my hands.

"I don't like her," she said simply. "She doesn't feel right."

"What do you mean, kiddo?" Nate asked.

Paige was quiet for a moment, trying to find words for something she felt but couldn't fully explain. "She wasn't asking about me because she wanted to know. She was asking because... because she thought she was supposed to. Like when kids at school pretend to be your friend because the teacher told them to include you."

Out of the mouths of babes. My eleven-year-old had just perfectly diagnosed narcissistic manipulation.

"You did great in there," I told her, squeezing her hand. "You were honest and polite, and that's all anyone can ask."

"Are we going to have to do that again?" Paige asked.

Nate and I exchanged glances over her head. "I don't know, sweetheart," he said honestly. "I hope not."

But even as he said it, I could see the wheels turning in his head. Paige's clear rejection of Sarah would look bad in court. A judge might see it as evidence that Nate had poisoned his daughter against her biological mother, rather than what it actually was—a child recognizing that someone claiming to love her actually felt nothing for her at all.

Sarah had gotten exactly what she needed from this meeting. The question was: What was she going to do with it?

thirty-two
nate

THAT EVENING, after Paige was safely in bed, I sat at my kitchen table staring at my phone. I'd been holding it for twenty minutes, Sarah's contact information pulled up, cursor hovering over the call button.

"You're not actually thinking of calling her," Tasha said from the doorway.

"She'll want to know how I thought it went."

"*How you thought it went!?*" Tasha moved into the kitchen, settling across from me. "Nathan James, your daughter told her biological mother to her *face* that she didn't want a relationship with her. That woman got angry at an eleven-year-old for not performing gratitude. How do you *think* it went?"

I set the phone down, scrubbing my hands over my face. "It was a disaster."

"For Sarah, yes. For us... it was Paige being honest about what she wants. Which should matter more than some legal strategy."

"You saw her face when Paige said that about you being her mom."

"I saw her calculating how to use it," Tasha said grimly. "That wasn't a hurt mother, Nate. That was someone realizing their plan had hit a snag."

My phone buzzed.

SARAH

> Nate, I think today went well, all things considered. Paige just needs time to warm up to me. Perhaps we could try again next weekend? - Sarah

I showed the text to Tasha, who read it with growing incredulity.

"Went well?" she said. "Your daughter literally rejected her to her face, and she thinks it went well?"

"She's delusional."

"No," Tasha said, her voice sharp with sudden understanding. "She's not delusional. She's playing a longer game. Think about it. If she acknowledges that today was a disaster, she has to explain why. But if she pretends it went fine and asks for another meeting, and you say no..."

"Then I'm the one being difficult. The one keeping them apart."

"Exactly." Tasha leaned forward. "She's setting you up, Nate. Every text, every request, every 'reasonable' suggestion—it's all building a case that you're the obstacle."

I stared at the phone, feeling trapped. "So what do I do? If I agree to another meeting, I put Paige through that again. If I refuse, I hand Sarah ammunition."

"You talk to a lawyer. Tonight. Tomorrow at the latest."

"It's Friday night—"

"Then Monday morning, first thing. Because I have a very bad feeling about what comes next."

As if summoned by her words, my phone buzzed again. This time it was an email notification.

Subject: AMENDED PETITION FOR MODIFICATION OF CUSTODY

My blood went cold as I opened the attachment. The legal

language was dense, but one phrase jumped out at me like a neon sign: *PETITION FOR PRIMARY PHYSICAL CUSTODY.*

Not joint custody. Not visitation. Primary custody.

"Tasha," I said, my voice barely above a whisper. "*Tasha.*"

She was already reading over my shoulder, and I felt her body go rigid. "That *fucking* bitch," she breathed. "She filed this before the meeting even happened."

The timestamp on the document was 4:47 PM. We'd still been in the coffee shop.

"She was never planning to take it slow," I realized. "The whole thing was a performance. Make me look unreasonable for refusing, then ambush me with this."

Tasha's face had gone pale, and she was gripping the edge of the table so hard her knuckles were white. "I think I'm going to be sick," she said, and rushed toward the bathroom.

I sat alone in my kitchen, staring at legal papers that threatened to take away my entire world, listening to the woman I loved being violently ill in the next room.

This wasn't about Sarah wanting a relationship with Paige. This was about Sarah wanting Paige, period. For whatever reason, for whatever purpose, she was going to try to take my daughter away from me.

And I had no idea how to stop her.

But as I listened to Tasha retching in the bathroom, one thing became crystal clear: I wasn't going to fight this battle alone.

We had built something beautiful together, the three of us. A family that worked, that loved each other, that made each other better.

Sarah could bring her lawyers and her money and her calculated manipulation.

But she was about to learn that some things were worth going to war for.

And she'd just declared war on the wrong family.

thirty-three
tasha

THE LAW OFFICE on Fifth Street had marble floors and leather furniture that probably cost more than Nate's car. The receptionist, perfectly coiffed and wearing what I recognized as a designer blazer, smiled at us with the kind of professional warmth that came with a price tag.

"Mr. and Mrs. Crawford?" she asked, and I didn't bother to correct her. "Mr. Harrison will see you now."

James Harrison looked like central casting's idea of a high-powered attorney—silver-haired, expensive suit, diplomas covering one wall like trophies. He listened to Nate's explanation with the kind of focused attention that made you feel like your case was the most important thing in the world.

Right up until he quoted his retainer.

"Fifty thousand dollars," Harrison said matter-of-factly. "That covers initial case preparation, discovery, and court appearances through resolution. Additional fees may apply depending on complexity."

I felt Nate go rigid beside me, saw his Adam's apple bob as he swallowed hard.

"That's... most of what I make in a year," Nate said quietly.

Harrison's expression didn't change, but something shifted in his eyes. The calculation of a man who'd just realized this wasn't going to be a profitable client.

"I understand that family law can be expensive," he said, already reaching for his calendar. "You might want to consider attorneys who work on a sliding scale basis."

Translation: *Get the fuck out of my office, you can't afford me.*

We left with a brochure for legal aid and a crushing sense of defeat.

The second office, in a strip mall between a nail salon and a tax preparation service, was more promising. The lawyer, Janet Wexler, seemed competent and genuinely sympathetic. Her fee was reasonable—only five thousand up front.

"The problem," she explained apologetically, "is timing. Your hearing is in six days. I'd need at least two weeks to properly prepare a defense for a case this serious. Primary custody modifications require extensive documentation, witness preparation, expert testimonies..."

She trailed off, seeing the desperation on Nate's face.

"I could try to get a continuance," she offered, "but given that you've already had the initial meeting with the child, the judge might not grant one. And if I'm not prepared..."

We thanked her and left. Nate was quiet on the drive to the third office, his knuckles white on the steering wheel.

By the fifth law office, a pattern was emerging that made my stomach drop.

"I'm sorry," the receptionist at Morrison & Associates said, not looking sorry at all. "Mr. Morrison isn't taking new clients in family law matters at this time."

"We haven't even explained the case yet," I said.

"He specifically asked me to tell you that he's had a consultation regarding this matter and would be conflicted out."

The words hit like ice water. "A consultation? With whom?"

"I'm not at liberty to say."

Outside, Nate leaned against the car, running his hands through his hair. "What does 'conflicted out' mean?"

My mind was racing, pieces clicking together in a way that made me feel sick. "It means they've already talked to Sarah. Or her lawyer. Which means they can't represent you."

"But we never—"

"No, Nate. We never talked to them. But she did." I pulled out my phone, scrolling through the list of family attorneys I'd researched. "How many have we called?"

"Seven or eight?"

"And how many have been available and affordable?"

The silence stretched between us as the implications sank in.

I started making calls right there in the parking lot, working through the list with growing horror. One after another, the responses were variations on the same theme:

"Already consulted on this matter."

"Conflict of interest."

"Not taking new family law clients."

By the tenth call, my hands were shaking.

"Nate," I said, my voice barely above a whisper. "She's done this on purpose."

He looked up from where he'd been staring at the pavement. "What?"

"Sarah. Or her lawyer. They've consulted with every decent family attorney in the city. They're not actually seeking their services. They're just having initial consultations to create conflicts of interest."

The color drained from his face. "That's... that's legal?"

"Technically, maybe. Ethical? Hell no. But if no one reports it..." I felt rage building in my chest, white-hot and consuming. "She's been planning this, Nate. The timing, the lawyer consultations, everything. This isn't about wanting a relationship with Paige. This is about destroying you."

Nate slumped against the car like all the air had been knocked out of him. "So what do I do? I can't afford the expensive ones. The affordable ones aren't available or conflicted out. The hearing is in six days."

The words hung in the air between us, heavy with implications: a single father, representing himself against a woman with money and a high-powered attorney.

"I don't know anything about family law," he said. "I'll lose. She'll take Paige."

"Maybe. Or maybe the judge will see what she's doing. The consultation thing, the timing, the way she's been manipulating everything." Even as I said it, I didn't believe it. Judges dealt with facts and legal arguments, not righteous indignation.

Nate straightened up, and I recognized the expression that crossed his face. Military bearing, kicking in when everything else failed. The same look he'd had when he'd defended me from that racist patient.

"Okay," he said quietly. "I'll do it myself."

"Nate—"

"No, it's okay. I'll figure it out. I'll research family law, I'll prepare arguments, I'll..." His voice cracked slightly. "I'll do whatever it takes."

I wanted to tell him it would be okay, that love and dedication would triumph over money and manipulation. But standing there in that parking lot, looking at this good man who was about to walk into a legal slaughter, I couldn't find the words.

Sarah had played this perfectly. She'd taken away our options, our time, and our hope, all while maintaining the facade of being the reasonable one.

And the worst part was, it was probably going to work.

thirty-four
nate

"DADDY, can you sing the bird song?"

Paige was already tucked into her bed, her stuffed axolotl under one arm, but she was looking up at me with those eyes that could make me do absolutely anything. The "bird song" had been our bedtime ritual since she was maybe three years old, though I hadn't done it in months.

"I figured you were getting too old for lullabies," I said gently, smoothing her hair back from her forehead.

"No. And it's not a lullaby, it's about not worrying." She paused, studying my face with that uncomfortable perceptiveness eleven-year-olds sometimes had. "You look worried, Dad."

She was right. I was worried. Terrified, actually. In five days, I was going to walk into a courtroom and try to convince a judge that I deserved to keep the daughter I'd raised alone for eleven years. Against a woman with money and lawyers and a story that would sound reasonable to someone who didn't know the truth.

"Okay, kiddo," I said, settling on the edge of her bed. "But just this once."

I started to sing softly. *Three Little Birds*, Bob Marley's words carrying the same comfort they had for years.

By the second verse, Paige's eyes were getting heavy. By the time I reached the final line, she was breathing deep and even, her face peaceful in the glow of her nightlight.

I kissed her forehead and whispered what I'd been whispering every night for eleven years: "Sweet dreams, baby girl. Daddy loves you."

In the hallway, I found Tasha leaning against the wall, tears streaming down her face.

"'*Three Little Birds*,'" she said softly. "Bob Marley."

I nodded, not trusting my voice.

"How long have you been singing that to her?"

"Since she was little. She used to have nightmares, and it was the only thing that would calm her down." I wiped my eyes with the back of my hand. "She probably doesn't even need it anymore, but..."

"But you do," Tasha finished gently.

That's when it hit me. All of it, at once. The fear, the helplessness, the crushing weight of everything I stood to lose. The sob that came out of me was ugly and raw, and suddenly I was collapsing into Tasha's arms, years of carefully maintained control finally cracking apart.

"She used to make this noise when she was pretending to sleep," I said through the tears, the words tumbling out in a rush. "Like cartoon characters, you know? 'Zzzzznk-pspspspsps.' And I always knew she was faking, but I never told her because she was so proud of fooling me."

Tasha held me tighter, her hand stroking my hair.

"And in nursing school, I carried this pink and purple diaper bag with glitter hearts on it. Got it at a thrift store because it was the best one I could afford. People would stare at me on campus, and I never understood why until someone finally pointed out what it looked like. But I didn't care. It held everything she needed."

The memories kept coming, a flood of moments I'd treasured and feared I might lose.

"One time she was on my shoulders, maybe four years old, and she started crying. Really sobbing. I was panicking, trying to figure out what was wrong, and she kept saying 'my feet are wrinkled.' Took me forever to realize she meant pins and needles." I laughed through the tears. "She didn't know the word for it, so she called it wrinkled feet."

"Nate—"

"She's everything, Tasha. Everything good about my life, it all comes back to her. The reason I got sober, the reason I went to nursing school, the reason I get up every morning and try to be better than I was the day before." The words were coming out broken, desperate. "What if I'm not enough? What if the judge looks at Sarah with her money and her house and her stability and decides Paige would be better off there?"

"Stop." Tasha's voice was firm but gentle. She pulled back to look at me, her hands framing my face. "You are enough. You have always been enough. You're the best father I've ever seen."

"But what if—"

"No." She cut me off. "What if nothing. You love that little girl more than anything in this world, and it shows in everything you do. Every bedtime song, every carefully packed lunch, every science project you've helped with, every tear you've dried. That's what makes a parent, Nate. Not money or houses or lawyers."

I wanted to believe her. *God*, I wanted to believe her.

"I'm so scared," I admitted.

"I know. I'm scared too." Her voice was thick with unshed tears. "But I need you here with me, okay? Present. Fighting. Whatever happens in that courtroom, we'll face it together. All three of us. You can't do anything stupid. Okay? Please, *please* tell me you won't."

I recoiled, shaking my head furiously. "No! No, Tasha. I wouldn't do that. I couldn't... not with you here. I couldn't do this without you," I said, and meant it with every fiber of my being. "I love you, Tasha."

"I love you too," she whispered. "And we're going to get through this."

But as she held me in the dim hallway outside Paige's room, both of us could feel the weight of what was coming. In five days, everything we'd built together could be gone.

The only thing we could do was fight like hell to keep it.

thirty-five
tasha

SLEEP WAS IMPOSSIBLE. Every time I closed my eyes, I saw Sarah's calculated smile and pictured Paige being led away by strangers. The digital clock on Nate's nightstand mocked me—10:47 PM, 11:03 PM, 11:15 PM.

Beside me, Nate's breathing was steady but not deep. He wasn't sleeping either, just lying there in the dark, probably running through legal arguments he'd never had to make, strategies he didn't know how to execute.

I slipped out of bed as quietly as I could, padding to the kitchen for water. The house felt different in the dark—heavier somehow, like it was holding its breath along with us. This could be the last night we spent here as a family.

The thought made my knees buckle, and I found myself gripping the kitchen counter to stay upright. We were going to lose. Nate was walking into that courtroom with nothing but his love for Paige and some hastily researched legal precedents. Sarah had money, lawyers, a plan that had been months in the making.

It wasn't fair. It wasn't right. And it was going to happen anyway.

I needed air. Needed space to fall apart where Nate couldn't see me doing it. He was barely holding himself together as it was.

The back deck was cool and quiet, the summer night air carrying the scent of Mrs. Swanson's roses from next door. Normal suburban life, continuing as if our world wasn't about to implode.

I pulled out my phone, scrolling to Sophia's contact. It was late... too late to be calling anyone. But I couldn't just sit here and do nothing while everything we'd built crumbled around us.

She answered on the fourth ring, her voice alert despite the hour. "Tasha? What's wrong?"

"I'm sorry for calling so late," I said, my voice already shaking. "I know it's—"

"Don't apologize. What's happening?"

My voice broke. "I need your help."

The morning of the hearing arrived gray and drizzling, which felt appropriate for what was probably going to be the worst day of our lives. I stood in front of my bathroom mirror at 5 AM, trying to decide between the conservative navy dress that made me look older or the black suit that made me look more professional.

In the end, I chose the suit. If I was going to watch the man I loved fight for his daughter, I was going to look like someone who belonged in that courtroom.

My phone buzzed. Text from my mother:

> MOM
>
> Praying for you all today. Remember, you're stronger than you know.

Somehow she always knew exactly what to say.

After getting out of the shower, I found him in the kitchen making coffee with the same methodical precision he brought to everything else. He was wearing his best suit—the one he'd worn to job interviews and Paige's school performances—and he looked like he was preparing for battle.

"How'd you sleep?" I asked, though the shadows under his eyes already gave me the answer.

"I didn't." He handed me a cup of coffee, his hands steady despite everything. "You?"

"About the same." I set the cup down and pecked him on the cheek. "Where's Paige?"

"Still sleeping. I thought... I thought maybe it was better if she didn't see us leave. She knows something's happening today, but not what."

We'd agonized over this decision for days. How do you tell an eleven-year-old that her biological mother is trying to take her away from the only parent she's ever known? How do you explain that after today, there was a chance—however small—that she might not come home with us?

In the end, we'd decided to tell her we had some "grown-up business" to take care of, and that Mrs. Swanson would watch her until Maya's mom picked her up for a day of fun and a sleepover. Normal summer plans, as if this was just another Tuesday.

"Mrs. Swanson should be here any minute," Nate said, checking his watch. "Maya's mom is picking Paige up around ten for their day out."

As if summoned by his words, there was a soft knock at the front door. Nate opened it to reveal Mrs. Swanson, looking unusually fierce despite her perfectly coiffed silver bob and floral cardigan.

"Morning, you two," she said, stepping inside with the kind of determined energy that suggested she was ready for battle. She looked between us, taking in our formal attire and obvious tension. "So today's the day that worthless twat waffle thinks she can waltz back in after eleven years and steal my Paige?"

Despite everything, a startled laugh escaped me. "Mrs. Swanson!"

"Over my dead body," she continued, setting her purse down with emphatic finality. "I've been thinking about this all night, and I want you both to know—if things don't go the way they should today, that woman will have to go through me to get to our girl. And

I didn't survive thirty years of middle schoolers to be intimidated by some entitled princess with a law degree."

Nate's mouth twitched, the first hint of something other than despair I'd seen from him all morning. "Marion, I—"

"No," she cut him off, reaching up to straighten his tie like a mother sending her son off to war. "You listen to me, Nathan Crawford. *You* are that child's father in every way that matters. You've earned that title through sleepless nights and scraped knees and homework battles. Some DNA donor doesn't get to swoop in and undo eleven years of love just because she finally decided being a mother might be convenient."

The fierce protectiveness in her voice, combined with her continued use of "twat waffle," made my throat tight with unexpected emotion. This woman, who owed us nothing, was ready to go to war for our family.

Suddenly, the reality of it all hit me like a physical blow, and I had to fight down waves of nausea. There was a real possibility that we wouldn't see Paige tonight. That Sarah's lawyers and money and manipulation would win, and an eleven-year-old girl would be ripped away from the only family she'd ever known.

"We should go," Nate said, checking his watch. "I want to get there early, maybe observe the courtroom before..."

He didn't finish the sentence. Before the slaughter, I thought grimly.

The drive to the courthouse was quiet, both of us lost in our own thoughts. Nate had spent the past five days researching family law, printing out case studies, preparing arguments that would probably sound amateur compared to Sarah's high-powered attorney. But he'd tried. God, he'd tried so hard.

"Whatever happens in there," I said as we pulled into the courthouse parking lot, "I want you to know that you're an incredible father. The best man I've ever known. And I'm proud to fight alongside you."

He reached over and took my hand, squeezing gently. "Thank you for being here. For being part of this family."

Family. The word hit me differently this morning, weighted with everything we stood to lose.

Inside the courthouse, we found the family court waiting area, a beige nightmare of uncomfortable chairs and fluorescent lighting. Sarah was already there, looking polished and confident next to a man in an expensive suit who could only be her lawyer.

She caught sight of us and smiled... the same practiced, empty smile she'd worn during that disastrous coffee shop meeting. Like she'd already won.

Maybe she had.

thirty-six
nate

THE COURTHOUSE STEPS felt like walking toward my own execution. Each step up the concrete stairs brought me closer to a room where strangers would decide whether I deserved to keep the daughter I'd raised from birth, whether eleven years of bedtime stories and scraped knees and homework battles counted for anything against biological claims and legal maneuvering.

The folder of legal precedents I'd hastily printed felt laughably thin under my arm, my amateur-hour research a pitiful shield against the professional demolition I knew was coming. Five sleepless nights had bled into days spent trying to make sense of impenetrable terms like "best interests of the child" and "parental fitness." I'd rehearsed arguments in my head until the words lost all meaning, arguments I'd inevitably fumble in front of a judge... and worse, in front of Sarah's incredibly pricey lawyer. Tasha had found a local review calling him a "shark with a heart of darkness," and the description felt chillingly accurate.

The courthouse lobby was all marble and echoing voices, designed to intimidate. I checked in with a clerk who looked at me with the kind of professional sympathy reserved for people about to be flattened by the legal system.

"Family Court, Courtroom 3," she said, handing me a visitor's badge. "You can wait in the gallery until your case is called."

I found Courtroom 3 and slipped inside, immediately spotting Sarah near the front. She looked like she was attending a business meeting—perfectly pressed blazer, hair styled with that casual-but-expensive look that probably took an hour to achieve. Next to her sat a man who could have stepped out of a yacht club catalog: blonde hair, perfect teeth, a suit that clearly cost a sizeable fraction of my yearly salary.

This had to be her lawyer. Bradford Kensington, according to the papers. He was leaning back in his chair with the casual confidence of someone who'd never lost a case, occasionally murmuring something to Sarah that made her nod seriously.

I took a seat in the back, trying to project the kind of military bearing that had gotten me through worse situations than this. Shoulders square, spine straight, hands steady on my knees. Don't let them see you sweat.

But inside, I was drowning. This wasn't a medical emergency where my training kicked in, where muscle memory and protocols could carry me through. This was a different kind of battlefield, one where the rules were written in a language I barely understood.

The judge entered—the Honorable William Morrison, according to the nameplate—and I felt my heart sink further. He looked like every conservative authority figure who'd ever dismissed my concerns: silver-haired, stern, the kind of man who probably thought single fathers were an aberration against the natural order.

"Good morning," Judge Morrison said, settling behind his bench with the kind of casual authority that filled the room. "We're here for Crawford versus Davis, regarding modification of custody for the minor child Paige Crawford."

Sarah's lawyer—Brad—stood with practiced ease. "Good morning, Your Honor. Bradford Kensington representing petitioner Sarah Davis."

"Nathan Crawford," I said, rising awkwardly. "Representing myself."

Judge Morrison's eyebrows rose slightly, and I caught the brief look he exchanged with the court clerk. *Amateur*, his expression said. *This should be quick.*

"Very well," the judge said. "Mr. Kensington, you may proceed with your opening."

Brad smiled—the kind of smile that probably charmed judges and juries but made my skin crawl. "Thank you, Your Honor. My client is not here to tear down a family, but to reunite one."

The words were delivered with perfect sincerity, as if Sarah hadn't walked away eleven years ago without a backward glance.

"Ms. Davis has undergone extensive personal growth since the difficult period following Paige's birth," Brad continued, his voice warm with manufactured compassion. "She's established a stable career in the medical technology field, purchased a beautiful home in an excellent school district, and most importantly, she's ready to provide Paige with the maternal influence every young girl needs."

He gestured toward Sarah, who nodded sadly, as if her absence had been some tragic circumstance beyond her control rather than a deliberate choice.

"My client isn't seeking to remove Paige from her father's life," Brad said, his tone suggesting he was being incredibly reasonable. "She simply wants to provide the stability and resources that a single father, however well-intentioned, cannot match."

The implication hung in the air like poison gas. *Single father. Well-intentioned but insufficient.*

"Mr. Crawford," Judge Morrison said, turning to me. "Your response?"

I stood, my folder of research suddenly feeling like tissue paper in my hands. "Your Honor, I've been Paige's sole parent since she was three months old. I've never missed a parent-teacher conference, never missed a doctor's appointment, never failed to be there when she needed me."

The words came out steady, but I could hear how inadequate they sounded compared to Brad's polished presentation. Love versus legal strategy. Devotion versus dollars.

"Ms. Davis abandoned her parental responsibilities when Paige was an infant," I continued, trying to channel some of the authority I felt in the ER. "She's had no contact with Paige for eleven years. No birthday cards, no Christmas presents, no phone calls. She doesn't know Paige's favorite book or her best friend's name or what makes her laugh."

"Your Honor," Brad interrupted smoothly, "my client was struggling with postpartum depression during a very difficult period in her life. She made the responsible choice to remove herself from a situation where she couldn't provide adequate care."

Responsible choice. As if abandoning a three-month-old baby was an act of selfless heroism.

"She's spent the intervening years building the stability and resources necessary to be the mother Paige deserves," Brad continued. "Meanwhile, there are serious concerns about Mr. Crawford's fitness as a primary caregiver."

The bottom dropped out of my stomach. Here it came.

"Mr. Crawford was recently the subject of disciplinary action at his workplace following an incident where he verbally assaulted a patient," Brad said, consulting his notes with theatrical precision. "The incident required his supervisor to physically remove him from the emergency department."

The words hit like physical blows. I wanted to explain about the racist slur, about watching someone attack Tasha, about the red haze that had descended when I'd heard that word. But the truth was complicated, and Brad was painting a picture in broad, damning strokes.

"Furthermore," Brad continued, his voice taking on a note of false concern, "Mr. Crawford is a combat veteran who has acknowledged struggles with Post-Traumatic Stress Disorder. While we certainly respect his service, the question before this court is whether an individual dealing with trauma-related mental health issues can provide the stable environment a child requires."

Judge Morrison leaned forward slightly. "Mr. Crawford, is it true that you were involved in a workplace incident requiring disciplinary action?"

My throat felt like sandpaper. "Yes, Your Honor, but—"

"And do you suffer from PTSD related to your military service?"

The question hung in the air like a trap. Deny it, and Brad would produce evidence. Admit it, and I'd just handed him ammunition.

"Yes, Your Honor," I said quietly.

Brad's smile widened fractionally. "Your Honor, with the court's permission, I'd like to enter into evidence certain military incident reports that speak to the severity of Mr. Crawford's psychological trauma."

"Objection," I started to say, then realized I wasn't a lawyer and had no idea what I was objecting to.

"There's no one here to object, Mr. Crawford," Judge Morrison said unkindly. "Mr. Kensington, proceed."

Brad pulled out a folder with the kind of theatrical flair that suggested he'd been planning this moment. "Mr. Crawford, you served in Fallujah during Operation Phantom Fury, did you not?"

"Yes."

"And during that deployment, you were present during incidents involving the deaths of Lance Corporal Daniel Hernandez and Private First Class Luis Alvarez?"

The names hit me like shrapnel. I could see Hernandez's face, could hear his voice saying "*I got him, Doc*" before running into that kill zone. Could feel Alvarez's blood on my hands as I tried desperately to save him.

"Yes," I managed. Barely.

"Perhaps you could share with the court the details from this incident report," Brad said, sliding papers across the table toward me.

"The one documenting how you were physically restrained from attempting a rescue because, and I quote, 'Corpsman Crawford's emotional state posed a risk to mission success.'"

The words on the page blurred as I tried to read them. Somewhere in the gallery, I could hear Tasha's sharp intake of breath.

"Mr. Crawford?" Brad pressed, his voice dripping with false sympathy. "Or perhaps you'd prefer to discuss the incident involving the civilian child caught in the crossfire? The one that led to your initial PTSD diagnosis?"

I was back there suddenly, in that dusty room, watching a little girl die while her parents screamed. The smell of cordite and blood. The weight of failure pressing down on me like a physical thing.

"Mr. Crawford," Judge Morrison said, and his voice seemed to come from very far away. "Are you all right?"

I forced myself to breathe, to stay present. Paige needed me here, in this moment, not lost in memories of a war that ended before she was even born.

"I'm fine, Your Honor," I said, though I could hear the tremor in my own voice.

Brad nodded sympathetically, as if my obvious distress proved his point. "Your Honor, while we have tremendous respect for Mr. Crawford's service to our country, the evidence clearly shows that he suffers from significant psychological trauma that affects his ability to—"

My head began to spin. I turned desperately to find Tasha. Her face was pale, her hands clenched into fists, but she caught my eye and nodded slightly. *I'm here. You're not alone.*

The small comfort of her presence steadied me enough to face Brad's assault, but I could see the trap closing around me. Every word he spoke was technically true, but stripped of context, twisted into a narrative that painted me as unstable, unfit, dangerous.

"Your Honor," Brad continued, "my client seeks only what any loving mother would seek: the opportunity to provide her daughter with the stability, resources, and maternal guidance."

I tried to find my footing, to explain what Paige meant to me, what we'd built together. "Your Honor, I understand Ms. Davis has made changes in her life, but Paige is thriving. She's happy, she's healthy, she knows she's loved. I've built my entire life around being her father—"

"Mr. Crawford," Brad interrupted smoothly, "no one questions your... emotional attachment to the minor child. But surely you can see that a stable two-parent household, with the financial resources to provide the best education, the best opportunities—"

"I provide for her," I said, my voice sharper than I intended. "She has everything she needs."

"Basic needs, perhaps," Brad conceded with patronizing sympathy. "But what about her emotional needs? What about the guidance only a mother can provide? Particularly as she enters adolescence?"

I felt myself losing ground with every exchange, Brad's legal training running circles around my desperate sincerity. The folder of precedents in my hands might as well have been blank paper.

"Your Honor," I tried again, "Paige herself has expressed that she doesn't want a relationship with Ms. Davis. During their meeting, she was clear that—"

"Children often resist change initially," Brad said dismissively. "It's natural for a child to cling to familiar patterns, even when those patterns aren't in her best interests. That's precisely why courts exist, to make decisions based on legal standards rather than the temporary emotions of an eleven-year-old."

I caught movement in the gallery and almost did a double take as I turned to see Sophia sliding into a seat next to Tasha. She met my eyes briefly, her expression tense but encouraging. *Help is coming*, her presence seemed to say, though I couldn't imagine what form that help might take.

Judge Morrison leaned back in his chair, his expression thoughtful in a way that made my stomach clench. "Mr. Crawford, while your dedication to your daughter over these years is noted, the law also recognizes the unique and foundational bond between a mother and her child, particularly a young daughter."

No.

Please, no.

"There is a long-standing principle," the judge continued, "the Tender Years Doctrine, which suggests that, all else being equal, a child of tender years benefits most from the care of her mother. Ms. Davis has expressed her desire to rectify her past absences and provide that maternal care."

The words hit me like a physical blow. The Tender Years Doctrine. I'd read about it in my frantic research, seen it mentioned in old cases, but every source had been clear that it was outdated, legally unsound, struck down by modern courts that recognized fathers as equal parents.

But this judge was invoking it anyway, hiding his bias behind archaic legal theory that had no place in a twenty-first-century courtroom.

Brad was trying not to smile, but I could see the satisfaction in his eyes. He'd gotten exactly what he wanted: a judge who would rubber-stamp his client's claims based on nothing more than biological sex.

In the gallery, I saw Tasha start to rise, her hand half-raised as if to object, to shout that wasn't valid law anymore. But Sophia caught her arm, shook her head slightly, and Tasha sank back down, her face a mask of barely controlled fury and terror.

Sophia was checking her phone discreetly, her own expression growing more anxious by the moment. Whatever plan she had, whatever help she'd promised, it was cutting dangerously close.

"Therefore," Judge Morrison continued, "I'm prepared to grant temporary primary custody to Ms. Davis, pending a full evaluation—"

"Your Honor, if I may—" I started desperately.

"Mr. Crawford, the court has heard your position. Ms. Davis has demonstrated the stability and resources necessary to provide appropriate care, while concerns have been raised about your own mental health and recent workplace conduct. Combined with the natural preference for maternal care in cases involving young girls—"

The courtroom door opened with a soft but decisive click.

Every head turned toward the sound, and I felt my breath catch as a woman in an impeccably tailored suit strode down the aisle with the kind of confidence that commanded immediate attention. She was maybe forty-five, auburn-haired and sharp-eyed, moving with the focused intensity of someone who'd never lost an argument that mattered.

Behind her walked a younger man in an equally expensive suit, both of them carrying themselves like sharks who'd just scented blood in the water.

"Your Honor," the woman said, setting her briefcase down with a decisive click that seemed to echo through the suddenly silent courtroom. "Eleanor Hayes, appearing for Mr. Crawford. I apologize for my tardiness, there were some urgent matters requiring immediate attention."

Brad's confident expression dropped immediately, uncertainty creeping in around the edges of his face. "Your Honor, Mr. Crawford indicated he would be representing himself pro se. This is highly irregular—"

"Mr. Crawford is entitled to representation, Mr. Kensington," Ms. Hayes said smoothly, her voice carrying the kind of authority that made Brad's objection sound petulant. "Surely you're not suggesting otherwise?"

Judge Morrison looked between them, clearly annoyed by the disruption to what had been shaping up as a quick victory for Sarah. "Ms. Hayes, this is most unusual. The hearing is already in progress."

"With respect, Your Honor," Ms. Hayes replied, opening her briefcase with practiced efficiency, "I believe my client's interests have been significantly prejudiced by the proceedings thus far. If I may have a moment to confer with my client and review what's been presented?"

I stared at her, not understanding how this was happening or who had sent her, but knowing with absolute certainty that the cavalry had just arrived.

The question was: Would it be enough to save everything I'd fought eleven years to build?

thirty-seven
tasha

I **WATCHED** Judge Morrison's expression tighten as Ms. Hayes settled in. Calculations were happening behind those eyes, silent and fast. He'd been caught red-handed invoking outdated legal doctrine, probably assuming he was dealing with an unrepresented father who wouldn't know better. Now he had a lawyer who clearly *did* know better, and his reputation was suddenly on the line.

Ms. Hayes leaned over to confer with Nate, her voice too low to hear, but I could see Nate's shoulders straighten slightly as she spoke. Whatever she was telling him, it was giving him hope for the first time all morning.

"Your Honor," Ms. Hayes said, rising with the kind of fluid grace that suggested she'd done this a thousand times before, "I'd like to address several irregularities in today's proceedings, but first I believe we should hear from Ms. Davis herself. After all, she's asking this court to uproot a child from the only home she's ever known. Surely the court would benefit from understanding her motivations directly."

Judge Morrison looked like he'd rather eat glass, but he nodded curtly. "Ms. Davis, please take the stand."

Sarah stood, smoothing her designer blazer, her practiced smile flickering slightly. For the first time since this nightmare began, she didn't look completely in control.

Brad shot to his feet. "Your Honor, my client is prepared to answer questions, but—"

"I'm sure she is, Mr. Kensington," Ms. Hayes said pleasantly. "This shouldn't take long."

Sarah was sworn in, settling into the witness chair with the kind of composed demeanor that probably worked well in business meetings. But I could see the tension in the way she gripped the armrests.

"Ms. Davis," Ms. Hayes began, consulting her notes, "you've presented yourself to this court as a reformed woman, ready to embrace motherhood. Is that accurate?"

"Yes, that's correct."

"And when did this transformation occur? This sudden desire to be a mother?"

Sarah's smile tightened almost imperceptibly. "It wasn't sudden. It's been a gradual process over several years."

"I see." Ms. Hayes pulled out a tablet, swiping to something that made her eyebrows rise slightly. "Interesting. Because according to the incorporation documents for VitalFlow Therapeutics—that's your company, correct?—you founded it eighteen months ago."

"Yes."

"And you're currently seeking Series A funding for this venture?"

Brad was on his feet. "Your Honor, I fail to see the relevance—"

"I'm establishing timeline and motivation, Your Honor," Ms. Hayes said smoothly. "I'll connect it momentarily."

Judge Morrison waved Brad down. "Continue, counselor."

"Thank you." Ms. Hayes turned back to Sarah. "Now, Ms. Davis, as part of your funding efforts, you've created extensive marketing materials, haven't you? Press releases, website content, investor presentations?"

"Standard business practice," Sarah said, her voice still steady, but I caught the slight tightness around her eyes.

"Of course." Ms. Hayes consulted her tablet again. "In fact, you've been quite vocal about your personal life in these materials. Would you like me to read some examples?"

Sarah's knuckles went white against the witness chair. "That won't be necessary."

"Oh, but I think it will be." Ms. Hayes's voice remained pleasant, but there was steel underneath. "Quote: 'As a devoted mother, I understand the importance of family balance in achieving true wellness.' End quote. That's from your website's About section, published six months ago."

I felt my stomach drop. Sarah had been using Paige as a marketing tool while fighting for custody.

"Another quote," Ms. Hayes continued relentlessly. "From your press release announcing your Series A funding round, dated two weeks ago: 'VitalFlow's mission is deeply personal to me. Every innovation we pursue is driven by my desire to create a better world for my daughter.' End quote."

Sarah's practiced composure was cracking. "I don't see what—"

"But perhaps most interesting," Ms. Hayes said, producing a stack of photographs, "are these images used in your marketing materials. Mr. Crawford, do you recognize these photos?"

She handed me several printed pages, and my blood ran cold. There was Paige at her favorite playground, but the background had been digitally altered. Paige at her science fair, but I'd been completely edited out of the photo. Paige's school picture from last year, professionally retouched and used in what appeared to be a company brochure.

"These are photos I sent to her parents," I said, my voice hollow. "But they've been... changed."

"Photoshopped, yes," Ms. Hayes confirmed. "Ms. Davis, you've been using digitally altered images of a child you haven't seen in eleven years to promote your business venture, haven't you?"

"I..." Sarah's face had gone ashen. "Those images represent my hopes for reconnecting—"

"They represent fraud," Ms. Hayes cut her off sharply.

Sarah's practiced composure was cracking. "I don't see what—"

"Ms. Davis," Ms. Hayes interrupted, her voice sharp now, "when was the last time you spoke to your daughter before filing this custody petition?"

"I—that's not—"

"The answer is eleven years ago, isn't it? When she was three months old and you abandoned her?"

"Objection!" Brad shot up. "Inflammatory language—"

"Sustained," Judge Morrison said, but his voice lacked conviction.

"I apologize, Your Honor," Ms. Hayes said pleasantly, "Let me rephrase. Ms. Davis, prior to filing this custody petition, you had no contact with Paige Crawford for eleven years, two months, and sixteen days. Is that correct?"

"I was going through a difficult time—"

"Yes or no, Ms. Davis."

"Yes, but—"

"Yet you've been publicly claiming to be a 'devoted mother' while seeking millions in venture capital funding. Isn't it true that your investors expect to meet this daughter you've been featuring so prominently in your marketing materials?"

Sarah's face went pale. "I don't know what you're implying—"

"I'm not implying anything. I'm stating facts." Ms. Hayes produced a stack of papers. "These are emails between you and your lead investor, Meridian Capital. Would you like me to read the one where they specifically mention wanting to meet your family at the closing dinner?"

Brad was practically vibrating with objections, but Ms. Hayes pressed on.

"Isn't it true, Ms. Davis, that your entire funding round depends on maintaining this fiction of being a devoted mother? That losing this custody case would expose you as a fraud to your investors?"

"That's not—I genuinely want to be in Paige's life—"

"For Series A funding purposes."

"No!"

"Then explain to this court why, after eleven years of complete silence, you suddenly developed maternal instincts precisely eighteen months ago—the same month you incorporated VitalFlow Therapeutics."

Sarah opened her mouth, closed it, then opened it again. No sound came out.

"Furthermore," Ms. Hayes continued, her voice building momentum, "isn't it true that you systematically consulted with family law attorneys throughout this jurisdiction for the express purpose of creating conflicts of interest that would prevent Mr. Crawford from obtaining adequate representation?"

Judge Morrison leaned forward, his expression sharp. "Ms. Davis?"

"I... my attorney handled—"

"Your attorney? Who's sitting right there?" Ms. Hayes gestured toward Brad, who suddenly looked like he wanted to disappear into his expensive suit. "Mr. Kensington, did you or did you not engage in a pattern of consultations designed to prevent opposing parties from obtaining counsel?"

The courtroom was dead silent. I could see Brad calculating, trying to figure out if there was any way to salvage this.

"Your Honor," Ms. Hayes said, her voice cutting through the silence like a blade, "I have documentation of sixteen separate consultations between Mr. Kensington's office and family law attorneys in this jurisdiction, all occurring within the two weeks prior to filing this petition. None resulted in retained counsel. This is a clear pattern of obstruction designed to deny Mr. Crawford his right to adequate representation."

Judge Morrison's face had gone from annoyed to furious. "Mr. Kensington, is this accurate?"

Brad's famous confidence had evaporated entirely. "Your Honor, we were simply exploring our options—"

"By poisoning the well against the opposing party? In *my* courtroom?" The judge's voice could have frozen hell. "Ms. Hayes, please continue."

"Furthermore," Ms. Hayes continued, and her voice took on a tone that could have cut steel, "I find it unconscionable that opposing counsel has spent considerable time attempting to weaponize my client's military service and trauma against him. Mr. Kensington has deliberately attempted to trigger a combat veteran suffering from post-traumatic stress *in open court* by reading incident reports for *theatrical effect*."

Brad's face went pale, but Ms. Hayes wasn't finished.

"Your Honor, if we're going to discuss Mr. Crawford's service record, then by all means, let's discuss *all* of it." She pulled out an official-looking document. "Since Mr. Kensington seems so interested in my client's military history, perhaps the court would benefit from hearing this citation."

Judge Morrison leaned forward, his expression shifting from annoyed to intrigued.

Ms. Hayes's voice rang clear and strong: "The President of the United States of America takes pleasure in presenting the Navy Cross to Hospitalman Apprentice Nathan James Crawford, United States Navy, for extraordinary heroism in action against the enemy while serving as Corpsman, First Platoon, Company G, Third Battalion, Fifth Marines, in support of Operation Phantom Fury on November 15th, 2004."

The courtroom went dead silent. I felt my breath catch as she continued reading, my heart hammering as I heard about Nate—*my Nate*—exposing himself to enemy fire to reach wounded Marines, carrying two wounded civilians over open ground while under sniper fire, evacuating his patients and immediately returning with another unit to the battle lines to treat other wounded.

This is why he never talks about it, I realized with stunning clarity. *Not because he's ashamed, but because to him, it was just doing his job.* The man who sang "Three Little Birds" to his daughter every night, who packed her lunches with surgical precision, who'd taught her about periods with color-coded charts, *that same man* had run through enemy fire to save lives. Had been willing to die for strangers.

And he'd never once mentioned it. Never used it to make himself look good, never brought it up during our worst moments. Never. He'd let Brad Kensington try to destroy him with his trauma rather than reveal the heroism that had caused it.

I looked at Nate and saw him sitting rigidly straight, his face flushed with what looked like embarrassment rather than pride. He kept glancing around the courtroom as if he wanted to disappear, completely uncomfortable with the public praise. *Of course he is,* I thought. *He probably thinks this is showing off.*

I watched Sarah's face go ashen. Brad looked like he might throw up. Even Judge Morrison had straightened in his chair, his previous dismissive attitude completely evaporated.

"His timely and effective care undoubtedly saved the lives of numerous casualties," Ms. Hayes concluded. "Hospitalman Apprentice Crawford's actions reflected great credit upon himself and upheld the highest traditions of the Marine Corps and the United States Naval Service."

She set the citation down with deliberate precision. "Your Honor, Mr. Kensington has spent this morning attempting to destroy the reputation of a Navy Cross recipient—an honor held by *fewer than seven thousand Americans*—by weaponizing the very trauma he sustained while saving the lives of Marines and Iraqi civilians. I submit that this behavior is not only unprofessional but morally reprehensible."

That's my man, I thought fiercely, tears in my eyes. The pride that swelled in my chest was so intense it was almost painful. This quiet, honorable man who'd been willing to walk into this courtroom alone to protect his daughter—*our* daughter—was a genuine American hero.

And somehow, impossibly, he was *mine*.

Judge Morrison cleared his throat, visibly shaken. "I... had no knowledge of these commendations, Counselor. Let the record reflect that the full citation has been entered into evidence."

Brad looked like he wanted to sink through the floor. The confident smirk he'd worn all morning had been replaced by something that looked suspiciously like shame.

"Now then," Ms. Hayes said, turning back to Sarah with the kind of smile a shark might wear. Sarah looked like she was about to be sick. "Ms. Davis, I'll ask you one final question. If Mr. Crawford were to agree to seal these proceedings and sign a non-disclosure agreement—meaning the public and your investors would never know the outcome—would you be willing to withdraw your petition?"

The question hung in the air like a bomb with the pin pulled. Sarah's eyes darted to Brad, to the judge, to anywhere but Ms. Hayes's penetrating stare.

"I... I..." Sarah stammered.

"Take your time," Ms. Hayes said pleasantly. "Though I should mention that Meridian Capital's due diligence team is quite thorough. I imagine they'll be very interested in these proceedings regardless."

And that's when Sarah Davis—venture capital darling, devoted mother, reformed woman—finally broke.

"This isn't fair!" she burst out, her carefully cultivated composure shattering completely. "I'm her mother! I gave birth to her! I have *rights*!"

Her voice climbed higher, more desperate. "You can't just—I need this! Do you understand? I NEED this!"

"Ms. Davis," Judge Morrison warned, his voice sharp.

But Sarah was beyond hearing him now, beyond caring about appearances. "Twelve years ago, I was *nobody*! I was *nothing*! Working at a fucking *coffee shop*, taking classes I couldn't afford! I was drowning, and I made a choice! I made the only choice I could!"

Tears were streaming down her face now; not the calculated tears of a manipulative mother, but the ugly, desperate sobs of someone watching their carefully constructed world collapse.

"And now I finally have something! I *built* something! And my investors expect, they need to see—" She looked around the courtroom wildly. "You don't understand what you're taking from me!"

"Your Honor," Brad said weakly, rising to try to salvage something from the wreckage, but Sarah wasn't finished.

"She's MY daughter!" Sarah screamed, pointing at Nate. "Not his! Mine! I MADE her! *SHE EXISTS BECAUSE OF ME*!"

The mask was completely off now. No maternal love, no desire to nurture—just raw, narcissistic ownership. The ugly truth of what she saw Paige as: not a child to be loved, but a possession to be claimed.

Judge Morrison's gavel came down like thunder. "That's *enough*! Ms. Davis, control yourself, or I'll have you removed from my courtroom!"

But the damage was done. Sarah Davis—venture capital darling, devoted mother, reformed woman—had finally shown everyone exactly who she really was.

And it was exactly what Ms. Hayes had been waiting for.

thirty-eight
nate

THE SILENCE in the courtroom after Sarah's breakdown was deafening. Judge Morrison looked like he'd witnessed something that would haunt his dreams, while Brad Kensington appeared to be contemplating a career change.

"Your Honor," Ms. Hayes said smoothly, as if Sarah hadn't just imploded spectacularly in front of everyone, "I believe my client would be amenable to sealing these proceedings in their entirety in exchange for Ms. Davis withdrawing her petition permanently and agreeing to no further contact with the minor child."

I found my voice somehow. "Yes. Yes, Your Honor. I agree to those terms completely."

Sarah, still sobbing but now looking utterly defeated, managed a shaky nod. Brad whispered something urgent in her ear, and she nodded again, more emphatically.

"Very well," Judge Morrison said, his voice carrying the weight of a man who knew he'd just dodged a professional bullet. "The petition for modification of custody is hereby withdrawn. These proceedings are sealed. Court is dismissed."

The gavel came down with finality, and suddenly I couldn't breathe. It was over.

Paige was safe.

She was mine.

She was coming home.

Tasha was there before I'd even fully stood up, her arms around me, both of us crying openly now. The relief was so overwhelming it felt like drowning in reverse—like surfacing after being underwater for so long I'd forgotten what air tasted like.

"It's over," I whispered into her hair. "She's safe. We're safe."

"I know," Tasha sobbed against my chest. "I know, baby. We did it. We did it."

A polite clearing of the throat made us separate. Ms. Hayes stood nearby, her expression professional but not unkind.

"Mr. Crawford," she said, extending her hand. "I need you to understand something. Without intervention, you would have lost today. Completely. Judge Morrison was about to grant temporary primary custody to Ms. Davis based on archaic legal theory that hasn't been valid in this state for decades."

The words hit me like cold water. "I... I thought maybe if I just explained—"

"No." Her voice was firm but not harsh. "Mr. Kensington had you outgunned from the moment you walked in here. The consultation conflicts, the PTSD ambush, the Tender Years Doctrine? You were walking into a slaughter." She glanced at Tasha with something that might have been approval. "You should listen to Ms. Williams' advice more often. And you should be *very* grateful you have friends like Mr. McKenzie."

I blinked, confusion cutting through the relief. "Mr. McKenzie? I don't know anyone—"

"Jack," Sophia's voice came from behind me. I turned to see her approaching, looking relieved but tired. "Jack McKenzie. My partner. He's the one who arranged for Ms. Hayes to represent you."

"But how did he... why would he—"

"Because that's what family does, Nate," Sophia said simply. "Tasha called me last night, desperate. I put Jack on the phone, and within an hour, he had his people working on this. Ms. Hayes is one of the best family law attorneys on the East Coast. Jack's family has... resources."

Ms. Hayes smiled slightly. "Mr. McKenzie was very persuasive about the urgency of the situation. And very generous about my fee."

Sophia shrugged. "Besides, he told me he 'owed you', Nate. Apparently, you gave him good advice once?"

I stared between them, trying to process that people I barely knew had moved heaven and earth to save my family. "I don't know how to thank you. Any of you."

"You don't need to," Sophia said. "We protect our own."

Ms. Hayes gathered her papers efficiently. "Mr. Crawford, the sealed proceedings mean this can never come up again legally. Ms. Davis has no recourse. But I'd strongly recommend being *very* careful about your social media presence and sharing any public information about your daughter going forward."

After she left, it was just the three of us- me, Tasha, and Sophia- in the emptying courtroom. The weight of what had almost happened was starting to hit me... how close I'd come to losing everything.

"Nate," Tasha said softly, and something in her voice made me look at her more carefully. She looked nervous, excited, scared, all at once. "There's something I need to tell you."

"What is it?"

She took a deep breath, her hands fidgeting with the hem of her jacket. "I'm pregnant."

The words hung in the air for a moment while my brain tried to process them. Pregnant. Tasha was pregnant.

We were going to have a baby.

"You're..." I stared at her, then at her still-flat stomach, then back at her face, then did it all over twice again. "Really?"

"Really." She bit her lip. "I found out a few days ago, but with everything happening, I didn't know how to tell you. I was terrified we might lose Paige and then have to tell her she was getting a sibling she might never see—"

I didn't let her finish. The joy that exploded in my chest was so intense I thought I might burst from it. I swept her up in my arms, spinning her around right there in the courthouse, both of us laughing and crying at the same time.

"We're having a baby!" I yelled, setting her down but keeping my hands on her face. "We're having a baby, and Paige is safe, and we're a family!"

"We're a family," she agreed, tears streaming down her cheeks.

Sophia cleared her throat delicately. "Should I assume this means you two have some news to share with Paige when we get home?"

"Home," I repeated, and the word had never sounded so perfect. "Yeah. Let's go home."

As we walked out of that courthouse together, I thought about how much had changed in a single morning. I'd walked in as a desperate single father about to lose everything. I was walking out as a man with a family—a real family, chosen and fought for and precious beyond measure.

Sarah could have her startup. I had my daughter, my partner, my child on the way.

And nothing would ever take them from me again.

thirty-nine
tasha

THE HOUSE FELT different when we walked through the front door—lighter somehow, as if the weight of Sarah's threat had been physically lifted from the walls. Nate set his keys down with the same careful precision he brought to everything, but his hands were shaking slightly.

"I can't believe it's over," he said, leaning against the kitchen counter like he needed the support. "I keep waiting for the other shoe to drop."

"It's over," I said firmly, moving to stand in front of him. "Sarah's gone. The legal papers are sealed. She can't touch us."

He nodded, but I could see the shell shock in his eyes. The morning had been a whirlwind of terror and triumph, and now, in the quiet of our home, the reality was finally sinking in.

"A Navy Cross," I said softly, reaching up to touch his face. "You never told me."

His cheeks flushed, and he looked away. "It wasn't important."

"Not important?" I laughed, but there was no humor in it. "Nate, you're a genuine war hero. You saved lives under enemy fire. You—"

"I did my job," he interrupted, his voice tight. "That's all. Just... doing what I was trained to do."

And there it was—the essence of Nathan Crawford. A man who'd run through gunfire to save Marines and Iraqi civilians, who'd raised an incredible daughter alone for eleven years, who'd been willing to walk into that courtroom with nothing but his love for Paige to defend himself. And to him, it was all just doing what needed to be done.

"You're extraordinary," I whispered. "Do you know that? You're the most extraordinary man I've ever known."

Something shifted in his expression then, some of the tension leaving his shoulders. "I love you," he said simply. "I love you so much, Tasha. When I thought I might lose Paige, when I thought Sarah might take her away from us—"

"She didn't," I said, stepping closer until I was pressed against him. "She can't. We're safe. All of us."

His hands found my waist, pulling me closer. "All of us," he repeated, and his eyes dropped to my still-flat stomach. "We're really having a baby."

"We're really having a baby." I covered his hands with mine. "Are you happy? I know this wasn't planned, and with everything that just happened—"

"Happy?" He laughed, and this time there was pure joy in the sound. "Tasha, I'm terrified and thrilled and completely over-whelmed. But yes, I'm happy. God, *I'm so happy*."

He kissed me then, soft and reverent, his hands cradling my face like I was something precious. When we broke apart, he rested his forehead against mine.

"I was so scared today," he admitted quietly. "Not just about losing Paige, but about losing you too. About losing this family we've built."

"You didn't lose us. You won't lose us." I took his hand, guiding it to my stomach. "This baby is going to grow up knowing they're wanted, knowing they're safe, knowing their father would do anything to protect them. Just like Paige."

His eyes filled with tears. "What if I'm not good enough? What if I can't give them everything they need?"

"Stop." I silenced him with another kiss. "You gave Paige everything she needed. You turned yourself into exactly the father she deserved. You'll do the same for this baby."

"We will," he corrected softly. "We'll do it together."

The word hung between us, heavy with promise and possibility. Together. A real family, chosen and fought for and earned through fire.

"I need you," I whispered against his lips. "I need to feel that we're real, that we're here, that we made it through."

His response was immediate and fervent. He lifted me easily, my legs wrapping around his waist as he carried me toward the bedroom. Every step felt like a celebration, like claiming something that was ours by right.

In his room—our room—he set me down with infinite care, his hands trembling slightly as he reached for the buttons of my blouse.

"Are you sure?" he asked, his eyes searching mine. "After today, if you need—"

"I need you," I repeated, covering his hands with mine. "I need this. I need us. I need to know I belong to you, and that you belong to me."

We undressed each other slowly, reverently, mapping the familiar territory of each other's bodies with new understanding. This was the man who'd almost lost everything to protect his daughter. This was the woman carrying his child. This was love tested by fire and emerged stronger.

When he laid me back on the bed, his touch was worship, his kisses prayers of gratitude and relief. Every caress spoke of how close we'd come to losing this, how precious it was to have survived intact.

I breathed him in deeply, savoring the familiar warmth and scent that had become my home. His fingers trailed across my skin, each touch a gentle affirmation, chasing away lingering fears, anchoring me firmly in this moment of absolute safety and love.

His hand settled carefully over my stomach as he kissed me, reverent and gentle. "You're giving me another miracle," he whispered. "I'll spend every day proving I deserve it."

"I love you so much, Nathan," I whispered back, so caught up in emotion I was barely able to find my voice.

"I love *you*," he murmured against my neck, his voice thick with emotion. "I love you and Paige and this baby we're making. You're my whole world, Tasha."

I arched beneath him, pulling him closer, needing to feel every inch of him against me. "Show me," I whispered. "Show me we're real."

And he did. With hands that had saved lives in wartime and packed school lunches with surgical precision. With the same quiet intensity he brought to everything that mattered to him. With love that had been tested in a courtroom and emerged unbreakable.

He moved slowly above me, careful and deliberate, and when he joined us together, it felt like coming home. We moved gently at first, savoring each second, each brush of skin against skin, each whispered endearment, each tremble of pleasure. The rhythm built gradually, steadily, drawing us deeper into a profound intimacy neither of us had ever fully known before.

"Nathan," I breathed, wrapping myself tightly around him, needing him closer still. "Please, never let go."

His lips brushed mine tenderly, urgently. "Never."

Together, we climbed higher, every movement filled with aching sweetness and fierce determination. When we fell over the edge, we fell together, my cry mingling with his whispered promises, our hearts beating in perfect sync.

Afterward, tangled together in our quiet sanctuary, Nate's fingers traced slow patterns down my spine, his heartbeat steady beneath my ear. For the first time in months—maybe ever—peace enveloped us fully, a profound sense of completeness filling me.

I'd never imagined happiness could feel so complete.

"When will we tell Paige?" he asked softly.

"Tomorrow, when we pick her up from Maya's. She'll be so excited." I smiled against his skin. "She's going to be an amazing big sister."

"Paige is going to lose her mind," Nate chuckled softly, fingertips tracing lazy circles on my shoulder. "She's probably going to start planning the nursery tomorrow."

I laughed quietly against his chest. "You realize we're never going to hear the end of her baby name ideas."

"Good," he murmured warmly. "I can't wait."

"Me either," I agreed, smiling.

"You know she's going to be protective," he said with a chuckle. "God help anyone who tries to mess with her baby brother or sister."

"She gets that from you."

"She gets that from *us*," he corrected, and the pride in his voice made my heart flutter. "She's ours, Tasha. Really ours."

I lifted my head to look at him, seeing the wonder in his eyes, the disbelief that this was really his life. "What are you thinking about?"

"Everything," he said simply. "A year ago, I was just a single dad trying to get through each day. Now I have you, and Paige loves you, and we're having a baby together. Sometimes I can't believe this is real."

"It's real," I assured him, pressing a kiss to his chest. "We're real. This family is real."

"Our family," he repeated, like he was testing the words. "I like how that sounds."

As the afternoon faded into evening, we stayed wrapped around each other, making plans for the future. Names for the baby. How to rearrange the house. Whether Paige would want to help decorate the nursery.

Normal things. Beautiful, ordinary things that a few hours ago we'd thought we might never get to experience.

When we finally dozed off, it was with Nate's hand resting protectively over my stomach and my fingers intertwined with his. Two people who'd found each other in the chaos of an emergency room, who'd built something beautiful from the wreckage of their pasts.

Tomorrow we'd pick up Paige and tell her she was going to be a big sister. Tomorrow, we'd start planning for the arrival of our baby. Tomorrow, we'd begin the next chapter of our story.

But tonight, we were exactly where we belonged.

Home, safe, and completely, perfectly whole.

forty
nate

MAYA'S HOUSE was a modest ranch split-level in a neighborhood that screamed "normal suburban family"—basketball hoop in the driveway, bikes scattered on the front lawn, the kind of place where kids could be kids without worry. I sat in the car for a moment, hands still trembling slightly from the morning's adrenaline crash.

"You ready for this?" Tasha asked, squeezing my hand.

"Are we ever ready to tell an eleven-year-old her life is about to change completely?" I managed a smile. "Again?"

We'd rehearsed this conversation during the drive over. How to explain that the woman who'd tried to take her away was gone forever. How to share the news about the baby. How to gauge her reaction to both pieces of information that would reshape our family.

Maya's mom, Jennifer, answered the door with the harried expression of someone who'd been supervising a sleepover. "Thank *God* you're here," she said with a laugh. "They've been up since six AM making friendship bracelets and planning some elaborate dance routine. I think they've had enough sugar to power a small city."

"Sorry," I said automatically. "Paige didn't give you any trouble, did she?"

"Are you kidding? She's an angel. Maya could learn a thing or two about cleaning up after herself." Jennifer called up the stairs. "Paige! Your dad's here!"

The thundering of feet on stairs announced Paige's arrival before we saw her. She appeared at the top of the staircase, hair in a messy braid, wearing the same clothes from yesterday but with the addition of about fifteen friendship bracelets covering both wrists.

"Dad! Tasha!" She bounded down the stairs and launched herself at both of us simultaneously. "We had the BEST time! Maya's mom let us make pancakes and we watched three movies and we stayed up until midnight talking about everything and—"

"Breathe, kiddo," I laughed, catching her in a hug that felt more precious than usual. Twenty-four hours ago, I'd been terrified I might never get to do this again.

"Thank you so much, Jennifer," Tasha said, hefting Paige's overnight bag. "We really appreciate this."

"Anytime. Maya's already asking when Paige can come back." Jennifer grinned. "Fair warning though, they're planning some kind of science experiment for next time. Something involving volcanoes."

"Of course they are," I said, ruffling Paige's hair. "Ready to go home, scientist?"

In the car, Paige chattered nonstop about the sleepover, the movies they'd watched, Maya's older brother's girlfriend, who was "so cool" and had painted their nails. Normal eleven-year-old stuff that felt like the most beautiful sound in the world.

"So," she said as we pulled into our driveway, "what was the grown-up business you had to take care of? Was it boring?"

Tasha and I exchanged glances. Here we went.

"Actually," I said, turning in my seat to face her, "we need to talk to you about something. A couple of things, actually."

Paige's expression immediately shifted to concern. "Am I in trouble? Did someone call about the friendship bracelet incident?"

"The friendship bracelet incident?" Tasha asked.

"*Nothing*," Paige said quickly. "What did you need to talk about?"

I took a deep breath. "Remember how we talked about your biological mother? How she wanted to meet you?"

Paige's face scrunched up slightly. "The coffee shop lady? The one who didn't know anything about me?"

"Yes. Well, she decided she didn't want to try to be part of your life after all. So that's done. She won't be contacting us anymore."

I waited for the questions. For confusion, or hurt, or curiosity about why Sarah had changed her mind. For some kind of reaction to the fact that her biological mother had just disappeared from her life again.

"Great," Paige said, and immediately pivoted. "So what's the other thing? You said a couple of things."

That was it. No follow-up questions. No interest in details. No apparent emotional investment whatsoever. The person who had tried to tear our family apart had been dismissed with all the consideration Paige might give to a weather forecast.

And for the first time since I'd met Sarah Davis, I believed, *truly* believed, that Paige was whole, untouched by the storm that nearly tore us apart.

"Well," Tasha said, reaching for my hand, "the other thing is pretty big news."

"Good big or bad big?" Paige asked, her attention fully focused now.

"*Very* good big," I said. "Tasha's pregnant. You're going to be a big sister."

The silence in the car stretched for exactly three seconds. Then Paige's face exploded into the biggest grin I'd ever seen.

"REALLY?!?" she shrieked, loud enough that I worried about my eardrums. "Really? *Really*, really? I'm going to have a baby brother or sister?"

"Really, really," Tasha confirmed, laughing at Paige's excitement.

"When? How big is it now? Can I help pick names? Can I help decorate the nursery? Will it be able to share my room? Oh my God, Maya and Zoe are going to be SO jealous!"

The questions tumbled out in a rush, and I felt something that had been wound tight inside me finally release. This was the reaction I'd hoped for but hadn't dared to expect.

"The baby will be here in about seven months," I said. "And yes, you can absolutely help with everything. We're going to need the best big sister in the world."

"I'm going to be the BEST big sister," Paige declared with the confidence only an eleven-year-old could muster. "I'll teach them everything I know about science and books and how to make friendship bracelets and how to avoid getting in trouble for the friendship bracelet incident."

"What exactly was this friendship bracelet incident?" Tasha pressed.

"It's really not important," Paige said airily. "What's important is that I'M GOING TO BE A BIG SISTER!"

She unbuckled her seatbelt and launched herself between our seats to hug us both again, her excitement so pure and infectious that I found myself grinning like an idiot.

"Can we go inside and start planning?" she asked. "I have SO many ideas. And I need to call Grandma Rose, she's going to flip! And Mrs. Swanson! And—"

"Slow down there, kiddo," I laughed. "We've got plenty of time to tell everyone and make plans."

But as we headed into the house, Paige practically bouncing with excitement, I kept waiting for her to circle back to the Sarah conversation. To ask why her biological mother had changed her mind, or what that meant, or how I felt about it.

She never did.

Over the next hour, as we sat around the kitchen table making lists of potential baby names and discussing nursery themes, Sarah Davis never came up once. Not even in passing. It was as if she had never existed, as if that coffee shop meeting had been a minor inconvenience quickly forgotten.

And maybe, for Paige, that's exactly what it was. She had her family. Her real family. What need did she have for anyone else?

"I think we should name the baby something strong," Paige was saying, her notebook already half-filled with possibilities. "Like Alexander if it's a boy, or Diana if it's a girl. Oh! Or we could do a science name! Like Newton! Or Curie!"

"Curie Crawford?" I asked, raising an eyebrow.

"It has a nice ring to it," Paige said seriously.

Tasha was laughing so hard she could barely speak. "Maybe we should stick to more traditional names for the first name and save the science names for middle names."

"Fine," Paige sighed dramatically. "But I get to help pick the middle name, right?"

"Absolutely," I promised.

As the afternoon wore on, I marveled at how natural this felt. The three of us, planning for our growing family, making decisions together. Paige had already appointed herself Chief Big Sister and was taking the role very seriously, asking practical questions about feeding schedules and diaper changes and whether the baby would need its own night light.

"The baby's going to love having you as a big sister," Tasha told her, and the pride in Paige's face was worth everything we'd been through to get here.

"I'm going to protect them from everything," Paige declared. "Like you protect me, Dad. Nobody's going to hurt our baby."

Our baby. Not "the baby" or "your baby." *Our* baby.

I caught Tasha's eye across the table and saw the same wonder I was feeling reflected in her expression. This was our family. Messy and complicated and absolutely perfect.

And Sarah Davis, who had tried so hard to destroy it, had been dismissed with a single word: "Great."

Sometimes the most devastating victories were the quietest ones.

forty-one
tasha

"SO," I said, settling onto Paige's bed as she organized her collection of friendship bracelets by color, "want to go on a girls' day tomorrow? Just you and me?"

Paige looked up from her rainbow array of embroidery floss, eyes lighting up. "Really? What kind of girls' day?"

"I was thinking we could start shopping for baby stuff. Maybe get lunch somewhere fancy, do some planning." I paused, suddenly nervous. "I mean, if you want to. I know you probably have other things you'd rather—"

"Are you kidding?" Paige abandoned her bracelet project entirely, bouncing on her knees. "I've been waiting my ENTIRE LIFE to go baby shopping! Can we look at cribs? And those little tiny clothes? Oh! And car seats! Did you know there are like fifty different kinds of car seats and Dad's probably going to research them for six months?"

I laughed, the nervous flutter in my chest settling. "He's already started. I caught him reading 'Consumer Reports' at breakfast."

"Of course he has." Paige rolled her eyes fondly. "He researched my bike helmet for three weeks. Three weeks! For a helmet!"

"Well, safety is important," I said, channeling Nate's earnest tone.

"You're starting to sound like him," Paige grinned. "That's good. Mom-like."

The word hit me like a gentle wave. Mom-like. Not "like a mom" or "motherly"—mom-like. As if being Paige's mom was simply a fact, as natural as breathing.

"Is that okay?" I asked softly. "Me being... mom-like?"

Paige tilted her head, looking at me with that serious expression she got when she was really thinking about something important. "Tasha, you've been my mom for months. Like, actually my mom. You came to school when I got my period. You held my hand at the doctor. You make sure I eat vegetables and help me with homework and sing along to terrible songs in the car." She paused. "You love Dad, and you love me, and you're having our baby. That's what moms do."

Actually my mom. The words, so casually delivered, so certain, landed with the force of a physical blow, but the good kind. The kind that rearranges everything inside you for the better.

All my life, I'd been the invisible middle child, the one expected to achieve without needing too much, the one who learned to build walls around her heart because overt emotion was seen as a distraction. And here was Paige, this incredible kid, not just accepting me, but claiming me. Defining motherhood not by biology or obligation, but by presence, by care.

By love.

A wave of emotion, so potent it stole my breath, washed over me. It wasn't just gratitude; it was a profound sense of healing, a validation I hadn't known I was starving for. This wasn't just being liked; this was belonging.

This was family.

"I do love you. So much, Paige. More than I ever thought I could love someone else's..." I stopped myself.

"Someone else's what?" Paige asked, but her tone was curious, not hurt.

"I was going to say 'someone else's child,' but that's not right, is it? You're not someone else's child. You're mine. Ours."

"Exactly." Paige flopped back on her pillows with the dramatic flair only eleven-year-olds could manage. "Plus, you're way better at the mom stuff than the coffee shop lady ever would have been. She didn't even know what axolotls were! I mean, *come on*."

I snorted with laughter. "That is pretty unforgivable."

"Right? And she kept talking about herself. Like, I asked her about sloths, and somehow she made it about her trip to Costa Rica. It was weird." Paige wrinkled her nose. "You always listen to what I'm actually saying."

"Because what you're saying is interesting," I said honestly. "You're brilliant and funny and thoughtful, and I like hearing how your brain works."

Paige beamed at that, then suddenly sat up straight. "Oh! Can we go to that fancy baby store? The one in the mall with all the expensive stuff? I want to see everything. Even if we don't buy anything, I just want to look at all the tiny baby things."

"Absolutely. We'll make a whole day of it."

"And can we get our nails done? Maya's mom took her for a manicure last month and she felt so grown up." Paige examined her currently chipped purple polish. "Maybe something baby-themed? Like pink or blue or yellow?"

"We don't know what we're having yet," I reminded her.

"But we will soon, right? When do you find out?"

"At the next ultrasound. About three weeks." I smiled at her eager expression. "Want to come with us?"

"Can I? Really?" Paige's eyes went wide. "I want to see the baby! Even if it's just a blob! Dad showed me pictures of ultrasounds and they're so cool, like little aliens!"

"I think Dad would love to have you there."

"This is going to be the BEST baby," Paige declared. "I'm going to teach them everything. How to ride a bike, how to make friendship bracelets, all the constellations, the best books to read. Oh! And I can teach them sign language! Maya's learning it in her summer program and it's so cool."

I watched her plan out her future sibling's entire childhood and felt my heart swell almost painfully. This child who'd been abandoned by one mother had embraced me so completely, so naturally. She wasn't just accepting me as her father's girlfriend or even as a stepmother—she'd claimed me as her mom, full stop.

"Paige," I said softly, "I need you to know something. Being your mom... it's the best thing that's ever happened to me. Even better than falling in love with your dad."

"Even better than the baby?"

"The baby is amazing, but you came first. You're the one who taught me I could be a mom. You're the one who made me want to be part of a family." I reached over and tucked a strand of hair behind her ear. "You made me brave enough to love your dad, and you made me believe I deserved to be loved back."

Paige was quiet for a moment, and I worried I'd said too much, gotten too emotional.

"That's really nice," she said finally. "But also, like, duh. You're awesome. Of course we love you." She grinned. "Plus, you make Dad smile all the time now. Like, all the time. It was getting weird."

I burst out laughing. "Getting weird?"

"He used to be so serious. Like, all the time. Responsible Dad Mode, twenty-four seven. But now he laughs at stupid stuff and sings in the shower and yesterday I caught him dancing while he was making dinner." Paige shuddered dramatically. "Dad dancing, Tasha. It was traumatic."

"I'll talk to him about that," I said solemnly.

"Thank you. Some things children should never have to see."

We dissolved into giggles, and I marveled at how easy this was. How natural it felt to joke and plan and just be with this incredible kid who'd somehow become mine.

"So tomorrow," Paige said, settling back into planning mode, "baby shopping, manicures, fancy lunch. What else?"

"Whatever you want," I said. "It's our day."

"Can we take pictures? For the baby book? I want them to know about all the planning we did before they got here."

"That's a perfect idea."

"And can we buy something little? Like a onesie or a stuffed animal? Something to put in the nursery so it feels real?"

My chest tightened with emotion again. "Absolutely."

"This is going to be so fun," Paige said, already reaching for her phone. "I'm going to text Maya and make her jealous. She doesn't have any baby siblings. All she has is her annoying older brother."

As I watched her type excitedly, sharing our plans with her best friend, I thought about how much my life had changed. A year ago, I'd been focused on my career, keeping people at arm's length, protecting myself from getting too attached to anything or anyone.

Now I was planning a girls' day with my eleven-year-old daughter, preparing to shop for my unborn baby, completely and utterly part of a family that had claimed me as fiercely as I'd claimed them.

"Hey, Tasha?" Paige said, looking up from her phone.

"Yeah?"

"I'm really glad Dad found you. Like, really glad."

"Me too, baby girl," I said, my voice thick with emotion. "Me too."

And as I kissed her goodnight and headed back to Nate, who was probably researching cribs or strollers or baby-proofing techniques, I realized that I'd never been more grateful for anything in my life.

I'd found my family.

And they'd found me right back.

forty-two
tasha

"I'M glad we chose the reveal cake," Paige said, consulting the checklist she'd made on her phone with scientific precision. "It's way more dramatic than balloons."

We were standing in the middle of my mother's backyard, which had been transformed into baby shower central. Streamers in every shade of yellow and green hung from the trees, tables groaned under the weight of food, and enough presents to stock a small baby store were piled on a dedicated gift table.

"Dramatic is definitely what we're going for," I agreed, watching Nate arrange chairs with the same methodical care he brought to everything else. "Your dad might have a heart attack from the suspense."

"Dad loves suspense. Remember how he made me wait until Christmas morning to open that chemistry set?" Paige grinned. "Besides, he's been trying to guess for weeks. Yesterday I caught him googling 'early signs of baby gender' at breakfast."

The guest list was perfectly us, a mix of hospital family and actual family that showed just how intertwined our lives had become. Maria had claimed the beverage station and was already holding court with my aunts, comparing stories about difficult doctors. Sophia and Jack had arrived early with Madison in tow, who was currently teaching some of my younger cousins card tricks that probably counted as mild gambling.

"Oh, honey," my mother said, appearing at my elbow with a plate of her famous deviled eggs, "you need to eat something. You're eating for two now."

"Mom, I'm almost halfway there. The baby is the size of a bell pepper."

"A bell pepper needs nutrients," she said firmly, then softened. "You look so beautiful, baby girl. Glowing."

And I *did* feel beautiful. The yellow sundress Nate had picked out hit just right, and my small but definite bump was perfectly framed by the empire waist. More importantly, I felt settled in a way I never had before. Surrounded by people who loved me, carrying the child of the man I adored, watching my daughter—*my daughter* —orchestrate this entire event with the enthusiasm of a party planner.

"Tasha!" Mrs. Swanson approached, looking unusually fancy in a floral dress instead of her usual cardigan. "Where do you want me to put this?" She gestured to a beautifully wrapped box that was clearly a handmade *something*.

"The gift table is perfect, thank you so much for—"

"Nonsense. I've been knitting baby blankets since I retired. This one's special, though." Her eyes twinkled. "Gender neutral on the outside, but there might be a little surprise border that'll make more sense after the reveal."

Before I could ask what she meant, Paige appeared at my other side, practically vibrating with excitement. "It's time! Everyone's here! Dad's ready! The cake is perfect!"

I looked around the backyard and felt my heart do that swooping thing it had been doing a lot lately. Everyone we cared about was here: Sophia and Jack, deep in conversation with my brother Marcus about something medical. Madison, showing my grandmother photos of New Zealand on her phone. Maria and my cousin Aisha, bonding over their shared opinion that all men were basically toddlers in disguise.

And Nate, standing near the cake table, looking nervous and excited and so handsome in his button-down shirt that I wanted to drag him inside and remind him exactly how we'd gotten into this situation in the first place.

"Okay everyone!" Paige called out, her voice carrying across the yard with surprising authority. "Time for the gender reveal! Mom and Dad, get over here!"

Mom and Dad. She'd been saying it so naturally lately that I barely noticed anymore, but today it hit me like a gentle wave. To everyone here, that's exactly what we were. Parents. Partners. A family.

Nate materialized beside me, his hand finding mine automatically. "You ready for this?" he asked softly.

"Are we ever ready for anything?" I smiled up at him. "But yeah. Let's find out if we're having a son or daughter."

The crowd gathered around as Paige presented us with a knife that was probably overkill for cake cutting but definitely added to the drama. "Everyone count down from three!" she instructed.

"THREE!" came the chorus of voices.

"TWO!"

Nate's hand covered mine on the knife handle, his thumb stroking gently across my knuckles.

"ONE!"

We sliced through the white fondant together, and the inside of the cake revealed itself in a burst of blue so vibrant it was almost electric.

"IT'S A BOY!" Paige shrieked, jumping up and down like she'd just won the lottery. "I'M GETTING A BABY BROTHER!"

The yard erupted in cheers and applause. My mother immediately started crying happy tears. Mrs. Swanson looked smugly satisfied in a way that suggested her surprise border definitely involved blue. Madison was already taking pictures, documenting everything for posterity.

But all I could focus on was Nate's face. The wonder and joy and slight terror of a man who was about to become a father again, eleven years after the first time.

"A son," he said softly, just for me.

"A son," I agreed. "Paige is going to be insufferable. In the best possible way."

"I'm going to teach him EVERYTHING!" Paige announced to anyone within hearing distance. "Baseball, science, how to make the perfect s'more, all the constellations—"

"How to avoid the friendship bracelet incident?" Sophia suggested with a grin.

"We are NEVER speaking of the friendship bracelet incident," Paige said with dignity, then immediately abandoned all pretense of sophistication. "But yes! I'm going to be the best big sister EVER!"

The afternoon dissolved into the kind of controlled chaos that only family gatherings could produce. Presents were opened and exclaimed over. Everyone had opinions about names (Paige was still lobbying hard for "Newton Crawford" as a middle name). My aunts interrogated Nate about his intentions while simultaneously praising his obvious devotion. Jack and Marcus discovered a shared love of obscure medical trivia and were deep in a debate about cardiac surgery techniques that was probably fascinating to them.

"Having fun?" I asked Madison, who was sitting slightly apart from the adults, scrolling through her photos.

"It's cool," she said with teenage nonchalance, then grinned. "Actually, it *is* really cool. Paige is going to be such a good big sister. And your family is..." She paused, looking for the right words. "They're loud. But like, good loud. Like they actually care about each other."

"They do. Sometimes to an annoying degree."

"Yeah, but..." Madison's expression grew thoughtful. "My dad's family was never like this. All quiet and polite and weird. This feels real."

Before I could respond, a commotion near the gift table caught our attention. Dr. Cameron Lee—somehow Sophia had convinced him to show up—was examining the baby monitor we'd received like it was alien technology.

"This has video capability," he was saying to Jack with the same intensity he probably brought to surgical consultations. "And smartphone connectivity. And temperature monitoring. Do babies really need this level of technological surveillance?"

"Wait until you have kids, mate," Jack laughed. "You'll want satellites tracking their every movement."

"I can't imagine," Cameron said, then caught sight of us and waved. "Congratulations on the future quarterback!"

"He could be a scientist," Paige called out defensively. "Or a doctor! Or an engineer!"

"All noble professions," Cameron agreed diplomatically, though I caught him exchanging an amused look with Jack.

"The cardiovascular monitoring features are actually quite sophisticated," came a crisp voice from behind him. "Though I'd argue the real innovation would be integrating early warning algorithms for respiratory distress patterns."

We all turned to see Dr. Delaney Ward approaching, looking perfectly put-together despite the casual outdoor setting. She wore dark jeans and a white blouse that somehow managed to look both relaxed and professional—a trick I'd never mastered.

Cameron's expression shifted, surprise flickering across his face. "Ward. I didn't expect to see you here."

"Sophia invited the ER staff," she replied smoothly, though I caught a slight tension in her voice. "I thought it would be... educational to observe normal family dynamics."

"Educational?" Cameron raised an eyebrow, and something in his tone made me think there was history there I didn't know about.

"Some of us didn't grow up in environments like this," Ward said, gesturing toward the controlled chaos of my family reunion. Her voice was neutral, but there was something almost wistful in her expression as she watched my cousins' kids chase each other around the yard.

"Right," Cameron said, and was it my imagination or did his voice soften slightly? "Well, if you're studying family dynamics, you picked a good one. The Williams clan could power their own anthropological research study."

Ward's lips curved in what might have been the beginning of a smile. "The intergenerational bonding patterns are quite remarkable. And the way they've integrated Mr. Crawford and Paige so seamlessly..." She trailed off, seeming to catch herself being too analytical.

"Sometimes the best families are the ones we choose," Cameron said quietly, and I definitely didn't imagine the way Ward's eyes sharpened on his face.

"Yes," she agreed, her voice equally quiet. "I suppose they are."

As the afternoon wound down and people started trickling out, I found myself in the kitchen helping my mother wrap up leftover food. Through the window, I could see Nate and Paige in the backyard, cleaning up streamers and collecting the mountain of gifts we'd somehow accumulated.

"He's a good man," my mother said quietly, following my gaze.

"The best."

"And Paige adores you."

"The feeling's mutual."

"You're happy." It wasn't a question.

I watched Nate laugh at something Paige said, watched him ruffle her hair with the absent affection of a father who'd been doing it for eleven years. Watched them work together to fold up chairs, their easy partnership the result of years of just the two of them against the world.

Soon it would be the three of us. And then four.

"I'm terrified and overwhelmed and completely out of my

depth," I said honestly. "But yes. I'm happy. Happier than I ever thought I could be."

My mother squeezed my shoulder. "That's what love is supposed to feel like."

An hour later, we were finally home, the car loaded with enough baby gear to supply a small daycare. Paige had claimed the passenger seat and was reading aloud from a baby name book, providing running commentary on her favorites.

"Okay, what about Oliver? That's nice and normal, but not boring. Oliver Crawford." She tried it out thoughtfully. "Oliver Newton Crawford, if we go with my middle name suggestion."

"We'll consider it," Nate said diplomatically.

"Or James? That's your middle name, Dad. James Newton Crawford?"

"Paige," I said gently, "maybe we should wait to see what he looks like before we decide?"

"But I want to start calling him something! I can't just say 'the baby' for five more months!"

"How about 'little brother' for now?" Nate suggested.

Paige considered this. "Little Brother Crawford. I can work with that."

Back home, as we carried presents and leftover cake inside, I felt that same sense of contentment that had been growing stronger every day. This house, these people, this chaotic, beautiful life we were building together—it was everything I'd never known I wanted.

"Best shower ever?" Paige asked, flopping dramatically onto the couch.

"Best shower ever," I agreed, settling beside her. "Though I think Mrs. Swanson might have spiked the punch."

"Grandma Rose definitely did," Nate said, joining us with three glasses of water. "I saw her adding something from a flask."

"Family tradition," I said with a grin. "No Williams celebration is complete without Grandma Rose's 'special ingredients.'"

Paige curled up against my side, her hand resting gently on my small bump. "Hi, Little Brother," she said softly. "Today was your first party. You're going to love being part of this family."

And as Nate settled on my other side, his arm coming around both of us, I realized that Paige was absolutely right. Our son was going to love being part of this family.

Because it was the kind of family worth fighting for, worth building, worth believing in.

The kind of family that turned a scared single father, a guarded nurse, and an abandoned little girl into something bigger and stronger and more beautiful than any of us had ever imagined possible.

The kind of family that would never, ever let him go.

epilogue: nate

Five months later

THE FIRST CRY cut through the quiet of the delivery room at exactly 3:47 AM, and I felt my entire world shift on its axis for the second time in my life.

"He's perfect," Dr. Martinez announced, placing our son on Tasha's chest. "Absolutely perfect."

Oliver James Crawford—Paige had won the name debate through sheer persistence and the logical argument that "Oliver Newton" flowed better than any of our other combinations—was red-faced and furious and the most beautiful thing I'd ever seen.

"He's so little," Tasha whispered, tears streaming down her face as she touched his tiny fist. "And so mad."

"He gets that from you," I managed, my own voice thick with emotion.

"The mad part or the little part?"

"Definitely the mad part."

Paige, who'd been permitted to wait in the family lounge despite it being well past midnight on a school night, appeared in the doorway with Sophia and Mrs. Swanson flanking her like bodyguards.

"Can I see him?" she asked, her voice unusually small. "Is he okay?"

"He's perfect," Tasha said, shifting carefully so Paige could get a better view. "Come meet your little brother."

I watched Paige approach the bed with the kind of reverence usually reserved for religious experiences. When she got her first good look at Oliver, her face went through approximately seventeen different expressions before settling on pure wonder.

"He's so tiny," she breathed. "Look at his fingers! They're like little sausages!"

"Attractive little sausages," I corrected.

"The most attractive little sausages ever," Paige agreed seriously. Then, to Oliver: "Hi, Little Brother. I'm Paige. I'm going to teach you everything I know, which is a lot, so you better be ready to learn."

Oliver chose that moment to open his eyes; dark blue like all newborns, but something about the shape already reminded me of Tasha. He blinked owlishly at Paige, and I swear his expression suggested he was already resigned to whatever his big sister had planned for him.

"I think he likes me," Paige said with satisfaction.

"He'd better," Tasha said. "You're going to be his favorite person in about a year when he realizes you're the one who'll sneak him extra cookies."

"I would never," Paige said with mock indignation, then immediately added, "Okay, I totally would."

Mrs. Swanson stepped forward with the blue-bordered blanket she'd knitted, the one she'd hinted about at the baby shower. Up close, I could see tiny embroidered sailboats along the edges, a nod to my Navy service that made my throat tight.

"For Master Oliver," she said formally, then broke into a grin. "Though I suspect he's going to be running the household within a week."

"He's a Crawford," Sophia observed from the doorway. "Of course he's going to be running things."

The next few hours passed in a blur of visitors and phone calls and the surreal adjustment to being a family of four instead of three. My mother-in-law (and wasn't that still a strange and wonderful phrase!) arrived with enough flowers to stock a florist shop. Maria showed up with coffee and gossip from the ER. Even Drs. Lee and Ward made a brief appearance, the former looking slightly uncomfortable and the latter ecstatic, both offering genuine congratulations.

But it was the quiet moments I treasured most. Watching Tasha nurse Oliver for the first time, both of them figuring it out together. Seeing Paige hold her brother with the careful concentration of someone entrusted with the most precious cargo in the world. The way Oliver's tiny hand wrapped around my finger like he was already claiming me as his dad.

"No second thoughts?" Tasha asked during one of the rare moments when it was just the four of us.

"About what?"

"Going from one kid to two. Losing all pretense of having your life together."

I looked around the hospital room, at our son sleeping peacefully in his bassinet, at Paige curled up in the chair reading a book about baby development she'd checked out from the library, at the woman who'd turned my carefully controlled world upside down in the best possible way.

"Not a single one," I said honestly. "This is exactly where I'm supposed to be."

"Even when he's screaming at 3 AM and Paige has a science project due the next day and I'm covered in spit-up and questioning all our life choices?"

"Especially then."

She smiled, the soft, tired smile of a woman who'd just brought life into the world. "Good answer."

Three days later, we brought Oliver home to a house that had been transformed by Paige's enthusiastic preparations. She'd made a "Welcome Home, Little Brother" banner that covered most of the living room wall. The nursery was perfectly organized, every outfit sorted by size, every book arranged by reading level for when he was older.

"I've prepared a schedule," Paige announced, producing a color-coded chart that would have impressed a Marine drill instructor. "Feeding times, nap times, tummy time, reading time—"

"Paige," I interrupted gently, "babies don't really follow schedules for the first few months."

She looked genuinely confused. "But how will he know what he's supposed to be doing?"

"He'll figure it out," Tasha said, settling into the rocking chair with Oliver. "Trust me, he'll let us know what he needs."

As if to prove her point, Oliver chose that moment to start fussing. Paige immediately sprang into action, consulting her chart.

"According to my calculations, he's not due for feeding for another hour, but maybe he needs a diaper change? Or tummy time? Oh! Maybe he wants me to read to him!"

"Maybe he just wants to complain about being evicted from his warm, cozy apartment," I suggested.

"That's fair," Paige conceded. "I'd probably complain too."

That first week was everything people warned you about and somehow still a complete surprise. The sleep deprivation, the constant laundry, the way Oliver could go from peacefully sleeping to screaming like his world was ending in approximately 0.3 seconds.

But it was also magic in ways I hadn't expected. The way Paige appointed herself Oliver's official translator, providing running commentary on what she thought he was trying to communicate. The sight of Tasha, sleep-deprived and wearing one of my old college t-shirts, singing lullabies at 4 AM like she'd been doing it her whole life. The moment Oliver first smiled—probably gas, but we all chose to believe it was genuine—and Paige nearly cried with excitement.

"He smiled at me!" she announced to everyone who would listen. "I made him smile! I'm officially the best big sister ever!"

"You definitely are," I agreed, watching her show Oliver a book about the solar system, complete with sound effects for each planet.

Two weeks in, as I sat in the nursery during a late-night feeding, Oliver in my arms and the house finally quiet, I thought about how much had changed since that first day Tasha had walked into the ER.

I'd been so afraid then. Afraid of letting anyone in, afraid of disrupting the careful balance I'd built with Paige, afraid that opening my heart would just lead to more loss.

Now, listening to my son's soft breathing and knowing my daughter was safely asleep down the hall and my wife—*wife*, we'd have to do something about that soon—was finally getting some rest, I realized that fear had been the biggest enemy all along.

Not Sarah's lawyers or custody battles or the thousand daily challenges of raising children. Just fear. Fear of believing I deserved this kind of happiness, this kind of love, this kind of family.

Oliver stirred in my arms, making the soft snuffling sounds that Paige insisted meant he was dreaming about rockets. His eyes opened briefly, unfocused but somehow seeming to see me anyway.

"Hey there, buddy," I whispered. "Welcome to the family. We're all a little crazy, but we love real big and we don't give up on each other. I think you're going to like it here."

His tiny hand curled around my finger again, and I felt that same overwhelming surge of protectiveness I'd felt the first time I'd held Paige. The bone-deep certainty that I would do anything, sacrifice anything, fight anyone to keep this small person safe.

But this time, I wasn't facing it alone. This time, I had partners in the fight. This time, I had a family that chose each other every single day, through sleepless nights and scary mornings and all the beautiful, chaotic, perfectly imperfect moments in between.

"*Three Little Birds*" came drifting softly from down the hall— Tasha's voice, singing the lullaby she'd heard me sing to Paige that first night she'd stayed over. The night that had changed everything.

I smiled, holding my son a little closer, and realized Bob Marley had been right all along.

Everything was going to be alright.

Everything already was.

THE END

epilogue: tasha

The night before court

THE THOUGHT HIT me like a physical blow, and I found myself gripping the kitchen counter to stay upright. We were going to lose. Nate was walking into that courtroom with nothing but his love for Paige and some hastily researched legal precedents. Sarah had money, lawyers, a plan that had been months in the making.

It wasn't fair. It wasn't right. And it was going to happen anyway.

I needed air. Needed space to fall apart where Nate couldn't see me doing it. He was barely holding himself together as it was.

The back deck was cool and quiet, the summer night air carrying the scent of Mrs. Swanson's roses from next door. Normal suburban life, continuing as if our world wasn't about to implode.

I pulled out my phone, scrolling to Sophia's contact. It was late... too late to be calling anyone.

But I couldn't just sit here and do nothing while everything we'd built crumbled around us.

She answered on the fourth ring, her voice alert despite the hour.

"Tasha? What's wrong?"

"I'm sorry for calling so late," I said, my voice already shaking. "I know it's—"

"Don't apologize. What's happening?"

My voice broke. "I need your help. Sophia, you were right. About everything. Sarah, the playbook, all of it."

Where could I even start? The custody papers, the lawyer consultations, the coffee shop meeting where Sarah had shown her true colors exactly like Sophia had predicted?

"The coffee shop meeting was a disaster," I managed. "Sarah played it exactly like you said she would. Perfectly reasonable, understanding, just wants what's best for Paige. And then she filed for primary custody the same day. She was never planning to take it slow."

"Shit," Sophia breathed. "When's the hearing?"

"Tomorrow morning. Nine AM. And we can't find a lawyer. Every decent attorney in the city has either been bought off or conflicted out. Sarah's people made sure of that."

"Hold on, Tasha," came Sophia's voice. "I've got Jack here. Can I put you on speaker? I think we might need his input on this."

"Of course," I said, grateful for any help, from anyone.

"Hey Tasha," Jack's warm voice came through the phone, carrying that slight accent that usually made everything sound calmer. Tonight it just sounded concerned. "Sophia's been filling me in on some of this situation. What's the current status?"

And then it all came pouring out. Everything. How Sarah had systematically sabotaged our legal options. How the coffee shop meeting had been theater from the beginning. How Paige had innocently handed Sarah exactly what she needed by rejecting her so clearly.

"She was twenty-eight when she left," I said, my voice thick with tears. "Twenty-eight years old, and she just walked away from a three-month-old baby because it was too hard. And now she wants to take Paige away from the only parent she's ever known.

"And the worst part is... I think she's going to win," I whispered. "Nate's representing himself against someone with unlimited resources and no conscience. He's the best father in the world, but that's not going to matter in that courtroom.

"There's something else," I said, my voice breaking completely. "Something I haven't even told Nate yet. I'm pregnant."

The silence on the other end stretched for what felt like forever.

"How far along?" Sophia asked softly.

"Seven, eight weeks, maybe? I just found out." I sank into one of Nate's carefully arranged patio chairs. "And it's my own stupid fault. I had an ear infection, took antibiotics. I should have known better. I'm an ER nurse, for God's sake, and I made the most basic rookie mistake in the book."

My voice was rising now, pregnancy hormones and stress combining into a toxic cocktail of self-recrimination. "What kind of mother am I going to be if I can't even manage my own birth control properly? What if I screw up something important with the baby? What if—"

"Stop," Sophia said firmly. "Tasha, listen to me. You made a human mistake that happens to healthcare professionals all the time. You think I haven't seen doctors and nurses make the exact same error? It doesn't make you stupid or incompetent or a bad future mother."

"But—"

"No buts. You're dealing with an impossible situation, you're pregnant, you're scared, and your brain is doing what brains do under stress—catastrophizing." Her voice gentled. "The antibiotic thing? That's just life being messy. The baby you're carrying? They're going to be lucky to have you as a mom."

I wiped my eyes, feeling slightly steadier. "I was waiting for the right moment to tell Nate, and then this happened. What if we lose Paige, Sophia? What if there's no good moment to tell him about the baby?"

"We're not going to lose Paige," Jack said quietly, and something in his voice had changed. More serious, more determined. "Tasha, what's the exact courthouse and time tomorrow?"

I gave him the details, my hands shaking as I scrolled through the legal papers on my phone. "Family Court, downtown. Nine AM. Judge Morrison presiding."

"Morrison," Jack repeated. "And Sarah's attorney?"

"Bradford Kensington. From Kensington, Walsh, and Associates."

There was a pause, then Jack said, "Right. I need to make some calls. Tasha, I can't promise anything concrete, but... we might have some options."

"What kind of options?" I asked, hardly daring to hope.

"The kind that require some very specific phone calls to some very specific people," Jack said carefully. "But Tasha, I need you to understand something serious. This is a longshot. We might not be able to pull anything together in time."

"But you'll try?"

"We'll try," Sophia confirmed. "Tasha, go back inside. Try to get some sleep if you can. And don't give up hope yet."

"But what if—"

"One crisis at a time," Sophia said gently. "We protect our own. And you and Nate and Paige? You're family now. All of you."

"The baby too," she added quietly. "That little one you're carrying is going to grow up knowing their sister, in the house where they belong. I truly believe that."

Tears were streaming down my face now, but for the first time in days, they weren't entirely tears of despair. "Thank you," I whispered. "Both of you."

"Don't thank us yet," Jack said, and I could hear movement in the background. "Wait until we see what tomorrow brings. But Tasha? Get some rest. Whatever happens, you're going to need your strength."

The line went quiet, and I stood there on the deck, staring at my phone in the darkness. It wasn't a guarantee. Jack had been careful not to promise anything. But for the first time since this nightmare began, I felt like we weren't completely alone.

Maybe that would be enough.

Maybe it would have to be.

epilogue: sophia

AFTER I HUNG up with Tasha, I found Jack already at his laptop, fingers flying over the keyboard with the kind of focused intensity I recognized from his paramedic work. But this was different. This was Jack McKenzie, son of a New Zealand business dynasty, not Jack the charming Kiwi who made incredible coffee and left his socks on my bedroom floor.

"You're calling Charlotte," I said. It wasn't a question.

"Among others," he said, checking his watch. "It's 3 PM Wednesday in Auckland. Charlotte will be wrapping up her after-noon meetings."

I settled into the chair beside him, watching him navigate what looked like an encrypted messaging system I'd never seen before. "Jack, are you sure about this? I mean, what if you can't—"

"Sophia." His voice was gentle but firm. "What did you tell me about Troy? About how you felt when he was threatening Madison?"

The memory made my chest tight. "That I'd do anything to protect her."

"Right. And what did I do?"

I thought about Troy's sudden departure from the state, the way his harassment had stopped so abruptly it was like he'd simply vanished. Jack had never told me exactly what had happened, just that "the situation was handled."

"You made him go away," I said quietly.

"I had him *made* to go away," Jack corrected. "There's a difference. And Sophia, what Tasha just described? This Sarah woman systematically trying to destroy a good man and steal his daughter? That's not just cruel. That's evil."

The laptop chimed with an incoming video call. Jack accepted it, and suddenly the screen filled with the face of Charlotte McKenzie—Jack's older sister, and the real power behind the McKenzie empire.

"Jackie," she said without preamble, her accent thicker than Jack's, her expression sharp with intelligence. "This better be important. I'm supposed to be reviewing the quarterly reports."

"It's important, Char. Family emergency. Sort of."

Charlotte's eyebrows rose. "Sort of?"

"Sophia's colleague. Good bloke, single father, being fucked over by his ex and her expensive lawyers here. They're trying to steal his kid using some very underhanded tactics. Hearing's at 9 AM local time tomorrow—that's about midnight our time tonight."

Jack quickly outlined the situation—Sarah's abandonment, the custody grab, the lawyer conflicts, the systematic sabotage of Nate's legal options.

"Bradford Kensington," Charlotte repeated when Jack mentioned the attorney's name, making notes. "And you need an American lawyer who can handle family court. On about eight hours' notice."

"I know it's asking a lot—"

"Jackie, you remember Alex Hayes? The Sydney barrister Dad helped out of that mess with her ex?"

"The one whose husband was embezzling from her firm's trust accounts?"

"That's the one. Well, her daughter lives in Washington D.C. now. Brilliant family lawyer, handles high-stakes custody cases for politicians and diplomats. Alex calls her 'the American version of herself.'"

Charlotte's fingers were already moving over her keyboard. "Let me see... yes, here we go. Eleanor Hayes. Just made partner at Hayes, Winters & Associates last year. She owes her mother everything, and her mother owes Dad everything."

"Think she'll take a midnight phone call?" Jack asked.

"She'll take the call if I have to wake her up myself." Charlotte paused. "But Jackie, even if Eleanor agrees to this, there's no guarantee she can pull it together in time. Eight hours to prepare for a custody modification hearing? That's barely enough time to read the file, let alone build a defense."

"We have to try, Char."

"Right then." Charlotte's expression hardened with determination. "I'll call Alex now, she can reach out to Eleanor. But I'm also putting Rawiri on this. If we're going into battle, I want to know everything there is to know about this Sarah Davis woman."

Jack opened another messaging window, this one labeled simply "R."

"Already on it," he said, typing quickly. "Rawiri's one of the best intelligence gatherers in the Southern Hemisphere. If there's dirt to be found, he'll find it."

The laptop chimed with Charlotte's call ending, then immediately chimed again with an incoming message from "R."

"Brief received. Already running preliminary searches. This Bradford Kensington character has an interesting reputation. Give me two hours for full workup on all parties."

"Jack," I said carefully, "what exactly are you asking your people to do?"

He looked at me, and for a moment I saw past the easy charm to something harder underneath. "Research, Sophia. All legal, all above board. But thorough. If Sarah Davis has skeletons, if Kensington has a history of sharp practices, if there's anything that might help Nate's case—we're going to find it."

The laptop chimed again. A message from Charlotte: "Eleanor is in. She's pulling an all-nighter and gathering her team. Says she'll be in the courthouse at 9AM sharp. She sounds absolutely furious about the lawyer consultation conflicts—apparently that's a career-ending ethical violation if it can be proven."

Jack smiled, but it wasn't his usual warm grin. It was something sharper. "Looks like Ms. Davis picked the wrong family to fuck with."

Another message from Rawiri: "Preliminary findings: Sarah Davis is running a startup funded by venture capital. She's been suspected of using digitally altered photos of the child in her marketing materials. This is potentially massive fraud if her investors believe she's an active parent. Full financial analysis in one hour."

Jack paused, reading another message that had just come in. His eyebrows shot up.

"What?" I asked.

"Rawiri just sent Nate's military background check." Jack's voice was quiet, almost reverent. "Sophia, did you know Nate has a Navy Cross?"

I blinked. "A what?"

"Navy Cross. It's the second-highest military decoration in the US. Only one step below the Medal of Honor." Jack was still reading, his expression growing more amazed. "Jesus Christ. He ran through enemy fire in Fallujah to reach wounded Marines. Carried two wounded civilians to safety under sniper fire. Rawiri says even he was impressed, and he's ex-NZSAS, spent months in the mountains of Afghanistan."

"I had no idea," I breathed. "He never... Nate never mentioned anything like that."

"Of course he didn't," Jack said softly. "That's exactly the kind of man who would never bring it up. But Sophia, if Sarah's lawyer tries to paint him as unstable because of his PTSD..."

"They'll be attacking a genuine war hero," I finished, under-standing dawning.

"Exactly. And if Eleanor can get that into evidence..." Jack's smile was sharp. "Well, let's just say judges tend to take a very dim view of attorneys who attack decorated veterans. And venture capital firms, even moreso."

I leaned back in my chair, watching this man I loved coordinate what was essentially a precision strike to save people he'd never met. "Your family really doesn't mess around, does it?"

"When it matters? Never." He pulled me close for a quick kiss. "Besides, Nate gave me advice once that helped save our relationship. I owe him."

"What advice?"

"To own up to my mistakes and hope you'd forgive me." Jack's expression grew thoughtful. "He said that sometimes showing up means admitting you fucked up. Best relationship advice I ever got."

As I watched him work, I realized I was seeing a side of Jack McKenzie I'd only glimpsed before. This wasn't just my charming paramedic boyfriend. This was someone who'd grown up understanding that, as the saying went, with great power came great responsibility— and that sometimes the right thing to do was use every resource at your disposal to help good people.

Tomorrow, Sarah Davis was going to learn that the McKenzie family never fought to lose.

author's note

The character of Nate Crawford was inspired in part by real-life Navy Corpsmen, and especially one my husband knew as "Doc Speedy," a decorated combat medic who received the Navy Cross for extraordinary heroism but returned home to face an entirely different war: PTSD, alcoholism, and the daily struggle of surviving the aftermath.

Nate's story is fiction. But for thousands of veterans, especially those who served in Iraq and Afghanistan, the trauma is very real—and ongoing. The silence around their suffering has cost too many lives. We owe them more than gratitude. We owe them action.

A portion of the proceeds from every copy of this book will be donated to support organizations that provide mental health care, trauma recovery, and peer support for veterans living with PTSD.

If you or someone you love is struggling, please know you are not alone. There is help. There is hope.

Semper Fi. We don't leave our people behind.

afterword

Dear Reader,

Thank you for joining me for *No Greater Love*, the second book in the Code Blue Hearts series. Whether you followed Nate and Tasha here from Sophia and Jack's story or this is your first glimpse into the world of Metro General, I'm grateful you chose to spend your time with this family that fought so hard to find each other.

This book holds a special place in my heart because it's truly a collaboration. My husband—a GWOT-era veteran and ER nurse—wrote the Fallujah scenes that form the backbone of Nate's trauma. While I've spent almost twenty years in emergency services, his military experience brought an authenticity to Nate's story that I wouldn't have achieved alone. (And yes, this is the same husband whose romance scenes I mentioned in the first book needed... *significant* editorial intervention. His combat scenes, however, need no such help.)

The medical cases you've read—from the heartbreaking pediatric situation to the everyday chaos of triage—come from the collective experiences of nurses across the country. Early on, I made a decision that no patient interaction I was personally involved in would appear in any of these books. But after years of listening to colleagues share their stories, of witnessing the patterns of pain and resilience that define emergency medicine, I've tried to capture the emotional truth of what we face without exploiting individual tragedies. My beta readers helped ensure we honored the reality of what emergency workers endure daily while being mindful not to traumatize you, our readers. It's a delicate balance, showing the weight of this work without making it unbearable to witness.

The next book, *Burn Notice*, follows Izzy, a female firefighter and Lieutenant who's damn good at her job. Before I became an ER nurse, I was an EMT and a firefighter. It's a demanding profession that shaped who I am today, and I have nothing but respect for everyone who runs into burning buildings when others run out. Izzy's story explores what it means to lead in a traditionally male-dominated field, to earn respect through competence and courage, and to navigate the unique challenges that come with breaking barriers. I hope I've done justice to the incredible women in the fire service who excel every single day, proving themselves through their actions, their leadership, and their unwavering commitment to the job.

Thank you for letting these characters into your heart. For understanding that heroes aren't perfect—they're just people doing their best with the wounds they carry. And for believing, like I do, that love and family can be found in the most unexpected places, often right when we need them most.

From our family to yours (including Sunny the dog),

Cari

sneak peek

BOOK THREE, CODE BLUE HEARTS: BURN NOTICE

IZZY

The first day off after a forty-eight-hour shift was always a disorienting limbo. My body, still humming with the ghost vibrations of the engine and the phantom shrill of alarm tones, didn't know what to do with stillness. My apartment, a small but meticulously clean one-bedroom in a quiet part of the city, felt like an alien planet compared to the controlled chaos of Station 2. Here, there were no checklists, no urgent calls, no crew to manage. There was only me.

I spent the first few hours in a ritual of decontamination, both physical and mental. My dirty station uniform went straight into the washing machine on the sanitary cycle, a habit ingrained so deeply it was second nature. I stood under the spray of a scalding hot shower for a solid twenty minutes, methodically scrubbing away the grime and the lingering smell of smoke that seemed to seep into my pores. It wasn't just about being clean; it was about washing away the shift, shedding the skin of Lieutenant Delgado to find the woman underneath.

The woman underneath, I reflected as I pulled on a pair of worn-out sweatpants and a threadbare academy t-shirt, was a lot less sure of herself.

At the station, I was in command. My orders were followed without question because my crew trusted my judgment. My world was a series of problems with tactical solutions: a fire required water, an entrapment required hydraulics, a medical emergency required a clear protocol. I knew the steps. I knew the rules.

Here, in the quiet of my own living room, the problems were messier. There was the ever-growing stack of paperwork for my Captain's promotion exam, a mountain of policies and procedures I had to memorize. There was the low-grade hum of anxiety about BC Evans and the political games being played by Lieutenant Santoro. And then there was the biggest, most unsolvable problem of all: Cap.

I sank onto my couch, the worn leather sighing under my weight. I picked up my phone, my thumb hovering over his contact. I'd seen him yesterday for his treatment, and he'd looked... tired. More than tired. The strength that had always seemed to radiate from him, the quiet confidence that had mentored half the department, was fading, eroded by the relentless poison of his illness and the equally toxic poison they pumped into his veins to fight it.

My job was to run into burning buildings. To face down chaos and wrestle it into submission. But I couldn't fight this. I couldn't command the cancer to stand down. I couldn't force a solution. All I could do was drive him to his appointments, sit with him in sterile waiting rooms, and pretend I wasn't watching the best man I'd ever known slowly disappear before my eyes. The helplessness was a physical weight, a crushing pressure in my chest that no amount of training could prepare me for.

I forced myself up, busying my hands to quiet my mind. I cleaned my already-clean kitchen. I organized my bookshelf by color, then by author, then back by color. I did a brutal HIIT workout in my living room until my muscles screamed and my lungs burned, the physical pain a welcome distraction from the emotional kind. By the time I finally collapsed back onto the couch, exhaustion had won. I fell into a deep, dreamless sleep, the kind that only comes after forty-eight hours on duty.

I woke up three hours later, still restless, my body refusing to accept true rest. The afternoon sun streamed through my windows, highlighting the sterile functionality of my living space. No photos on the walls, no personal touches that might reveal who I was beneath the uniform. Just clean lines and practical furniture.

Unable to sit still, I grabbed my keys and headed down to the parking lot.

My father's 1995 Ford F-150 sat in my assigned space like a shrine to everything I'd lost and everything I was trying to become. Miguel Delgado had restored this truck with his own hands, teaching me to hold a wrench before I could properly hold a pencil. The forest green paint still gleamed despite its age, the chrome bumper reflecting the afternoon light.

I popped the hood and began my ritual inspection. Oil levels, coolant, belts, hoses—everything Miguel had taught me to check. The mechanical precision of the engine was soothing in a way that promotion study materials never could be. Here was something I could understand completely, something I could fix if it broke.

"That's a beautiful truck."

I looked up to find Mrs. Park from apartment 3B standing nearby with her small dog, both of them watching me with friendly curiosity.

"Thank you," I said, wiping my hands on an old rag. "It was my father's."

"Was he a mechanic?"

"Firefighter. But he liked to tinker." I closed the hood, signaling the end of the conversation. Mrs. Park meant well, but I wasn't looking for neighborhood friendships.

"Well, he did beautiful work. Have a nice day, dear."

I watched her walk away, feeling the familiar pang of guilt that came with keeping people at arm's length. But letting people in meant letting them see your vulnerabilities, and in my line of work, vulnerabilities could cost lives.

Back in my apartment, I made a simple dinner—grilled chicken, steamed vegetables, brown rice. Fuel, not pleasure. As I ate, my phone rang with a number I recognized but dreaded.

"Hi, Mom."

"Mija," Carmen's voice carried that particular mix of love and disappointment that only mothers could perfect. "How are you? You sound tired."

"Just got off shift. I'm fine."

"Are you eating enough? Taking care of yourself?"

"I'm fine, Mom." I could hear the edge creeping into my voice.

A pause. "I heard about Captain O'Sullivan. Ramona Martinez's daughter works at the hospital. She said he's been in for treatments."

Ramona Martinez. Of course. The Latino community in our city was small enough that everyone knew everyone's business.

"He's fighting it," I said carefully.

"Ay, mija. This job..." Another pause, heavier this time. "Maybe this is a sign. You could go back to school, get your nursing degree like you always talked about. David has connections at the hospital where he works."

David. Her new husband, the accountant. Safe, stable, everything my father hadn't been.

"I'm already in school, Mom. For my Captain's exam."

"That's not what I meant, and you know it." Her voice softened. "I just worry. First your father, now Captain O'Sullivan. This job takes the good ones, Izzy. It takes them young."

The conversation we'd been dancing around for years finally lay bare between us. Carmen had loved my father, but she'd also spent every shift terrified that he wouldn't come home. When the structure fire took him—when that burning roof collapsed—it had confirmed every one of her worst fears about the job. Now, watching Cap waste away from cancer caused by decades of breathing smoke and chemicals, it felt like the job was claiming its victims in every way possible.

"I know you worry," I said quietly. "But this is who I am, Mom. This is what I'm meant to do."

"You're meant to be happy, mija. You're meant to have a family, a life outside of that station."

"I have a life."

"You have a job. There's a difference."

The conversation ended the way it always did—with careful "I love yous" and the unspoken understanding that we'd never see eye to eye on this. After I hung up, I sat in my kitchen feeling the weight of her words. Maybe she was right. Maybe I didn't have a life so much as a series of duties and obligations.

But it was my choice to make.

I spent the evening reviewing promotion materials, memorizing policy numbers and command structures until my eyes burned. By nine PM, I was ready for sleep, grateful for the exhaustion that would keep my mind from wandering to darker places.

The shrill ring of my phone jolted me awake. The room was pitch black, the glowing numbers on the cable box reading 1:17 a.m. My heart hammered against my ribs, my body instantly flooded with adrenaline. A call at this hour meant one thing: something was wrong.

It was Margaret, Cap's wife. Her voice was thin, stretched tight with panic.

"Izzy? I'm so sorry to call so late, but it's Michael. He's in so much pain, and... oh, God, Izzy, he's yellow."

The floor dropped out from under me. Jaundice. That meant his liver was failing.

"I'm on my way," I said, my voice all business, the calm, commanding tone of Lieutenant Delgado taking over. "Don't try to move him. Just keep him comfortable. I'll be there in fifteen minutes. We're going to Metro General."

I was dressed and out the door in under three minutes, my mind a blur of tactical assessment. Abdominal pain, jaundice, pancreatic cancer—it was a straight line to the worst-case scenario. As I sped through the deserted city streets, the familiar route to Cap's house felt different, fraught with a new and terrible urgency.

When Margaret opened the door, her face was pale and tear-streaked. I gave her a quick, firm squeeze on the shoulder. "Where is he?"

"In the bathroom."

I found him kneeling on the floor, leaning over the toilet, his body wracked with tremors. The bathroom light was unforgiving. His skin, normally weathered and tan from years of outdoor work, was a ghastly, sallow yellow. His eyes, when he looked up at me, were the same awful color. The pain was etched into every line on his face.

"Hey, Cap," I said softly, my professional calm a thin shield over the terror clawing at my throat.

"Izzy," he rasped. "This is... this one's bad."

"I know," I said, my hand instinctively going to his wrist to check his pulse. It was thready and weak. "We're going to get you some help. Can you stand?"

With my help and Margaret's, we got him to his feet. Every movement was a fresh wave of agony for him. Leaning heavily on me, we shuffled slowly out to my car. The fifteen-minute drive to Metro General was the longest of my life. Cap was quiet, his breathing shallow, his focus turned inward on the pain. I kept one hand on the wheel and the other on my phone, ready to call 911 if he crashed on the way.

The emergency bay at Metro General was an oasis of bright, fluorescent light in the dark of the night. I pulled up to the ambulance entrance, a place I'd been a thousand times in the engine, but never like this. Never as the terrified loved one.

I helped him out of the car while Margaret went to the triage desk. A nurse in dark blue scrubs met us at the door with a wheelchair. He had a kind face and an air of calm that seemed to soak up some of the panic radiating from me.

"What's going on?" he asked, his voice steady as he helped me ease Cap into the chair.

"This is Michael O'Sullivan," I said, the words catching in my throat. "History of pancreatic cancer. Acute onset of severe abdominal pain and jaundice."

The nurse's eyes met mine, and in them, I saw an immediate, professional understanding. He wasn't just looking at another sick patient; he was seeing the whole picture. He was seeing Cap, and he was seeing me.

"Alright, Michael," he said, his voice gentle but firm. "Let's get you inside and get you some help. My name is Jimmy. You're in the right place."